T0284437

PRAISE FOR
LITTLE CREEPING THINGS

"Chelsea Ichaso has without a doubt written the breakout thriller of the year."

—Dana Mele, author of *People Like Us*

"Ichaso's debut is a riveting whodunnit…a psychological thriller worthy of mystery aficionados."

—*School Library Journal*

"Thrilling…will satisfy the appetites of all manner of mystery fans."

—*Booklist*

"Everyone's a suspect, and no one is safe in this twisty debut from a compelling new voice in YA, Chelsea Ichaso. Don't miss it!"

—Kit Frick, author of *See All the Stars, All Eyes on Us,* and *I Killed Zoe Spanos*

ALSO BY CHELSEA ICHASO

They're Watching You
Dead Girls Can't Tell Secrets
Little Creeping Things

THE SUMMER SHE WENT MISSING

THE
SUMMER
SHE
WENT
MISSING

CHELSEA ICHASO

Content warning: depiction of violence and descriptions of physical abuse.

Published by Sourcebooks Fire, an imprint of Sourcebooks
P.O. Box 4410, Naperville, Illinois 60567–4410
(630) 961-3900
sourcebooks.com

Cataloging-in-Publication Data is on file with the Library of Congress

Printed and bound in Canada.
MBP 10 9 8 7 6 5 4

For Ann and Bill

PART 1

LAST SUMMER

1

PAIGE

The wolf is standing just off the road, something dead and bloody hanging from its jowls. Its amber eyes lock onto mine through the van window, so cold that a chill ripples through me. But before I can get a word out, the wolf's gray hide vanishes into the trees as our van clunks ahead.

So fast, I start to wonder if I even saw it at all.

"Did anyone else see—"

"We're almost there!" my younger sister, Lucy, says, tugging her earbuds free. She tucks them away and smooths her long russet-colored hair in her phone's camera.

I look ahead to see that she's right. We've driven this route every summer of our lives and know the telltale white rock. It marks the end of the road that winds up the mountain and leads to our destination: Clearwater Ridge.

To me, summer in Clearwater Ridge has always meant three things.

One, the cool, sparkling river that runs through it, sun

beating through the wisps of trees overhead as you float down-stream; the sounds of the birds, laughter, and the roar of the rapids in my ears. Two, the droves of wealthy vacationers fill-ing the homes that remain locked and empty for nine months of the year. Three, my favorite people in the entire world.

One of those people hugs me the instant I step out of the van.

"I can't breathe," I mumble through a laugh. Audrey Covington smells of sunscreen and her coconut leave-in con-ditioner. The scent brings back a hundred memories of her and this place. I nearly forget about the horrible drive up here until I attempt to pull away, and my arm sticks to hers. "I'm sweating all over you." The van's air-conditioning broke halfway up the mountain, which prompted not only a near bout of heat exhaustion but an hour-long tirade from Mom. She'd been telling Dad to take the hunk of junk to the shop for a month. "Help me get my stuff to the room so I can cool off."

We're still in the driveway, and though the lush canopy of trees offers plenty of shade, the water slaps against the rocks in the distance, calling me.

"Sorry," she says, only squeezing me harder. "I just can't believe you're here."

"I know. But seriously, let go." She does, pulling back and looking over me the way my grandmother does every Christmas. "You're being weird."

Still, I look at her too: she's the same Audrey as always. She's wearing ripped jean shorts and a lacy white crop top over a floral bikini. Her face is bare, save a swipe of shimmering bronzer and a coat of pink lip gloss. Her blond hair is pulled up in a bun that's somehow perfectly messy. The kind that would take me forty-five minutes to replicate, which is why my long sweaty brown hair is in a ponytail, as usual. My ponytail is never *perfectly* messy—just the regular kind of messy.

"Paige!" Mom calls from the front porch. "Bring that IKEA bag to the kitchen." Mr. Covington waves at me before taking one of the suitcases from Mom and heading through the door.

I duck my head back into the stifling car and, with Audrey's help, lug the bags toward the chalet-style mansion that the Covingtons refer to as "the cabin." My gaze sweeps up the limestone facade, which sparkles in the sunlight. The entire place was renovated a few years back. The regular old pool was replaced with a fancy infinity variety. All new stonework and reclaimed timber were done to create a semblance of that rustic log vibe the Covingtons think they've got going on. When Mrs. Covington has had one too many glasses of chardonnay, she can't help but repeat the story of a certain celebrity whose Realtor came by, asking to buy the place.

My parents, after having enjoyed an entire summer of luxury, like to gossip about their best friends on the drive back home. "Can you imagine shelling out millions of dollars on a home you don't even live in for most of the year?" my dad whispered last summer, when he thought Lucy and I both had our earbuds in.

Mom scoffed; there wasn't really much she could say. Of course she could imagine it; anyone could dream. We hadn't even updated our kitchen once. Our dishwasher was broken, and sometimes, the panels on the ceiling came loose and crashed to the nasty linoleum floor.

I drag the massive IKEA bag over the natural stone floors

here, the grout somehow still blindingly white. I doubt Audrey or her siblings even know what linoleum is.

"I'll unpack this stuff." I open the stainless-steel refrigerator with glass doors. It looks like something I saw in an episode of *The Kardashians*. But Mrs. Covington glides into the kitchen, her floral-print summer dress fluttering about her ankles. "We've got it, Paige. Go on, get your suit on."

"Yeah, hurry up," Audrey says, shooing me along.

"Thanks." I heft my bag over a shoulder and make my way to the stairs.

When a low voice calls out, "Hey, Paige," my heart jolts. But it's only Nate, Audrey's fourteen-year-old brother, sitting with Lucy at the high bar in the game room. His dark blond hair is shaggier this summer, and he's grown. He isn't the skinny kid who used to join forces with Lucy to pester us.

"Hey, Nate. You...sound older," I say, causing him to redden.

At least I didn't say, "My, you sure have grown," which is the line my brain fed me. I have this tendency to talk like an old lady, thanks to all the time I spend at my after-school job at a nursing home, Sunshine Park Care Center. Nate goes back to showing Lucy something on his phone, and I resist the urge to ask the question that's been rolling through my mind on a constant loop: *Where's Dylan?*

Everyone else made an appearance for our arrival, the way they do every year. It's a first-day tradition. All the kids go down to the river, and all the parents eventually join us, once they've helped my parents unpack and filled their thermoses with Mrs. Covington's sangria. But Dylan isn't here, and I'm not going to play the part of his little sister's clingy friend by asking about him. Instead, I heft my suitcase up the stairs to the room I've shared with Audrey since we were toddlers.

Once dressed in my navy blue and white polka-dot bikini and cutoff shorts, I stuff a wrinkled tank top and sunscreen in a tote bag. There's a spring in my step as I head out the door, swinging my bag to the beat of the Beach Boys song they always play at Sunshine Park. As I near the stairs, my bag sweeps back in a grand arch, then launches forward.

Smack into someone's face.

"What the h—" comes the deep voice, and I cower in horror as Dylan Covington grabs at his jaw. "Paige?"

I debate stepping back inside the bedroom, closing the door, and going to sleep for all eternity. "Hey, Dylan," I say instead, cringing.

"Where was that hit during last year's pickup game?" He rubs a knuckle along his chin, which I must've bruised with my feral girl antics. *Why am I such a klutz?* But then he looks up at me with his pretty blue eyes and winks.

My heart speeds up so much that I have to steady myself against the railing. "I've been training. You obviously haven't been."

He punches my arm softly. "How are you?"

"Less bruised than you, I suppose." I match his smile. "Glad to be here, ready for a swim." I gesture toward my bikini top and immediately go hot with embarrassment.

His eyes lower for the briefest moment before flicking back up. I don't think I'm imagining the pink blush painting his cheeks. "Same," he says, choking on the word slightly.

"Can you believe that in one more year, you'll be a college guy?"

His forehead creases. "A college guy?"

This is the problem. The old lady–isms get stronger with nerves.

But he laughs and pulls me into a hug. "I've missed you, Paige."

"I've missed you too," I say, trying to sound casual. I am completely, buzzingly aware that half my torso is bare against his T-shirt, through which I can feel his swimmer's muscles.

"Let's roll!" Audrey calls from the bottom of the stairs, causing Dylan and I to wrench apart.

Down in the kitchen, Lucy and Audrey are stocking a cooler with sodas and snacks. I catch Audrey slip a few beer cans into the mix, burying them beneath the ice and water bottles. Every year, someone tries it, and every year, that someone gets caught. But the consequence is never more than a stern talking to, which is why we always try again.

Summer in Clearwater Ridge isn't like regular life. Here, we're too carefree, too far removed from the rules of school and jobs and society in general. No one—not even our parents—can be bothered to dole out a punishment.

Audrey shuts the lid, and Dylan takes over, rolling the cooler along as his sister hooks her arm through mine.

The five of us head out the back French doors, straight through the large patio with the white gazebo and the crystal-blue infinity pool. Immediately, the sound of the waterfall, the singing of the birds, and the scent of pine hits me. The woods press up against the gate, infringing on this civilized space with their wild and savage beauty. Their branches weave through the iron bars, and if it weren't for the gardeners who tend to the place twice a week, the patio would be covered in pine cones and needles.

The inner tubes lean against the gate. Dylan grabs one and loops it around an arm. The rest of us follow suit, heading through the gate and onto the path down to the rocky bank, where the synthetic whoosh of the pool's waterfall gives way to the river's roar. We leave the trail and the canopy of trees to hike down the ravine, which is carpeted in shrubs and fallen logs. The twigs scrape my bare legs as mosquitoes buzz at my ears, but my focus is on the water ahead. This part of Clearwater Ridge is calm. The knee-deep water runs clear, perfect for floating. It foams and gushes over the rocks, creating mini waterslides. The sunshine stipples through the overhanging branches to glimmer off the water, and Lucy snaps a photo that will no doubt be up on her Instagram account momentarily.

At the bottom of the ravine, we toss our things onto some large rocks. Nate and Dylan continue to the water, while Audrey digs into the cooler. I apply a quick coat of sunscreen, because it's the responsible thing to do. When Lucy kicks off her sandals and starts after Nate and Dylan, I drag her back by the arm and spray her down.

"Thanks, Mom," she mutters, reaching into the open cooler to retrieve a beer.

I slap at her hand until she drops it. "You're too young," I say, taking up the can and cracking it open.

"So are you," she retorts. But Nate's laughter rings out

through the gully, snagging her attention. He's already coasting ahead downstream, and she grabs an inner tube and chases after him.

Dylan is standing in the shallows near the shore, inner tube looped over a shoulder. "You girls coming?" he asks.

I start to nod, ready to abandon my beer and all earthly possessions to join him. But Audrey says, "You go on ahead. We've got some catching up to do."

My heart sinks. Dylan shrugs and wades out into the deeper water. Letting my sunglasses slide down the bridge of my nose, I glare at her. "Very funny, Covington."

"It was." She laughs and takes a swig of beer.

Audrey has known about my crush on her older brother for years, and she's made it her personal mission to thwart my every effort. All in fun, of course.

At least, I think it is. She has said it would be cool if I dated him one day, or even married him, because then we'd be sisters.

This year, I sort of wish she'd give the shenanigans a break. This summer doesn't feel like every other summer. It doesn't feel like three years ago when I got all dressed up, hoping he'd ask me to come with him to Tripp Shaw's annual party in the Pines. I tiptoed downstairs, strategically placing myself between him and his pathway to the front door. The moment he reached the bottom step and our eyes met, Audrey emerged from the kitchen to shout, "Paige, are you wearing lipstick? Does this mean the tummy trouble cleared up?"

Part of me wanted to die, and part of me wanted to take her mother's precious vase off the table in the foyer and chuck it at her head. I couldn't speak. I could only stare at the ground and stammer that I didn't have tummy trouble before running past Dylan toward the stairs.

Later, Audrey swore that Dylan knew she was joking and that one day, he and I would be together. That it was obvious, written in the stars. Her games were just that—games.

"You know," Audrey says, dusting an insect off her thigh, "I could've interrupted you two earlier, when you assaulted him. Nice work there, by the way. A bizarre cry for attention, but effective."

My mouth drops open. "That wasn't—I didn't. You were *watching* us?"

She smiles to herself in that omniscient sort of way. "I may have eavesdropped for a second. But I did good, didn't I? Let you lovebirds have your moment?"

"We're not lovebirds." I take a sip of beer and resist the urge to spit it out. I forgot I don't actually like this stuff. "He still sees me as your stupid little friend. And he's going to college in a year." Like Audrey, I'm headed into my junior year of high school. Two years left in high school may as well be a lifetime.

"Then you've got to up your game," she says, leaning an elbow back onto the rock.

"We both know I don't have any game." *Must change the subject before I spontaneously combust.* "Have you seen Kurt yet?" Last year, Audrey and Kurt Winfield were a summer item. They worked together at the Clearwater Ridge Rafting Company. Kurt is one of the few locals who's managed to find his way into the summer people crowd. But things fizzled out quickly once summer ended and Audrey went back to her real life.

"Nah, we only got here yesterday." Audrey tips her head back, finishing the dregs of her beer before stashing the can in her bag. "I've managed to avoid town."

"Well, you can't avoid town forever. I need a banana split from Carlson's as much as I need oxygen. Maybe more."

"I know," she groans. "If we go later today, he'll probably be rafting."

"Tripp's party is tonight. Do you really have to avoid Kurt all summer? I thought things ended on a not-so-horrible note."

"That's the problem," she says, tipping her head back dramatically. "I'm worried he thinks we're just going to pick up where we left off."

"Would that be so bad?"

She glances up at the trees contemplatively, then shrugs. "I just want to go riding, eat banana splits, and hang out with you."

"Same." I toss a baby pine cone at her. "Minus the riding part, obviously." Audrey has always had this fascination with horses. She's in the equestrian club at her private academy, competes on weekends. Her horse obsession never rubbed off on me, mostly because I'm allergic to hairy animals. I can barely be around Audrey after she's been riding. My eyes itch, I sneeze, get hives. It's not pretty.

"Still working on getting your own?" I ask. Part of the reason Audrey worked at the rafting company all last summer was to earn the funds to buy her own horse. Her parents believed she'd take better care of one that had been purchased by her own sweat and blood.

"Still working." Her eyes avert to the weeds that spring up between the rocks. "They're not cheap, especially not the one I've had my sights set on." She once showed me a picture of the breed she'd been interested in. It looked like…a horse. "I was thinking about getting a job at the club this summer. The waitresses make way better money than I ever made at the rafting company."

"Sounds good. Free smoothies for me." I raise the beer I've barely touched.

"And…" Audrey's eyebrows waggled playfully. "I was thinking maybe you could get a job with me."

"Me?" I slap my chest, feigning a heart attack. "A workin' girl? I have so much lounging to do this summer."

"Just part-time. We'll have plenty of hours to lounge."

I twist my lips. I was really looking forward to a relaxing vacation. Unlike Audrey, with her equestrian competitions and SAT prep courses, I work as an orderly at Sunshine Park all year long. That's five afternoons a week of getting yelled at by elderly people who don't like steamed cauliflower, believe they're being held hostage, or can't remember why they're mad. And that's after I'm already beat from water polo practice. It's the reason my parents never force me to find a summer job; Clearwater Ridge is my break from waiting on people.

But Audrey's curling her lower lip at me like a sad baby, her blue eyes wide and unblinking.

"Fine." I put my beer down and cross my arms. "Guess there's no point in lounging if you're not here."

"None whatsoever," she says in a singsong voice, peeling

off her crop top. She shakes out her long blond hair and grabs my hand.

I tug down my shorts and kick off my sandals. Together, we take our matching inner tubes and dash toward the water.

2

Audrey and I coast along, passing the occasional couple or lone fisherman on the thin golden strands of beach. For the most part, though, we have the river to ourselves. I lean back, shutting my eyes against the sun and letting the water carry me.

When my tube snags on a log, I dip my hand into the cold water and paddle around it. "Wait up, Audrey!" I call out, noting how far ahead she's gotten.

"Oh, sure! I'll just step on the brake!" Her laughter echoes through the gorge, but she grabs hold of a large rock until I catch up.

Together, we bump along down a series of small frothing rapids, water spraying our skin. When we reach the section where our tubes catch on the rocks, we hop down. Picking up the tubes, we wade the rest of the way to where the granite walls form Haver's Gorge, a natural swimming hole. It's here that our siblings' voices ring out.

We toss our inner tubes onto the beach. Audrey clambers

over the slippery boulders first, and I follow. We make our way between two waterfalls, emerging to face the stone wall. Scaling it, we find our footing in the crevices, as we have hundreds of times.

Audrey reaches the top and stands with her hands on her hips, like some sort of intrepid adventurer. I climb up after her, taking in the glassy green water that shines like a gemstone.

On my right is a granite cliff; to the left, a smaller boulder— the one I like to jump from. Dead ahead, the river continues, eventually becoming deeper and more treacherous this time of year. That's where the whitewater rafting happens.

I take a seat on the boulder, ready to sun myself like a reptile. Beside me, Audrey yells, "Bombs away!" and flings herself into the water.

"Finally!" Dylan shouts from the top of the high cliff to my right—the cliff our parents declared off-limits years ago. "Thought you two got lost." He takes two large steps toward the edge and then dives, plunging pin-straight into the water with barely a splash.

My heart stops, the way it does every time he makes that dive. It's only when his head breaches the surface, his mouth in a stupid grin, that my pulse starts up again.

"Show-off!" Nate yells from the other lower rock formation, across the pool, as Dylan swims toward me. "Totally trying to impress *someone*." Nate glances pointedly in my direction, and I look away, pretending not to have heard.

Only I *did* hear. Tiny bubbles of hope and nerves float up in my chest. Audrey has always teased me about Dylan, but no one's ever teased *him* about *me*. Did he say something to Nate?

Probably not. I'm overthinking this. "Eight point two," I say as Dylan clambers up onto my boulder.

"What?" he asks, feigning outrage. "That's ridiculous."

"You lost an entire point for breaking the damned rule."

"But I always break the damned rule."

And I always die a little inside. "Do it again, and I'm telling your mother."

"You wouldn't." His eyes linger on mine long enough to heat me through.

"Try me."

In response, he shakes the water from his hair all over me until I shriek.

"So, is your dad staying long?" he asks, lowering beside me, palms behind him on the granite.

"Yeah, he'll be around."

My mom and Mrs. Covington—Eleanor—were college friends. When they graduated, Mom married Dad, and Eleanor married Spencer Covington, heir to a pharmaceutical fortune. Mom had to move upstate for Dad's job, but the friends vowed that they'd always reunite for the summer.

My parents kept their vow, though in the beginning, it wasn't easy. Dad worked long hours, so he had to make the drive to and from on weekends, leaving Mom and us girls here with the Covingtons. I was little, but I can still remember the arguments between my parents.

Now, though, Dad has worked his way up in his job and has the flexibility of working remotely. He only has to return home a couple of times, just to make sure things are running smoothly at the plant.

"Are you working this summer?" I ask, trying not to stare at his muscular chest.

"Nah. I've got to train for season, so there isn't much time. Why, are you?"

I shrug. "Sounds like Audrey's going to make me get a job at the club."

"Tell her no. We need more time to hang out."

A flutter goes through my stomach. "Okay," I say stupidly, knowing Audrey always has the final say. She isn't the oldest, but she bosses both of her brothers around. At her school, she's in charge of everything too. She's in student council and heads two clubs. When she directs, people obey.

In fact, her bossiness is how we became friends in the first place. I mean, we'd always been "friends" in the sense that we'd been placed together every summer since we were born. But it wasn't until the summer after first grade that it felt real—that she'd chosen me and I'd chosen her. Our parents had dropped all of us off at our various Clearwater Ridge Country Club summer camps: Dylan chose swim, Nate and Lucy golf. I opted to stick with Audrey at tennis camp, foolishly thinking that anyone could hit a fluorescent-colored ball with a racquet.

Of course, Audrey ended up queen of the court, and I ended up getting whacked in the face with a ball and tripping over my untied laces more times than I could count. A particularly vicious group of country club kids taunted me, calling me "ball girl" and pressuring me to quit. I was on the verge of tears when Audrey stepped in. She told them if they bullied me again, she wouldn't invite them to the pool party her mother was planning. I don't know how that threat managed to pack such a punch, but it worked. Those kids were nothing but nice to me the rest of camp, and Audrey went from this distant glowing star sitting high on a pedestal to the friend I now carry with me in my heart.

But boy is she bossy. Right now, for example, she's shouting my name and pounding her fists over the surface of the water. "Paige! Stop flirting and get your ass in here!"

I consider rolling into a ball and pretending to be just another rock. Instead, I get up, face hot from more than the beating sun, and get my butt in the water.

———

After a sunset dinner of barbecue chicken beneath the Covingtons' gazebo, Audrey, Dylan, and I head over to Tripp Shaw's annual Summer Kickoff party. Dylan drives, navigating the winding roads to the Pines, a small community of the richest of the rich when it comes to Clearwater Ridge's summer society.

At the door, Tripp, a tall sturdy blond with a year-round tan and professionally whitened teeth, answers the door. "Bro!" he booms at Dylan, high-fiving him before pulling him into a hug. Tripp, whose full name is Preston Winthrop Shaw III, is eighteen, having recently graduated high school. He's headed to UCLA on a football scholarship, even though his family can more than afford tuition.

Tripp's summer house is even more impressive than the Covingtons', having both an indoor and an outdoor pool. This means there's an extremely good chance that some drunk kid will end up knocking someone into one before the night is over.

I'm not too worried, since one of my repeat fantasies involves falling into the pool and Dylan diving in to rescue me. Sure, I'm a varsity water polo player and wouldn't actually need to be rescued. But because I'd be soaking wet and there's a chill to the summer air, Dylan would have to hold me to keep me warm. Basically, this mansion is where dreams really could come true.

Tripp greets us girls next, lingering a little extra on his hug with Audrey. There was a summer, back before Kurt, when Audrey liked Tripp and all signs pointed to them becoming an item. But then we caught him sharing a raft with another girl—that's not a metaphor.

Tripp leads us into the kitchen, placing red cups of beer in our hands. He slings an arm around Dylan's shoulder, showing off a massive football championship ring. "Dude, there's someone you have to meet tonight."

My insides knot. Of course, Tripp found Dylan a pretty, rich girl to hang out with this summer. No need for me. The two of them amble off down the hall together, crushing my falling-in-the-pool dream to bits.

"Well, we should probably find a sad couch to sit on until this is all over," I say, gesturing toward the living room.

"He'll be back," Audrey says, a playful lilt to her voice.

"Yeah, right."

She takes a sip of her beer and then purses her lips, her blue eyes dancing with something like eagerness. "Okay, so I wasn't going to say anything. I just...really believe these things should happen organically. But you're my best friend, so I think it's more important that I—"

"Spit it out, Covington."

"Right. Sorry." She grins. "When we got back after the river, Dylan asked me something."

"Okay," I say, dragging out the word.

"He asked if I thought there was—" Audrey's eyes widen, and she shields her face with her hand. "Kurt alert," she whispers, turning her shoulder to me.

I glance across the kitchen to the doorway that leads to the dining room. Audrey's ex, a stout seventeen-year-old with severe brows and muscular rafter's arms, is reaching for a red cup.

"Paige!" He drops the cup and crosses the kitchen, craning his neck when he spots Audrey, who's frozen on the threshold. "Audrey?" he says, coming closer yet.

Her spine stiffens, but she spins around, forcing a smile. "Kurt! Hey. Good to see you." He embraces her, and I try to think of an excuse to get her out of the kitchen. Audrey clearly needs saving. And I need to know what she was about to tell me.

"Hey, Kurt," I say, forcing him to tear his gaze and his hands off my friend.

"Oh, hey." He offers me a fist bump. "What's up?"

Awkwardly, I switch my cup to my left hand and fist-bump him back. "Uh, Audrey, remember how we were going to find that girl about that thing?" Super smooth.

"That's right," she says, making a pouty face at Kurt.

"Are you working at the rafting company this summer?" Kurt asks in a flirty voice, completely ignoring our fake excuse.

Audrey purses her lips and slings me an apologetic look. "Maybe you should see that girl without me."

"Well, she's your friend, the girl. So...that would be..."

She gives me a bashful smile. "I'll catch up in a sec."

"Great." I take a swig of beer and skulk out of the kitchen. I know it's childish, but all we have together are our summers. Weekly video chats during the school year aren't the same thing as hanging out in real life. Last summer, she had her job and Kurt; I hoped this summer would be different.

The worst part is, she never told me what Dylan said. Now my insides are knotted in anticipation. I wander into the living room, thankful for this beer to occupy my hand. There are people, most of whom I've never seen before, scattered around the room in little clusters. Tripp likes to brag that he keeps the townies out, but I know that isn't true. They're here. Word gets loose, and they infiltrate. For one night, we aren't townies and summer people; we're just a bunch of kids gone wild.

Audrey can spot townies from a mile away though. It's her *gift*. "The shoes," she'll tell me. Or "The dress." It's not like she avoids them, but for whatever reason, she feels the need to point them out.

Bored, I take a seat on a formal-looking wingback chair and attempt to play Audrey's game. Near the far wall, a tall curly-haired guy wearing khaki shorts and one of those stiff button-up shirts is bobbing his head to the music. A girl with shoulder-length brown hair and a white minidress enters by way of the foyer, wasting no time before tossing her sweater and bag onto the nearest chair and joining the guy in bouncing to the beat. I analyze the girl's attire first, channeling my friend's powers. The girl tilts her head back, smiling up at the ceiling as her body sways. But as I start to inspect her shoes, the guy glides in front of her, blocking my view. Doesn't matter, anyway. I definitely don't have Audrey's radar. I couldn't tell a five-hundred-dollar handbag from the ones Grandma picks up at Walmart.

Adjacent to me, a girl with a skirt so short it could be underwear is sitting on a guy's lap. He whispers in her ear, and she laughs so hard she spits beer all over the expensive leather couch.

Across the room, a bunch of guys are playing beer pong. I spot Brent Haywood, another one of Dylan's longtime country club friends, throwing his hands into the air after what he deems an "epic shot." With his light blue polo shirt, khaki shorts, and boat shoes, he looks ready to step onto a yacht. It's a far cry from the boy we used to play hide-and-seek with as kids.

Before I can look away, he spots me staring. "Paige!"

I smile brightly, acutely aware of how pathetic I look sitting on this grand chair all alone. He passes his paddle off to another guy and strides over.

"Hey," I say as he pulls me up by the hand into a hug.

"How are you?" Drawing back, he peers intently through his tortoiseshell frames, causing me to blush. Brent is tan with dust-brown hair and stunningly green eyes. He's a soccer player and probably the king of his high school. Unlike Tripp, who's constantly loud and showy, Brent has a…less loud side. I think that's why I've always liked him more than Dylan's other Clearwater Ridge friends. Two years ago, when Dylan had a girlfriend back home and I spent all summer moping about it, Audrey tried to pair Brent and me up. But then he turned up at the swimming hole with a gorgeous raven-haired girlfriend named Larissa.

At the last Summer Kickoff, when Audrey was off with Kurt

somewhere in this mansion, Brent and I ended up together in the outdoor pool. We sat on the steps for a good hour. I asked about his ex, Larissa, and he relayed how she'd dumped his ass a week into the school year. He told me how she was now dating some blond, perfect football quarterback from Iowa State. When I told him he needed to stop looking at her Instagram, he lowered his head into his hands, body wracked with silent laughter.

"It's not *that* pathetic," I assured him, patting him on the back like you would a puppy. "You'll get through this." I had no idea what I was talking about; I'd never even had a boyfriend.

Still don't.

A rambunctious partygoer bumps into my shoulder now, causing my beer to slosh around and yanking my mind out of the past. "I'm good." I smile up at Brent.

"You know, we were just talking about you," he says, crossing his arms.

"Me?"

And who's *we*?

"Paige Redmond," he says. "The one and only."

"And what exactly were *we* saying?"

He laughs. "I'm not about to spill Summer Kickoff secrets. But some of us guys were in the wine cellar, and *someone* might have asked if you were single." He puts a hand to his heart. "I made a vow in that cellar not to relay a single word of our communication. But"—he checks over his shoulder conspiratorially—"someone *else* might've said to stay away from you."

I try to keep my stare as blank as possible, but there are multiple mystery figures in this story, and Brent is being very coy.

"And the second someone," he adds, "maybe, probably lives in the same house as you every summer."

A flurry of hope spirals through my chest. Still, I shrug. "He's the protective older brother type."

Brent shakes his head, letting out a chuckle. "Sure, Paige. That's definitely it."

Now I have to know what Audrey was about to tell me.

"Let's go swimming." Brent snatches my beer right out of my hand, holding it out like bait.

"I'm waiting for Aud—" I start, cutting off when I spot my best friend in the kitchen doorway, lips pinched as she stares down at her phone. "Audrey!" I call out, but she doesn't hear me over the clamor.

"Be right back," I tell Brent before crossing the room to stop in front of her. "Everything okay?"

She finally glances up from her phone. "Oh, hey." The inscrutable look on her face lasts another beat before she nods. "Yeah, just about to text Tripp. Some idiot knocked over his mom's fancy-looking plant. It's a goner." She cringes. "Have you seen him?"

"Uh, not since earlier. Brent and I are headed to the pool. You coming?" I make to loop my arm through hers, but she pulls back.

"In a sec. I've got to get Kurt."

"Kurt?" I can't help it. After everything Audrey said today by the river—all the promises she made about spending the summer together—I feel deceived. She can't even stick with me for one evening.

"He's back there cleaning up the mess." A new song starts,

this one louder, the bass line deeper than the last. Distractedly, her head bobs, her gaze skimming the room.

So much for Audrey wanting to avoid Kurt like the plague. "I thought you were over him."

"I was—I *am*." She licks her lips. "I told you. We're just catching up."

"Right. Well, see you in there, I guess."

"Yep." She turns and strides off through the kitchen, and all I can do is watch her go.

3

"Kurt again, huh?" Behind me, Brent's voice rises over the din. He hands me back my beer, like that will fix whatever girl drama is going on here, and adjusts his glasses. "Not sure what she sees in that guy, honestly."

I shrug. Kurt is fine, as far as guys go. But right now, I wish Audrey didn't see a thing in him. Not one single thing.

"Shall we, then?" he asks, tipping his head toward the doorway.

"Let me grab another drink first."

He squints down at my full beer. "Okay, well...see you in there." He takes off through the hall toward the indoor pool.

I make my way back to my special chair only to find that it's now occupied by a lanky guy watching a video on his phone.

Just then there's a tap on my shoulder.

"What are you doing by yourself?" Dylan asks, scanning the room as if my hordes of friends will suddenly appear.

"I—uh, had to see a girl about a thing."

He cocks a brow. "You're so weird, Paige."

"Thank you?" I move to lean against the wall, but Dylan's hand darts out, nudging me forward.

"Where's Audrey?" he asks.

"With Kurt."

"Ah. Well, guess we all saw that coming." Hand still on my back, he begins to steer me past the beer pongers, down the hall.

"Did we though?" I ask, wondering how I missed the signs. "Also, where are we going?"

"To the cool kids' club," he says.

"Oh, I'm not cool." I shake my head. "This isn't even my beer."

Dylan laughs, removing his fingers from my back to take my hand. It sends a current of electricity through me. "Come on."

Voices trickle from a wide set of double doors, followed by splashing. Dylan tugs me along into the room with the enormous indoor pool. The ceiling opens to a skylight, surrounded by hundreds of starlike bulbs, which reflect off the surface of the pool. Underwater lights paint the pool green, then purple a few seconds later. The walls are made almost entirely of glass, and at this hour, the moonlight streams through. The Jacuzzi is filled with people, and I spot Tripp among them, holding his red cup.

Ten or so partygoers fill the pool, including two girls in their bras and underwear.

"I actually did my hair today," I lie, motioning to my bedraggled ponytail.

One corner of Dylan's mouth lifts. "So did I." He peels off

his shirt, and I avert my eyes again, focusing on this beer that I don't even want. He discards the shirt against the wall and kicks off his flip-flops.

"You're a guy. You're, like, born with your hair done."

"Right." He rolls his eyes and dives into the pool. My heart skips at the thought of him abandoning me here, but he wades back over. Propping himself up on the edge with his elbows, he frowns. "So you're going to make me swim all by myself."

"You're not by yourself. All your friends are in there." I glance over to where Tripp shoves Brent into the pool before taking a victory lap around the edge, raising his red cup like a trophy on his way out the door.

"What if I don't want to swim with them?" The way he's looking at me now—it's different. In fact, I don't think Dylan Covington has ever looked at me this way before. His blue eyes are narrowed, intense. Pleading.

I huff and tug my shorts down. Thank the good Lord I wore a swimsuit, because I would not look like those girls across the pool in my underwear. Earlier today, I had on the granny panties with the dancing panda bears that my actual grandmother found on sale at Walmart.

Once my white T-shirt and shorts are strewn atop Dylan's belongings, he taps the water, and I take a running leap to cannonball beside him.

The pool is warmer than I imagined, nothing like the river earlier today. No sooner do I come up for air, when I hear him call out, "You're little fish!"

A jolt of adrenaline rushes through me. I start to swim, knowing it's hopeless. Dylan is on me in seconds, hand on my back. When we were little, and he played the role of big fish, he used to let me believe I could outswim him, at least for a minute or two. There are no such illusions now as he spins me around in the water to face him.

"You know you're supposed to give me a twenty-minute head start."

"Paige," he says, and I feel his fingers dust my waist. "You could swim twenty laps in this pool in that amount of time." Dylan's the one who encouraged me to try out for water polo freshman year. I'm not much of an individual sport–type person, but it turns out that water polo suits me just fine.

"Still," I say, melting at his touch.

I'm vaguely aware of people climbing out of the pool, carrying their booze as they exit the room. But I can't focus on that, because Dylan pulls me in close to him. My heart is racing so fast it could probably propel through the water. His gaze is locked on mine, so intense I almost have to look away.

When his grip tightens around my waist and he starts to lift me, all of my hopes spring up in my chest.

But then he tosses me backward.

I land with a splash, shame burning despite the tepid water as I catch my breath.

I'll always be like a younger sister to him, one he has to protect from other boys. One he chases around the pool.

But when I blink away the droplets and gain my bearings, I find him hanging on to the pool's edge, right where he was a moment ago. His eyes meet mine for an instant before he looks away. I wade over to him, anchoring myself to the edge with an elbow. "Everything okay?"

He nods. "Yeah, I guess I wasn't expecting...I mean, I *knew* how I felt about you. But I thought I could just...turn it off."

"What do you mean?" I ask, realizing with a quick surveying glance that everyone's cleared out, leaving the two of us alone. The glowing lights beneath the water shift from yellow to blue.

He turns to face me, eyes searching mine. Though his feet reach the bottom, I have to keep one hand on the edge. "I'm sorry," he says. "I got nervous. *You* make me nervous."

"You threw me because I make you nervous," I say, nodding slowly.

With a soft smile, he reaches out to push a bedraggled strand of wet hair behind my ear. "It's how little I trust myself around you. I thought I could ignore everything. But now that you're here, the only thing I can think about is"—his gaze lowers to the water between us, cheeks blushing in an adorably sheepish way—"kissing you."

"What?" This sounds suspiciously like something dream-Dylan would say.

"Sorry. We should probably just...go inside with the others."

I remove my hand from the edge, so scared of ruining the moment that I don't dare kick my feet. Instead, I hold on to his arm, letting his sturdy frame keep me afloat. "Probably shouldn't," I say, my voice barely a whisper.

Carefully, as if Dylan's body might detonate, I reach my other hand out, letting it settle onto his shoulder. He stiffens under my touch.

But then he grabs my waist with both hands and drags me

closer. My body crushes against his, arms looping around the back of his neck.

Then his eyes fall shut, head tilting as his lips meet mine.

It's better than I imagined.

When we exit the pool, Dylan leads me to one of the lounge chairs. "I'll find you a towel," he says, sitting me down. "And," he adds, glancing at my stale cup of beer, "something else to drink?"

"Water would be lovely," I say, arms wrapped around my torso.

"Be right back." He kisses my forehead before hurrying off through the double doors.

I wait, replaying the kiss in my mind, enjoying a silent moment until a group of kids rush into the pool room, shouting and peeling off their clothes. I think about leaving to find Dylan, but I don't want to seem too desperate. The questions start to pile up as I sit, the air hitting my damp skin and chilling me through.

Will things be awkward now? Will he regret this night forever? When we see his friends, will he play it cool, like nothing's going on between us? Or will he want to make it official?

As the minutes pass, my shivering intensifies. Maybe I'll go find myself a towel.

Arms wrapped around my midsection, I slip on my flip-flops and head out the door and down the hall. The bathroom is a mess, beer bottles spilling out of the trash can and used towels in a heap in one corner. But there's still a huge stack of plush, clean towels. I grab one and drape it over my shoulders.

I head toward the living room in search of Dylan. In the hallway, laughter trickles from the door up on the right. The game room.

Inside, Brent and a bunch of guys are seated at a round table, playing cards. "Thought you could pull a fast one on me," Brent says with a laugh, slapping his cards onto the table. The others groan and lower their hands. "Almost had me too," he adds, glancing over at the door. "Care to join, Paige?"

"Oh, no." I shake my head, causing my damp hair to drip over the wood floor. "I'm bad at cards. No poker face." Not to mention, I'm broke and I happen to know these guys play for money. "I'll leave you to it."

"It's over," one of the other guys says, chair screeching as he gets up from the table. "I'll Venmo you."

"Gentlemen, it's been a pleasure." Brent chuckles and ambles over to the doorway, still in his swimsuit.

I motion to the card table. "The gift must be in the blood." Brent's older brother, Oliver, is a Harvard student and somewhat of a poker legend. He doesn't usually spend summers in Clearwater Ridge anymore. Now, he travels the world, gambling and getting even richer than he was to begin with.

"Oliver may have taught me a few tricks." Grinning, he lifts his brows. "So, you and Dylan seemed to be having fun in the pool."

Heat rushes over me. "Yeah, until he ditched me."

Brent frowns. "Everyone else was headed to the backyard pool. Maybe he's there."

I don't bother arguing that Dylan wouldn't have gone out there, because he said he'd return to me. Instead, I follow Brent down the hall and into the living room. The music is still blasting, though the dancing has turned slower and sloppier.

Still no sign of Dylan. We wade through, past the kitchen and the stairs, reaching a dimly lit hall. I head down it, Brent behind me, our flip-flops crunching over shards of glass and the contents of a Cheetos bag. Mrs. Shaw's broken plant is going to be the least of Tripp's worries by the end of the night.

At a fork, I glance down a corridor that presumably leads outside toward the woods. Brent nudges me. "Backyard's this way." He gestures toward the other hallway, this one dimly lit.

That's when I see them. Audrey and Kurt, standing together. His back pressed up against the wall, her hand on his shoulder. Their faces mere inches apart.

I freeze. Part of me wants to be upset with Audrey for saying one thing earlier today and then doing the complete opposite. The other part is glad she'll be too occupied with Kurt to try and ruin things between her brother and me.

Brent spots them and shakes his head, letting out a low laugh. "Coming?" he asks me.

"Nah. I should've just waited in the pool room. You go on."

I return to the pool room to find Dylan standing there, looking lost. Towel draped over his arm, water bottle in hand. "There you are."

The anxious knot in my stomach loosens. "I got cold."

"I'm sorry," he says, sad blue eyes working their way into my very soul. "I got dragged into a conversation out there, and then I couldn't find a towel."

"You mean this towel?" I ask, removing mine and hitting him in the stomach with it.

He catches the end of the fabric and tugs on it, easing me toward him until his arms are around me. His T-shirt brushes my bare stomach, and his hands roam to my bare shoulders. I shut my eyes, inhaling the chlorine scent of him.

Quickly I grab my clothes, throwing them on over my swimsuit. When I return to him, he finds my hand, sending a bloom of warmth through me. We're barely through the doors when he spins me to face him. Pulling me closer, he kisses me again.

4

When I wake the next morning, Audrey's bed is empty.

Panic streaks through me, and I check my phone. There aren't any new messages.

Last night, Audrey texted that she'd get a ride back with Kurt and we should head home without her. At first, neither Dylan nor I liked the idea. But it got so late that we gave in.

I throw on some shorts and a tank top and hurry down the stairs. Turning the corner, I see her. She's seated on a barstool at the countertop, nursing a steaming mug of coffee.

"Good heavens, Audrey," I say, sounding like old Mrs. Flannigan from Sunshine Park as I move to the cabinet to find my own mug. "You scared the living daylights out of me. What time did Kurt drop you off?"

"I don't know. Late." Her face is still in her mug, but I spot the dark bags beneath her eyes.

"You two must've been having fun." Part of me wants to

give her a hard time for abandoning me the entire night, but the other part is grateful she did.

"Yep."

My tongue itches to spew all the details of my own evening. The way Dylan and I wandered the mansion hand in hand until we found Tripp's parents' ridiculous balcony. How we talked for hours beneath the stars. How he wrapped his arm around me to keep me warm. The way he kissed me.

But the second I get situated in the barstool beside hers, her phone dings on the countertop. She snatches it up, eyes on the screen.

"Everything okay?"

Audrey smiles. "Just Hannah."

"Oh." I try to ignore the pinch of jealousy at hearing this name. Hannah is Audrey's best friend the other nine months of the year. They attend prep school together, do student council together. And the *best* part about Hannah is that she has a massive crush on Dylan.

Every summer, Hannah's come to Clearwater Ridge for a week to visit Audrey, leaving me the third wheel. "When does she arrive?" I ask.

Audrey slides down from the stool. "She's still working out the details. Scored a modeling gig in New York, which is awesome. So she'll probably swing by after that." She rinses her mug out in the sink and grabs a water bottle from the fridge. "I'm headed to the rafting company. They're calling it a job interview, but it's just a formality. I mean, Solomon's going to hire me again."

I practically drop my mug. "What about the club?"

"Oh, um," she says, frowning. "I was thinking this would be better, since I already know the ropes."

I arch a brow. "And Kurt will be there."

She blushes. "Yeah. But don't look at me like that. You didn't want to work at the club anyway. Now, you're free to lounge around all day."

"Gee, thanks." She's right though. I didn't want a summer job, and this will give me more time with Dylan. "Will you be around later? Should we wait for you before heading to the river?"

"Nah. I'm not sure about my hours yet."

"Okay, but—" Forget being patient. I've waited years to be able to blurt the words now dancing on my tongue. "Last night, Dylan and I—"

"I've got to go, Paige," Audrey says, voice reed-thin and cold.

I flinch, the words a whip to my chest.

"I'll text you later about the river," she says, leaving me in the kitchen, my mind reeling and my heart sore.

———

Audrey does not text me later.

I try not to let that moment in the kitchen bother me. She must already feel bad about blowing me off. Sure, Dylan is her brother, and it's all a bit new and strange. But she's my best friend. Deep down, she's happy for me. She'll return, begging for forgiveness. Then she'll ask to hear everything and tease me about it until the sun comes up.

When Dylan finally bumbles down the stairs at noon, hair disheveled and eyes sleepy, I'm reading a book on the living room couch. That panicked feeling returns, setting my nerves ablaze. I think of last night: holding hands on the drive back home, sneaking in at 2 a.m., Dylan walking me all the way to my bedroom door. The thrill of one last kiss in the dark hall, knowing that if we made a single sound, we could be caught. After so much time wishing for this, the whole experience felt like a dream.

What if he wishes that's all it were?

But he spots me, and his eyes brighten. Grinning, he looks suddenly awake as he crosses the room to sit beside me. "What's up?" he asks, leaning his head on my shoulder. "Where is everyone?"

I set the book in my lap and smooth his hair with my fingers. "The parents are on a hike. Lucy and Nate are having lunch in town, and Audrey is interviewing for her old job at the rafting company."

His lifts his head to look at me, brows furrowed. "No country club, then?"

"No country club."

He slips an arm around my waist and tugs me closer. "Good." A creak sounds out in the hall, and he releases me, running his hand over the back of his neck. I examine my fingernails, trying too hard to look casual as our younger siblings wander in.

Nate, carrying a familiar bag from Bianca's, the sandwich shop in town, narrows his eyes as he glances between his brother and me. "What's going on?"

"Nothing," Dylan says. "What's going on with you two? I thought you were eating in town."

"We decided to picnic at the river," Lucy says, unable to keep the suspicion out of her voice. "We brought sandwiches for you guys, if you want to join us. Audrey too."

"Audrey isn't here." Dylan stands, only to take my hand and pull me up off the couch. "But we'd be delighted to accompany you. Wouldn't we, Paige?"

"We certainly would."

———

Two weeks later, Dylan and I are sharing a booth and a banana split at Carlson's Ice Cream Parlor when I get a text from Audrey. Can't make it to ice cream. Sorry. Solomon put me on a multiday trip. I leave in an hour.

I slide the phone across the table, letting Dylan read it. "Why is Solomon being such a killjoy?" I ask. We've barely seen Audrey at all. She came with us to the river once, but she was quiet and moody. When Nate teased her about being away from her boyfriend, she practically bit his head off. "She promised she'd hang out with us today."

"We could always go to her," Dylan offers. "Drop by with an Italian soda."

I nod. "You're always full of great ideas."

We order a strawberry Italian soda to go. The kid behind the counter is Jesse Villareal, who created a bit of a stir last summer when his neighbor caught him doing some sort of chant in the backyard the day before her cat was killed in "ritualistic fashion." The rumor mill took off, accusations about satanic practices turning into an all-out witch hunt. Audrey and I became immersed in the story on the Clearwater Ridge

Forum, this site where the same people who gossip in the diner all day long can share even more scandalous theories from the comfort of their homes and the anonymity of the internet. We stayed up way too late, reading and theorizing. The whole situation amounted to naught a week later, when another neighbor spotted a mountain lion on Jesse's street.

If Audrey were here now, we'd be speculating on the new subject of town gossip: this teenage girl who went missing. My gaze wanders to her flyer stuck to the corkboard on the wall. Madison Blake, a seventeen-year-old brunette with hazel green eyes, went missing a couple of days before I arrived here in town.

Her flyers went up a week ago, but there haven't been any developments in the case. Apparently, this girl lives in Shadow's Pass, a.k.a. the Shadows. It's also known around here as townie central. Kurt lives in Shadow's Pass, though he's one of the rare townies to infiltrate the summer kids' social circle. Most of the people who live there only come to this side of town to work in the vacation industry.

Madison is a different apple. I read all about her case on the forum—by myself this time. According to one comment, the second Madison's story broke loose, a handful of people came forward, saying that they'd been swindled by this girl. Accounts varied, but most of them were anonymous wealthy men who'd dated her, only to be duped into paying apartment bills or car payments that, in the end, never existed. These guys had no idea that Madison and her mother lived on the other side of town.

One comment said that the sheriff's department shouldn't waste resources looking for trash like Madison Blake.

It made my insides churn. Maybe the person who'd posted that had been conned by her, maybe not. When I glance at Madison's flyer on my way out, all I know is that she doesn't look like the monster this side of town has painted her as.

She looks like a teenage girl. She looks like me.

We pay for Audrey's soda and take Dylan's truck out to the Clearwater Ridge Rafting Company office. It's a small office in a tiny shopping center with a desk and a locker where they keep all of the rafting equipment. "I wonder why Solomon has Audrey on a multiday trip," I say. "Don't they have *older* guides for that?"

"She won't be the only guide," Dylan says, though I catch the wariness in his voice. "Solomon probably wants her to get more experience. Like an apprentice." He tries the office door, but it's locked.

That's when I see the small sign taped to the window. CLOSED FOR THE DAY.

"There's your answer," Dylan says. "They must've all gone on this overnight thing."

I glance down at the bright red Italian soda that's sweating all over my hand. "Perfect."

He reaches out to lift my chin with an index finger. "Hey," he says with that hopeful half grin that reaches straight into my chest cavity and squeezes. "I'm no Audrey, but is there something I can do to help?"

I twist my lips as his fingertip runs along my jawline, sweeping up to tuck a loose strand of hair behind my ear. "Well, Audrey always braids wildflowers into fashionable jewelry with me on the riverbank."

"I guess I was thinking more along the lines of…going for a swim." He blushes, which makes me blush. We're both thinking about Tripp's pool and all the *swimming* we did that night.

"A swim would be good," I say with feigned nonchalance.

Laughing, he presses a kiss to my forehead.

5

The weeks pass, and Dylan and I manage to keep our relationship a secret, at least from the adults. If they catch on, my parents will undoubtedly freak out and start imposing boundaries. Our carefree summer haze, effervescent and ethereal as a dream, will evaporate.

We've spent nearly every moment of every day together, off at the river or in town. Evenings at home have been a different matter, filled with whispers and stolen kisses in the halls, secret looks exchanged at the dinner table. Fingertips brushing on the couch.

As for Audrey, whatever worries I've had about her coming between us have proved unfounded. She's scarcely seen. Any free time she has is filled with Kurt or riding at the stables in the Pines. If she's not wearing her rafting company T-shirt, she's decked out in her riding gear.

When she misses dinner yet again, Nate brings it up at the table. "I feel like Audrey is never around."

"That's because she isn't," Dylan mutters under his breath.

Mrs. Covington sips her wine. "Well, I think it's great that Audrey's finally learning some responsibility."

Responsibility? Audrey runs two clubs, is captain of the equestrian team, and holds a seat on the student council.

Mom must be just as confused. "But isn't this a bit extreme, Eleanor? Audrey's missing the entire summer."

Mrs. Covington's lips pinch, her eyes darkening. "I don't need you to tell me how to raise *my* daughter."

I flinch, spine digging into the backrest. I've never heard Mrs. Covington snap at my mother—at anyone, really.

Mom is equally shocked. Her face turns a ghostly hue as the men at the table merely stiffen, averting their gazes to the tablecloth. Finally, my mother clears her throat. "I'm sorry, Ellie. You're right. I overstepped."

Mrs. Covington rubs at her face, creating a red splotch. "No, *I'm* sorry. I just—we've had some issues with Audrey this past year."

Issues with Audrey? Heat fans over my cheeks, down my neck. Audrey and I are supposed to be best friends, yet she never mentioned any problems with her parents.

Before I can pry, Mrs. Covington takes up her wineglass again. "But you're right. I could tell her to take it easier. Cut back on her hours a bit." She tips back her rosé. "Besides, she promised to help me with the deck next week."

Every summer, Mrs. Covington invites her country club friends over for an afternoon tea by the pool—except the tea is actually cocktails. She goes all out, from the theme to the menu. Since Audrey has an eye for decor, she's always in charge of that aspect.

"I can help you, Mrs. Covington," I offer, though decor is another of Audrey's gifts that I lack.

"Aw, thanks, sweetie," she says with a look of pity. "I was hoping you and Audrey could team up."

"I'll talk to her about it," I say. Inside, though, I'm starting to wonder if I'll ever get the chance.

———

Audrey still isn't back by midnight. I've been trying to stay up and catch her, but my heavy eyelids refuse to cooperate. Dylan is already asleep beside me on the couch, our second movie of the night still playing on the living room TV. Lucy and Nate, however, are wide awake, eating popcorn and drinking soda.

Oh, to be young.

I pad over to the kitchen to grab a glass of ice water, hoping the cold will jolt some life back into me. But something stops me in my tracks. Voices coming from the study. Audrey must be home.

I tiptoe closer and press my ear up against the cracked door. "Have you seen a dollar of this money, Eleanor?" Mr. Covington's low voice.

"No, but we will," Mrs. Covington says. "She's working hard, but it takes time to earn five thousand dollars at a summer job."

Guilt ripples through me. I definitely shouldn't be eavesdropping. But that niggle of curiosity keeps my feet planted to the wooden floor.

"Who's to say she's really going to pay us back, Elle?"

"She has no choice. She has to earn back our trust."

"I don't know. She's with that boy all the time. She doesn't even bother showing up for dinner. I think she's headed down that dark path again." He clears his throat. "This time, I don't know if we're going to get her back."

"I'll talk to her in the morning," Mrs. Covington says. "I'll enforce a curfew. It'll be okay, Spence. Audrey learned her lesson last summer."

At the sound of footsteps within the room, I back away from the door. My pulse pounds so forcefully in my ears that I can't hear my own steps on the wood as I scurry down the hall, slipping into the kitchen.

Of course, when I get into bed, I can't sleep. What were the Covingtons talking about? Audrey hasn't ever set foot on a dark path—not even a dimly lit one.

But they spoke about five thousand dollars that she needed to pay back. What could she have done with the money?

It's not like I can even ask her about it. Audrey hasn't exactly been her usual chatty self. Any time I try to talk to her, she blows me off, saying she has to get a riding session in before work. Or that she's off to meet Kurt. Audrey has had boyfriends, jobs, and hobbies in the past. In fact, she's had these *exact* boyfriends, jobs, and hobbies.

But she never treated me like a stranger. She made time for me. This summer, Audrey isn't just busy; she's avoiding me.

I have to stay awake until she comes back so I can confront her about it. If I fall asleep, she'll be gone in the morning, and I'll never have the chance.

When the door finally creaks open, I'm nearly out, despite my best intentions. I sit up and check my phone, its light casting a green glow about the room. 1:05 a.m. "Hey," I rasp.

Audrey jumps, startled. "You're still awake," she whispers, shrugging off her shirt in the corner of the room.

"Yeah, I was waiting for you. Is everything okay?"

"What do you mean?" The dresser rattles as she opens a drawer. Fabric rustles.

"I haven't seen you all summer. You've completely vanished off the face of the earth."

"Don't be dramatic," she says, and it stings. It's something she always says to me. Only this time, it wasn't in fun.

She ducks into the bathroom, the sound of the running water mimicking my rushing thoughts. They just keep falling, whooshing, beating down on my brain until I can't remember what I'd planned to say.

When she returns, crawling into the bottom bunk, she speaks before I can get a word out. "I need you to take the guest room at the end of the hall."

I roll my eyes in the dark. "Okay, sure, I'll just grab my pillow."

"No, I'm serious, Paige. You can move your stuff tomorrow."

Her words hit me like a blast of cold air. "Wait—what? Is it because I left my wet swimsuit on your desk chair? It was a momentary lapse of judgment, but it didn't ruin the chair."

"Paige, no. It's not because of the swimsuit."

"Is it about Dylan?" I should've known since that day she blew me off in the kitchen. "Are you upset that we're together? Because you always said—"

"No," she cuts in, the word riding on a sigh. "It's nothing like that. I'm happy for you guys, really. I just need my space this summer. I think it'll be best for both of us."

It feels like she reached straight inside my rib cage and squeezed my organs. "I don't understand. What did I do wrong?"

"You didn't do anything wrong, Paige." She sounds exhausted. "Just...stop overthinking everything."

"Does this have something to do with last summer? I heard your parents talking about five thousand dollars."

"No—*god*, Paige. Will you just leave me alone?"

"Why won't you talk to me? We've always tell each other everything."

Except that obviously isn't true. Because the person the Covingtons whispered about downstairs sounded like a total stranger. That person didn't sound like Audrey.

That person sounded like the girl lying on the bunk beneath me. The one I don't know anymore.

My eyes flood with tears that fall down my cheeks, spilling onto my pillow. This was supposed to be the summer I'd finally have it all. Best friend on one side, boyfriend on the other.

But I think I just lost the one I'd always taken for granted.

6

August arrives, and with the sweltering heat comes the knowledge that our time in Clearwater Ridge is finite. Lucy and Nate have long since been on to us, never growing tired of making faces at the smallest display of affection. Dylan and I start to discuss how to make a long-distance relationship work. How often he'll come to visit me. I start to envision the looks on my friends' faces when they see us together. I even plot to drag him along to Sunshine Park.

But with the winding down of summer comes something else: a change in Audrey.

I head downstairs for breakfast one morning and find her humming and slathering cream cheese on a toasted bagel. Instead of her rafting company T-shirt or riding gear, she's wearing a tank top. Beneath it, the hot-pink strap of a bikini pokes out.

"Hey, Paige," Audrey says brightly. "Want me to toast you a bagel?"

I try to play it cool, even though my heart is leaping with joy. Maybe the weird stuff is behind us. This can't be the Audrey who banished me to another bedroom without so much as an explanation. "Sure, thanks. Are you coming to the river with us today?"

"Oh." She frowns, glancing down at her attire. "Actually, I'm going with Kurt."

"Can't we all go together?" That's what we always did last summer. That's why it never felt like Audrey had completely abandoned me. Sure, Kurt was attached to her like an extra limb, but at least she was there. And this summer, I have a guy of my own.

"Well, I'm not sure when we're going," she says, already headed toward kitchen door. "But I'll text you."

Ah, right. The famous text that never comes. "Sounds good."

———

Dylan walks me to my bedroom a little after midnight. His arm is slung around my shoulders as we stop by Audrey's parted door. It's dark inside, no signs of Audrey's return from a long day and night with Kurt. "Your parents are far cooler than mine," I whisper. "If I were out with a guy all night, there would be a padlock on my door."

His body tenses beside mine. "Audrey's always been pretty trustworthy," he says, his tone suddenly clipped.

I know Audrey always *seems* pretty trustworthy. But I think about the hushed conversation I heard between Mr. and Mrs. Covington a few weeks back. Maybe Dylan doesn't know about the five thousand dollars. Ever since that night, I've been curious about that money. About why Audrey had to earn it. It could've been an innocent enough situation—paying her own way to some equestrian team competition abroad.

But the way her dad spoke about a "dark path," it doesn't add up.

As we reach my door, though, Dylan's fingers intertwined with mine, I shove the question aside. I don't want to talk about Audrey anymore, especially not as he turns to face me, his hands moving to the small of my back, his lips lowering to meet mine.

———

The following morning, I find Mrs. Covington and Mom seated at the dining room table. Both sets of eyes dart up to mine as I enter.

"Have you heard from Audrey?" Mrs. Covington's eyes are red and puffy. It's 10 a.m.

I shake my head. "I don't think…" I pull out my phone and check. "No, sorry. I don't have any texts from her. Did she not come home?"

Mrs. Covington shakes her head. "When Audrey didn't answer any of our calls, I had Dylan text Kurt, asking him to send Audrey home. But Kurt said she isn't at his place."

"What?" That can't be right.

"Did Audrey say anything to you yesterday, about her plans?"

I think back to our short conversation in the kitchen. "Just that she was going to be at the river with Kurt at some point."

At this, Mrs. Covington pales. "But he—that doesn't…" She lowers her head into her hands and mumbles, "Kurt said he never saw Audrey yesterday."

I get the sudden disoriented feeling of rocking in a boat at sea, despite being on dry land.

Mom reaches over to grab Mrs. Covington's hand. "I'm sure there's a reasonable explanation, Elle."

"Did you try the rafting company?" I ask. "Maybe she had another overnight trip and forgot to tell you."

"Spencer's headed to the rafting office now. It must not be open yet. No one's answering the phone."

"Where's Dad?" I ask.

"Driving around, looking for Audrey," Mom says. "Dylan and the kids too. If we haven't heard from her in an hour, we're going to alert the authorities."

Now it's like the entire boat flips over, sending me deep into the frigid water. Dread whooshes through me, followed by a needle of guilt. I noticed that Audrey wasn't in her room last night, and I did nothing about it. Dylan was there, holding me and consuming my every thought. "I'm sorry I slept so late. I had no—"

"It's fine, honey," Mrs. Covington says. "I'm sure she's just…at a friend's house. Her phone must be off."

I nod, even though Audrey doesn't really have other girlfriends in Clearwater Ridge. Here—outside of Hannah's annual visit—I'm the only girlfriend Audrey has. Mrs. Covington knows this too.

"She'll turn up," Mom says, rubbing her friend's back now.

"Yeah," Mrs. Covington says, her eyes telling an entirely

different story. "Then she'll be grounded for the rest of the summer." She lets out a hollow laugh and goes back to staring down at her phone, pressing the home button repeatedly. Her foot jounces against the legs of the chair.

Seeing her, watching her fidget—it's all making me physically ill. "I'll go look," I say, earning a grateful look from Mrs. Covington.

I slide my flip-flops on and head out the front door. As I descend the steps, Dylan's truck pulls into the driveway. He drops down, slamming the door and hurrying toward me.

"Any word from her?" I ask, reaching my hand out and expecting him to take it.

Instead, eyes dark, he brushes past me in the direction of the side gate. "Not yet," he mutters.

My empty hand is still lingering in midair when I spin around. "Where are you going?"

He pauses at the gate, shoulders slumped. "To check the river."

"You really think Audrey spent all night down by the river?"

He grasps at his hair, raking his fingers through and tugging much too hard. "I don't know, Paige. Where do *you* think she'd be?"

I rack my brain, flipping through the mental pages of what I know about my best friend this summer and finding them all blank. "We can drive around some more," I offer timidly.

"You know what?" He turns, removing his keys from his pocket. "You should check the river. We'll cover more ground if we split up. I'll take the truck over to the club."

"Good idea," I say, my doubts half strangling the words.

Something tells me Audrey isn't at the river or at the club. Only I don't have a better idea. The truth is that I have no clue where to search for my friend. I don't know where she really went, and I don't know why she lied about it.

Because this summer, I lost Audrey Covington in more than one way.

And I'm afraid I may never find her.

Search for 16-year-old girl in Clearwater Ridge

Officials are asking the public for help locating 16-year-old vacationer.

August 7

CLEARWATER RIDGE, CROWN COUNTY—Sixteen-year-old Audrey Covington was reported missing on Monday, August 5, when she failed to return to her family's vacation home in Clearwater Ridge. Covington was last seen Sunday morning, around 9 a.m., before leaving to spend the day with her boyfriend on the river.

When family members discovered the teen was not home the following morning, they became concerned and contacted her boyfriend. "He said he never saw her on Sunday," the girl's mother, Eleanor Covington, stated. "I knew something was wrong."

At a press conference this morning, Sheriff Dean Bolton of the Crown County Sheriff's Department said that Covington's phone has been out of service. "She could've fallen into the river or gotten lost on a hike. We're treating this with utmost urgency because we simply don't know what transpired."

A Missing Endangered Person Alert (MEPA) went out Monday to anyone in a ten-mile radius of Clearwater Ridge, and law enforcement later pushed the alert out to social media. Covington is described as 5 feet 5 inches tall, weighing around 120 pounds, with long blond hair and blue eyes. She was last seen wearing a white tank top over a pink bikini and cutoff jean shorts.

Sheriff Bolton has asked the public for help locating Covington. Anyone with information regarding her whereabouts is encouraged to call the CCSD tip line listed below or email CCSDtips@id.gov.

PART 2

THIS SUMMER

7

PAIGE

No one is chatty on the drive this year.

I'm miles deep into my newfound world of knitting, an art passed down to me by the great Matilda Wigsworth—a resident of Sunshine Park Care Center. My newest project is a hat that no one will be able to wear for at least six months, when the weather cools off.

Lucy and I both have our earbuds in, too willing to drown out the echo of the ongoing fight our family has had about this trip. It isn't about the air-conditioning this time.

When the Covingtons invited us back to Clearwater Ridge for the summer, we were all surprised. We'd just assumed that this year's visit would be canceled. No one expects a fun, relaxing time on the river.

Not with Audrey still missing.

But the Covingtons said that if we forgo our tradition this year, we may never get it back. They insisted on reuniting this summer in Audrey's honor. To remember her, to keep hope alive.

Dad said it would be too awkward, rubbing his two perfectly healthy daughters in the Covingtons' faces all summer. Ten weeks of tiptoeing around them would be unbearable.

Mom, on the other hand, argued that we needed to be there for the Covingtons. They were best friends, after all, and though Mom has made the drive several times over the past year to support them and the investigation, it's not the same as actually staying with them.

Lucy took Mom's side. Nate is her best friend, summer their one time to hang out in person. I understood her feelings; after all, it's how I used to feel about Audrey.

In the end, I took Dad's side. Only not for the same reason.

We pull up into the long driveway, and Nate is the first to greet us. Lucy yanks out her earbuds and exits the car, hurrying into his arms.

The rest of us begin to unload, me packing my knitting supplies away. The front door swings open and Mrs. Covington, a ghost of her former self, steps onto the porch. I drop my suitcase where I stand and walk to her, ready to get this part over with.

"You made it," she says in an easy voice that defies her weary, slumped posture. She embraces me, all bones, before gazing down with lifeless eyes. "It's good to see you."

"You too," I say, the lie sitting heavy in my throat.

The truth is that I'd do anything to get back in that car and gun it all the way home. Despite the difficulty of this moment, the worst is yet to come.

When Mom comes up behind me, sniffling, I take my leave. Dragging my suitcase behind me, I make the trek beneath the canopy of trees. The pine scent, the whistling of the birds, that gurgle of running water in the distance—it's all the same as last year.

But I know that's where the similarities end.

I enter the house, too on edge to breathe. I'm not ready to see this place again, to inhale the vanilla-meets-wood scent. Even crossing the foyer sends a current of memories through me. It's the excitement of arriving, the promise of adventure. It's Audrey and me attempting to sneak out this door to go to Tripp's party when we were fourteen.

I force in a breath, force my feet to carry me and this suitcase up the stairs. I only have to make it to the guest room. Then I can stick my earbuds in and nap the rest of the day away.

At the top of the stairs, I lift my suitcase so that the wheels won't announce my presence. It's heavy, but I push through, tiptoeing past Dylan's room to the end of the hall. I make it, lowering my suitcase and reaching for the doorknob.

But a click sounds behind me, and my heart jolts. "Paige?"

I take a deep breath, running through my options. I can pretend I didn't hear him. I can walk through this door, shut it behind me, and never confront this moment.

Instead, I spin to face the boy I loved last summer.

"Hey, Dylan." Meeting his eyes brings on a pang so acute I have to look away. Instead, I smile at my suitcase like a weirdo.

"How was the drive?" He doesn't move toward me. Doesn't even offer the *friends* hug of old.

"Oh, you know." I don't move toward him, either, even though every bone in my body craves his embrace.

"How have you been?" As he leans against the doorframe, I lift my gaze enough to see his board shorts and white T-shirt, muscular physique still seemingly intact. Unlike his mother, who lost her appetite over the past year, Dylan took out his feelings in the pool. In his division, he placed in every event he competed in.

Of course, I didn't hear this from *him*. I only know from stalking his team's Instagram account. After Audrey went missing, my family stayed in Clearwater Ridge as long as we could. Eventually, though, we had to return home. I assumed Dylan and I would video chat regularly. And we did, at first. But things never felt the same after Audrey went missing. I sensed it that day we started to search for her—that we were no longer a team.

Dylan and Nate moved back home, while their parents stayed in Clearwater Ridge to be present for the investigation. Their grandmother helped out with Nate here and there. For the most part, though, Dylan took on the role of parent. He grew up quickly. Our conversations soon became forced and awkward. New responsibilities piled up, constantly distracting him. He grew distant.

That close connection we'd developed over the summer came apart, like two cords on an old rope. It loosened and unraveled until, one day, our talks ceased to exist and we weren't together anymore. There was no official breakup. Life had become so consumed with finding Audrey that any time Dylan and I spoke, it was about her. We never had a chance to discuss *us*.

Maybe it was too painful. Maybe I reminded him too much of his sister.

The long and short of it is, I didn't just lose my best friend. I lost him too.

Saying that Dylan broke my heart isn't quite accurate, since it had already been cracked clean through. A more accurate assessment is this: When Audrey disappeared, my heart broke. Then Dylan came along and smashed it into millions of minuscule pieces.

This past year was a living hell.

"Okay," I answer. "How are you?"

He shrugs. "Glad to have my family all back together under one roof." My eyes flick up to catch the horror in his expression. "I mean, not *all* of us, obviously."

"How are your parents?"

"Pretty defeated, since everything slowed down."

Mom told me about the day that Detective Ferrera admitted to being out of leads back in March. "The investigation is still open though, right?"

"Yeah, but they're not doing anything. The case is basically cold, though they won't label it that yet."

My mind darts back to last summer, to all the so-called leads we were certain would direct us to Audrey.

How, in the end, the only place they led was utter confusion.

Because Audrey Covington—straight-A student, captain of the equestrian team, member of the student council at Mayberry Prep—had lied about everything.

According to Solomon at the rafting company, he never rehired Audrey last summer. There had never been any long hours or training, never any overnight trips.

Even Kurt said he hadn't seen Audrey the night she went

missing, nor the entire day she was last seen. He denied knowing anything about Audrey's plan to go to the river with him.

And that wasn't the only surprise thrown at us. Kurt went on to claim that he and Audrey never even got back together last year. Since the first day the investigation opened up, he's stuck to the story that he hardly saw Audrey last summer. Not on lazy days by the river, not on long evenings on his couch. Not anytime, not anywhere.

Everyone—Audrey's family, me, the cops—had to face the terrifying fact that Audrey had been *somewhere* all summer. Yet no one had a clue where that was.

"I should probably go down and help your parents unload." Dylan looks off down the hall, running his fingers through his dark hair.

"Okay," I say, choking on my disappointment. This is really how it's going to be.

I guess part of me still held out hope that once we saw each other, that spark from last year would reignite. That the two of us, though in need of repair, could still fit together, like two pieces of a jigsaw puzzle. Broken and jagged apart, but whole together. I head to the guest bedroom door, rolling my suitcase over the threshold.

Dylan's footsteps creak down the hall, stopping abruptly. "Hey, Paige? Any chance you're up for a banana split from Carlson's?"

Nerves kick up. He's already got me melting faster than a marshmallow over fire.

I can't let him win this easily. The least he can do is crack that smile I can't stop thinking about. "Well, I'd hate to miss my program," I say, impersonating Mrs. Dobbs, a nursing home charge who used to swipe desserts from her fellow charges and never missed a *Murder, She Wrote* rerun. I pull out my phone, squinting at the time. Dylan used to love my stories about her.

"Program?" Dylan quirks a brow.

"It's fine. I can have Lucy tape it."

"Yeah, we don't have a VCR, Paige. I don't think my parents have owned one since before I was born."

"Well, maybe I can find it on the Netflix."

"Maybe."

And there it is. That smile.

——

I'd hoped that Carlson's would somehow reset everything between Dylan and me. But we've become celebrities in Clearwater Ridge, and not the kind people ask for autographs or selfies. We're the kind that passersby like to stare at and whisper about. Case in point: three elderly women seated in a booth across the shop aren't even attempting to be discreet about it. They watch our every bite, turning to one another only to discuss the case in what they may believe are whispers.

The one with the fluffy white curls and pink floral blouse thinks that Audrey's just a runaway. "Teens these days," she says knowingly. In the next breath, she adds, "Or you know, the boyfriend did it. It's always the boyfriend."

The woman across from her, hair dyed a vibrant shade of red that matches her sundress, has her own theory. "No." She shakes her head. "It was an animal. Remember that bear that killed two hikers back in the eighties? It was months before anyone discovered the bodies. Until the authorities search every cave in a ten-mile radius, they'll never find her."

An icy tingle licks up my spine. It's not a new theory; Clearwater Ridge is as wild and savage as it is picturesque. Audrey was young and active. Detective Ferrera's first pitch out of the gate was a hike gone wrong.

Only we did, in fact, scour the forests and trails—even caves off the beaten path. Could we have missed something out there in the endless pines?

Easily.

The third woman lifts a trembling index finger. "That Madilyn Baker girl is still missing. Fred says we've got a serial killer on our hands. He's been saying it since November. That detective won't listen."

"And to think," I say in a hushed voice, offering Dylan the cherry, "Fred cracked the case all those months ago. And investigators just ignored him."

Dylan chuckles softly, declining the cherry. "If only they'd allowed Fred to join the team."

"I think the problem is that this entire time, the police were searching for a girl named *Madison Blake*."

"Actually," Dylan says, a serious note to his voice now, "they aren't even doing that. They closed the investigation into Madison's disappearance."

"Closed it?" I guess I've missed a lot. It was easier to follow the case when I was living here. "They found her?"

"No, but they're saying they have reason to believe she's a runaway. According to the sheriff who was investigating, Madison's last con failed, and she skipped town. That's why the state police never took over her case like they did with Audrey."

"I guess that's good news though, right?" Immediately, embarrassment sweeps up my neck, hot and prickly. "Not *good*, obviously. But it means we're not looking for a serial killer."

"Except half the town thinks the sheriff's department is lying. Or at the very least, deceptively optimistic. They haven't shown any proof that Madison Blake is alive. The town thinks they're spreading this runaway theory to keep everyone from panicking."

The door chimes, and Kurt Winfield walks in wearing his blue rafting company T-shirt. He doesn't see us as he heads to the counter and begins chatting with Liz, the waitress.

Dylan's lips go taut. I study him, unsure how he feels about Kurt these days.

Initially, Dylan assumed Kurt was lying about Audrey's whereabouts on the night she vanished. That she'd been with him, something bad had happened, and he was covering his own hide. When Detective Ferrera told us what Kurt said about not even having a relationship with Audrey last summer, Dylan and Nate hopped in the truck and hunted him down. Dylan got in Kurt's face. According to Nate, things got really heated. Dylan might've even hit the guy had Nate and Solomon not stepped in.

I struggle to picture Dylan getting that upset—that violent. But his sister was missing, and all signs pointed to Kurt as the deceiver.

Eventually, Dylan apologized. Detective Ferrera interviewed most of the town; no one admitted to having seen Kurt and Audrey together after the night of the Summer Kickoff.

From the stiffening of Dylan's shoulders now, though, it seems like he's still unconvinced.

Across the parlor, Ethel and company call Liz over for the check, and Kurt turns to find his own seat. That's when our eyes meet, his widening before darting to the window. Then, with something like resignation, he paints a smile on his face and trudges over to our booth.

I take in his slumped posture, his shifty eyes. He isn't pleased to see us. Maybe he's not over what happened with Dylan last summer. Maybe he simply doesn't know what to say.

But what if it's something else? What if this obvious anxiety is fear of being found out?

"Hey, guys," he says, shoving his hands into his pockets. "When did you arrive?"

"Today." I wipe at my lips with a napkin.

"My family's been here a week," Dylan says. "Haven't gotten out of the house yet."

"Yeah, it's—I don't blame you. How's the investigation going?"

"Fine, good," Dylan says. "They're about to look into someone whose story last summer didn't quite check out." A buzzing sensation picks up at the back of my neck; I haven't heard Dylan lie since I was eight and accidentally knocked over his mother's entire tray of fresh-baked cookies. Before my lower lip had time to quiver, he took the fall for it.

"Oh, really?" Kurt scratches at his hairline. "Who?"

Dylan takes a bite of ice cream, forcing Kurt to wait as he swallows. "They're pretty tight-lipped about it. But we're all really hopeful it will lead to Audrey."

Kurt glances over his shoulder before turning to us again. "Well, that's great news. Look, I've got to get back to work. Just came to grab a root beer float on my break."

"See you around," I say.

"Yeah, bye, Paige."

"See ya," Dylan adds with a wave.

The second the door clangs shut behind Kurt, I cross my arms. "You want to tell me what *that* was about?"

"I don't know," he says, rubbing a hand over the back of his neck. "*You're* the one who made me watch all those detective shows last summer. That's what they do. Get the suspect nervous so he'll slip up."

"Hey, you said you loved those shows," I say with mock astonishment. "You still don't believe Kurt's story?"

"Do you?"

It's a question I can't really answer. Kurt has always been a nice guy, a hard worker. It's been easy for everyone in town to take his side. He's *one of them*. Sure, Audrey was the golden child at her school, but in Clearwater Ridge, she's been an outsider. A summer person. And even to her own best friend, she wasn't exactly trustworthy. At least, not last summer.

But there has always been one problem with Kurt's story. *I* saw Audrey with him the night of the party. I saw them together twice, and I told Detective Ferrera as much. Seeing him just now brought it all back, clear as day. The way Audrey went off with him, the way they were perched together in the hallway, bodies brushing. So I find it hard to believe that nothing was going on between the two of them last summer.

"If we'd only searched harder for her that day we showed

up at the rafting office," Dylan says, dropping the spoon onto the table with a clatter, "we could've figured out that she wasn't working there. *I* should've realized. I'm her brother."

"Hey." I reach across the table to take his hand, then remember with a flush of embarrassment. I withdraw my fingers, tilting my head until he looks at me. "It isn't your fault, okay? Audrey lied to everyone. She worked there two summers ago. No one would've thought to question her."

He lets out a hard sigh that rustles my hair. The pained look in his eyes twists my insides. But he is wrong. It can't be Dylan's fault that Audrey is missing.

Because it's mine.

8

What kind of person doesn't know their best friend is lying?

Something was wrong with Audrey last summer—that much was clear to me. But I didn't try hard enough to draw the truth from her. I let her push me away after a lifetime of friendship. I stayed off in my own world of first love and summer bliss, content in my self-indulgent ignorance. It was too much work to fight with Audrey. So I left her alone to grapple with whatever was going on until it stole her away forever.

That's why it's *my* fault she's gone. I'm the only one who could've coaxed or even wrestled the truth from her last summer, and I failed.

Earlier, Lucy texted that she and Nate are down at the river. So, when Dylan and I get back, I change into my swimsuit, throwing shorts and a tank top over it. Dylan politely declines to join us; apparently, an hour with me in town was enough.

I should head out the back doors and join the others.

Instead, I tiptoe down the hall and stop to face Audrey's closed bedroom door.

Last summer, this room was off-limits. First, when Audrey kicked me out. Then, when the sheriff's department marked the entire thing off as evidence.

Social mores would say it's still off-limits. Audrey could be—*is*—still alive out there somewhere, and this room is full of her private things.

Despite this, I find myself turning the knob and slipping inside her room. I don't know why I do it, not even as I ease the door shut behind me. Maybe because this room is the closest thing I have to my best friend. I step farther inside, finding everything neat, the way Audrey would've kept it. This is obviously Mrs. Covington's doing.

Before I left for home last summer, I caught a glimpse of what the investigators did to this room. They'd rifled through all of Audrey's drawers, removing things, sending them off to the lab for testing. Her laptop was confiscated for a time. The mattress was removed, desk torn apart. Her belongings were strewn about the desk and the floor.

Mrs. Covington has since reorganized the room, piece by piece.

I was always the messy one; it was our one point of contention. I liked to fling my clothes onto the bed; she liked everything tucked away, in its proper place. I never made my bed, which is why she gave me the top bunk. Her bottom bunk was always pristine, the white knitted blanket folded, and not just any old way. She folded it with one end tucked into the other, forming a pillow, a method that Mrs. Covington failed to replicate.

I lift the blanket off the foot of the bed and refold it, tucking the ends into the center first, then flipping it in half. Then I try to remember the next step, Audrey's instructions. I end up with more of a burrito than a pillow, pushing it into the corner. Taking a turn of the rest of the room, I see that the only object out of place is Audrey's sunscreen. It's on the desk when it should really be stowed inside her beach bag, which hangs on the hook in her closet. I open the tube, squirting a drop onto my hands and rubbing it away. Then I crawl onto the bed, facing the top bunk that used to be mine.

Shutting my eyes, I let the coconut scent and the memories in this space wrap around me. The time Audrey forced me to sleep down here with her after Dylan's scary movie gave me a nightmare. How she talked me through getting ready for my first formal school dance over video chat, giving me hair-curling and makeup tutorials until she ended up late to her own academic award ceremony. How she never gave me hell for it.

I let the memories twist and circle like a vine, pulling me under until all I can do is cry.

When the sniffles turn to body-wracking sobs, I turn over, muffling my cries in Audrey's pillow. This only makes things worse, since the faint scent of her shampoo still lingers in the pillowcase fabric.

I have to get out of here. Dylan's room shares a wall with this one, and I can't keep it together. Sitting up, I smooth out the comforter and the pillow. I give the room one last scan, knowing that I can't return—that I shouldn't even be in here.

That's when I see it. A bookcase pressed up against the narrow space of wall between the bed and the far corner. I don't remember that bookcase being there before. Not last summer nor any summer before that. Did Mrs. Covington add it after Audrey went missing?

But that doesn't make sense.

I move closer. Actually, it looks more like a cheap IKEA model than the antique oak pieces that Mrs. Covington has an eye for. There are four shelves stocked with paperbacks, books Audrey used to read by the river when she was twelve. Nothing important enough to merit her finding and building a bookcase.

Unless Mrs. Covington has made it into some sort of shrine. I shudder. Can she really have given up hope?

Anxious to get out of here, I swivel on my heel when the board beneath my foot gives a *pop*.

I step on it again, feeling the slightest give. Kneeling, I dig my fingertips in between the slats, but I can't lift the loose board. The bookcase is covering the other end, weighing it down.

Leave. Just leave.

I debate with myself for another minute until, finally, the side of me that can't let this go wins out. I take a deep breath and lift the end of the bookcase nearest me. Hefting it up and dragging it toward me, I set it down.

Only it's more of a drop. The bookcase lands with a thump, sending some of the books sprawling about the room.

I hold my breath, waiting for the moment to pass. But the creak of footsteps sounds in the next room over.

My heartbeat accelerates. I can't be seen in this sacred shrine room. A door creaks open, and footsteps pad down the short stretch of hall between Dylan's room and this one.

I have to hide.

Frantic, I look to the closet. If I sprint to it, he'll hear me. He will know someone is in the room, and he'll find me hovering like a burglar in the dark closet.

Instead, I make a much wiser choice and crouch, frozen in shame by the bookcase.

Dylan opens the door, head drawing back when he spots me. "Paige? What are you doing in here?"

"I left my, uh…pearls in here last summer."

"Pearls," he says with a head tilt.

"A classy string of saltwater. Audrey took one look and had to borrow it." Crossing the room, I tug him inside. "Just— never mind the reason." I peek my head out to check the hallway before shutting the door behind us.

"Do you know where this bookcase came from?" I ask, moving to where it stands, skewed at a forty-five-degree angle with the wall.

Dylan's brow furrows. "I don't know, Paige. Decor isn't really my thing."

"So you didn't help her build it last summer?"

He scratches his head. "No. But…now that you mention it, I saw Nate helping her carry furniture from the driveway once. I figured it was for Mom's tea party thing."

"When was this?"

He shuts an eye. "July, maybe? August? I don't know." He scans the room, drawing his shoulders in close, like he's nervous. "Why don't we put this back and get out of here?"

"Because I think there's something under it."

He frowns. "What?"

"Yeah, just—" I drag it farther from the wall, straining with the effort. Dylan, sighing audibly, nudges me aside and takes over.

"I don't see anything," he says, fingers trailing over the back of the bookcase.

"Not *behind* it." I step on the exposed board, which tilts like a seesaw, exposing the hollow space beneath it. "Below."

Dylan's eyes widen, and he lowers to examine the board.

"Here, keep your foot on it." He complies, and I kneel down, attempting to peer through the narrow slit. When that fails, I wrestle my phone from my back pocket, shining its flashlight over the hole. "I think there's something down there."

"Like a rat?" he asks, causing my body to recoil.

"I've had all my shots." I hesitate a moment. Then, taking a deep breath, my insides clenched into a tight knot, I stick my hand into the dark shallow space.

The splintered edge of the board scrapes my skin as my hand glides down. I wince, but my fingers light on something cold, flat, and very unratlike. "I've got it," I say, drawing the object back until my fingers curl around it.

Like a squirrel with a nut, I try to slide my hand through the slot, only to drop the object back into the depths again. My hand is sore and raw from the splinters, but Dylan's massive man hands would never fit. So, I try again.

This time, contorting my fist the way Houdini would, I manage to tug the object free, finding a black Nokia flip phone. "It's a phone," I say, confusion drawing the words out.

"But it's not Audrey's."

We settle onto the bottom bunk to get a better look. I press the home button but nothing happens. "It's dead." Of course, it's dead. It's likely been down there since last summer.

Dylan looks at me, lines drawn over his forehead. "This could be evidence. We have to give it to the cops."

I nod. "Yeah, we'll give it to Detective Ferrera." Suddenly, the entire screen lights up.

Not dead. Just powered down. And there's no passcode protection; I'm on the home screen.

My fingers itch to search the phone. "Maybe we could take a quick look ourselves. It couldn't hurt, right?" I, for one, am curious as to why this would be buried here.

When Dylan doesn't contest, I navigate through the contacts, finding only one. It isn't a name though. It's a number, ending in 4477.

The phone doesn't have a name assigned either. Not Audrey's, not anybody's. Just a phone number ending in 2328. "Only one contact," I say. "No name."

Dylan peers over my shoulder. "Yeah, it's a…prepaid phone." He avoids the term we're both thinking. *Burner phone.* Only criminals have those.

I start to scroll through the texts exchanged between the two anonymous numbers, and immediately a sickening sense of guilt rolls through me.

Sunday, July 7, 11:15 p.m.

4477: I had fun today

2328: Me too, see you soon

Sunday, July 14, 10:00 a.m.

4477: Meet me at our usual spot in an hour. Got
    something for u

2328: Can't wait

Dylan leans closer. "Got something for you? What the hell
does that mean?"

"Could be a secret boyfriend with a present. Or...you
know, a drug dealer." I pick up my own phone and type the
full number into the search bar above my contacts.

"What are you doing?" Dylan asks.

"Checking to make sure this isn't someone we know." But
no results are found.

Dylan conducts an identical search in his phone, coming
up empty. "Could be another burner."

We return our attention to the Nokia. The exchanges
continue in much the same way. Planning secret rendezvous,
4477 having "something" for 2328. Everything short and to
the point. Apart from the flirty messages thrown in, it seems
to be a phone used to buy illegal substances.

I feel light-headed, almost woozy trying to process the idea.
Did Audrey have a secret drug addiction? One so bad that she
had to flirt with her dealer?

"I guess this explains where she was all summer," Dylan
says, sighing. "And what she did with all that money she stole
from my parents."

"You knew about the money?" Instantly, I regret the question. *I'm* not supposed to know about the money.

Dylan's gaze sinks to the rug. "They argued with Audrey

about it, when my parents realized what she'd done. It was impossible not to overhear." His fist balls up at his side. "I can't believe we didn't see it. We have to get the cops looking at whoever deals in Clearwater Ridge. Or maybe they can trace the number."

I nod, my shock contending with a sudden burst of clarity. In a way, everything makes sense. Audrey wasn't herself all summer. She must've kicked me out of the room we shared for privacy. If anything, I feel like an idiot for not realizing what she was doing in this room.

A sense of purpose begins to form inside me, solidifying as I continue to scroll through the text messages.

But I reach the last exchange, dated August 2, 4:15 p.m., and my heart ricochets in my chest.

2328: What are we going to do about Madison?

4477: Everything's under control

THE GIRL

The phone began to buzz in the girl's purse, and she withdrew it. At the name on the screen, irritation needled at her, followed quickly by guilt. She hit Ignore.

She'd walked all this way, and she was going to enjoy the peace and quiet. Here, where the river swept past the outskirts of town, was a place to which she could escape. Here, she could clear her head as she walked among the aspen trees, their thin white trunks like a million standing matchsticks.

Tired, she found a rock in the shade beneath the heart-shaped leaves of the aspens. The leaves whispered in the breeze, and it seemed as though they were telling her to stay with them.

Never return, they told her.

The girl was more than happy to obey. The trees understood her better than her own parents, who pretended to care about her, but were completely selfish. Better than her best friend, who would only judge her. Better than her ex, who'd been badgering her about getting back together.

The trees listened. They knew about the Bad Stuff. The stuff she tried not to think about, because it sent shivers of terror through her. The stuff that kept her up at night until finally, when she drifted off to sleep, it haunted her dreams.

The trees—unlike anyone in the girl's life—knew why she'd had to lie.

And she had lied, about all of it. She'd lied about where she was going, what she was doing. She'd had to.

Unfortunately, the trees couldn't offer the girl a drink, and she'd grown thirsty. The downtown strip was only through the woods and across the slender stretch of road. It was charming and well-maintained—it had to be, for it was frequented by the summer people.

The girl thought a soda from Carlson's Ice Cream Parlor would suffice, but then a new inclination kicked up, bringing with it an invigorating sense of risk. She'd felt bolder since the lies had begun.

Instead of stopping inside the parlor, the girl removed a tube of lipstick from her purse. She applied a coat in her phone's mirror, blotting the way she'd learned in the school bathroom. Though her mother knew a lot about makeup, she'd neglected to show her daughter how to put any of it on.

Satisfied, the girl passed the ice cream parlor, pressing on until she reached Terry's Saloon, constructed in the shape of a log cabin. There were a few umbrella-covered tables dotting the patio area, though they were empty.

Inside, the dimly lit saloon maintained a rustic style in line with its exterior. Large wooden beams stretched across the ceiling, and wood paneling covered the walls. The stone fireplace wasn't in use due to the summer heat, but overhead, tiny flames flickered from candelabras formed of antlers.

An elderly couple occupied a booth at the back, and a waitress in a white blouse and tight black pants tended to them. The girl held her head high, shoulders back as she strode up to the bar, taking a seat on a stool at the end nearest the door. Two young men sat at the opposite end of the bar, deep in conversation. The bartender set a bottle of beer in front of each of them and made his way toward the girl.

When he nodded at her, she asked for a beer. "Whatever's on draft," she said, repeating a line she'd once heard in a movie.

The man reached for a mug but stopped to narrow his eyes at her. "You got some ID?"

The girl's heart sank. "Not on me," she said, hopeful that the man might let it slide.

"This bar's twenty-one and over. Try Carlson's." He flicked his head toward the door.

Defeated, the girl slid down from the bench and skulked across the saloon. Her head hung low, hair covering her eyes and sticking to that fresh coat of lipstick.

She made her way back to the rock, convinced yet again that this place among the aspens was the only one where she would ever be accepted.

For what she'd done. For everything.

Her eyes had fallen shut when the crack of a branch startled her. Wide awake now, she looked up to find *him*.

He was holding out a bottle, the cap already removed. "It isn't draft, but it's nice and cold."

9

PAIGE

I tear my gaze from the screen, my heart somewhere up in my throat. "*Madison?* Why was Audrey asking about Madison?"

"Maybe it's a different Madison," Dylan says, sounding dubious.

"Right." Because Audrey didn't even know Madison Blake.

Still I can't shake the questions sneaking into my brain. This text message was sent in August; Madison went missing in June. Could Audrey have known something about the girl's disappearance?

According to the sheriff's department, though, Madison was never missing. Not officially. She's been ruled a runaway. She's a con artist who skipped town in search of new, unsuspecting victims.

But what if the sheriff was wrong?

What if 4477 isn't simply some drug dealer? It certainly sounds like this person was something more to Audrey. If the

Madison in the text message refers to Madison Blake, then 4477 could be linked to two missing girls.

Finding this person could be the key to bringing them both home.

"We have to find out who 4477 is," I say, powering the phone down, either to save what remains of the battery life or because I can't look at it anymore. "The cops never mentioned a *prepaid* phone. This could be someone they never interviewed. This guy could have information about all of those days Audrey spent that went unaccounted for. Let's take it to the station. Have them give it to Detective Ferrera." I stand, tossing the phone onto the bed and moving to the bookcase. "Help me put this back."

Dylan nods but stays seated on the bed, staring down at Audrey's pink patterned rug in the center of the room.

"Dylan, the bookcase."

His eyes slide over to the phone on the comforter beside him. "What if we didn't give the phone to the cops?"

I blink at him. "Then we'd be no closer to finding Audrey. This could be a lead, Dylan. Ferrera needs to know about this guy if she's going to bring Audrey home."

"It looks bad, Paige." His gaze is back on the rug now. "Really bad. You and I both know Audrey was into something shady last summer. Why else would she lie every day for months? Why would she steal five thousand dollars from my parents? Madison Blake went missing. Audrey and this 4477 were talking about *doing* something to her!"

"Doing something *about* her," I correct. But yeah, I see his point.

"What if Audrey did something horrible to Madison? Something so horrible she had to..."

Leave. Finishing his thought sends a shiver through me. I wrap my arms around myself and sit down beside him. Now we're both staring at that swirling pattern on Audrey's rug.

I think of Audrey defending me to those bullies on the tennis court years ago, struggling to reconcile that image of her with the one Dylan just offered up. "But what if that's not it?" I finally ask. "Are we really going to forfeit this chance to find her based on some...*fear?*"

"We don't have to forfeit the lead," Dylan says.

"I'm not following you."

"What if...?" He digs his fingers into the hair at his temples. "What if the cops don't follow the lead, but *we* do?" I crinkle my brow, to which he adds, "You and me. We could try to find this guy."

I lift a hand. "How do you propose we do that? We don't know how to trace a burner phone. I don't even know if it's possible. I don't underst—"

"Clearwater Ridge isn't that big," he interrupts. "According to the text exchanges, Audrey was meeting this guy almost every day. All we have to do is ask around. Someone's sure to have spotted her with this 4477."

"The cops already interviewed everyone."

"Yeah," he says as if I'm missing something, "and people lie to authority figures all the time. They get scared. But you and I are different, Paige. We're not cops, just a couple of kids, and all we want to know is who Audrey was seeing last summer. That's it." He shifts to face me now, blue eyes pleading. He's close enough beside me on the bed that I feel the warmth of his breath, the fear radiating off his body, his need for my help. I want to lean in and wrap my arms around him, to tell him it'll be okay.

I understand his worry. Despite her parents' feelings on the matter—despite most of the town and the authorities' view of her as an innocent victim—Audrey could very possibly be a runaway. The cops never found a body. If she left town on purpose, she might not want to be found. Tracking her down could get her into serious trouble.

And yet, I know I should give this phone to the police. It's a missing piece in their puzzle. I should grab it, get up, and drive my parents' van down to the station.

Wracked with indecision, I pick at my fingernails until finally, I come up with a compromise. "We make a list of people to talk to," I say. "We talk to them." Dylan starts to nod, but I hold a hand up. "If our investigation leads nowhere by the end of the week, we show your parents the phone. They deserve to make the final decision on what to do with it."

The glimmer of a smile shifts onto his face. "That sounds like a sensible plan."

Nerves beyond frazzled, all I can do is quote old Mr. Crawley from room 29 of Sunshine Park: "Sensible as a good pair of loafers."

———

There was never any question as to who we'd interview first.

When Dylan and I hop down from his truck in the parking lot where the rafting company office is located, the sun is high in the sky. In the anxious rush to begin our investigation, I forgot my sunglasses, so I hurry toward the door, using my hand as a shield. Spotting our subject typing away at the ancient computer on the desk, relief swoops through me. Kurt Winfield glances up at us, his shoulders drawing back into his chair. "Hey, guys. Here to book a trip?"

Dylan and I agreed that I should take the lead on this one, considering that heated dispute between the boys last summer. What we *didn't* agree on, exactly, was using television detective tactics to coax our subjects into talking. "Actually," I say, my voice wobbly as I channel the no-nonsense, middle-aged male detective from the show that's always playing in the Sunshine Park activities room, "we just wanted to ask you a few questions. About Audrey." Discreetly, I remove the pocket-sized notebook and pen from my purse.

"Oh." He frowns at my notebook; guess I wasn't *that* discreet. "Well, like I told the cops, I didn't see much of Audrey last summer. Almost never."

"You saw her at the Summer Kickoff," I contest. "You were with her practically the entire night."

"Yeah, we caught up. I guess we thought maybe something was still *there*." He shrugs. "But at the end of the night, we agreed to stay friends."

"Okay, good, good," I say, flipping to the next question in my notebook. "Do you, uh, know if Audrey ever fooled around with illegal substances?"

"Audrey?" Kurt's brows furrow.

"You know. Like..." I clear my throat, trying to remember

the street names for drugs and coming up with only this story that old Mr. Samuels from room 14 told me about his troubled grandson. "The dope?" Beside me, Dylan, who's been quietly standing by, lets out a sigh.

Kurt's head droops forward in irritation or boredom. "Yeah, I know what *illegal substances* means, Paige. But why are you asking?"

"No reason," I say, making little scribbles. "Do you happen to know anyone who does? Take illegal substances, I mean."

"You just want me to give you a list of names of people in town who do drugs?"

"Pretty much."

Dylan skirts in front of me now. "Look, we think Audrey may have been hanging around with a…"

"An unsavory type of fella," I cut in, accidentally over-channeling my TV detective persona.

He shoots me a look, then turns back to Kurt. "I know you told the cops you never saw Audrey. But if you *did* see her and kept it out of your statement because of the sort of person she was with, we need to know. We won't mention your name. But this guy could have information about what happened to my sister." His voice goes raspy at the last few words, and he glances off in the direction of the wall full of rafting photographs.

"Please, Kurt," I say. "We swear, we didn't hear it from you."

Kurt blows a puff of air through his teeth, not making eye contact with either of us as he folds his hands on the desk. My heart starts to lift in my chest.

Because he *knows* something.

"Like I told the cops," he says through the slit between his lips, "I didn't see Audrey after that party in the Pines. Sorry I couldn't be of more help." There's a dismissive note to his voice. I press a little harder anyway. "Did Audrey ever mention Madison Blake to you?"

Kurt looks up, a flicker of surprise in his brown eyes. But his shoulders ease, the expression vanishing so quickly I might have imagined it. "Madison Blake? You mean that girl who went missing for, like, a day? You think Audrey knew her?"

"I'm not sure," I say. "She never mentioned Madison?"

His lips twist in thought. "Not to me, no. Why are you asking?"

"Oh, you know. Some people in town think that the same person who took Madison took Audrey. I thought maybe if we could establish a connection between the girls—where they met or hung out or whatever—we could figure out who took them."

Kurt scoffs. "Madison Blake wasn't taken. Not even the cops think so."

"Just double-checking every angle, Kurt." I turn to Dylan; we didn't exactly discuss how to proceed if Kurt chose to be difficult.

But the door swings open behind us, sending a wave of hot air into the small space.

Solomon McCleary, a muscular twentysomething with short red hair and freckled arms, walks through the door. His eyes widen upon seeing us, but then he smiles broadly. "What's up, you two?"

Solomon is the easygoing owner of the rafting company.

When Audrey worked for him two summers ago, she said he always stayed late, passing out beers to whichever employees would hang back with him. The rafting company is a hand-me-down from his father, who has the funds and the know-how to run the business side of things from a safe and air-conditioned location, whereas Solomon is the guy in charge of showing people a good time on the river.

Conveniently, he's also the guy up next on our interview list.

"Hi, Solomon." I'm already flipping to a clean page in my notebook. Dylan nudges me, and reluctantly, I stand down.

"Actually," Dylan says, "is it okay if we talk to you outside?"

Smart. If Solomon was ever going to set Kurt's story straight, it wouldn't happen right in front of him.

Solomon's narrowed gaze flits from Dylan to Kurt, sticking to his employee for another beat. Then he shrugs and spins back in the direction of the door.

Out in the beating sunlight, Solomon resumes his laid-back vibe. "What can I do for you?"

"We're on an errand of sorts," Dylan says. "For my mom."

"Ah, does Elle want to host a ladies' trip down the river?" A squirming sensation rolls over my skin at his use of Mrs. Covington's nickname. "Because I can give her a discount on a party of twelve or more."

"No, nothing like that." Dylan takes a deep breath and lets it out slowly. "It's more of a personal matter. She says the cops aren't doing enough to find Audrey, so she asked us to follow up on a few details."

"Right." Solomon's affable expression falters. "How is your mother doing?"

Changing the subject—classic diversion tactic. But why, Solomon?

"Not great, to be honest. We're coming up on a year at the end of summer. That's why I have to do this errand, even though I know it's pointless. Is it okay to ask a few questions, just so my mom *believes* someone is still working on the case?"

He shrugs. "Anything to help bring Audrey home."

"Thanks." I smile, ready to take over now. "So Audrey told us about your little after-work parties." At this, Solomon fidgets. I pretend not to notice, focusing on my pad. "Don't worry. We won't say anything to Mrs. Covington about them. I'm just wondering if Audrey was ever particularly friendly with any of the guys at these parties." I glance in the direction of the office. "Guys who weren't Kurt."

Solomon's freckled forehead wrinkles. "I don't think so. She and Kurt were all over each other two summers ago. She only had eyes for him."

I want to ask if there were ever drugs at these parties, and if so, who delivered the goods. But he's already on edge. Instead, I pretend to cross something off a nonexistent list in my notepad and ask, "Did she come around here last summer looking to get her job back?"

"No, never. I totally would've rehired her. I showed the cops all the payroll stuff."

"And she never came by to see Kurt? Not even as friends?"

He gives us a sympathetic smile. "Not that I saw."

"To see *you*, maybe?"

Solomon's jaw clenches now; I've gone too far. "I'm not into underage girls," he says in a gravelly voice, pulling out his phone. "Actually, I've got to be on the river in twenty minutes. If you'll excuse me." He starts back toward the office, then turns as if suddenly remembering himself. "I hope you'll have more luck elsewhere."

10

Seated in the suffocating cab of Dylan's truck, we stare out the windshield, wallowing in our defeat.

Dylan inserts the key into the ignition without starting the truck. Instead, he turns to me.

"Can I take a look at your notes?" he asks, straight-faced as he holds out a hand.

"Wha—why?" I clutch the notepad to my chest like it's a precious heirloom and not a few squiggles, four lines of gibberish, and a darn good likeness of the turkey needlepoint that hung on the back wall in the office.

"You were scribbling pretty fiercely back there. It looked like you were really onto something."

"It's more theories and hunches at the moment," I say, thinking of the zigzags that represent the stubble of Solomon's chin and the very poor sketch of Kurt.

"Ah." He scratches at his neck, then starts the engine. We head out of the tiny parking lot and onto the main street that runs through town. "I guess what I'm really wondering is how exactly the turkey factors into all of this."

My mouth falls open. "You peeked!"

He finally cracks a smile. "I may have looked over your shoulder, yes. That point you made, comparing Solomon to a squirmy worm? Top-notch detective work."

I punch him lightly in the shoulder, feeling a prick of nostalgia. It's the kind of play fighting we used to do as friends, the kind we used to do as *more* than friends. Now that we're neither of those things, it just feels wrong. "The scribbling was a tactic, okay? And I was onto something with the worm. That guy was definitely nervous."

"Yeah, about his sketchy parties."

"I don't know," I say. "I think we need to keep Solomon in the persons of interest column."

"Well, maybe don't dramatically x him out." Dylan slings me a wry look as he turns onto the road that leads to the downtown strip.

"I didn't…do that," I say, my grip on the notebook tightening. "Hey, where are we going?" This isn't the way to his house.

"Thought maybe we could plan our next move a lot better over burgers at the diner."

"Good idea," I say, only now noticing that my stomach is growling after skipping our annual first-day lunch at the river.

He parks in front of the diner, and I hop down before he has a chance to grapple with the whole *should I open her door now that we're not a couple* dilemma. Striding ahead of him, I spot *our* booth open at the back.

I slide down into the one in front of it.

Dylan sits across from me, his gaze wandering to that back booth. I know it's stupid. I've been with him all day, so avoiding our table isn't exactly going to put a damper on the memories. I couldn't do it though. I couldn't sit and drink a chocolate milkshake, remembering the way we shared one last summer in that back-corner booth. Remembering the way we play fought over the fries and how he would always start out sitting across from me, the way he is now, but would mysteriously end up beside me halfway through the meal.

"So," he says. "The usual?"

"Sounds good." I have no idea what *usual* he's referring to. Our usual from two summers ago, when we would come with Audrey, Nate, and Lucy, and everyone would order individually? Or the usual from last summer, when we shared a milkshake and a basket of fries?

The waitress is a girl I've never seen before with gorgeous brown spiral curls and a friendly round face. She looks a little older than me, and her name tag says *Katie*. "Hi, there. What can I get for you?"

"Two cheeseburgers, one without pickles, two orders of fries, and two chocolate milkshakes, please," Dylan says.

My heart sinks, even though I know we're not together anymore. The waitress nods and heads back to the kitchen.

"We have to find someone close to Madison," I say, attempting to focus on the job at hand before I spiral. "We need to know what the people closest to her think. If she's alive and well, can she lead us to Audrey—or at the very least, to this 4477 guy? And if she's never heard of Audrey, then can we turn the phone in to the cops in good conscience?"

"I guess so. But how are we supposed to find someone close to Madison? She's not on social media. We checked."

The waitress returns, setting two glasses of ice water in front of us. "Food will be up in a minute," she says before hurrying off to take the next table's order.

I reach for my water, parched after sitting in the hot truck. Downing half of it, I set my sweating glass back on the table. "I guess we start with whatever we can find online. We know she's from the Shadows, so a—" I catch the waitress glance over at us before going back to jotting down orders. "A local," I say, lowering my voice. "We could probably head over there and start asking around."

I've only been to Shadow's Pass twice. The first time was when we followed a bike trail through its outskirts. The second was when Audrey needed an emergency hem fix on her dress for a dinner at the Hilltop—this fancy restaurant the Covingtons treat us to at the end of summer. There isn't an actual tailor for miles, but someone at the club mentioned a seamstress who works out of her home in Shadow's Pass. I accompanied Audrey, who didn't want to cross the tracks alone.

It's always made me uncomfortable, the way the Covingtons and the other country club kids talk about Shadow's Pass. Maybe because they make it sound like the depths of poverty, when really, it's just a neighborhood that looks a lot like mine back home. And, unlike my suburban spot, Shadow's Pass boasts some truly incredible scenery.

Or maybe it's the way they talk about the people who live there, people who could never be worthy of their company.

People who live merely to serve them, who are made to sound lesser than rodents.

I catch the waitress watching us on her way back to the kitchen this time. Annoyance spikes in me. She must recognize Dylan from the news or from the social media posts asking for help finding Audrey. Some of those posts contain family photos.

Dylan must notice her too. He leans forward with his elbows on the table, using his fists to shield his mouth. "Clearwater Ridge isn't that big a town. Someone we know must've met Madison before, right?"

"You would think. Except we're talking about Shadow's Pass."

I don't have to explain what I mean. Dylan knows. Shadow's Pass is only on the other side of town, but it might as well be another state. Our friends do not interact with townie kids—apart from Kurt, that is.

"Plus," I add, "we would've heard about it. Everyone likes to brag that they knew the missing girl." Last summer, I stopped into the coffee shop and overheard a girl announce to her group of friends that Audrey Covington had once been her river rafting guide. This waitress is probably dying to blab about the time she waited on Audrey Covington's brother.

"Yeah, you're right."

I don't notice the waitress sneak up on us until a plate clanks onto the table before me. "Two cheeseburgers, two fries, and two milkshakes. Need anything else?"

Some privacy would be nice. I bite back the remark, nodding. "Thanks, we're good."

"Sorry for intruding," Katie says, transferring the milk-shakes from her tray to the table, "but I thought I heard you mention Madison Blake."

So not just staring but also eavesdropping. I don't respond because lies—even of the little white variety—are not my forte. Dylan and Audrey discovered this when we were kids and an illicit game of nighttime hide-and-seek led to a round of inter-rogation from our parents. I'd been the first to cave and admit the reason our shoes were so muddy. It's why I'm not allowed to speak to any of the adults the day after the Summer Kickoff. I'm simply not the person to answer questions about alcohol or what time we got home.

"Yeah," Dylan says, simultaneously saving and stunning me. "We were, actually. Do you know her?"

"Not really." She frowns. "We went to school together, Clearwater Ridge High. So I know of her. We had a class or two together, but she hung out with the artsy kids. I'm assuming she stole from you."

"Stole from us?" I ask. "No, nothing like that."

"Oh, good. Because a friend of mine has been looking for Madison too."

I straighten in my seat, my fingers itching to pull out my notepad now that there may actually be something real to write down. "Which friend?"

She reddens. "Probably shouldn't say. But Madison stole like two grand from him."

"Really? He hasn't been able to track her down?"

"Nope," she says, fiddling with the pen clipped on to her apron pocket. "I think she took off right after she scammed him."

Back in the kitchen, something clatters, like a dish breaking. Katie's head turns toward the sound, but I attempt to reel her back in. "You don't happen to know where she used to live, do you?"

"No, but Madison and I have a mutual friend—Britta Clark. She was in art club with Madison. She'll know her address."

"Do you think Britta would speak to us?"

"I could ask her." Katie's eyes narrow suddenly. "Though you never did say what this was about."

No, we definitely didn't. I'd foolishly hoped she wouldn't notice. In a panic, I glance at Dylan.

"I'm Audrey Covington's brother," he says, eyes drifting down to his untouched meal. "She's the girl who went—"

"Missing, yeah." Katie nods. "I'm so sorry. You must want to find out if there's a connection between the two disappearances, like the people in the Clearwater Ridge Forum are saying."

"Exactly," Dylan says. "If there's any chance that Madison's really missing, and that whoever did this—" He breaks off, and I can't tell whether he's actually struggling with the words or a really good actor.

"I just—I hate to say this, but I think you're getting your hopes up for no reason," Katie says. Apparently, this waitress is an expert on the case after having scrolled through the stupid gossip forum.

"Any hope is better than none." Dylan's eyes glisten in a way I'm certain isn't fake.

The door chimes as two tweens walk in, and Katie turns, remembering herself. "Look, this guy I told you about? My friend? He pressed charges. *That's* why Madison skipped town."

"Really?" I ask. Maybe Katie really is an expert on this. "Are you sure you can't tell us this guy's name? Not even if there's a chance he could help us find Audrey?"

"Sorry, I have to get back to work," Katie says. "If you give me your name and number before you leave, I'll pass it along to Britta. Maybe she can help you find Madison's mother." She tucks a stray curl behind an ear and scurries off to the tweens' table.

"Well," I say, picking up a nearly cold fry. "That's one more person who thinks that Madison Blake is fine and dandy."

"Then we have to find her," Dylan says. "Whatever connection she has to my sister, we have to figure out what it is."

On our way out of the diner, I leave my cell number along with the paid bill. Not that I'm holding out hope in the waitress's friend.

Back in the truck, Dylan and I decide to call it a day. Tonight is the annual first-day-of-vacation dinner, followed by Tripp Shaw's Summer Kickoff. I have no desire to attend either of these affairs, but Mom said we need to be there for the Covingtons. We enter the house just as Nate and Lucy are making their way through the back French doors, towels wrapped around their waists. "You guys never showed," Nate says, lugging the cooler to the kitchen.

"Sorry, we weren't feeling up to it," Dylan says.

An ache spreads through my chest; this is the first year I've skipped the river on day one. It shouldn't be a big deal, but after Audrey, after Dylan—it feels like one more piece of the life I used to know to crumble and fall away.

Lucy continues on to the stairs, but I catch the way she

looks from Dylan to me. My sister and I don't share everything, but we do share a wall back home. She heard me shed tears over Dylan this past year. Now, she's wondering why we were off alone together.

I follow her up the stairs, hoping she'll drop the issue and opt for a hot shower. But she pauses in front of her bedroom door. "What's going on with you and Dylan?" she asks, putting a hand on her hip.

I debate telling her about the investigation. It would get her off my back. But I'd have to keep the burner phone from her. It would be too much to put on a fifteen-year-old.

I could tell her that Dylan and I were merely catching up, but that would involve lying. "We got burgers at the diner," I say, knowing that this small truth is far from an answer to her question.

"Okay," she says, obviously unsatisfied.

"We talked, mostly about Audrey."

"Oh." She blinks, like the answer should've been obvious. Audrey is my best friend and Dylan's sister. It makes sense that *she* would be the topic of conversation upon our reunion.

Guilt floods my chest, because Audrey *was* the topic of conversation. But deep down, I'd been hoping that Dylan and I would talk about more.

"Well," she says, spinning to grasp the door handle. "I'm glad you guys got to talk. We did miss you at the river though."

"Yeah." I want to promise to be there tomorrow, but it's not a promise I can make.

Tomorrow, Dylan and I have plans to track down 4477.

11

Dinner with the Covingtons was nothing short of excruciating. A suffocating sense of unease saturated the room. No topic seemed safe.

Being here again has everyone in a fragile state—no one more than Mrs. Covington, who cried when Nate casually mentioned getting sunburnt on the river today.

"Remember that summer when Audrey's shoulders burnt so bad they blistered?" Mrs. Covington asked through a sniffle. "I'm sorry. She just…has such a fair complexion."

Mr. Covington tried to change the subject, bringing up Dylan's trip to Berkeley in a few days for orientation. "He might be the only freshman starter on the roster," Mr. Covington said, tired eyes failing to match his enthusiastic tone. "Isn't that right, son?"

Dylan merely shrugged, face reddening.

The sound of clanking silverware turned to stifling silence, and I had to get out of the dining room. It was like being trapped underwater, my oxygen-deprived lungs begging for air.

Dad suggested an after-dinner cocktail, and I wasted no time offering to do the dishes.

"I'll help," Dylan said, following me to the kitchen.

Now, the three of us work in silence, Dad's tense posture as he mixes drinks a reflection of how we all feel. He guzzles down a shot of rum before adding lime to the daiquiris. When he leaves, tray in hand, I glance over at Dylan. He's returning a clean plate to a cabinet, and my eyes linger a moment on the muscles in his arms, those broad shoulders. "I didn't know you were leaving for orientation."

He shrugs, picking up the towel. "Just for a couple days."

"That's exciting, right?"

"Yeah, it is. It should be. But with everything going on—"

"What time are we leaving?" comes a voice from the doorway.

I startle, the plate nearly slipping from my grasp. Nate is standing there, rubbing the back of his neck nonchalantly.

"Leaving for what?" Dylan reaches a hand out, and I place the dripping plate into it for him to dry.

"Tripp's party," Lucy says, sliding up beside Nate with an expectant grin.

Dylan dries the dish and puts it away in the cabinet. "We're not going."

"Why?" Lucy squeaks. "You guys *have* to go. If not, our parents will never let us!"

"Good." Water still running, I spin to face her. "You shouldn't go. You two are only fifteen."

The instant Lucy's lips part, I know what she's going to say. "You were fifteen when you first got to go!"

She's right. Audrey and I attended our first Summer Kickoff when we were their age. Dylan chaperoned us.

"You really want to go to a party, Luce?"

"Yes," she says, the sentiment quickly echoed by Nate.

"Dinner was so depressing," he says. "We just want to take our minds off the Audrey stuff for one night. *Please.*"

Inhaling a steam-filled breath, I shut off the faucet. I turn to Dylan, letting my eyes ask the question, hoping he can't see what else hovers in my mind. The slew of painful memories the party will surely bring back: kissing him in the pool, Tripp's parents' balcony, Audrey abandoning me for Kurt, the tornado of confusion that would follow.

"Whatever you want to do, Paige," Dylan says, tearing his gaze from mine.

I don't want to go. But it is a party full of Clearwater Ridge vacationers, townies undoubtedly sprinkled in. If we're going to get anywhere in our investigation, we have to find the connection between Audrey and Madison. The more I think about it, the more this party is the perfect place to start.

"Well," I say, offering Lucy a half smile, "after that dinner, I guess we could all use a distraction."

That's how we all end up on Tripp's doorstep an hour later. "Do not do anything I wouldn't do," I hiss at Lucy.

She side-eyes me. "So, basically, I'm allowed to sit in a corner all night."

Before I can respond, Tripp answers the door, surprise lighting his eyes. "Hey!" He catches himself a moment too late and gestures to Lucy and Nate. "The babies escaped their cribs, huh?"

"Funny," Nate says, rolling his eyes.

Tripp laughs and side-hugs him. When he furls his hand toward the foyer, Nate grabs Lucy by the hand and tugs her along.

"So, how are you guys doing?" Tripp asks as we follow him inside.

Dylan shrugs. "All right, man. You?"

"I mean, I'm on my third beer, so can't complain. You need to catch up." He slaps Dylan on the chest and leads us into the kitchen. Filling two cups from a shiny stainless-steel keg dispenser, he hands one to each of us. "Dad told me about Audrey's investigation. I can't believe they're just giving up. I'm really sorry."

"Thanks," Dylan says, looking down at the foamy liquid.

"Did your dad mention trying to talk to Detective Ferrera?" I ask. If Tripp Shaw and his dad were truly torn up about Audrey's investigation, they would *do* something about it. Tripp's parents have more sway in this town than anyone. His mother is on the Clearwater Ridge town council, and the family is the biggest charitable donor.

Tripp's lips quirk. "Yeah, I think he tried, but the detective's hands are tied." He shrugs, like that's that.

I grit my teeth, ready to press him on the subject. But I spot Kurt in the doorway at the far end of the room, and a sense of déjà vu rattles me so hard that I stumble.

"You okay?" Dylan says, turning to take my arm.

Tripp laughs and lifts his beer. "I can see you two already got started back at the Covington pad."

"No, it's—I'm not drunk." Face scorching, I remove my arm from Dylan's grasp and take a swig of my beer. "I'm fine."

"Sure you don't want some water instead?" Dylan asks, eyes narrowed in concern.

"I'm sure." I take a defiant swig, even though the bitter taste of beer is the last thing I want. It roils in my stomach to the beat of the too-loud music.

It's better than him looking at me this way though. Like he actually cares.

"Well, I'm going to let you two sort that out," Tripp says. "But enjoy yourselves. I'll be in the pool, if you're up for a swim." He trots off, and by the time I remember to look, Kurt is long gone.

Of course he is. After our interrogation earlier today, he'll be avoiding us at all costs.

I turn toward the door, and Dylan touches my elbow. "Are you really going swimming?"

"Um, no. I'm going to pretend to drink this beer and then"—I scan the area and lean in closer—"try to get a leg up on tomorrow's mission."

"How?"

"If Katie knew Madison from school, some other townie at this party will know her too. Maybe someone can tell us where she used to live."

"That's not a bad idea," Dylan says, nodding. "Except I already found the hotel where Madison's mom works."

"Wait, what? When?"

"While you and Lucy were getting ready," he says. "I just Googled 'Madison Blake' and found her mother, Delilah Blake. Then I searched for her, and the address popped up."

"That's crackerjack detective work."

A corner of his mouth quirks up.

"Okay, so we ambush this poor woman at her place of work." My gaze wanders the living room now, where a couple of guys on the couch are lazily pointing at the ceiling as if they're counting stars in the night sky. Doug Rayburn and Todd Morales. "Maybe we can still get some answers while we're here." If Audrey somehow got into drugs last summer, those two might know about it. "Stay here."

Dylan protests, calling my name, but I'm already halfway across the room.

"Hey, Doug," I say, sidling up like he and I are the best of friends. I get a strong whiff of body odor and stifle a gag. "Todd. What's up, guys?" I raise my beer in salute.

"Hey, um..." Todd gives me a blank look and turns to Doug.

"Paige," Doug says, straightening. He tries to focus his bloodshot eyes. "What's going on?"

"Oh, nothing much. It's a clear ceiling kind of night, my favorite." When they fix me with another vacant stare, I add, "Just in need of some of the good stuff." I aim for a knowing look, despite my cluelessness as to how to buy drugs. "I've got my guy back at home, but I could use a contact out here. Who's the go-to?"

"What are you looking for?" Todd asks calmly. He has a broody look about him, dark hair and eyes. Audrey always joked about wanting to date a bad boy, and Todd Morales could quite possibly fit the bill. I picture her dressed in a plaid skirt and Mayberry Prep polo, hanging on to his scruffy black sleeve.

I think back to my blunder with Kurt earlier today and internally wince. "Molly mainly."

"Oh, I can handle that," Doug says to my dismay. There is zero percent chance that Doug Rayburn, with his greasy hair and body odor, is Audrey's mystery guy.

"Actually..." I channel that television detective again, undercover this time. "I've got a long list that needs filling, so a proper dealer is more what I'm looking for."

"Fortunately, that's me too." Doug smiles, like he's just made my day.

"Great. Hey, uh, you sold to my friend Audrey last summer, right? I think she mentioned you."

"Audrey Covington? The missing girl?" Doug frowns. "No, I definitely would've remembered her." He and Todd share a sleazy grin.

"Right. Well, let me get your number, then, and I'll hit you up once I have the cash."

Doug types his number into my phone. Unsurprisingly, it does not end in 4477. I plod back over to Dylan, defeated but also slightly underwhelmed by my first encounter with a real-life drug dealer.

"Well, it's not looking like drugs," I report. "Apparently, Clearwater Ridge's resident dealer is Doug Rayburn."

Dylan arches a brow. "Does it count as dealing if he does all the drugs himself?"

"A fair question. I can't see Audrey getting within two feet of that guy." I tried, and the stench nearly killed me.

"So, the dealer thing is a dead end."

"One we never should've entertained in the first place," I

say, guilt nagging at me. "We should've known Audrey didn't spend all last summer getting high or whatever."

Dylan scratches his head, neither agreeing nor disagreeing. "Let's stick with the Madison angle. We've got to connect the girls before we get anywhere."

"Tomorrow," I say. "Right now, we have other matters to attend to."

"Such as?"

"Checking on Nate and Lucy."

Dylan cracks a smile. "You mean *spying* on Nate and Lucy."

"Semantics. I think I saw them headed to the pool."

He starts to follow me, but pauses to scan the room. "I lost my beer. You gonna drink that?" he asks, indicating the nearly full cup I'm clutching tighter than a bag of pearls.

"No," I say, tucking it behind my back and spilling a little. "But I need it." Babies have pacifiers and stuffed bears; I have this beer. It's even more necessary now that I don't have a certain guy's hand to hold anymore.

We stop by the kitchen to grab Dylan a drink before making our way to the pool room. The moment we step inside the palatial space with the blinking colored lights, it's like the wind has been knocked out of me.

I suck in a deep breath of chlorine-filled air and sidestep over to the wall, pressing my back up against it.

"You okay, Paige?" Dylan nears me.

"Yeah." I nod, shaking it off. "I was trying to be covert," I say over the sounds of splashing and laughter. "Blend in with the scenery."

"That's a white wall, and you're dressed in a lime-green shirt."

"Like one of those little geckos, right? Any sign of the young'uns?"

He turns to face the pool. "Nope. Where'd they go?"

"I don't know, but I'm five seconds away from texting Lucy."

"That would make you a very ineffective spy," Dylan says, tipping his head toward the door.

I follow him into the hall again, feeling relieved to be out of that room but also a bit anxious. After Audrey, that niggling worry that it could happen again is always with me. Though it's silly in this case. Lucy is with Nate, and he'd never let anything happen to her.

We reach the game room, barely making it two feet inside when Dylan nudges me. "Over at the card table," he whispers, his breath tickling my ear and sending a shiver down my spine.

I look to find Lucy and Nate at the round table, intently studying their hands of cards. A few guys are seated around their table, including Brent and Tripp. "That better be water," I say, indicating the red cups before our siblings.

"And they'd better not be playing for money," Dylan adds. "Last summer, Brent was almost as good as his brother."

Unlike Brent and Oliver Haywood, however, my little sister doesn't have loads of her parents' money to gamble away. "Should we run interference?" If Lucy spends our parents' money, *I'm* the one they'll murder.

"Nah. They're not that stupid." He makes to leave, but halts in the doorway. "Are they?"

"I don't know. At least they're playing a card game and not a drinking game."

"Which is *your* favorite kind of game." He grins, glancing at the now-stale beer sloshing around in my cup.

"I'm up for whatever game you throw at me," I say, lifting my brows. Immediately, heat rushes into my cheeks.

I hope he's not thinking of last summer and all the games we played. About water polo in the Covingtons' pool, parents against kids, back when his parents still had their hearts intact. About tube racing down the river, laughter ringing through the ravine. About how the loser had to do the dishes, but we ended up doing them together anyway, passing dishes and sneaking kisses while our parents chatted in the next room. The game in Tripp's pool that ended with our lips meeting and our limbs entwined. "I mean, I…"

Before I can stutter my way out of this, something at the pool table in the far corner of the room catches my eye. Solomon McCleary. It isn't his presence here that stands out. He parties wherever and with whomever he can. It's the girl he's canoodling with that's throwing me for a loop. "Hey," I whisper to Dylan, "isn't that the waitress from the diner?"

Dylan's gaze follows my discreet thumb sign. "Oh, yeah. Katie."

Envy pricks up at the way he remembered her name so easily. Then I feel foolish, yet again. Of course he notices pretty girls. He and I aren't together anymore. For all I know, he had a whole slew of girlfriends his senior year of high school.

I turn my attention back to Solomon, whose arms are wrapped around Katie's waist. Clearly, neither of them is interested in the pool lesson. Solomon's face is buried in her neck. She giggles, spinning to face him as he pins her body over the table.

"They look...close," I say, wanting to cover my eyes. Back in the diner, Katie mentioned a friend, a guy who'd been swindled by Madison Blake. Could this guy have been a bit *more* than a friend? After the way Solomon shut down when we asked about Audrey, though, I doubt he'd talk to us.

"That's Solomon." Dylan reaches for my hand to tug me along, and for a second, the act feels entirely natural.

Then we both freeze. "Sorry," he says, releasing my hand to run his fingers through his hair.

"It's fine," I say, though my pulse is pounding. "I'm going to find a bathroom." I leave him in the doorway, regretting coming here with every fiber of my being and wishing for my best friend.

12

In the morning, Dylan and I slip out bright and early. We left a note saying we're on a hike. Dylan wrote it, since I can't even *write* a lie.

Madison's mother, Delilah Blake, works as a front desk clerk at the Landmark Hotel, a waterfront property on the outskirts of the Pines. We aren't sure what hours she works, but we found a photo of her on the internet. We're looking for a middle-aged brunette with green eyes and somewhat over-plucked brows.

The drive is silent, apart from the occasional yawn. Last night, dragging Lucy and Dylan from the party was like tearing two toddlers away from their favorite cartoon. We were fools, indulging far too many pleas of "just ten more minutes."

Now, we're paying for it. In the driver's seat, Dylan is showered and ready for our mission in a button-down sky-blue shirt that matches his eyes. Unfortunately, he keeps rubbing at those eyes with his free hand, turning them red. Before we left,

I attempted to paint some life into my corpse-like face with undereye concealer and blush. I don't think it worked.

The parking lot is free only to guests, so Dylan parks in the makeshift dirt patch used by river-goers, and we make the trek. The Landmark Hotel is one of those luxury lodge varieties, large timber beams framing intricate stonework and immaculate cream-colored paint. If you drive by this place at night, you'll catch millions of twinkly lights strung from the beams and a colorful water fountain display. We head beneath the wooden portico fit with stone columns to approach the gleaming double doors, and I tug my flimsy white cardigan over the spaghetti straps of my sundress. I smile at the doorman, feeling like I'm headed into church or a funeral; this dress is the only thing I packed that's not a bathing suit or ripped for the sake of fashion.

"Good morning," the large man answers, pulling the door open for us. Just like that, we've passed the first part of the test. Only I don't feel relief. That's the man who's going to pick us up and drop-kick us out of this place when Delilah Blake orders us from the building.

If she's even here.

Across the grand lobby, a fire blazes in the stone fireplace. With the luxurious air-conditioning whipping through my ponytail, you'd never know it was eighty-five degrees and climbing outside.

The front desk is off to the right. Together, Dylan and I approach the woman sitting there. Unlike the online photo, this woman wears glasses and has short, thinning gray hair. I start to doubt that it's her at all until I get close enough to read her name tag: *Delilah*. The worry evaporates. Her gaze flicks up, green eyes peering at us over the black rims. "Checking in?" She smiles warmly, but a flicker of judgment lights her gaze. Clearly, Dylan and I are too young to be sharing a hotel room.

"Actually," I say, playing with the top button of my sweater, just in case she missed my wholesome vibe, "we were looking for your daughter, Madison Blake?"

The woman's breath hitches audibly, and her eyes fall to the desktop. "I suppose you're friends of hers."

"Yes, ma'am. Anna and Peter from art club at Clearwater Ridge High. I've been trying to get in touch with her for a while now. Do you know if she changed her number? "

Delilah presses her lips flat. "You two went to Clearwater Ridge High?"

"Go Coyotes," Dylan says brightly, laying on the charm. The woman looks unconvinced, however. This is the exact reason I told him not to wear anything name brand. "We were inseparable in school. Me, Anna, Madison, and Britta."

At the name, the woman's rigid stance falters. "Britta?" Her scrutinizing gaze roams over us again. "Why do you need to get in touch with Madison now?"

"There's this exhibition coming up," I say. "Over in Melville Falls." My lips go numb the way they do after a tooth filling. I'm completely blowing this attempt at a lie. "We really think Madison should apply. Her work would be perfect." The truth is that after scouring the internet for an example of Madison's work, I found one photo of a painting from three years ago on the art club's public Instagram account. "Maddie Blake" was in the caption. "Only we haven't been able to get in touch."

"I see." The stiff posture is back, only now Delilah is crossing her arms. "Look, my daughter dropped out of art club her sophomore year and, to my knowledge, hasn't painted a thing since. I don't know what she stole from you, but I can't help."

Panic bolts through me. "It's nothing like that," I say, shaking my head. "She didn't steal from us. We're her friends."

"All the same," she says, no longer looking at me but focusing on Dylan, "I can't help you."

"Can you at least tell us if she's okay?" I ask. "There was talk that she'd gone missing a while back."

Delilah pauses her study of Dylan to lift a drawn-on brow. "What does *your friend Britta* say?"

My insides flip. "Britta's lost touch as well. Did Maddie"—I give the nickname a spin, hoping it'll land—"change her phone number by chance?"

Delilah takes a handkerchief from her pocket and covers a cough. "Give me a minute," she says, turning to her computer. "As you can see, I'm working, and there are things that need my attention." She begins typing away on her computer before either of us can answer. We stand around, admiring the wood carvings along the walls and the animal sculptures speckling the room. "I knew it," she says so suddenly that I flinch.

She spins her computer screen to face us, and my heart plunges into my gut. The article on the screen is titled "Vacationer Still Missing." The captioned photograph at the top shows all five smiling members of the Covington family, including Dylan. "This is you," Delilah says, pointing him out. "So are you going to tell me what this is really about? Or do I need to ask Rick out there for some assistance?"

I lift my hands. "No, ma'am. We mean no harm." Lowering my gaze, I add, "But you're right. We don't actually know your daughter or Britta Clark. Dylan is Audrey Covington's brother, and I'm her best friend. Recently, the state police slowed down their investigation into Audrey's disappearance, so—silly as it sounds—we wanted to look for her on our own. We know Madison went missing just before Audrey did, so we're starting with her."

The lobby door opens, and an elderly couple meanders in. Rick follows, dragging their bags along.

Delilah clears her throat. "I have to get back to work." She turns her head dismissively, and my shoulders slump in defeat. As we start to let the couple pass, Delilah says, "Excuse me. I think you forgot this." She pushes a pink sticky note across the desk to Dylan, who palms it.

The moment we exit the hotel doors, we read the note: *54 Sunny Place. Come after 7.*

———

It turns out that "after 7" is the exact time that Mr. and Mrs. Covington really want everyone to have a game night, complete with cocktails for the adults. Apparently, Dylan is the only one who can make the perfect lemon drop. I'm antsy to talk to Delilah, but in the kitchen, Dylan promises we'll only stay for one game.

"I don't mind," he says when I throw a critical look from his setup on the kitchen counter back to the door his mother just wandered through. "It's an unspoken rule that if I make the martinis, I get to sample them."

"That's exactly why it's messed up, dude."

He laughs. "Calm down, Paige. Here, have a sip. But only one. You need a clear head tonight." He pushes the glass he's been sampling from toward me.

I take a tentative sip, and *damnit*, it tastes delicious. I try to sneak another while he garnishes the real martini glasses with lemon slices. "So how did you become a eighteen-year-old bartender?"

He shrugs, placing all the glasses onto Mrs. Covington's casually chic, rustic wooden serving tray. "I became a lot of things when Audrey went missing." A knot forms in my throat. I cough, trying to find words to smooth things over, but Dylan continues. "A counselor for one. Nate's chauffeur and often-times parent figure for another. Handyman, designated driver, grocery shopper. It's been quite a year."

"I'm sorry. I can't imagine." And I'm definitely not winning any awards for sensitivity tonight.

He smiles, but his eyes go distant, like he's trying to see through that kitchen window even in the dark of night. "They took care of me for almost eighteen years. It's only right that I take care of them now."

"You lost a sister too," I say, reaching out to touch his arm. "Who's taking care of you?"

"I don't need anyone. I don't—" He sucks in a breath. "I don't *deserve* anyone. Not after last summer." He lifts the tray, effectively shaking my hand from his arm.

"What does that mean?" I ask, stepping in front of him.

But he doesn't answer. Instead, he navigates around me, carrying the tray across the kitchen and out to the sitting room.

After a game of Pictionary, Dylan and I finally head out. It's 8:15 p.m. I strap on my seat belt, the same question from earlier in the kitchen dancing on my tongue. What did he mean by "Not after last summer"? Does he mean after what happened with *us*? Does he know something about Audrey that he hasn't shared with me?

I've nearly mustered up the courage to ask when his voice shatters the silence, along with my resolve. "So what's the plan here?"

I blink. That's what I should've been pondering instead of Dylan's cryptic words from the kitchen. "Well, the jig is already up, right? She knows we're looking for Audrey. As long as we stick with the whole *we believe there's a serial killer out there* theory, she'll never suspect anything else is going on."

Audrey's the good girl; Madison's the thief. No one would ever suspect that the two might've known each other.

"I guess." Dylan's GPS instructs him to turn right onto the next street. He does, casting us in utter darkness.

"So, no streetlamps on Sunny Place, huh?" I squint into the void, trying to locate number fifty-four. When the GPS lady says, "You have arrived at your destination," we've already passed it.

Dylan backs the truck up onto the corner, and we sit and stare at the house with only one lit window. The rest of the place could be invisible, for all I can tell. "Do you think it's rude to use our phones as flashlights?" I ask.

"No ruder than Delilah Blake not bothering to turn on a porch light when she invited us here."

Sold, I hop down from the truck, shutting the door and

turning on my flashlight mode. I shine it ahead, illuminating the rusted fence and the swinging gate that creaks with the breeze. Dylan is already on the porch, pressing the doorbell.

"I think it's broken," he whispers, pulling on the screen door. Its torn mesh flaps as he knocks on the wooden one behind it. We wait, and I continue to flit my light over the oxidized paint on the exterior panels, the shattered window to our left.

Dylan's feet fidget over the mangy doormat. He lifts a fist to knock again when the knob begins to rattle. The door creaks open, and Delilah Blake stands before us in black sweatpants and a gray and white striped T-shirt. A blue scarf, knotted at the base of her neck, now covers her hair. The makeup from earlier today has been washed off, revealing a hollowness around her eyes and an ashy pallor to her skin. "Come in," she says, motioning us forward.

We step into a cozy living room that smells faintly of cigarette smoke. It's painted sea green, and Delilah has us take a seat on the beige couch as she pads over to the kitchen in her house slippers. She returns with a tray full of tea and cookies, setting it down on the coffee table beside an ashtray shaped like a cat. "Sorry about the front of the house. Madison left more than her share of unhappy customers. And since she's not around for them to take out their frustrations, they work everything out on my home." She sits across from us on a coral-colored accent chair. "Please, take a cookie."

"They vandalized your home?" Dylan leans forward to take two of the stale-looking cookies, passing one to me.

"Not since last summer. I just haven't...uh, had a chance to get started on repairs."

"You live alone here?" I ask, knowing that I've already overstepped.

"I'm divorced. Madison's father took off a while back."

"I'm sorry. Any idea who trashed the house?"

She shakes her head. "The sheriff's department said they'd look into it, but you know how that goes. A car drives by late at night while I'm half-asleep. There's nothing to go on. But no one's attempted a thing since Madison left town."

"Left town?" I ask. "So then, you agree with the sheriff that she ran away?"

"I know she did." Delilah folds her hands over her lap. "Look, I'm the one who reported Maddie missing in the first place. I'll admit, when she up and disappeared one day—never come home, never answered any of my calls—I worried that something was seriously wrong. Britta hadn't heard from her either. She'd been Maddie's best friend since kindergarten, the one person who seemed to look the other way when it came to my daughter's"—the woman's lips twist as she carefully chooses her word—"*habits*. So when I saw how concerned Britta was, I filed a missing person's report. The sheriff started an investigation. Every morning, I went down to the station to follow up. But then, a month later, out of the blue, she called me."

"Madison called you?" I ask, bobbling my teacup and nearly spilling scalding liquid all over my bare legs. "From her cell phone?"

Delilah coughs, a harsh bark that turns into a fit. "Sorry," she says, taking a deep breath. "Asthma." She bends forward to pour herself some tea, and my gaze settles on the ashtray. As far as I know, asthmatics aren't supposed to smoke. "No, this was from a number I didn't recognize. And when I tried to call back, it was disconnected. Anyway, she said she was fine, but it was better if I didn't know where she was."

"You didn't think that was strange?" Dylan asks.

"Everything about my daughter is strange to me," Delilah says, blowing on her tea. "Though, if I'm honest, it's not entirely her fault. I credit her father for imparting his *skills* on her before he took off for good."

Skills? "Her father was a grifter?" I ask.

Delilah nods. "Before we met, that was his life. Running cons and moving on. Then we got married, and he found a job at the car repair shop here in town. For the most part, I believed he'd changed. But it was always part of him, who he was. When Madison was little, he thought it was funny, teaching her little scams, like how to turn a five-dollar bill into a twenty at the county fair. *Party tricks*, he called them. He never realized what an aptitude his daughter truly had for that lifestyle." Shrugging, she sips her tea. "Now, I imagine he's back at it. Living from con job to con job. Hell, for all I know, he and Madison could be working together."

"I just don't understand why she couldn't at least tell you where she was," Dylan says.

Delilah tugs at a loose thread on her shirt. "On the call, she mentioned something about plausible deniability. I hate to think this about my own child, but it seemed like she was either in trouble or about to be. I hear the whispers in town, and sadly, I think those people are right. Madison went somewhere else, to try her old tricks on new people."

"But," I say hesitantly, "how did you know it wasn't a

kidnapper forcing her to make the call? In order to halt the investigation?"

"I just knew," she replies in a clipped tone. "Madison is my daughter. I could tell by her voice that she was telling the truth for once."

Dylan's gaze reflects my own skepticism. "Did you ever ask the sheriff to follow up on the number?" he asks. "To confirm that she was okay?"

"Madison told me not to."

I can feel my grip on the teacup growing precariously tight. She can't honestly be this stupid. Her daughter told her that she was fine and not to come looking for her or call her. The circumstances practically scream *kidnapping*. Madison could've been held at gunpoint for all Delilah Blake knows.

I set the cup down on the table before it shatters in my hand. "What does Britta make of all this?"

Delilah takes a slow sip of tea. "She was obviously upset that Maddie hadn't called her. She kept bothering the sheriff's department, saying that Maddie hadn't run away. In her mind, it was impossible for Madison to be okay and not call *her*."

"We'd really like to talk to Britta," Dylan says, shifting in his seat. "Do you know how we can get in touch with her?"

"She works over at the liquor store out in the Den," the woman says indifferently. "She'll either talk to you or she won't."

"Thank you," I say. "That's really helpful—*you've* been extremely helpful."

My lie practically rattles the room, but Dylan adds, "And these cookies are amazing."

"Yes," I say, closing a fist around what's left of my rock-hard shortbread. "Delicious."

At Dylan's lead, I get up, following him toward the door, past a trio of abstract paintings featuring bold colors. I think of what Katie said about Madison in high school, and I'm about to ask if she painted these when my gaze drifts to an antique console table pressed against the wall. I didn't notice it on the way in, but various candles and knickknacks adorn it, along with a trio of photographs, all of the same girl.

The first is a close-up of the girl dancing. She's smiling, round cheeks rosy, head thrown back, arms in the air. Her long brown hair and the silver chain on her wrist bounce and leap, as if escaping their 2D confines. In the next, the girl wears a graduation cap and gown. Her green eyes are serious in this one, expression as stiff as the crisply ironed white-collared shirt peeking through the gown. The last photo features Delilah and a man—presumably Mr. Blake—with the girl, though she's years younger, sitting on a sandy beach. I stop, my gaze trickling back to the first photo, the one with Madison in motion. I must study it for a beat too long because Dylan taps my arm.

I struggle to wrench my eyes off the laughing girl. I've seen her photograph before, on the internet, under old articles from when she was considered missing. School photos where Madison sits with her back rigid, giving forced smiles beneath titles like "Seventeen-Year-Old Girl Vanishes." Titles and photos like the ones that ran about Audrey.

But *this* Madison—the one who moves and laughs—jogs something in my memory. I've seen Madison Blake before, in person. Only I can't remember where.

Delilah coughs again, a wet sound that stirs me from my trance.

"Paige," Dylan hisses, tugging on my wrist now.

"Sorry," I say, commanding my feet to move. Madison Blake lived in Clearwater Ridge her entire life, up until last summer. I've spent every summer of my life here. Of course I've seen her around—maybe even spoken to her.

Delilah opens the front door for us, choking back the next cough, and we thank her for her time. We thank her for being so forthcoming, though I'm not sure she's been forthcoming at all.

Delilah Blake's story sounds flimsy. So flimsy you could knock it over with a breath.

Only I can't come up with a reason why she'd lie. If Madison were truly missing or...*worse*, wouldn't her mother want to find her? Wouldn't she want to seek out whoever did this?

Then again, the woman could be right. Perhaps she does know when her daughter is telling the truth, and the girl simply skipped town.

But if she's wrong, Madison could still be in very grave danger.

And if Delilah is lying, someone out there could be trying to cover the disappearance up.

The worst part is, I still don't know how Audrey fits into any of this.

THE GIRL

The girl knew the boy. At least, she knew *of* him. She'd seen him around town.

He was gorgeous, and anyone could tell he was beyond rich. She knew the boy wasn't twenty-one, either, though he was older than she was. Either the bartender believed he was of age, or he'd been able to get the beers simply by being a boy.

Normally, the thought would've made the girl's insides clench. But as the boy stood there, smiling and offering the sweating bottle, she felt only a swell of excitement. "Thanks," the girl said, accepting the drink. She took a swig and, finding the boy still hovering over her, patted the space beside her on the rock.

He assented, glancing around the trees as though he'd never seen these woods before. Of course, she knew that he vacationed in Clearwater Ridge every summer. "What's a girl like you doing all alone on a day like this?"

The girl dragged her feet in the dead leaves that blanketed

the dirt. She drew a faint sketch of her ex with her toe before crossing it out with her heel. "Just thinking. I needed to get away." She drew two intersecting circles to represent the Bad Stuff next, and a series of dots that trickled beneath them. The dots were tears—*her* tears.

The dots were blood.

Then, just as with the first sketch, she smudged it all away with her heel.

"You ride horses, don't you?" the boy asked.

She narrowed her eyes at him in response.

He laughed. "I'm assuming, only because everyone in Clearwater Ridge rides horses. You do, don't you?"

The girl tipped back her beer, letting the bubbling liquid try and inevitably fail to quench the thirst that lay deep within. She wasn't sure what exactly would ever quench that thirst. Only that it would take something more than this drink.

It would take more tears, that was certain.

It would take a great deal more blood.

13
PAIGE

At 8:15 in the morning, Dylan is still in bed. I sit on one of the stools at the kitchen bar, sipping my coffee, so jittery that I whack my shin against the iron leg. I send off a text that he won't read because his phone is likely on silent: Time to go!!!

Last night, when he and I wandered in late, Lucy started acting clingy. She made me sit with her through the end of a rom-com we'd already seen three times. I know she and Nate thought they'd be hanging out with us more. That even though it couldn't be the five of us, at least it would be the four.

If Dylan doesn't hurry up, those two will cajole us into some activity, and we'll miss the opportunity to seek out Britta.

When my coffee is down to dregs, I drop from the barstool and wander to the staircase. For a moment, I merely watch Dylan's door from this safe distance, willing it to open. But it stays shut. Hasn't he ever heard of an alarm?

Hearing movement from Lucy's room, I tiptoe up the stairs. Sweat blooms over my forehead as I lift my hand to knock on

Dylan's door. The vague stirring noises from Lucy's room turn into definite footsteps.

Frantic, I pull open the door and slip inside. Easing the door shut behind me, I press my back up against it and let out a too-loud breath.

Over on the bed, Dylan's sheets rustle, and he bolts upright. Morning light trickles in through the blinds, casting a glow over his bare torso and disheveled hair. He rubs his eyes and squints into the muted light. "Paige? What's going on?"

"Sorry," I hiss. "I was about to be compromised."

He continues to squint.

"Lucy almost spotted me. We were supposed to be out of here and on our way to the liquor store before anyone else woke up! Operation 7-Eleven, remember?"

"We never named it that." He gets out of bed, his boxer shorts and bare body on full display.

My cheeks scorch, and I avert my eyes as he rifles through his drawers. I pretend to admire the painting his mother must've hung in here, though I can barely see it.

"Can you get the light?" he asks.

I switch it on, not only the painting but my ex-boyfriend's swimmer's arms and torso now visible with perfect clarity. He turns from the dresser to catch me staring, tired eyes crinkling as he smirks.

"Sorry. I-I would leave, but she could be out there."

"Right." He's still grinning softly as he tugs on a T-shirt. "So how are we going to sneak out?"

"How high is your window?"

He tilts his head. "You can't be serious. We can always

make something up, Paige. We wanted breakfast at the diner. Coffee in town."

"They might try to tag along."

"Not if we tell them we're on a da—"

His eyes widen as he catches himself, but not before my entire face combusts. The mortification is quickly replaced by pulsing fury. This isn't one of Lucy's rom-com movies. Fake dating is only cute when it didn't already happen for real.

"Window," I sputter.

He turns to face the dresser as he tugs on a pair of shorts. When he slips into the bathroom, I take a few long deep breaths. I can't shut down. Audrey needs me. She could still be out there.

But I'm not sure I can do this with *him*.

Dylan emerges from the bathroom, sliding his feet into his flip-flops. When I make for the window, he moves in front of me, blocking my way. "I don't think we need to climb out of my second-story window," he says. "One of us can just play lookout, and we can sneak out the front door."

"Sure." I turn for the door, but he skirts around me again.

"That was really insensitive of me," he says, not bothering to clarify *what* was insensitive, since it's the trillion-ton dinosaur in the room.

"It's fine," I say, refusing to meet his gaze.

"No, it's not. Look, Paige, I know I was a jerk this past year." He steps closer, and I can smell the ocean-fresh scent of his deodorant and his spearmint toothpaste. His flip-flops inch into my line of sight; he's close enough that if I lifted my head, our noses would touch.

"Your sister went missing," I mumble, trying not to move a muscle. "It's understandable."

"No, it's not. You're the one who made everything bearable. The last person I should've pushed away. Without you, I felt..." He trails off.

Involuntarily, my gaze sweeps up as if in search of the rest of his words. What is he saying? That he needed me as a friend? Or is he saying he made a mistake about *us*?

He doesn't answer my questions with words. All I can do is feel the closeness of his body, his warm breath rustling my hair. I feel that inch of space left between us, the need for him to pull me closer, to close that space, to wrap his arms around me.

Then, all that matters is that space. Because it never diminishes, only hangs there. Like a bottomless pit or a black void.

That space is the answer to my questions as he pulls away.

———

"Audrey once told me that two teens from Clearwater Ridge came up here to go canoeing but got lost," I say as the truck bumps along the unpaved road. "And a bunch of inbred cannibals cooked them up and ate them."

"Audrey fed you the plot to *Deliverance* with a dash of *The Hills Have Eyes*," Dylan says.

"Damn that girl," I grumble.

"If you ever watched horror movies, you'd know this."

I scoff. "At my age? They'd scare the dentures right out of my mouth."

Devil's Den is what the locals call a nearby mountain town in the backwoods that makes Shadow's Pass look like the lap of luxury and that casual, onetime vacationers to the area will never even know exists. It's well below the poverty line, with people living in shanties, tents, or whatever they can find. I've only ever heard about it, and now that I'm seeing it with my own eyes, I can't reconcile how a place like this could exist a mere ten miles from the mansions in the Pines.

Another question gnaws on my mind. Most of the kids from Clearwater Ridge High end up working jobs in the vacation industry. That means they work in the nicer parts of town. So how the hell did Britta end up working—possibly even living—out *here*?

Delilah didn't give us an address, and cross streets don't seem to exist in these parts. But after winding up the same road for twenty minutes, we finally reach the run-down liquor store called Al's Mart. We get out of the truck, and suddenly, I understand how Devil's Den got its name. The beating of the sun up here is relentless. Rock formations shoot up on every side, surrounding us and making even the great outdoors feel claustrophobic.

Then there's the stench. Instead of pine, the area reeks of waste. I get an image of a cave up in the woods, ground covered in excrement and the rotting bones of prey.

On one side of the lot, I find the source—an overflowing garbage can, its contents baking in the sun. A man with leathery skin steps out from behind it, fixing us with a hard stare.

My heart races as Dylan and I pick up our steps to enter the tiny store. The place is empty at 9:05 a.m. on a Monday, apart from the blond girl manning the register.

Dylan and I approach her slowly. I debate grabbing a pack

of gum, partly so that we qualify as paying customers and partly because I'm out of gum. The clerk wears thick black eyeliner and burgundy lipstick as well as an ugly red and white collared Al's shirt. Once again, the name tag saves the day.

"Britta?" I ask.

The girl looks up, squinting at us. Her face is thin and angular. Not even her heavy makeup covers the pink scar that runs along the left side, from her temple down to her jawline. I haven't seen her in Clearwater Ridge before; I would've remembered that scar. "Yeah, who are you?" Her eyes linger on Dylan for an extra second, and some possessive instinct awakens in me. I fight off the urge to run my fingers down his back or loop an arm through his.

"We're friends—well, I'm Paige, a friend of Audrey Covington. This is Dylan, her brother."

"Audrey Covington? I don't know her."

"Yes, well, she's missing. I'm not sure if you've seen the—"

"I know *about* her," the girl says, rolling her eyes. "I don't live under a rock. I just don't know her personally. And I haven't seen her, either, if that's what you're asking about. Shouldn't you have a photograph to pass around or something?"

"We're not really here to ask about Audrey," Dylan says. "We were wondering more about Madison Blake? I believe your friend Katie passed along our contact info?"

"Oh." Britta lets out a harsh puff of air. "Yeah. Must've ignored that message. What could the two of you possibly want to know about Madison? Did she scam you or something?" Britta picks up her phone and starts fiddling with it, and I think we've lost her for good.

"We're just wondering if the cases—Audrey's and Madison's—might be related," I say. "The authorities seem to think that Madison's a runaway, but we heard that you believe otherwise."

"Who told you that?" The girl lowers the phone now, suddenly interested in this conversation.

"Delilah Blake. She said that her daughter called to tell her she was okay, but that you weren't convinced the call had ever happened."

Britta laughs, head back in her phone. "I was a bit of a drama queen last summer." She turns to the cardboard box behind the desk, taking a handful of candy bars and pushing past the counter into the aisles.

"Does that mean you changed your mind?" Dylan asks as we follow her.

"Well, yeah," she says, like it's obvious. She stacks the candy bars on the shelf and then weaves past us back toward the desk. "She went a long time without calling me, which was weird. She's my best friend, so I guess I freaked out a bit, started making up conspiracy theories. But I can assure you, Madison is fine and perfectly safe. She isn't…" Britta bites her lower lip, her gaze still untrained. "Look, whatever happened to Audrey, I'm sorry. But it had nothing to do with Maddie."

"What made you change your mind about Madison? Did she call you? Did you see her?"

"She, um…" The girl goes back to her box, grabbing more candy bars. "Yeah, she called me."

"What did she say? Did she tell you where she is?"

"I don't really see how that's relevant," Britta says, fumbling a bar. It drops to the floor, and she stoops to retrieve it.

"Here, let me help you." Dylan is already skirting the desk. The girl blushes. "I'm really not supposed to allow customers behind the desk."

At this, Dylan backs up, folding his hands like a polite schoolboy and cocking his head to one side. "Then you pass me the bars, and I'll go stock."

She hesitates, then lets out a resigned sigh, unable to resist his charm. When she passes him a few candy bars, their fingers brush in the process, eliciting a shy smile from Britta. Either Dylan is an amazing actor, or he's completely forgotten that I exist. "So," he says, "how did you end up with this job?"

"Al's my grandpa." Britta points to the emblem on her shirt. "My family has lived up here and run this shop since 1952. When my dad ran off, my grandpa promised that when I graduated high school, the place would be mine. And now it is."

"So you're running this place all by yourself?" I ask, thinking of Mr. Glares-a-Lot outside.

"Yep. Thinking about changing the sign out front to *Britta's*." She starts to pass more bars across the desk, but stops. "Look, I've got to work, and I'm still not entirely sure why you're asking about Maddie. I already told you, she's not missing."

Frustration gnaws at my jaw. I can't tell Britta that Audrey could be with Madison—not without mentioning the burner phone. "This is going to sound totally random," I try, "but did Madison know Audrey? Did she ever mention Audrey to you, or did you ever see them together?"

Britta laughs again, a bitter sound. "Oh, sure, they were great friends. Audrey Covington just loved to take Maddie for spins around the club." She rolls her eyes. "Are you serious? A country club bitch like that wouldn't have spoken to a girl like Maddie if she were the last person on earth."

I bristle, fists curling at my sides. I want to defend my friend to this person who never even met her. My friend, who defended me in front of the country club kids at tennis camp, who didn't care that I wasn't one of them. But then I think about Audrey and her game at the parties, sleuthing out the townies. The way she'd point and whisper, "*The skirt*," and flash a knowing grin. I remember that in the end, *I* didn't really know Audrey either. My fists loosen. "Is there any way that we could call Madison? Just to make sure the two never had contact?"

"Can't help you there. Madison didn't give me a callback number."

Dylan starts to ask another question, but Britta cuts him off. "If you really want to know, my *best friend* only called to tell me she'd be unreachable." I catch the way she wipes at an eye with the back of her hand, smearing mascara before spinning to face the box. My heart pinches. It's all too familiar, this tale of a best friend drifting away.

Britta clears her throat. "Any time we spent searching for her was a complete and utter waste. Honestly, we're all a lot better off without her. Madison Blake is a lying, conniving bitch and a fraud. One thing Madison Blake *isn't*, though, is missing."

She seems as done with this conversation as she is with Madison, but there's still so much I need to understand. "Delilah Blake said you had a soft spot for her daughter," I try. "That you always found a way to forgive Madison's shortcomings."

She only stares down at the cash register. When the bell at the front door chimes, I stiffen, Audrey's stories about the Den rushing back into my mind.

But Britta's body practically heaves in relief; she'd rather deal with the cannibals than us. "Yeah, well, that was then. That was before she made herself unreachable. Now, Madison may as well be dead."

———

When I get into Dylan's truck, I take out all of my pent-up frustration by slamming his door as hard as I can and letting out a growl.

"You okay?" Dylan starts the ignition but pauses to watch me the way zoo-goers would a caged animal.

"We're getting nowhere. Both women claim to have heard from Madison, but there isn't any proof! Would she really refuse to disclose her location or contact number to her own mother and best friend?"

"I mean, yeah, maybe," Dylan says, backing the truck out of the space. "The sheriff thinks one of her con jobs went south. If that means she was caught stealing, it could be really bad. If whoever was after her was dangerous enough for her to skip town, she might have worried for her mother and Britta's safety."

"But what if Madison's *not* actually safe? What if someone was holding a gun to her head on the other line?"

Dylan sighs. "I don't think Delilah or Britta would have bought it. They would've demanded proof or had the sheriff follow up."

"Then…what if *they're* the ones being threatened? Someone else could be forcing Delilah and Britta to keep quiet. And if they tell the truth about their suspicions, someone— maybe Madison, maybe one of them—will get hurt?" The truck turns onto the main road through town; Dylan must know a shortcut.

"Or maybe it's not a kidnapping thing at all," he says. "We know Audrey stole a lot of money from my parents. What if she somehow got mixed up in Madison's dealings?"

"You really think Audrey would do that?"

Dylan parks on the curb of the downtown strip, throwing a hand up. "I don't know, Paige. Last summer, I never thought she could lie to my face. Two years ago, I never would've believed she could steal money from my parents." He shakes his head. "Now? I think it's possible. The whole *what are we going to do about Madison* text message could very well have been about a con. Maybe Audrey and 4477 were part of something, and Madison double-crossed them. It could explain that text and why Audrey was so distracted."

"That sounds ridiculous. Where's Audrey been all this time?" I squint out the window. "And why are we parked here?"

"Supplies," Dylan says, pointing to the diner. "I thought we could use a little hike and picnic in the Pines to clear our heads."

"Like a working lunch," I say in an attempt to void the fact that a picnic complete with a gorgeous view sounds exactly like a date.

We reach the viewpoint, taking a seat on the large rock that kids love to take Sharpies to. My behind is currently covering *Dan and Shiela 4Eva*. Instead of our usual burgers, we opted for sandwiches, given nothing stays nice and warm for the forty-five minutes it takes to get up here.

Dylan hands me a lukewarm water bottle and a soggy turkey club, then takes a seat beside me on top of *Brock C was here*. "Maybe Madison isn't the key to finding Audrey, after all," Dylan says, unwrapping his sandwich. "Maybe we have to switch our focus. Remember, there's a third person involved in all of this."

I nod. "You're right. 4477. Whoever that bastard is."

"Exactly. Kurt claims Audrey wasn't with him last summer. Solomon says Audrey never worked for him. So what was she doing? What are the facts we have about Audrey last summer?"

I take a bite of my sandwich and ponder this. "She wasn't around much."

"Right, but she was *somewhere*. If she'd been at the swimming hole, we would've seen her. There's plenty of river though."

"I don't remember seeing her in a swimsuit. She was always wearing that rafting company *costume*." I think back to all the times she purposely fooled us with that stupid collared shirt, and it's enough to make the turkey sandwich swim in my stomach. I guess wherever she was, she didn't care what she looked like. Or maybe she brought a change of—"Wait a minute," I say, spine straightening. "When Audrey wasn't wearing the rafting uniform, she was dressed in riding gear."

Dylan pauses midbite, swallows. "Then, either it was just another illusion…"

"Or we should be looking for someone with a horse."

THE GIRL

The girl did like horses, very much in fact. She rode in the passenger's seat of the boy's shiny, expensive car. In her gut, the girl knew that riding in cars with strange older boys was a bad idea. Yet she got an almost sick thrill from being with him, headed somewhere that no one—not her closest friend nor even her parents—knew about.

The girl had visited the town stables many times. She'd never owned a horse, though it had been a dream of hers since she was small. But she'd spent hours with other people's horses, stroking their manes and whispering her secrets into their flapping ears. She'd ridden many of the horses there, the ones whose owners had learned to trust her.

The boy owned several horses. He told her she could ride any one she chose but that Henry was special. Henry, the boy said, a beautiful Appaloosa, would be a perfect match for the girl.

The girl spoke softly to Henry as she ran her fingers over the hair on his neck. It was important to gain the horse's trust.

Almost as important as the decision to put your trust in someone new.

As the boy walked off to fetch the riding equipment, the girl squinted against the rays that slanted over the stable roof to watch him. Her gaze trailed his confident gait and his sturdy figure, and she thought about earning trust and giving it away.

About the consequences the last time she offered up her trust.

She wondered if today, it might finally be possible to try again.

14

PAIGE

After our hike, we're tired and sweaty, but we want to check the stables before the manager heads home for the day. Guilt worms through me as I ignore the three texts from Lucy, plus the one from Mom about how Lucy's looking for us.

I was last at the town stables three years ago, when Audrey was attempting to convert me to the religion of riding. Despite my protests about allergies and a general disinterest in horses, she dragged me along and stuck me in the whole getup. She swore that once I was up on the horse with the wind blowing in my hair, I'd never want to get down. Then she helped me onto the enormous beast, and I waited for the transcendental experience to occur.

Ten minutes later, I left with a bad case of hay fever that included itchy hives all over my body.

We find Lenny the manager, a gray-haired man with bushy eyebrows that end in curlicues, in his office. He smiles as we walk in, standing to reveal faded jeans and a blue polo shirt pulled taut over a round belly. "Hi, folks. What can I do for you?"

"Hello, sir," Dylan says, approaching the desk. "I'm Dylan Covington, and this is Paige Redmond."

At Dylan's name, the man's smile falters. "Covington. You're Audrey's brother."

"That's right. We were hoping to ask you a few questions about her."

Lenny motions to the two chairs before us. "I can sure try. My mind isn't as sharp these days as it once was. And I did speak to the police last summer when they came around."

"Anything you can remember would be great," I say, taking a seat. This is the first time it's felt appropriate to use my notepad since talking to Solomon, and I waste no time pulling it out. "Did Audrey come by the stables last summer that you can recall?"

Lenny nods immediately. "She did. Quite often."

"I see," I say, jotting this down. So then, the riding clothes weren't a costume. "And can you remember whose horse she rode?"

At this, he taps a pen against the desk, head angled in thought. "Everyone knew Audrey, as I'm sure you can imagine. She'd developed relationships with half the owners and had a standing invitation to ride most of the horses in this place."

I see Dylan's lips part, a follow-up question ready on his tongue. But Lenny continues, "Last summer was different though. Last summer, she rode the black and white Appaloosa almost exclusively."

"Appa-*what*?" I ask.

"Appaloosa," Lenny says, frowning like I've committed some sort of blasphemy. "It's a breed of horse. Gorgeous spotted creatures. Solomon's is a particular beauty."

"Solomon McCleary?" I practically spit, to which Lenny darts me a look that says *How many Solomons could there be in this tiny town?*

"Was Solomon ever with Audrey when she came to ride?" Dylan asks, keeping calm where I've failed.

"Oh, sure. Solomon would ride the black Arabian mostly, and they'd go off to the trails together."

"Did you tell the authorities all of this?" I ask.

Lenny's lips twist. "I believe so," he says unconvincingly. "It was hard to think straight back then. They just kept hounding me about that *Kurt* fella. Seemed to think he would be around here with Audrey. But Kurt hadn't come round since two summers ago, when he tagged along after Audrey. He didn't own a horse. Didn't even ride."

"So then, the state police never looked into Solomon?"

"I'm sure I told them." Lenny rubs at both temples, as if that will help him remember whether he actually committed this massive blunder. "Yes, I definitely mentioned the Appaloosa."

"Right." Can't forget the freaking Appaloosa, though apparently, remembering that a missing girl had been spending time with an older, completely sketchy dude is something that possibly slipped your mind. "Just one more question, sir." I pull up a photograph of Madison Blake on my phone. "Was Audrey ever with this girl?"

Lenny squints at the photograph for a long beat, then shakes his head. "No, I didn't see her with Audrey."

My heart starts to sink until he adds, "But I saw her with Solomon."

Dylan falls forward, palms landing on the desk. "When was this?" he asks. "Last summer?"

"Maybe?" The man winces. "Or spring, possibly. It was before Audrey started riding the Appaloosa."

My brain starts racing, speeding so fast that I can barely keep up with it.

Solomon knew Madison Blake.

Solomon spent time with Audrey, here at the stables.

Solomon could be our missing link: our 4477.

———

"We should give the burner to the cops," I say the moment my door clunks shut.

"Whoa, hold on. This information doesn't clear Audrey of any wrongdoing. You realize that, don't you?"

"Solomon is the key, Dylan! He was spotted at the stables with two girls who later went missing. He could know where both of them are." I don't dare speak my other, niggling thought aloud. That he might've *done something* to both girls. "What if they can tie him to the burner phone? We don't know how to do that, and we certainly can't strut up to Solomon McCleary and demand that he admit his involvement in all of this."

Dylan lifts his hand from the steering wheel to run it over the back of his neck. "We have to think. I get it, we're in a hurry. But we also have to be logical, rational. If we give the phone to the cops, they'll take the Solomon lead seriously."

I nod. "They could finally show us proof that Madison is

fine and we can put our worries over that text message to rest, once and for all."

"Somehow, I don't think Madison's fine," Dylan says. "And if she's not fine, and my sister had something to do with it"—his chest rises and falls slowly—"then we've put Audrey exactly where she never wanted to be."

"Look, her behavior last summer was...*odd*. Trust me, I know. But we're talking about *Audrey*, your sister." My friend, who—before last summer—was always there for me, despite the distance between us. "You can't really believe she'd hurt Madison and then go on to—what? Threaten Delilah Blake and Britta into lying about it?"

Dylan's knuckles go white over the steering wheel. "Maybe."

"Maybe?"

"It wasn't just the money, you know. Audrey, she..."

I'm hanging on to his every word like it's the next monkey bar over a pit of boiling lava. "She *what*, Dylan?"

"I spoke to Hannah at school last year."

"Oh." Hannah. Audrey's best friend from Mayberry Prep. The one with an obvious crush on Dylan. Last year, I was finally feeling okay about her annual summer visit—almost excited even—because I had Dylan and couldn't be left out for once.

But for the first time in years, Hannah didn't come.

Part of me always wondered if the reason Audrey gave me such a hard time about Dylan was because deep down, she wanted her brother to end up with her *other* best friend, Hannah, who's prettier and wealthier.

Audrey never would've admitted this to my face, and to be honest, it could simply be my insecurities spinning stories. Still, I've always wondered. "What did"—I swallow the urge to call her *Little Miss Flirt*—"Hannah have to say?"

Dylan nibbles on his lower lip. "She said she was feeling really stressed and horrible, because she'd kept something from the cops."

"What did she keep?" I ask, now genuinely interested in what Little Miss Flirt had to say. "What did *you* keep?" This whole time, he's held on to this secret information?

"It's part of the reason I didn't want you giving the burner to the cops. Hannah told me that Audrey didn't really talk to her last summer, but they'd had one conversation. And in it, Audrey was muttering about some *bad stuff*. Something she'd done that was too horrible to speak about."

His words send a chill through me. How was something like this happening to my best friend, when I never knew?

"So then, we have no choice," I say. "If we don't give the phone to the cops, we'll have to investigate Solomon on our own."

"How exactly?"

"I'm thinking. We need hard evidence of his relationship with Audrey." I stop and cover my eyes. "Oh my—" I hadn't actually taken this thought all the way to its nauseating end. If Solomon is 4477, that means he and Audrey were *involved*. "Yuck, I just...sorry. Does this mean he went through Madison, then Audrey...and now Katie?"

"Well," Dylan says, dragging the word out, "Solomon dates a lot of girls. This isn't news."

"Katie had a *friend*, remember? One Madison Blake cheated. What if this person wasn't just a friend? What if he was a boyfriend?"

Dylan sinks back in the driver's seat. "Then that would give Solomon a pretty solid motive to hurt Madison."

"He'd never admit it to us." My fingers fidget, aching to work out some of this frustration with a pair of knitting needles. "But he might tell someone else."

15

After the dishes are done and the young'uns are watching their movie downstairs, Dylan and I nestle onto his bed with a burner phone of our own.

"Here, I'll do it," I say once Dylan has removed it from the packaging. "Where's Solomon's number?"

Dylan reads out the numbers from his contact list, and I punch them in.

> **Us:** Cops are saying Madison Blake is missing, presumed dead. Their suspect list? Everyone she ever conned. That puts you at the top of the list, Mr. McCleary

With a whoosh, the text goes through. It remains unanswered for a whole minute, and my palms become slick with sweat around the phone. Just when I decide to set it down beside me, it dings.

Solomon McCleary: Who is this?

Us: Someone willing to tell the cops that Madison took thousands of dollars from you before she went missing

SM: I had nothing to do with her disappearance

Us: I'm sure the cops can decide if that's true

SM: What do you want?

Us: Information

SM: I'm listening

I hesitate. I can't mention Audrey, or it'll blow our cover.

Us: Tell me where she is, and I'll keep what I know about you secret

There's a pause, and then the little dots start up.

SM: How the hell would I know where she is?

"Damnit," I say, and Dylan lets out a sigh over my shoulder. "I told you he wasn't going to fall for this." I ignore him, typing out the next message.

Us: That's too bad

SM: Why are you doing this?

Us: I'm a friend of Madison's, and I don't believe she just ran away

The dots fail to pick up again. Dylan's right. He isn't going to play. But the moment I glance away from the screen, the phone buzzes in my hand.

SM: Britta?

"Oh, crap." My heartbeat accelerates. "If Solomon is dangerous—if he did something to the girls…"

Beside me, Dylan stiffens. "He won't hesitate to take care of Britta."

"We don't have her number. We can't even warn her." Frantic, I do the only thing I can think of. I type out one last message.

Us: Nope, let's just call me the Watcher. I watch people, and right now I'm watching you

I hit send, my heart galloping like horse hooves in my chest. "I hate to say this, but we're not going to bed right now."

Dylan shakes his head. "The Watcher doesn't sleep."

We waste no time sneaking out of the house and heading to Solomon's bro-pad two miles up the road. It's a one-story cabin with a flat modern roof and an entirely glass facade, so that it looks like we're peering into a shoebox diorama.

Our plan had been to park outside his house all night and make sure he didn't go anywhere. Upon arrival, however, we find a party in full swing.

"Of course, Solomon is using all of his booze and video games to lure in more unsuspecting teens." I watch as a group of girls in cutoff shorts and crop tops passes our truck to head through the back gate. "What do we do?"

Dylan doesn't answer at first, his gaze whipping to something down the road. He straightens in his seat. "We go inside." He picks up his phone from the dashboard and sends off a text message.

"Why? I hate these things." Audrey dragged me along once when she worked for Solomon, and the whole thing made me uncomfortable. His parties are on a small enough scale that you can't stand in a corner with a safety blanket beer and pretend like you don't exist. "We weren't invited." I peer out the window into the darkness, but it's just a horde of loud, obnoxious guys.

Dylan continues to stare down at his phone until a text message buzzes in his lap. "Because it's an opportunity to find proof that ties Solomon to the girls. Maybe Katie will be there and we can get her to confirm that Solomon was the friend Madison conned." Grinning, he shows me the screen.

Dylan: Hey what's going on 2nite?
Tripp: Solomon's place. Get over here!

I can only gape at Dylan. "*Tonight* with the number two? Who are you?"

———

We wait long enough to validate the whole Tripp-inviting-us cover story and exit the car. I've packed a small sling bag with my phone, notebook, pen, and raspberry lip balm.

Unlike at the Summer Kickoff, there's no host waiting at the front door to greet us and offer a beverage. Here, we knock and no one answers—probably because Solomon's music is blasting like a sonic boom through the whole house.

Following the lead of the girl in the bathing suit top and jean skirt who heads straight through the swinging side gate, we see ourselves back.

In the pool, we spot Dylan's friends, including Tripp and Brent. They wave us over, but Dylan shouts, "Grabbing a drink first!"

Tripp lifts a beer can in response, and Brent performs a running cannonball into the pool.

We enter through the back sliding door that opens to a living room. Instead of throngs of drunken partygoers, we find little groups of people scattered about, sipping wine coolers. Solomon really brought out all the stops. Though this place is technically in the Covingtons' part of town, it's half the size of their house. There aren't many places to hide. Everyone's pretty much congregated in the living room and in the pool, and we quickly discover that Katie the waitress isn't here.

Instead, Solomon is seated on his enormous sectional, flirting with another girl—one who looks even younger than Audrey. On either side of them, guys are playing video games. Solomon's lazy gaze drifts over to us. After a moment of eye narrowing that passes so fast I almost miss it, he shouts across the room, "Hey, come on in! Grab a drink!"

"Thanks," Dylan calls back. He tugs me along to the kitchen as Solomon turns back to his girl of the minute.

"Why did Tripp want to come here?" I whisper. "He doesn't really seem like the gamer type."

Dylan shrugs. "Free booze?"

"He's a millionaire, Dylan." I point down a seemingly uninhabited hallway. "Self-guided tour?"

"Sure."

We tiptoe down the dark hall, finding a bathroom on the left. Beyond it on the right is a guest bedroom slash office. "Stand guard and hold this," I say, pushing my bag at him. "Don't let it out of your sight. My lip balm is in there."

I duck inside and shut the door behind me. Flicking on the light, I head straight for the desk. The computer is timed out, so I jog the mouse until a password verification box pops up. I dig my fingernails into the hair at my temples. I don't know anything about Solomon. There's no way I can hack into his computer.

Instead, I start digging through the top desk drawer. If Solomon is Audrey's mystery guy, he might've stashed the burner phone in one of these drawers. My gaze snags on a small card taped to the side of the drawer that says *password*. My pulse quickens, but I look closer. It's only the Wi-Fi password: raftingislife42.

I try it on the computer screen anyway, clenching a fist when it inevitably fails. After striking out on the second drawer, I turn my attention to the large and surprisingly organized filing cabinet tucked away beneath the desk. It's fit with dividers containing labels such as *utility bills, medical bills, car loans,* and *home loans.* Apart from a handful of printed receipts from the Clearwater Ridge Day Spa, the files are empty.

Of course, he's got the bulk of his finances filed away on that computer.

The one I can't access.

I start to push in the drawer when the folders jostle,

revealing a sliver of blue. I dig down to find another, shorter divider, its blue tab labeled *miscellaneous*.

Hope starts to climb, a soft scale of notes that mingles with the trill of nerves. If there were ever a spot to stow a sketchy secret phone, it would be here.

But all I find inside are a few bills and scraps.

I'm an idiot. If Solomon is 4477, he probably trashed the phone the instant Audrey went missing. That's the whole point of a burner phone, isn't it? To leave no trail.

I sift through the papers one last time for good measure, finding a manila envelope labeled *cleaning receipts*. I stick my hand inside, finding that it does indeed seem to be filled solely with receipts. No burner phone.

Giving a grunt, I withdraw my hand, causing something small and white to flutter to the floor. When I pick it up, I find that it's a card for a private investigator named D. L. Shuler.

A nervous buzz runs over my skin. Why would Solomon need to hire a private investigator? Turning back to the drawer, I take the envelope and dump its contents out on the desk. I sift through the slips of paper, the first of which is dated February of last year. Then I find receipts from March and April. The company is called Marley's Cleaning. Each time, Solomon paid them two hundred and fifty dollars cash.

Apparently, Solomon wasn't satisfied with the company, because the final receipt is dated last May. After that, there's nothing.

No, that's not true. A white sheet of paper is still tucked inside the envelope, flush with the side. It seems to be a printout from a discussion board called Scam Alert. I skim the messages.

Ferdthenerd231: Hired someone from Caroline's Cleaners. Found out too late that the company doesn't exist 😕. The girl came and cleaned once, did a pretty good job. The second time I let her clean while I was out. When I returned, I paid her, and we scheduled another cleaning. I only realized she'd stolen my watch, my electric guitar, and my wife's jewelry a day later. Cleaner had receipts and business cards that looked so official. Wish I would've googled or checked yelp

> **RiverRat81:** Same thing happened to me except the company was called Marley's Cleaning. What did the cleaner look like? Maybe we can find this bitch
>
> **Ferdthenerd231:** DM me

The conversation ends there. I go back to the miscellaneous drawer, hoping to find a slip of paper containing Solomon's computer password so I can get into his private Scam Alert messages. When I start to check around the desk, the creak of the door launches my heart like a rocket. "Time to go," Dylan whispers.

Pulse thumping, I shut the drawer. I stuff the manila envelope beneath my T-shirt, thankful I didn't wear that crop top I first laid out. Still, the shirt doesn't fully conceal the wrinkled mass as I race to the door, slipping out to join Dylan, who's casually leaning an elbow against the wall.

Down the hall, a dark shape moves toward us. The hallway light flicks on, and I glance down at the obvious bulge beneath my T-shirt to what I can now see is Solomon's hulking figure.

Out of options, I spin to face Dylan. The envelope smashes between us as I loop my arms around his neck. He flinches against me. I'm desperate to whisper some sort of apology or message, but Solomon is too close.

So, I push up on my tiptoes and press my lips to Dylan's.

A tangle of panic, guilt, and exhilaration spins through me as the footsteps draw nearer and Dylan's body eases. His lips soften, the hands that were stiff at his sides moving to the small of my back.

"Get a room," Solomon's voice booms behind us, causing me to jerk away slightly. I turn my head to acknowledge him, unwilling to expose my stolen intel.

Solomon laughs. "Kidding, kidding. Carry on, children." He salutes us, then continues to strut past, entering what's likely his bedroom at the end of the hall.

Once he's shut inside, I wrench my head back. Dylan's hands slip from my waist, a curious, dazed grin lingering on his lips. "What was that about?"

I glance down from his blue eyes to my stomach guiltily. "Sorry, I-I…"

"Don't be sorry," he says, his fingertips grazing my cheek. "I'm not."

My stomach drops. "No, you don't—" Shame heats me through. "I took something, and I had to hide it."

Dylan's eyes widen as I flash a sliver of envelope beneath the hem of my shirt. Then his expression flattens. "Ah." He pulls his hand back, as if scorched by my cheek. "Nice cover."

He lets my purse fall from his shoulder, and when I take it, slides past me. "Dylan, I just couldn't let him see."

"It's fine," he says, his voice rough. "You were quick on your toes. Literally." He keeps walking without letting me catch up.

"Would you at least look at what I found?"

"I need a minute, Paige." Before the hallway's end, he spins to face me, pain glinting in his blue eyes. "Can you give me that?"

It hurts more than a slap. "Of course."

He trudges off in the direction of the living room, and I stay where I am, that crack in my heart splintering off in a thousand different directions.

16

I roll the envelope, fold it in half, and stuff it inside my purse. It refuses to zip shut, but at least I no longer look like I ate a large folder for dinner. I slump against the wall, sliding until I'm down on the ground with my hands wrapped around my knees.

Dylan asked for a minute. While he takes it, I should take a quick course on how to be less of an insensitive jerk. Why did I kiss him? Why do I always say the wrong thing?

And why the hell am I such a lousy detective?

The only thing I know for certain is that I can't stay here. I can't ride home with Dylan. I have to go out there and find someone else to drive me. Then I can send Dylan a text, and neither of us has to look the other in the eye until tomorrow. By then, hopefully, the morning light will have blurred the stark lines and painful edges of this night.

Resigned, I pull my pathetic corpse off the ground. "Hey!" a thunderous voice calls, causing me to thunk back down.

I land on my behind and proceed to slam my head against

the wall. "Ow," I moan, reaching up to delicately press a finger to the spot.

"Ooh, are you okay?" Solomon pads nearer, kneeling to inspect my head.

"Yeah, fine." My eyes dart to that sliver of manila envelope peeking out of my purse.

"You should probably lay off the booze," Solomon says, helping me to my feet.

"I'm not drunk," I say, covering the bag with my arm. "Just clumsy and stupid."

"Sure." He gives me a knowing grin.

I try to play it off by returning the grin, but end up wincing. "Man, this is going to be a headache tomorrow."

Solomon slides a hand behind my back, and I shudder at his touch. But he's surprisingly gentle as he guides me down the hallway, away from the room full of chattering people. Away from Dylan.

"Where are we going?" I ask, trying to keep my voice light as my brain and body rebel.

"You can wait in my room while I get you some ice. It's right here."

"Oh, I can wait in the living room." Surrounded by witnesses.

"Nah," he says, continuing to steer me like a shopping cart. "You need quiet. Those bastards will only make your head hurt worse."

I want to scream for Dylan, but a mixture of pride and curiosity keeps my mouth bolted shut. This man was seen with Madison and Audrey before they went missing. He may be responsible for whatever happened to them.

He opens his bedroom door and we enter a dark minimalist space. A black comforter covers a king-sized bed, and on the IKEA-like nightstand sit two dented beer cans, an empty vodka shooter, and a selection of pill bottles. He shuts the door behind us, and that urge to scream grows tenfold. For all I know, the girls' disappearances began with Solomon leading them to the back bedroom under the guise of helping.

I consider sending a text, but think better of it. Solomon wouldn't *do* something to me now—he couldn't. Not when he knows that Dylan is out there.

He sets me down on his bed, and my skin crawls. "I think I'm fine, actually," I say as he walks over to the nightstand and opens up one of the pill bottles.

But he takes two white ovular pills and presses them into my palm. "You'll feel even better after a couple of these."

"Oh, I don't need—"

"It's just stronger Motrin," he says with a laugh. "I got them after I dislocated my shoulder on the river."

"Really?" I ask, glancing down at the pills that dot my palm. I remember that injury. Audrey told me about it two years ago. So why would the pills be beside his bed now? "Thanks." I have no intention of taking them, regardless of what they really are. *RUGBY 4606* is inscribed on each one, which could stand for anything, quite honestly.

A vision flashes in my mind: Audrey taking these two pills and drifting off to sleep in this creep's bedroom. On this very fabric beneath me.

Solomon starts to lower onto the bed, but his phone dings in his back pocket. He tugs it free to read the message, then tosses the phone onto the bed before taking a seat dangerously close to me.

"Maybe you could get me some water while you get the ice?" Then I can get the hell out of here.

"Ice!" he says, slapping his forehead. "Almost forgot. Maybe I should lay off the booze too." He leans over me, waggling his ginger brows, and I shrink back. "Hey, where's Dylan? Weren't you two just all over each other out there?"

"Yes, we were," I say, grateful he's not too far gone to remember. "He went to grab a drink, so he's probably looking for me. I should go find him."

"Nonsense," Solomon says in an English accent. "I shall locate him, procure the ice and water, and return anon." He stands and staggers toward the door. Before exiting, he turns to me with narrowed eyes. The accent suddenly gone, he adds, "Don't you move."

He shuts the door, and I stand too fast. The room begins to spin. Maybe I have a concussion. Dizzy, I pull out my phone. But before I can send Dylan a *Let's go now* text, I spot a black object peeking out from between the wrinkles in Solomon's comforter.

His phone.

I reach for it, my heart thwacking against my ribs. The unlocked screen still hasn't timed out. I dart a look at the door, then turn my attention to the phone. I'll never get another opportunity like this.

I navigate to Solomon's text messages and type "Audrey" into the search bar. A text chain pops up. In it, he and Audrey make casual conversation, including several plans to meet at the stables. But on July 6 of last summer, the focus of the conversation takes a turn.

> **Solomon McCleary:** I've hired a PI to locate the girl. We could use whatever info you have.
> **Audrey Covington:** Not interested
> **SM:** That bitch stole 7K from you, Audrey
> **AC:** Can't talk here
> **SM:** Why not?
> **AC:** Let's talk at the stables, ok? Tomorrow around 3?
> **SM:** Fine.

The texts end there.

My hands are sweaty over Solomon's phone. The messages start to swirl in front of me. *This* is the connection between the girls. Audrey was one of Madison's cons. She lost seven grand to her.

Solomon wanted Audrey's help finding Madison. Audrey didn't want to talk to him on her personal phone.

So they switched to the burners.

The thought sends a wave of nausea through me. *What are we going to do about Madison?*

Kidnapping victim, runaway, murder victim. These were the words I'd toyed with labeling my best friend over the past year. Now, a new word creeps in—one with sharp talons that dig into the soft, permeable parts of my brain: *killer.*

What if Solomon persuaded Audrey to help him, and things took a turn for the worst?

Now it isn't simply the text messages lifting up off the

screen and swirling around—it's the phone itself. It performs a sweeping dance, and when I glance up, everything in the room is spinning.

I'm too dizzy to get up, but I have to try. I can't just take the phone; Solomon would figure out what happened eventually. Plus, I don't have his screen passcode. The second I stop messing with it, the phone will time out. I should send the messages to myself.

No. He'd find out. I have to take a photo of the messages with my phone.

I reach into my purse, but the giant envelope is in the way. A pulsing pain in my head amplifies by the second, so bad that if I had time, I'd consider downing those sketchy pills with Solomon's half-empty beer.

When I finally wangle my phone free, I go back to Solomon's, scrolling up so that the first batch of texts fills the screen. I snap a photo. Next, I get the final batch of texts, holding my phone up and trying to focus it as my own vision zigzags and blurs.

The second photo clicks, and behind me, something mirrors the sound.

The door. "What the hell are you—"

Solomon's hulking body is on me before I can blink.

17

Solomon wrenches his phone from my hand, the force knocking my unsteady frame to the floor. I land on the same bruise from earlier, letting out a groan.

Solomon turns from his phone to glare down at me. I'm an ant at this giant's mercy. Too bad he looks anything but merciful. "What the hell were you doing with my phone, Paige?" he shouts.

"I was, um…" I scramble away from him, pain tearing from my tailbone up through my skull. "I'm sorry, I was just checking the time." I turn to my own phone, frantically closing out the photos and opening a new app.

He steps closer, lifting his foot as if to kick my phone from my hand. Before I can part my lips to scream, the door swings open.

Dylan pushes into the room, taking in the scene before him with wide eyes. "Get the hell away from her," he growls.

Solomon lifts his hands. "Hey, it's not what it looks like, man."

"Then step away from Paige," Dylan bites out. "Quickly."

"Fine," he says, taking one lumbering step backward. "But she has some explaining to do."

"I don't think she does." Dylan shoves past Solomon to scoop me up. "Are you okay?" His concerned eyes peer down at me as he slings an arm around my waist.

I make to nod, but it sends another pang through my head. I clutch my temple, my body swerving. Dylan steadies me, then helps me toward the door.

"No way!" Solomon skirts in front of us to block the path out. "She's not going anywhere until I see her phone."

At my side, Dylan stiffens. "She's hurt. We're leaving."

"She *stole* something from me." Solomon crosses his arms, and that's when I notice that he isn't looking at his phone or at mine.

His eyes are on the manila folder, an entire corner of which pokes out of my sling bag. Panic slices through the pain and the dizziness. "I know you were in my office." Solomon says, focus still lasered on the folder. "I thought I saw you come out of there, but I was drunk. I told myself I only imagined it." He cocks his head. "Then I checked."

Once again, I'm a fool. There was never going to be any ice or water; Solomon was next door in the office this entire time. "Where's Audrey?" I ask, wanting desperately to flee but unwilling to do so without answers.

Solomon blinks. "Audrey? How the hell would I know?"

"You lied to us back at the rafting office. You did see Audrey last summer. You saw her a whole lot. You rode horses together. That's something I didn't need your text messages to verify. And"—I tug the folder free from my purse, wishing I'd taken photos of everything in here too—"you had something in common."

Dylan squints from me to Solomon. "What do you mean, Paige?"

"He wasn't the only person conned by Madison Blake last summer. Audrey was too. Right, Solomon?"

The man presses his fingertips to his forehead and laughs. "You're that anonymous texter, aren't you? The one trying to blackmail me into admitting something about Madison without any proof."

"I have it now though, don't I? Audrey got conned too, *didn't she?*"

"No, you're wrong."

Blood boiling, I start to push out a retort, but he continues. "Technically, Audrey got conned *two* summers ago." He flashes a smug grin.

"So then, you planned to get your money back whatever way you had to. And you wanted Audrey to help. That's why your texts cut off and you switched her over to the burner phone."

Solomon's grin falters. "No—what? Burner phone?"

"What did the two of you do to Madison Blake?" I ask, my voice an angry plea.

"Do—" His head jerks back. "We didn't *do* anything to Madison! Look, when I met Madison, she was going by another name. Marley. I actually thought she was a cool girl, so I let her take my horses out, took her for drinks a couple times. She said she was down on her luck, but didn't seem interested in working at the rafting company. She claimed to be starting her own cleaning company, so I threw her a bone and hired her to clean this place." His eyes darken as he gestures to my stolen folder. "As you're aware, that didn't turn out so well. She stole a ton of expensive shit, only I didn't realize anything was missing until weeks after her last job, when she'd already disappeared. That's when I realized *Marley* wasn't really Marley."

"That's when you hired a PI," I say. "D. L. Shuler."

Solomon nods. "Shuler identified the girl as Rose Lambert and I reported her, but no one—neither the cops nor my PI—managed to track her down. Last summer I found out why; she wasn't *Rose Lambert* at all. She was Madison Blake. Anyway, Audrey said she didn't need my help. She already had someone else on the job."

"Someone else?" Dylan asks, helping me to the bed. "Did she say who?"

"No. Anyone would've been better than my lousy PI—who I fired, by the way. But when I asked to get in on whatever Audrey had going, she asked me to back off. She also asked me not to text her anymore, and she stopped coming to the stables."

"No, but..." That doesn't make sense. "You met Audrey on July sixth. Audrey was wearing riding gear long after that."

"Well," Solomon says in a bored tone, "she wasn't riding *my* horse. And I never saw her riding anyone else's."

"So, what was the con?" Dylan asks, wrapping an arm over my shoulders. "How did Madison take Audrey's money?"

Solomon shrugs. "Madison put up an ad on every corkboard in town for a Dutch Warmblood for seven grand. They can cost upward of nine thousand, and Audrey, thinking she'd scored a deal, took the bait. She'd earned two grand the previous summer with me, and I guess she...*borrowed* the rest from the Covingtons." His chest balloons as he pulls in a slow breath. "Only there was no Dutch Warmblood. Madison made Audrey pay in advance, and the poor girl was so desperate, she bought it sight unseen. Madison never showed up to their meeting."

"Why didn't Audrey report her?" I ask.

"Why do you think?" Solomon says. "She stole most of that money from her parents. She couldn't exactly admit to letting someone else steal it from *her*. Last summer, she seemed really down. I didn't know what she was down about, but I let her ride my Appaloosa. I thought it might cheer her up."

"Aren't you the Good Samaritan?" Dylan mutters.

Solomon side-eyes him. "We hung out, rode together. I didn't even know about the horse con until I confided in Audrey about my cleaning lady fiasco. That was when she told me what had happened the previous summer."

Tailbone aching, I adjust my weight on the bed. "Why do you think Audrey didn't want to work on tracking Madison down with you?"

Solomon licks his lips. "It's hard to explain. But last summer, Audrey had this look in her eyes. Like she wouldn't be content with simply getting her money back." For a moment, he's silent. Just when I think he's done talking, he adds, "Like my way wouldn't fix anything. Not really. Because the only thing that would fix it for Audrey was...*revenge*."

I try to swallow, saliva sticking to my bone-dry throat. "That's not Audrey," I scratch out, even though the last subject on earth I can claim to know is Audrey Covington. "Why would she wait a whole year to set some big revenge plot into motion?"

"Because," Solomon says, like I'm missing something, "she needed a whole year to plan it."

A chill wends through me. Was Audrey really hell-bent on getting revenge for that stolen money? Did she succeed and then flee?

"You can take the cleaning receipts," Solomon says flippantly. "Madison Blake isn't missing. She's living her best life out there with all the money she stole from Audrey and me and a bunch of other poor fools." His expression darkens. "But I need to see your phone before I can let you leave."

"Why's that?" I ask, clutching it to my chest.

"Because Audrey is actually missing. And I know you'd love to try and misconstrue those text messages against me."

Or maybe you're scared, I think. Because I'm not misconstruing anything.

I look to Dylan, hoping he'll fight to keep the messages—ones he hasn't yet had a chance to read. But he simply nods at me.

Solomon jounces an open palm impatiently. "Unlock it."

Begrudgingly, I do, opening up the photo app and handing the phone over.

"Delete and delete," Solomon says, sneering as he passes it back. Finally, he shifts out of the way. Dylan keeps me steady as we make our way out into the hall, through the oscillating rooms, and into the black night.

"What was on the photos?" Dylan asks, helping me into the cab of his truck.

"I'll show you on the way."

Dylan frowns. "Show me? I thought he just deleted them."

"He deleted the ones saved to my phone," I say, trying to buckle my seat belt with a shaky hand. "But I backed them up."

"How?" He starts the car and pulls a U-turn.

"While you two were facing off, I managed to connect to his Wi-Fi—thanks, raftingislife42—and open up Google Photos."

Once we're a safe distance from Solomon's place, my vision clears enough for me to read off the texts to Dylan.

"These prove that he and Audrey cut off regular cell communication around the same time she started using that burner phone," I say. "They prove he had a motive to go after Madison. And…" My foggy brain struggles to latch on to the rest. "They make it seem like Audrey wasn't too keen on helping him find Madison. Maybe he confided in her—maybe *he's* the one who got revenge—and when Audrey threatened to report him, he…" The words die in my throat. I can't say them. Not ever, but especially not now, in front of Audrey's brother. "I mean, she had to run for her life, obviously."

"Listen, Paige, I know that guy is shady as hell. But if Solomon really *did* something to Audrey, wouldn't he have deleted those texts last summer?"

"He's definitely deleting them now! You saw that back there. He made me wipe the evidence. I'm sure last summer, he assumed he was above the law. He tried to drug me, you know."

Dylan glances over in horror. "With what?"

"That's what I'm going to find out." I free the pills from the pocket of my shorts and type "RUGBY 4606" into my search engine. The results start to pop up. After scrolling through, all I can do is slump back against the seat.

"It really is just Motrin." I stare down at the pills. "But eight hundred milligrams for a headache?"

"He wasn't trying to drug you, Paige."

"He knocked me down," I mutter.

"I'm not saying I wouldn't like to lock him up," Dylan says, reaching over to touch my arm with his free hand. "He's not a good person, probably even dangerous. I'm just not sure he's responsible for what happened to Madison or Audrey."

"So then, what do we do now?"

Dylan smiles softly. "We might need to take you to a hospital. How are you feeling?"

"Nausea's gone, now that we're out of the creep's lair. Headache's better too."

"You tell me if it gets worse, okay?" We reach the Covingtons' driveway and he turns off the engine.

"I repeat, what are we going to *do*?"

"We're going to keep our voices down so we don't wake up the whole house. Then we're going to put you to bed."

I want to argue, to press him on this. Yet I can only nod, the act of which brings on another bout of soreness in my skull.

We reach my door, and he follows me inside. "What are you doing?" I whisper, flicking on the light.

"Making sure you're okay."

"My bed is right there." My face warms, and I flick my eyes in the direction of the bed to avoid his gaze.

"I keep thinking I should've forced you to go to the hospital. I want to stay and make sure you're like...breathing and everything."

He's overreacting. Still, the sentiment sends a swell of

warmth through my stomach. "I think you're supposed to check the pupils, but I assure you, it isn't necessary. I just need sleep."

"Paige." He reaches for my hand, running his thumb over my palm. "For once in your life, let me have the final say. Please." The last word comes out low and frayed.

"Fine." I turn off the light and remain by the door. "But this room doesn't have bunk beds."

I wait in the darkness, feeling only his fingers trail over mine, his breath on my face. The urge to kiss him again but mean it thrums in me like an arhythmic song.

"I'll be fine on the floor," he says. My heart sinks as he inches away, but he interlocks his fingers with mine and leads me to the bed. Once he's tucked me in and I've assured him I don't need ice or an IV drip, he leaves to get me a glass of water.

A few minutes later, he returns, a pillow and a spare blanket tucked beneath an arm. He tosses them onto the floor and clicks on the desk lamp. Soft light spills over the room. "You sure you're okay?" he asks, handing over the water glass.

"Mhmm." I gulp it down. "Just extremely uncoordinated."

He laughs, likely remembering how I nearly knocked him down the stairs with my beach bag last summer. "You had me pretty freaked out tonight, you know. When I couldn't find you. And when I finally did, you looked so…" His voice wavers, and a torrent of guilt crashes over me.

"I'm sorry," I say. "I was trying to do one good thing in a slew of bad things."

"I'm just glad you're okay." His lips curve upward in the dim light. "But promise me you won't go off and play investigator on your own anymore."

"I promise."

"I'm going to need the official handshake."

I roll my eyes. He's referring to the one that the three of us—me, Dylan, and Audrey—had as kids. Withdrawing my hand from beneath the covers, I make a fist, and he knocks it twice before high-fiving me. We shake, make sparkler fingers, and then shake again.

Only when it's time to end the rite by dragging our fingers free, he keeps mine interlocked with his.

"Dylan?" I ask, feeling somehow nervous yet completely at ease with my hand in his.

"Yeah?" He takes the water glass from me.

"You don't really think Audrey would go on some sort of vengeance mission, do you?"

He sighs. "I don't know, Paige. Two summers ago, my sister spent hours and hours working to buy that damned horse. She ended up short, so she begged my parents to chip in the rest. They declined. Now, we know that she wanted that Dutch Warmblood so bad she stole the money from them." The blanket shifts as his free hand grips the edge, wringing it in his fingers. "Then Madison Blake swoops in and steals all of it away. Do you really think anyone would just...let it go?"

I want to say *yes*, that someone would let it go. That Audrey would let it go. But I can't, because after everything we've learned about Audrey and the way she treated us last summer, I don't really believe it. Tears start to pool in the corners of my eyes, and I sniffle.

"Hey," Dylan says, wiping at the trickling tear with a

calloused fingertip. "We're going to find her, okay? We will. After you get some rest."

"Okay," I mumble. He stirs beside me and I snuggle into my pillow.

"Good night, Paige," he says.

That's when his lips graze my cheek.

Before he pulls away, I shift onto my back. Reaching up, I slide my hand behind his neck and gently tug his face toward mine.

"Is this another cover story?" he breathes, his lips hovering a mere inch from mine.

"No," I say, fully aware that I've thrown myself at him. Knowing I've allowed this boy to hold my fate in his precarious grasp, the same way I did the first time. Knowing I don't care. "It's not a cover. I want this."

"Good, then." He kisses me.

A single kiss—soft and deliberate with his fingers in my hair—and yet, it's warmth and healing. It's comfort tangled with a sharp thrill, like dangling from a precipice.

It's everything.

THE GIRL

It was always in secret.

The boy took her places where they would be concealed from prying eyes and whispering gossip, and this was fine with the girl.

She loved a good secret, and she knew how to keep one.

His stables were private, and his property ran for acres and acres. The couple would take to the trail, side by side, her on the Appaloosa and him on the stallion. The girl loved the feel of the wind on her face, the way the boy kept turning to check on her.

When they weren't riding, they were often cooling off in a section of river that ran through the property. Secluded by trees, its banks private land, the place was very good at keeping their secrets.

He was fun, this boy. He splashed and laughed in the sparkling river. He leapt from rock to rock and beckoned the girl to join him. She loved to watch him, his strong, sculpted body. When he smiled, it filled her with a longing that almost hurt.

But the girl's most favorite secret spot of all was the wooded area behind the boy's home. After all, it was in the woods that they'd first met. It had since become the place they could spend hours wasting away the day, lost in conversation. The boy had a checkered picnic blanket and a woven basket, which he filled with champagne and crackers like in the movies. He poured bubbling liquid into fancy flutes, and the couple drank until the pain softened and the responsibilities the girl was neglecting faded like the skywriting just visible through the treetops.

The boy's voice was low and soothing, his words intelligent, carefully chosen and strung together like beads on a string. He told the girl about his father—a powerful man he was meant to become one day. He told her about his friends back at school, the teams he was on and the championships he'd won. She'd told the boy everything—about her parents, about school, and even her friendship drama.

The only thing she'd neglected to mention was the Bad Stuff. She wasn't exactly sure why. She had learned to trust the boy and even thought he might love her.

And yet…she wasn't certain she wanted him to know about *this*. She wasn't entirely sure how to say it. And it would change the way he looked at her; it had to.

But as they sat together, her legs crossed over his like a pretzel and his hand on her thigh, the girl thought he might be able to see past the Bad Stuff.

She hoped that he would help with her plan.

18
PAIGE

I wake in the morning with a dull ache at the back of my head. It all comes back in a whoosh. Hurting Dylan, him leaving me in the hallway. My head smacking against the wall. Solomon taking me to his room and that menacing look on his face as he towered over me.

But another memory floats up to the forefront of my mind, this one bathed in a halolike glow: Dylan's lips on mine before I drifted off.

I flip over to find him sleeping on the floor, and relief ripples through me. It wasn't just a dream. I don't know what last night means. Maybe he pitied me after my head injury, or maybe we want the same thing. Either way, we're in a better place. The realization gives me a nice, near-buzzed feeling that dulls even my headache.

Sunlight shines through the slits in the shutters. I have no idea what time it is, but I have to wake him. My family can't find out he slept in my room, even if it was on the floor.

My phone is beside my pillow, its battery dead. I wiggle out from beneath the covers and sit on the edge of the bed. When I grab Dylan's phone from the floor, a preview notification on the lit screen kills my pleasant buzz on the spot.

I can't access the message, but the preview says the sender is Hannah.

Why is *she* texting him? Then I remember, my chest pinching, that while Dylan and I were in our period of silence, he was talking to her. For all I know, she could be the reason for our period of silence. Maybe he'll wake up, see that text, and regret last night's kiss.

I'm so shaken, I nearly return the phone without checking the time. But I peek to find it's 9:00 a.m. Setting the phone carefully down the way I found it, I tap Dylan on the shoulder. "Hey," I whisper.

He lets out a groan, smiling with his eyes shut. "Just twenty more minutes."

"Not today, buddy. You and your pillow have to go before someone sees."

He opens his eyes and rolls his neck. "You're the meanest." Sitting up, he blinks at me. "And you're alive."

"Very observant."

"How's your head?" he asks.

"Better. Now scram." I swipe his pillow before he can flop back down again, shoving it into his stomach.

"You know," he says, fighting a yawn, "we used to have slumber parties all the time."

"When we were eight and not yet kissing each other." As soon as the words are out, I want to crawl back under my covers and hide.

A devious grin lights his face as he gets to his feet. The pillow falls to the floor, and he inches closer.

"What are you doing?" Legs dangling over the bed's edge, I use the pillow as a shield.

In one quick motion, he swipes the pillow from me, tossing it back onto the floor. With both hands free, he places them on my shoulders. Pressing closer still, his legs nudge mine until they're situated between my knees. My heart rate kicks up as his face lowers and his fingertips shift to the back of my neck. "To think that we were content with ghost stories and flashlights."

"Again, we were eight," I say, "so..."

He starts to close the space between our lips but stops. "I should go, like you said." Before I can grab him by the T-shirt, he straightens, backing away.

"But I—you—"

With a smirk, he bends down to grab his things. Then, he strides toward the door and, after peeking out to ensure the coast is clear, slips out into the hall.

Monster. An absolutely adorable monster that I can't wait to kiss again.

Still, as my eyes linger on the closed door, the thought of Hannah and that mystery text slither their way back into my head.

In the kitchen, I find Lucy sitting alone. "Are you eating with me?" she asks, beaming.

I get a pang at her open earnestness. "Yeah," I say, grabbing the loaf of bread. "I was thinking maybe I'd come to the river today. If that's what you guys are up to."

She nods emphatically. "Duh! What else is there to do? We made up this new game too. You throw one of those cheap bouncy balls down the river and then race to see who can grab it first. We've…lost a few."

"You don't say." I pour my coffee, my mind still on the events of last night, and a little on Dylan.

Speak of the devil, Dylan walks in, showered and ready for the day, in clean shorts and a T-shirt. He meets my gaze, a sheepish grin on his face, and it feels like last summer all over again. That uncertainty—not knowing how to act with him around our families or how he'll act with me—is exactly what I felt after we kissed the first time.

"Toast?" I ask him, holding up a slice of bread.

"Yeah, thanks." He gets coffee as I start the toaster, and we settle in next to each other at the bar. Unlike last summer, there's no show of affection to settle my worries, nothing to clarify our status. I don't know if we're still playing the game from my room or if he doesn't want to stir things up with our families just yet.

Then again, it could be something else entirely. He could be having second thoughts about us after reading that text from Hannah. "I was telling Lucy that a river day sounds nice," I say.

Dylan sips from his steaming mug. "Count me in."

Lucy grins. "Really? You'll come too?"

"Of course. I've missed the river."

The toaster dings behind us. I slide down from the barstool, but Dylan puts a hand on my arm. "Allow me."

Lucy slings me a look, then clears her throat. "You two,

uh, never really did say what you've been up to all this time. *Together.*"

Dylan glances over from the counter, looking unbothered. "Butter, Paige?"

"Yes, please." I turn back to Lucy like I have no idea what she's implying.

"Hikes, lunches, drives at late hours of the night. What's going on?"

"We're, um…" *Lucy, if you weren't my sister who I love so much I'd die for you, I would murder you on the spot.*

"It's adult stuff, Luce," Dylan says, placing a plate in front of me with utter nonchalance. "You wouldn't understand."

"Oh, wouldn't I?" she says. "Maybe it's kind of like when *your brother* kissed me."

"Lucy!" I nearly scream.

She slaps a hand over her mouth.

"I thought you were best friends," I say, stunned.

"We are," she says softly, all the fire from a moment ago drained. Only a timid girl looks up at me with wide eyes. "But now we're friends who…maybe kiss."

I shake my head like the seventy-year-old judgmental porch sitter that lives inside me, ready to chastise her or give her a good time-out.

But Dylan picks up his coffee and says, "To answer your question, Luce, *yes*. Our thing is a lot like that."

My entire body ignites, feelings of wanting to deck him and kiss him flaming up in equal measure.

After getting ready, we head out the back doors to the river, Lucy and Nate leading the way.

"I guess it's a good thing we're chaperoning this river trip," Dylan says, nudging my side with an elbow.

"How can you joke about something like this? They're only babies." The sun is high, baking the sage-green trees until they reach a glimmering neon. We shove aside the branches, our flip-flops squelching over the forest floor.

"Like you didn't know this would happen eventually."

I let out something between a growl and a sigh. "I knew, but...I thought we had time."

At the rocks surrounding the bank, Dylan says, "I didn't mean to tell Lucy. I realize we didn't actually talk about any of this, and you might be having second thoughts."

"Me?" I kick off my sandals, finding shade beneath a large willow. "I'm not the one texting someone else."

Dylan scratches at his eye. "Excuse me?"

"I saw that Hannah texted you this morning. I didn't realize your conversation was an ongoing thing."

"Ah," he says, lips forming a tight line. "So it isn't just potential suspects you're swiping phones from anymore, huh? You went through mine too?"

"No." Out of breath from the hike down, I take a seat on the nearest boulder. "I checked the time when I woke up. My phone was dead. I didn't read what she said, only saw that she'd texted."

"And this worried you," he says flatly.

"No," I argue like a stubborn toddler. "I don't know. She likes you, everyone knows that."

"So what?"

"So," I say, dragging the word along, "you broke up with me and started talking to her."

"I didn't—are you serious?" He faces me, devastatingly handsome in this indignant state. "I didn't start *talking* to her. I asked her about the case. I told you that already."

"And now? I suppose she's still texting you about the case. Like a pretty little long-distance informant?"

Dylan's shoulders relax. "She could be. I still think she knows more about Audrey than she let on the last time we spoke. But today she was helping with something else."

I don't prod; I already deserve an award for my role of jealous, annoying nutcase. In fact, even ninety-two-year-old Mrs. Frangelino, whose favorite pastime is cooking up conspiracy theories about Sunshine Park's kitchen staff, would tell me to go jump in the lake if she could see me now.

"Mom wanted some photos of Audrey for the vigil she's putting together at the end of the month," Dylan finally says.

"Vigil?" No one told me anything about a vigil.

"She's inviting everyone in town. It was Detective Ferrera's idea. She said it would generate awareness, remind everyone that Audrey is still missing. It seems like after a year, the whole town has forgotten. Plus, Ferrera's going to attend and keep an eye on everyone who shows up. Just in case the…*perp* makes an appearance."

"So Hannah was just sending photos?"

"Yep." He holds out his phone. "Go ahead, check for yourself."

"I don't need to—"

"Paige, just read it." The message app is already open to Hannah's text: Emailed you the photos! Wish I could be there for the vigil! 🖤🖤🖤

"Who even texts at eight thirty-two a.m. during the summer?" I mutter.

"You know," Dylan says as I hand the phone back, "I never got your jealousy there."

"I wasn't jealous." The lie makes me sweat so much that my T-shirt sticks to my back.

"I never saw Hannah that way." His gaze is on the purple wildflowers painting the bank. "It was always you."

My neck blazes, and my head drops into my hands. "I'm sorry. I need to go jump in a lake."

"What?"

"It's an expression. But also, I really do need to cool off. I'm so stupid."

"You're not *that* stupid," he says, punching me softly in the shoulder. "Just a little stupid. Because this isn't a lake town. So you'll have to settle for the river."

"That should do the trick." I bat away a fly, my mind slipping back to the case. "Do you really think Hannah could be an asset?"

"Spy talk again?" He tugs off his shirt, tossing it beside me on the boulder.

My stomach warms, and I avert my gaze from his shirtless figure to the sandy bank. "What makes you think she's hiding something?"

"I don't know. Those two told each other everything. I mean, *everything*." His words carve into me like a knife. Audrey told Hannah everything.

And she told me nothing.

"From what I gathered," he says, "when Hannah first

spoke to the cops, she didn't think Audrey was hurt, only in trouble. So, she stayed quiet out of loyalty. But maybe…" He runs his fingers through his hair, leaving it in disarray. "Maybe she'd talk to *us* now, if we could ensure secrecy."

"So we get her to go over her story, and maybe some detail will come out."

"Exactly."

Speaking to Hannah is the last thing I want to do. Audrey confided in her last summer from afar; meanwhile, I shared a room with her, and she not only shut me out completely but sent me packing.

Still, I know it has to be done. "I could really use a beer for some reason. Just to hold."

Dylan laughs. "Too bad Audrey isn't here to stock the cooler with illegal beverages."

Before I let the sadness of this statement seep any deeper, the others call us from downstream, their voices ricocheting off the rocks.

"Coming!" Dylan shouts back.

"We should make the call now though," I say. Otherwise, I have to spend the whole day dreading it.

"We promised Lucy a river day."

"And we're keeping that promise." I gesture around us. "We're standing on the riverbank."

Dylan bites his lower lip, his gaze trailing off down the river. With a grimace, he pulls out his phone. "Come closer. I'll put it on speaker."

"No, no, no. I'm here as backup. The little Jiminy Cricket feeding you the lines."

"You're doing this with me, Paige."

I grumble and shift beside him, trying not to panic at the realization that I left my pen and notebook back in my room.

"Hey, Hannah," Dylan says into the receiver. "Good, good. How are you?" For a while, Dylan merely nods along to whatever Hannah is blabbing about on the other end. Then he meets my eyes. "Listen, after being here for a few days, I've got some more questions about Audrey. I hate to bring all of this up again, but do you have a minute to talk?" He nods again, though the girl can't actually see him. "Awesome. Thank you. Paige is here with me. Is it okay if I put you on speaker?" Another pause. "Great."

Dylan tips his head toward me pointedly, and I clear my throat. "Hi, Hannah."

"Paige," comes the sugary-sweet voice. "So good to hear from you again. I was so sorry to miss last year's visit."

"Yeah, we missed you too." I sweep a bare foot over the pine needles coating the dirt. "You know, Audrey never did say why you weren't able to make it."

Hannah clears her throat. "Oh." Suddenly, I regret prodding. I'd meant it as a tactic to ease into the conversation and assumed it had something to do with her fancy modeling gig. But maybe she had some sort of medical condition or the type of community service that really posh prep school students get when they steal test answers. "I never really got the story there either. Audrey just...told me not to come."

"She did?" Dylan asks, forehead furrowed.

"Yeah, look," Hannah says, "I didn't say this before because she was missing and it felt *wrong* to focus on anything other than the positives. But Audrey wasn't particularly nice to me last summer."

Now I feel even worse than I did before this conversation. "How do you mean?"

"I mean, she pretty much stopped speaking to me. She barely ever answered my calls or texts. And then when she finally did answer, it was only to tell me not to visit."

"Wow," Dylan says. "I'm so sorry, Hannah. That's awful."

"She did the same thing to me," I offer out of some sense of communality or sympathy. Maybe out of an obligation to share, since she's been so open. "I mean, not exactly the same, because I was here. But she completely shut me out, even made me switch rooms."

"I just wish she'd spoken to one of us," Hannah says, sounding unfazed by my revelation. "Then, maybe we'd know what happened to her."

"But you did have that *one* conversation." Dylan tugs at a loose string on the pocket of his board shorts. "Was that when she told you not to visit?"

"Yeah," Hannah says. "I called her for the millionth time to check in, and she actually picked up. I think she'd been drinking. I doubt she would've answered or said anything otherwise."

"Can you remember the conversation?" I ask. "More or less?"

"I mean, yeah. It was short and sweet," Hannah says. "She told me it wasn't a good time, and I got upset. I told her it never seems to be a good time anymore, and she agreed. I still remember her saying, 'No, it never is.' When I asked why that was and if something had happened, she said, 'Yeah, bad stuff.'"

"What bad stuff?" I ask, a shiver snaking through me despite the warmth of the day.

"Audrey wouldn't tell me. Only that she didn't know what to do about it. She had to do something, but there was nothing to do. It was all nonsense, really. She kept talking in circles. She said it was all too horrible and that someone from that party might talk."

"Party?" I ask, meeting Dylan's wide eyes.

"Yeah, I assume she meant that Summer Kickoff thing at Tripp's, but who knows?"

"Hannah," I practically spit. "Did Audrey ever mention anything about a horse?"

"Oh," Hannah replies quietly. "You two know about that?"

Laughter echoes out on the water as a couple of kids coast by on tubes. Dylan wanders away from the bank, motioning me along before slipping into the trees. "Solomon told us," he whispers to Hannah. "Did this *bad stuff* have to do with the horse?"

"I have no idea, sorry."

I'm not giving up that easy. "Did she ever talk about Madison Blake?"

"That other girl who went missing?" Hannah pauses a moment. "No, Audrey never mentioned her by name. But"—her swallow is audible on the other end—"I think she might have come up."

"Come up how?" I ask.

"Audrey was mumbling about the bad stuff. Incoherent, drunk ramblings, but the last thing she said was, 'Now she's gone. And it's all my fault.'"

Gone. Dread thrums in the air around me. I didn't want to believe, but deep down, I knew.

Madison Blake isn't just some runaway. Something terrible happened to her, and my best friend is responsible.

"Hannah." Dylan's voice is graver and more urgent than I've ever heard it. His skin has taken on a sallow hue. "This is really important. If you've spoken to Audrey—if you know *anything* about where she is—we need you to tell us."

"What? I don't—"

"Hannah, please," he begs. "You won't get in any trouble. Audrey won't get in any trouble. We won't go to the cops, we promise, but you have to—"

"Is that what you think, Dylan?" She sounds genuinely hurt, and I feel for her. "You think I would keep that from you? From your parents?"

"No, I don't—I just had to make sure. Something really strange is going on here, and we're the three people closest to her."

"Except we weren't," I remind him. "There was a guy. Hannah, did Audrey ever mention a new guy? Or even her old guy, Kurt?"

"No," Hannah says, sounding upset now. "Like I said, we weren't exactly sharing those types of details last summer. I suspected she'd ditched me for a guy, but she never mentioned anyone."

"Is there anything else you can remember about that phone call?" I ask.

"I'm thinking. I know I kept pushing her to explain. To tell me about the bad stuff. But she started crying and repeating that she was so sorry. That if she could do it all differently, she would."

My gut twists. *Oh, Audrey. What the hell did you do?*

"Well," I say, feeling like we've taken one large stride forward, only to fall into a pit. "Thanks, Hannah." I have no clue how we'll crawl our way out.

"Yeah," Dylan adds. "And thank you for the photos. Mom's going to love them."

"Of course." Her voice is choked with emotion, all the pep from earlier gone. "Take care, you two."

We end the call, and I say the thing that's been cycling through my head since Hannah brought up the party. "Something happened the night of the Summer Kickoff. This *bad stuff*, whatever it is. Audrey was her normal happy self the day I arrived last summer. But after the party, she changed."

"What could've happened at that party?" Dylan asks, shutting his eyes and grabbing his temples. "We were there!"

"We were…a little distracted," I say, the nape of my neck heating. I think back to that night. In my mind, it was a blur of fluorescent-colored lights and Dylan's bright blue eyes seeing me as if for the first time.

I try to remember the rest of the night. Was Solomon there? I know he attended this year's Summer Kickoff, but I'm not sure about last year's. I work my way backward from Dylan, reaching Brent, who entertained me when Audrey ditched me. There was a room full of teens with booze, some dancing, some—*dancing*.

"The photo," I say, nearly breathless at the realization.

"Photo?" Dylan bats away a pine branch and leans in close.

"The photo of teenage Madison from Delilah Blake's living room. I couldn't stop staring at it because I recognized her, the way she was dancing. Head thrown back as she smiled. Only I couldn't remember where I'd seen her before."

But I remember now. I barely glimpsed her face but she was swaying to the music with some guy. Dancing like no one else was in the room. She wore a white minidress, and though her hair wasn't long like it was in Delilah Blake's photo, I'm certain it was her.

Madison Blake was the dancing girl. She was at last year's Summer Kickoff.

19

Once we're sufficiently exhausted and sunburnt, the four of us stop in town for a late-afternoon milkshake at Carlson's. Our siblings go ahead while Dylan and I drop by the gift shop on the corner under the pretense of purchasing sunscreen.

Aimlessly, we wander the aisles, recapping the facts of the case.

"If Madison Blake was at that party," Dylan says, pretending to inspect a bag of chips, "why did the missing posters say she'd disappeared earlier?"

"Because her mother reported her missing, remember? Delilah Blake didn't exactly keep close tabs on her daughter. And between all the cons, Britta probably hadn't seen her around much either."

"It sounds like that night was when everything fell apart for Audrey," Dylan says. "So what does it mean?"

"It means Audrey could've had something to do with Madison's disappearance. According to Solomon, Audrey had spent an entire year thinking up a way to exact her revenge. So the first night she gets to Clearwater Ridge, who just happens to show up at the party?"

"Madison. But Solomon said that Audrey was working on finding Madison with her *source* later on last summer."

"Of course she told *him* that. If she'd already done something to Madison—something too horrible to confide in anyone, even Hannah—then she had to pretend she was still searching for her, just like Solomon was."

"And this source?" Dylan asks. "If it was the burner phone guy, why didn't Audrey ask him what to do about Madison until August?"

I nod. "I've been stuck on that too. My only thought is that this guy might not have been involved in whatever Audrey did to Madison. His job may have been helping her clean it up and get away."

"He could've been both," Dylan says. "4477 could've been there with Audrey at the party. Then maybe they switched to burner phones."

"What if 4477 is the reason Madison's mother and Britta went silent on the whole disappearance thing? That text message could've meant: *What do we do to make the cops stop looking for her?*"

"Well, if Audrey put the burner phone guy on that job, I'd say it worked." We reach the sunscreen aisle, and I cringe at the $22 price tag. "Small-town shops are the worst."

"I'll get it," Dylan says, reaching for the bottle.

"No, that's not—" I dodge his reach, knocking a stick of deodorant off the shelf behind me. Wincing, I duck my head. "You realize I don't actually need sunscreen, right?"

"Honestly, I'd forgotten." He stoops to pick up the deodorant.

I tilt my head. "I've become one of those humans who tells untruths with relative ease."

"You mean a liar."

I gesture at the deodorant. "You should probably get that instead."

Dylan smirks and puts it back on the shelf. "The lies may be improving, but the jokes…" He rocks a hand in a so-so gesture, and I stomp on his sandaled foot, eliciting a yelp.

We exit the shop with our heads down, avoiding the owner's malicious gaze. Out in the beating sun, we stick to the cobblestone beneath the shops' overhangs.

"Hey!" Brent Haywood waves us down from the other side of the road, then crosses over to join us.

"What's up?" Dylan says.

"Not much." Brent wears his signature tortoiseshell glasses, navy chino shorts, and a jade-green polo that matches his eyes. His tan is more perfect than I remembered, his floppy, light brown hair somehow floppier this summer. "How are you two? You were at Solomon's, right? Not sure how I missed catching up."

"We weren't there for long," I say, hoping Solomon failed to mention my little robbery stint.

"How come you two never come to pickup soccer on Saturdays? It's coed. A bunch of us are there every week, rain or shine."

"Mostly shine, I'm guessing." I squint against the blinding sun. "We don't come because we don't play soccer."

"Get out of the pool for once. And come by the club tomorrow." Brent leans in to play punch each of us. "My dad left the tab open."

"Can't," Dylan says. "I've got to fly out to orientation day."

"Already? Man, mine's not until next month."

"Yeah," Dylan says, frowning. "Prospective swim team has its own day. I can't miss it."

"Bummer." Brent turns to me. "What about you, Paige?"

I freeze, put on the spot. What does Dylan want me to say? We never actually had the relationship talk; still, I doubt he'd want me hanging out with another guy all day, not even his friend. "Um…" is all I manage.

"That sounds fun," Dylan says to me.

I can't help but feel a stab of disappointment. He doesn't care if I go, which means he can't care much about *us*.

Then there's the fact that I hate the Clearwater Ridge Country Club. It makes me self-conscious of everything from my scuffed-up flip-flops to the little halo of frizz around my crown—an affliction from which, miraculously, none of the member girls seem to suffer. I'd much rather spend the day investigating. Too bad Dylan made me promise not to.

I force a smile to match Brent's. "Yeah, I'll think about it."

———

Before bed, I knock on Dylan's door.

"Come in," he calls.

I enter to find him, a pile of clothes, and a carry-on suitcase splayed open on the bed. "Do you really have to go?" I ask, plopping down beside the suitcase. "How can you leave me here for two days with these horrible children?"

"Look, if you can fit inside here"—he gestures to his luggage—"you can come with me."

"It's going to be depressing." I don't just mean that he'll be gone. I mean that here in this house without Dylan, I'll have to face what I've avoided since we found that burner phone.

This entire investigation has been about finding Audrey. Yet I've managed to avoid dwelling on the fact that she's gone. It's like the search has given me a purpose—both a goal and a distraction.

Without Dylan and my purpose, I'll be forced to sit around and miss her.

Dylan, understanding in his eyes, abandons his pile of clothes to shift in front of me. "Get out of the house tomorrow, Paige." He tucks a loose strand of hair behind my ear. "Do something to take your mind off her. Go to the river. Decimate those horrible children at a game of water polo. Or take Brent up on his offer."

"Ah, yes, the club," I say in my Scarlett O'Hara voice, pantomiming fanning myself and straightening my nonexistent collar. "It will do me such good to see my oldest and dearest friends for a round on the course."

Dylan laughs. "If a round on the course means eating nachos by the pool." He reaches out to grip me by the waist. "You know, you're mocking me and my family."

I clap a hand over my mouth. "Mr. Covington, I would *never*."

"Would you just shut up and kiss me already?" he says, pulling me from the bed.

"If you insist." I wrap my arms around his neck, and our lips meet. My eyes fall shut as I ease into Dylan's chest, his every touch igniting a million sparks over my skin.

This time, the kiss doesn't end right away. Our lips remained locked, our bodies pressed together as the world around goes blank and the sense of urgency between us grows.

I sink back onto the bed, tugging him with me. But my hip lands on something sharp. "Ouch." I reach back to rub my already bruised tailbone. Apparently, in the world's hottest move ever, I landed on Dylan's suitcase.

He feigns concern, even as he stifles a laugh. "Oh, Paige. What are we going to do with you?" He collapses beside me, and I bury my tomato-red face in his chest, letting him smooth my hair. "It's good you have a day off from your detective work. You need time to heal before you get back in the field."

"It'll be tough taking a day off," I say in a gruff voice, impersonating the Sunshine Park residents' favorite television detective again. "The job is my life, and my life is the job. It's why I spend every evening drowning the remnants of the day in strong bourbon." I glance up to find Dylan looking befuddled.

"I just…" He scratches at his hair. "I don't even—so what's the plan when I get back? We still have no idea who 4477 is. But he could be hiding Audrey."

"I haven't totally ruled out Solomon, but…" I sigh into his shoulder. "I keep coming back to Kurt. We know Audrey was with him that night in the Pines. I saw them together multiple times. They looked like they were having a very serious, *private* conversation. If he's not the guy, he at least knows something."

"Except he won't talk to us."

"Maybe someone else will. We should interview people who were at the Kickoff. Someone must've spotted Audrey. According to Hannah, even *Audrey* was worried about that."

"Okay, I guess we can each make a list?" Dylan says. "Everyone we remember from the party who might've seen Audrey. And when I get back, we'll go down it, one by one. We'll talk to everyone."

"That sounds good." I waggle my notepad at him, smiling despite the dark thought churning in my brain. The one I try to battle, to keep from winning out.

The one that would mean breaking a promise.

20

The next day, coffee mug and book in hand, I tiptoe out the back door and make my way down to the river. Summers in Clearwater Ridge mean you're always surrounded by people, noise, endless sources of entertainment. I rarely have a minute to myself, and since my investigation is on hold for today, I might as well steal a moment to sit and reflect.

I find a seat on a rock and, for a stretch of time, do nothing but sip my coffee and watch the way the sunlight glimmers over the surface of the water. Eventually, I pick up my book, letting my mind drift away like one of those leaves floating downstream.

At the buzz of a text message, I assume it's Dylan letting me know he's boarding the plane. But when I find my phone, the text is from Brent.

Are we hanging out today??

I don't respond. I'd hoped Brent would forget ever inviting me. In truth, part of me wants to accept the invitation. Only I know it's for the wrong reason.

I want to go to the country club so I can start with interviewee number one on my list.

Brent Haywood was at that party in the Pines last year. He saw Audrey with Kurt, but he could've seen more. He might even recall something that he doesn't realize is important. The cops interviewed all of Audrey's friends, but they wouldn't have known to trace all the way back to that party. The Summer Kickoff was more than two months before Audrey went missing.

But I promised Dylan I wouldn't conduct any more interviews on my own. We did our childhood handshake and everything. After what happened with Solomon, it seemed a reasonable deal.

This is Brent, though—a friend Dylan trusts enough to suggest I hang out with him today. If our topic of conversation *happens* to steer into investigation territory, it's not really my fault. Is it? He may simply tell me that he spent the entire night at the card tables, like he did this year. And that will be that— one interview checked off the list.

But if he does know something, why should I waste another day waiting around for Dylan? He wouldn't want me to do that. This is Audrey we're talking about.

Still, there's a pinch of guilt as I open the text conversation and type back a reply.

What time?

Dylan said I could borrow his truck for the day, so I drive myself to the club. A stone arch marks the entry to the Clearwater Ridge Country Club, from which hangs a sign: *Charity Dinner Tonight!* Navigating beneath it, I park in the lot. Then I grab my bag and head toward the pool house. Brent said he would sign me in with the attendant that guards it.

I arrive at the desk, and the attendant, a twentysomething kid with a smattering of freckles and a navy blue CRCC polo shirt, looks me up and down. "You can't come through here in that."

I'm not sure what "that" is referring to. "My flip-flops?"

He frowns and points to the sign perched on the desk, leaving me to skim all twenty-six of the pool facility rules. Finally, I get to number seventeen, "Proper Pool House Attire," which apparently does not include tank tops.

"Right." This is exactly the sort of thing that makes me avoid this place. I dig through my bag, knowing there's nothing else inside that will fit the non–tank top bill. Instead, I pull out my phone, ready to text Brent an SOS.

"Paige!"

I glance over to see Brent ambling through in board shorts and a short-sleeved button-down. That must be the proper attire for a fancy room that leads to a pool. "Hey," I call out. "Can't seem to get past the TSA here."

Brent squints at me until I clarify, pointing at my strap. "Dress code infraction."

He covers his mouth with a hand, feigning shock. "A tank top, Paige. Really?"

"You know me, stirring up so much trouble I took my sleeves clean off and left them at home. But now I hear they're important." I expect him to slip the attendant a fiver and tug me along inside, but Brent simply stands there, looking truly flummoxed. "Should I call the CIA?" I ask. Surely, he knows a girl outside that will lend me a shirt with sleeves for five seconds.

Finally, he grins with one side of his mouth and turns to the attendant. "She's with me. Paige Redmond."

The kid glances down at his list. "Yep, she's here. Her charge will be billed to your father's account."

"Great, and uh, it looks like we'll be needing a shirt."

The attendant nods before heading into what looks like a closet door. He returns, handing me a polo shirt like the one he's wearing.

I stare at him. "Seriously? You had this extra shirt the whole time?"

He shrugs. "I forgot."

"Mhmm." I tug it on over my tank top and follow Brent through the pool house. "How is this ugly shirt better than what I was wearing?"

Brent laughs. "You can't overthink this stuff, Paige. These people love their rules." He says *these people* like he isn't one of them. It makes me feel slightly more comfortable, even though I know he's country club to the core. "When my parents first became members, the restaurant manager made Oliver sit outside because his pants had this tiny, almost imperceptible hole."

"The training it must take to spot something like that."

"Years and years," he deadpans, leading us outside. "But that's what keeps us safe."

"Imagine what could've happened. How is Oliver, by the way? Off in Barcelona or London, I presume." Oliver Haywood goes wherever the biggest poker tournaments take him.

"Morocco." We pass the lifeguard chair and a couple of tables. "He promised to deign our family with his presence this Christmas."

"Still living the dream, huh? Any desire to join him after college?"

"Nah. I'm nowhere near as good as him."

"Sure you are. I witnessed you sucker my baby sister into a game the other day."

"Hey, *Lucy* asked *me* for a game." He stops at four lounge chairs that have been claimed by towels, articles of clothing, and bottles of sunscreen. He shoves everything from one onto another. "All yours."

When I hesitate, he points to the pool. "It's just Tripp's stuff. He isn't going to be lounging anytime soon." I glance to where Tripp and a brunette named Gwen Ortíz are splashing each other.

"Are you saying I am?"

He shuts one eye, like he's examining me beneath a microscope. No glasses today; he must've swapped them for contacts. It isn't a Superman versus Clark Kent type of transformation. Brent Haywood is good-looking no matter what he wears. "Forgive me," he says, mock cowering. "I forgot you were Paige Redmond, varsity water polo star at..." His lips quirk. "What's the name of your school?"

"Peyton Valley High."

"Ah yes, the elite and renowned Peyton Valley."

I remove the polo shirt and toss it onto my chair, the gauntlet thrown and my tank top on full display for all. "I don't suppose they let you play water polo in this pool."

"Of course not. Didn't you read and memorize all twenty-five rules? No pool toys."

"It was *twenty-six*, and yes. That's how I know there's a bylaw. Small balls, water guns, and flotation devices may be permitted, depending on the number of persons in the pool and the manner in which such toys are utilized. At the pool attendant or lifeguard's discretion." It's not a direct quote, but it was one of the rules that made me choke back a laugh.

Brent's eyes light up. "There's no one in the pool but us."

"Exactly."

What starts as a game of hot potato with a tennis ball soon turns into a water volleyball game of sorts, utilizing the lane line as a net. Tripp and Brent are as competitive as they are athletic, only Gwen keeps squealing and missing the ball, drawing the lifeguard's attention and making the teams uneven. Tripp has little patience for his teammate and keeps muttering that the game is unfair. But two more teens join in, and we really have a match.

When one of my spikes lands just out of Tripp's reach, ending the set in our favor, Brent picks me up and spins me around. I blush at the feel of his muscular arms on my bare skin, remembering how Audrey used to encourage the idea of the two of us. But I quickly return to game mode, ready to crush Tripp's team in the next and, hopefully, final set.

That's when an elderly woman in a swimming cap decides to wade into our lane. The game is promptly squashed by the lifeguard, and we all exit the pool. The two teens who joined us wave and wander off to their lounge chairs, and we find ours.

"We were just about to decimate you," Tripp says, slapping Brent on the back hard enough to leave a handprint.

"Doubtful." Brent reaches to touch the blooming splotch.

"Can't believe he wouldn't let us play one more point." Tripp casts a scathing glance at the lifeguard. "Might drop a tip with the manager about him." He picks up his towel and starts to dry off. "That got my appetite going though. Anyone want nachos or, like, a double cheeseburger?"

"Oh my god, a milkshake would be heaven." Gwen throws a dress on over her still-wet suit.

The two trot off together, leaving me alone with Brent.

"Let me guess. No food in the pool area." My heart rate climbs. It's now or never. Unfortunately, my plan to put him at ease worked a little too well. We've been having such a nice, relaxing time, it would be weird to bring up my missing best friend.

"Ha! You didn't memorize all the rules after all. Food may be consumed within the pool area, provided it is done so in designated zones and is purchased from the Poolside Café."

"Got me there." I begin to reapply sunscreen, just to busy my hands. "So, this is random, but Dylan and I found out that Audrey was seeing someone last summer before she went missing."

"Oh, yeah?" Brent spreads his towel out on the lounger beside me and lies down, seemingly unbothered by my line of questioning. "How'd you find out?"

I join him in getting comfortable. Might as well keep him at ease, even if my heart is attempting to burst free of my chest cavity. "Some love letters, hidden in this secret spot that only I knew about." I'm lying. I'm actually telling a flat-out lie right now, and though I feel slightly hot and faint, my mouth isn't betraying me. I haven't even stuttered.

"Wow, so you gave them to the cops?"

"Yeah, but they didn't really help. The letters mention the Kickoff at Tripp's last year. So we know the guy was there. Only I couldn't help with that, since I didn't see Audrey much at the party. Did you, by chance?"

Brent's eyes are closed beneath his sunglasses now. "I don't think so? I'm trying to remember."

I inhale slowly. This isn't going anywhere. As much as I didn't want to feed Brent my theory—it would be so much better if he remembered and conjured it up on his own—I have to. "I mean, apart from that time we saw her with Kurt."

"Ohh," Brent says. "I remember that, now that you mention it. Oof, yeah."

What does he mean by "oof"? "You know, he's denied being Audrey's boyfriend last summer. You don't think maybe he's lying, do you? I remember they were pretty close at that party."

At this, Brent sits up, letting the sunglasses tip slightly down the bridge of his nose as he looks at me. "Audrey didn't tell you what happened with Kurt that night?"

I want to spit out, *No!* To rip the answers from him like they're wiggly baby teeth. But there's a wariness to his voice. Like he's trying to ascertain why my best friend never told me.

I can't divulge the truth: that Audrey shut me out last summer. "She was very coy about the whole thing," I offer. "I didn't press her about it. Those two, with their on-again, off-again drama. I figured they hooked up and she was embarrassed about it. She swore to me she was done with him right before we walked through the door that night."

Brent shakes his head, his green eyes still narrowed. "Audrey and Kurt weren't *close* or hooking up that night. They were *arguing*."

I frown. "Arguing about what?"

He glances over his shoulder in the direction of the pool house. "I didn't, like, eavesdrop or anything. I didn't hear much." He leans closer, lowering his voice. "But I do know it was about Tripp."

THE GIRL

The boy spared no expense on their private night in—though, technically, the couple sat outdoors.

He had a wide backyard deck overhanging a man-made pond. The night sky overhead was filled with blinking stars, and hundreds of twinkly lights dangled from the wood railings, making the girl feel as though the night sky surrounded her. As if she were floating up in space.

The long rustic oak table was adorned in simple elegance: wineglasses, white porcelain plates, and silverware. The boy had set three tea lights in clear glass holders, and the girl felt touched that he'd gone to such lengths for her. "It's beautiful," she told him.

He poured them each a glass of dark red wine. As they drank, the wine buzzed through her veins, filling her with warmth.

When the boy poured himself a second glass, some of the liquid dribbled onto the table. The girl saw only blood—tiny droplets that soon gushed like the falls at Haver's Gorge, pouring and pooling. She remembered the Bad Stuff then.

She remembered what she'd come here to do.

Before she could allow the thoughts to engulf her, the boy took her hand. Gently, he caressed the delicate flesh between her thumb and index finger. "I know there's something on your mind. You can tell me anything."

As the pond's waterfall gurgled gently and the crickets chirped in the background, the girl considered this. She felt she truly could tell the boy anything. She also felt a strong tug in her chest, unlike anything she'd ever felt for her ex. It was a twinge that teetered somewhere between wanting and hurting, whenever the boy touched her. She craved that touch, the feel of his skin on hers, but she thought of losing him too.

She was afraid of this boy, of what he could do to her. Was this what it meant to love someone? To truly care?

The girl believed it might be. There was still time to guard her heart, and guard it she would. She wouldn't allow the boy's hand to wander or his words to drift any farther into her ears—to penetrate her soul the way he hoped to. Not until he'd heard her proposal.

That's how she would know. It was, after all, no ordinary proposal.

With her free hand, the girl took up her glass and sipped from it, letting it warm and embolden her. Then she chose her words carefully.

"Something very bad happened," she said, looking the boy in his beautiful eyes.

His eyes grew bigger, as she'd expected. His hand tightened around hers; she'd anticipated that too.

But it was the next line that truly counted. Everything hinged on it. She watched the muscles in his face, every twitch. Every flicker of light bouncing off his irises. She felt his hand on hers. Was it dampening? Stiffening? The girl scrutinized it all when she added, "I'd like your help in getting justice."

21
PAIGE

Tripp? Audrey and Kurt had been arguing, not rekindling their romance.

And the argument was about Tripp Shaw.

"Did you hear anything they said?" I ask Brent, who's still glancing nervously back like he wishes he'd never said anything.

"No, not really. I mean, I assumed something happened between Audrey and Tripp, but he never mentioned it."

"And you never asked?" As soon as the words are out, a sick feeling rolls through my gut. If anyone knows that sometimes best friends don't tell each other everything, it's me.

"Nah, I wanted to. But he disappeared the rest of the night, and the next time I saw him, whatever it was seemed over. He didn't say anything about Audrey. I didn't bring her up."

Except Audrey and her guy were a secret. It could've been Tripp. I remember the crush Audrey had on him a few years back, before Kurt, and how it seemed inevitable that the two of them would become an item.

The question is, if they did get together, *why* was it in secret? Was it because Kurt was jealous, so they decided to play it off like nothing?

Or was it because something happened that night with Madison Blake? Something in which Tripp was complicit?

"Brent," I ask, even though he's lying down again, sunglasses shielding his eyes. "Did Tripp ever mention Madison Blake to you?"

"The townie who went missing?" The sun's reflection is too strong for me to make out his eyes beneath the glasses. But I see the way his lips go taut. "You should probably talk to Tripp about that."

"Yeah," I say, gaze flicking over to the Poolside Café just as the subject in question emerges, carrying a plate in each hand.

———

As midday bleeds into afternoon, I watch Tripp Shaw. King of the young summer crowd, former varsity wide receiver and division champ, all-league electee three times over, rising star on UCLA's team.

"Take this party to my place?" he asks, sliding his feet into flip-flops and slinging his wet towel over a shoulder.

The others gather their belongings as I debate. If I tag along, at the very least I can continue my study of Tripp.

Let's be honest. There's no way I can simply walk up to Tripp and ask about Madison Blake. If he had something to do with her disappearance—or Audrey's—he'll never admit it.

And if he's dangerous and I give him the slightest indication I'm onto him, he could come after me next.

I tell the others I'll meet them at Tripp's house; I can always decide to bail and text an excuse later. In the truck, I debate calling Dylan and asking his advice. But he's busy with grown-up college stuff. Plus, he'd tell me to back off until he returns. He'd let me squander this opportunity.

I've already broken my promise. Might as well get some answers and apologize later. Two girls' lives could be at stake.

Instead of dialing Dylan's number, I Google "Al's Mart" in hopes of finding a contact number for Britta, the manager. Unsurprisingly, the mart has no website, only a handful of one-star Yelp reviews. There's no mention of a manager, but I do find a phone number.

I dial the number, which rings four times before a girl picks up. "Al's Mart," she says flatly.

Hope sparks in my chest. "Britta?"

There's a long pause before the girl finally asks, "Who is this?"

"Britta, this is Paige, from the other day. It's important. Does the name Tripp Shaw mean anything to you?"

"No," she says, dragging the word out.

"Madison never mentioned him?"

"Not to me."

I grit my teeth. "Is there any way you can give me your cell number so I can show you a photo?"

"A photo? Why?"

"Just in case it triggers a memory. I need to know if you ever saw this guy with Madison before she went missing."

"Madison isn't miss—"

"I know, I know," I say, mentally swatting myself. "That's

not what I meant. It has to do with Audrey. Can you please just let me show you the photo?"

"Look, I don't have time for this. I'm in the middle of a shift."

A horn honks, startling me. Brent drives by, waving at me through the window. I return the wave. "I promise," I tell Britta. "After this, I'll leave you alone. Please. I know you understand what it means to lose a best friend. I'm just trying to get mine back."

I hear Britta's breath on the other line, followed by a grunt. "Fine." She gives me the number, which I jot down in my notebook. Then she hangs up, leaving me to search for a photo of Tripp. It's not like I've snapped a bunch of selfies with him over the years; instead, I find a picture of him posing for an article about his high school football team in an online sports journal. I screenshot it and send it off to Britta.

If she knows something, I'll stay away from Tripp. I'll wait until Dylan gets back, and we can go to the cops together.

But I wait and wait, and Britta doesn't respond.

I'm starting to sweat in this truck, so I turn on the ignition. The air blows hot. All I can do is roll down a window. Once ten minutes have ticked by, and I'm sufficiently roasted, my mind is made up.

I send off a text to my mom. After everything with Audrey last summer, I'm surprised she's even letting me out of the house. This is the least I can do.

Hanging out with friends at Tripp's. Won't be back for
dinner

When I arrive at Tripp's mansion, the front door is parted. I see myself inside, following the voices to the game room.

The instant my foot lands on the room's lush carpet, Brent shouts, "You came!"

"I said I would."

Tripp stoops below the bar top, coming back up with a beer. He jogs over to me and shoves it into my hand. "We sort of assumed you'd bail."

I shoot Brent a look of shocked indignation. "Even you? After I laid down my life for you in the pool...*court* thing?"

Brent slaps a hand over his heart. "Please forgive a foolish boy his mistake."

I stare down my beer next, cracking it open and wondering how long I can reasonably get away with using it as a prop in such a tiny crowd. "You've got the house to yourself?" I ask Tripp, my conclusion based on all the underage drinking.

"Yep." He grins. "My parents just left for the club's fundraiser."

"Ah, yes, the extremely specific *Charity Event*," I say, taking a seat on the couch beside Gwen.

Tripp laughs. "I think it's to fight cancer. Maybe homelessness."

"It's good to have a cause," I say. "Even better when you know what it is."

He pats his back pocket like he's checking for his wallet and calls over to Gwen. "Need another beer?"

"Nope, I'm good." She does look pretty comfortable,

sprawled out on the couch with her beer clutched to her chest like a newborn baby. "Just a little sunburnt."

"Well, you girls relax. We'll pick up the pizza." The small-town pizza joint hasn't yet discovered the concept of delivery, but their pizza is so phenomenal, it's worth the drive.

"See ya," I call out as they amble out the door. I glance over at Gwen, who looks content to take a nap and never speak to me. "So, you and Tripp seem close. Are you two...an item?" I cringe at my word choice.

"No," she says, chortling. "We're just friends. I mean, not that he isn't boyfriend material. Only that I'm not one for summer hookups."

"Yeah, I suppose not," I say, though I know close to nothing about Gwen. Like the Covingtons, her family has a summer place up here. I've seen her around, at Tripp's parties and whenever Audrey would drag me to the country club. But Gwen is friends with Tripp, which means she could know how he's connected to the missing girls.

"Hey, Gwen? Did Tripp ever mention dating Audrey last year?"

"Audrey?" Gwen shakes her head. "No, last year, Tripp was still torn up over Rose."

"Rose?"

"Mhmm. His girlfriend."

The name triggers a memory, vague and distant. I struggle to latch on to it. "I didn't know Tripp had a girlfriend."

"Well, none of us really did. I think they met here at the end of summer, a couple years back. But they didn't really date until fall, so no one met her. Tripp kept talking about introducing us to her at the Kickoff last summer, but I guess Rose didn't want to come. They broke up, like, right after that."

I think back to Tripp's words to Audrey and me in the kitchen that night. *Dude, there's someone I want you to meet tonight.* I'd assumed it was a girl for Dylan, but Tripp was referring to his girlfriend.

"What was her last name?" I ask, already opening up Instagram.

Gwen shuts one eye. "Lambert, I think."

Where have I heard the name Rose Lambert? "Did you ever see her? Or a photo of her?"

"I wish. Rose was super private and camera shy." She points at my phone, where I have the app open. "You won't find her on there."

"Why did Tripp say they broke up?"

"I'm guessing it was because she sucks. I mean, who doesn't come to her boyfriend's party? But, um…" Her gaze rolls upward, like she's conjuring a memory. "He said he got to know the real Rose, and it wasn't pretty."

"Did he elaborate?"

"Not really," she says, sitting up slightly to guzzle her beer.

The real Rose. I do a quick search of her name on Google, but of course, there are thousands of Rose Lamberts. I add "Clearwater Ridge" to the search bar, getting nothing again.

"You're still looking her up? What, are you *into* Tripp or something?" In the slice of a second, her tone shifts from bored to teasing.

"No," I say, shaking my head. "Just, the name Rose Lambert sounds so familiar."

"He probably told you about her. He was in love with her, and honestly, my impression is that she was nothing more than a leech." Gwen leans in closer now. "Like, she followed him to school—well, technically, she got him to fly her out to his apartment a bunch of times. Hellooo? Can you say *stalker*?"

Inveigling herself into a guy's life. Getting him to pay for flights.

Suddenly I know where I've heard her name before.

Solomon's private investigator couldn't identify Marley the cleaning lady as Madison Blake of Clearwater Ridge. But he was able to connect her to a Rose Lambert.

"Definitely a stalker," I say, trying to stay present in this conversation while my mind is spinning off into the cosmos.

Tripp's girlfriend was a fake. She was Madison Blake the entire time. A con artist. And he was the target of what sounds like a long-term con. Who knows what she managed to claw away from him in all that time?

And what would a guy like Tripp have done after learning the truth?

According to Gwen, the couple simply broke up, and that was that. I'm not sure I buy it. This makes it sound like everything was fine that night in the Pines, and that all the drama with Madison unfolded elsewhere.

But I know something happened at that party last summer.

Madison was there, dancing like she didn't have a care in the world. She must've bought Tripp's claim that the party was free of townies—of anyone who'd recognize her from Shadow's Pass.

Audrey was looking for Tripp that night. If Audrey recognized Madison—if she somehow figured out that Madison was the one who stole her money—maybe she tried to warn Tripp. Then, the two of them might've gotten together to *take care of* the situation. To try to get all of their money back.

Or worse. Hannah's words from our phone call ricochet back to me now. *Now she's gone. And it's all my fault.*

I can't be certain of any of it. I don't even have definitive proof that Tripp was dating Madison.

"Did Tripp ever mention where Rose went after they broke up?" What story did you feed your friends, Tripp?

Shrugging, Gwen gets up and wanders over to the refrigerator beneath the bar. "Why would he? He didn't care where that bitch was."

"Well, he didn't just put her out on the street, did he? You said she was living with him."

"Part-time, yeah. But she has her own place here. She's loaded, like everyone in the Pines. They met at the club for god's sake. It's not like she *needed* Tripp's apartment."

So Madison hooked Tripp by pretending to be a wealthy summer person. But did Tripp figure out her whole scheme? The way things look now, Tripp could've simply decided to break up with her.

Desperate, I throw one last question at her. "Gwen, did Tripp ever mention Madison Blake to you?"

She frowns. "That trashy girl from the news? No, why would he?"

"No reason. Guess I'm getting caught up in the mystery like the rest of the town."

Gwen's eyes brighten. "You know—I'm not supposed to talk about this—but my uncle's a cop in Massachusetts, and he heard that Madison actually sent a fake ransom note to the Crown County Sheriff's Department. Her parents never could've paid it, obviously, so they're saying she was banking on the cops publicizing it and some rich vacationer forking over the money as an act of charity."

Ransom note? "How did they know the note was fake?"

Gwen shrugs. "It was so obvious. By that point, they already knew she wasn't missing. Even her own mother said the note had to be fake. Just a new ploy to take some gullible guy's money."

"Well, I heard no one's actually ever seen Madison Blake," I offer. "That there's basically no evidence that she's even alive."

Gwen stares at me for a moment and then laughs. "You're funny."

I smile despite my frustration. This isn't working. I need a better excuse to pry. "Don't you think a podcast about all of this would be cool?" I ask. "Maybe I could have your uncle's number. To interview him."

She shakes her head, the smile on her face gone. "Look, you can't say that I told you about the note. And *no*, you can't talk to my uncle. If you want content for your Madison podcast, go talk to Sheriff Bolton."

"Madison podcast?" comes a low voice from the doorway. Tripp.

I jump in my seat. "Oh," I say, my entire body flaming hot. "No. It was a stupid idea. I got carried away by town gossip. You know, some people think she's still missing."

"Which people?" He crosses the room, dropping the pizza boxes onto the coffee table with an unsettling thud.

It's not the reaction I'd expected. Maybe a laugh or an

eye roll. But not this directness, almost as if he's worried. Thankfully, I don't have to lie about this. "Some old ladies in town."

"And you," he says, taking up a slice of pizza and pausing to meet my gaze.

"Of course not. Gwen and I were just making small talk while we waited for you." But I catch the grave expression on Brent's face, and when I look at Gwen, her lips twitch, like they're itching to blab about my entire line of questioning.

This is why Dylan told me not to investigate without him. Now both Brent and Gwen—two of Tripp's closest friends—know about my fascination with Madison Blake and how it all relates to Tripp.

One of them is sure to tattle.

My phone buzzes in my back pocket, and I flinch. Tugging it free, I read the text message from Britta, replying to the photograph I sent her an hour ago.

Stay the hell away from that guy.

A tremor of fear wracks my body, and I glance up to see Tripp's slate-blue eyes, narrowed and trained on me.

22

I stand, shoving the phone into my back pocket. "That was my mom," I say, my voice shaky. "I guess the Covingtons want everyone home for dinner tonight. She says it would be polite for me to attend." Frowning, I set my beer down on the table.

"Aw." Brent cracks open a fresh can. "You just got here."

"I know. Parents."

"At least take some pizza for the road," Tripp says.

The last thing I want to do is eat. But I take a slice, just to get him off my back.

"I'll walk you to the door," he offers, following me.

"Oh, that's not necessary. I know my way." I keep moving, even as his footsteps near and overtake me.

He reaches past me to clutch the doorframe, his body now blocking my way out. "You know, it's funny," he says, and I'm positive he can hear the erratic thumping of my heart. "I could've sworn the Covingtons always attended the club's fundraisers."

His eyes brim with cockiness and an almost playful gleam. He's a cat, and I'm the mouse dangling by its tail. I clear the bundle of nerves from my throat and force out, "Probably couldn't make this year, after everything."

His hand moves from the doorframe, allowing me to pass as he lightly taps his forehead. "You're right. I'm an idiot."

I smile, but on the inside, I'm hoping with everything in me that I am right. If the Covingtons attend that fundraiser tonight, I'll be caught in a lie. And Tripp already seems wary of me.

Out in the hallway, I thank Tripp for the beer and the pizza. Then I book it through the house and out the front door.

I want to sprint to the truck, but an uneasy feeling settles over me. I sense his eyes on me from the window. I speed walk, not stopping until I'm safely locked inside. After starting the car, my gaze dares to wander up to the game room window.

The shutters are closed. No one's standing up there, watching me. Am I being paranoid?

Maybe. But I can't deny that Tripp started acting weird when he heard the name *Madison Blake*. That move in the doorway was a clear threat.

Once I'm on the main road, I get the overwhelming need to call Dylan and tell him everything. But he'd know that I broke my promise. I can't ruin his last few hours of orientation.

He'll be back tomorrow. Maybe by then, I'll know how Tripp fits into all of this.

I park beneath a tree in the Covingtons' driveway, staring at the closed garage door and praying that their cars are still in there. Grabbing my phone, I bring up the Scam Alert website. I have to find out more about the con Madison pulled with Tripp. As helpful as Gwen's speculations were, they *were* merely speculations. Everything about Madison's criminal side seems to come by word of mouth—an anonymous rich guy, a friend who was swindled. When I dug for information on her, all the articles from the time she went missing were sympathetic. The stories about her cons somehow managed to stay off the internet, maybe because she was a minor. Maybe because the powerful people she targeted wanted to stay out of the press.

Then there's the reason I'm working on. That one powerful person didn't bother going to the press or the cops, because he took care of Madison Blake himself.

I enter Rose Lambert's name on Scam Alert, but nothing comes up. Out of options, I dial the number of the last person in the world I want to speak to.

Solomon McCleary.

To my astonishment, he answers on the third ring. "What do you want, Paige?" he barks out.

"Solomon, I'm sorry to bother you. And I'm sorry about the other night. After what happened with Marley, the whole stealing your phone thing obviously would've hit a nerve."

"You think?"

"I just have one tiny question. But it's important."

"I've already told you everything I know."

"Yes, and I appreciate that," I coo in a way that turns my stomach. "Thank you again. Your PI came up with the alias Rose Lambert for Madison Blake. Do you remember any of the other aliases she used?"

Solomon clears his throat. "Why do you want to know?"

I answer as honestly as I can. "I think Madison's killer was dating her when she was under an alias."

There's a huff, followed by a sound like the shuffling of papers. Then, Solomon says, "Before she was Rose, she was Meredith Dolechek. No wait, *Marianne* Dolechek. One of the two."

"And did your PI mention Marianne's crime?"

"It wasn't a fake cleaning company. *Marianne* posed as this rich girl who attended a fancy boarding school."

"How did you finally connect this person to Madison?"

"I spoke to Sheriff Bolton," he says, his voice easier now. "Once Madison had officially been declared a runaway, he was more than willing to blab about all of her known crimes. Apparently, some guy from Green Rapids reported her. She went on a few dates with him, pretended to have all this money, but for some bogus reason that the guy fell for, she couldn't access her funds. She convinced the guy to pay her fancy school's tuition, in cash. Only, as you can guess..."

"The fancy school didn't exist," I say.

"Exactly. It was a Ponzi scheme. The sheriff had a load of accounts where Madison used some poor sap's money to look like a millionaire while she dated someone else. Every time, she'd use the school tuition thing."

So assuming Tripp was the final target in this entire scheme, it means he not only treated Madison like a queen while they dated—flying her out to his apartment, paying for her every need—he also forked over thousands of dollars for a fake school.

"Thank you, Solomon. You've been a huge help."

The question is, how and when did Tripp figure out Madison's game? And what did he decide to do about it?

Inside the house, everything is dead quiet. My heart sinks. I leave Dylan's keys, the notepad, and my sunglasses on the console table by the front door and make my way down the hall. The kitchen is empty. I glance out the back doors, finding only Lucy and Nate sitting on the patio table.

At the sound of the door, they flinch.

"Paige!" Lucy squeaks, turning crimson and glancing guiltily at the bottle of rum set on the table between them. Nate pushes his glass away from him, like that will exculpate him. "Mom said you were out tonight."

"Yeah, well, there was a change of plans. Where is everybody?"

"The Covingtons went to a fundraiser at the club," she says, and anxiety lances through me. "So Mom and Dad decided to eat at the Hilltop."

"Your parents went to the fundraiser?" I ask Nate, trying and failing to keep the panic from my voice. "I would've thought that after everything, they'd skip this year."

"Yeah," Nate says, his gaze still darting from me to the rum warily. "They were going to. But at the last minute, the club decided that this year's fundraiser would support kidnapping victims. Obviously, my parents had to attend. They're doing everything they can to draw awareness back to Audrey's case."

"Wow," I say, unsure whether to run back inside or collapse into an open chair. What I really need is a good place to scream.

Tripp knew about the charity the entire time. He knew I was lying, but he enjoyed watching me wriggle like a worm. And now, he could very well know that I'm onto him.

I rush straight through the patio toward the back gate. Maybe I'll stick my head under the frigid river water and scream where no one will ever hear me.

"Paige?" Lucy calls out. "Are you okay?"

"Yeah, fine. Just need some space." I stop at the edge of the patio. "Put the bottle away, and we never have to speak of this again."

"Oh, come on!" she whines, throwing a hand up. "Audrey always used to do it and you never cared."

My fists ball at my sides, so tightly that my fingernails dig into the soft flesh. "Maybe I don't want you to become Audrey," I spit.

Lucy's mouth drops open, and across from her, Nate's eyes widen in horror. Before either of them can muster a reply, I spin around. I unlatch the gate and grab an inner tube for good measure. Letting the gate clang behind me, I duck into the woods.

The pain in Nate's eyes at my words still takes my breath away. I want to turn back and apologize. But I can't deal with that right now. I can't deal with any of it. Everyone believes that Audrey was this perfect girl, when in reality, she may have been some vengeful, destructive force.

At the rocks, I pull my phone free and stare at it, like it will somehow tell me what to do. I start pacing, once again tempted to text Dylan.

Tripp is connected to both missing girls. Audrey was arguing with Kurt that night in the Pines. The subject of that argument was Tripp.

Madison was still dating him at the beginning of the night, but she never met any of his friends. At some point, Tripp must've learned that she was using him, the same way she'd used other men before.

So what went down at that party? I remember Audrey had been looking for Tripp. She had some story about a broken houseplant that's looking less and less credible. So why did she need to find him?

Did Audrey spot Madison and, knowing that she was behind the horse con, make some huge and violent mistake? Did Tripp help her once she'd disclosed the truth about his *girlfriend*, Rose?

Or was Tripp merely Audrey's new guy? Someone helping to keep her secrets.

I have no idea. All I really know is that Tripp is in our grasp, about to slip free because of my blunders. I should drop a tip with Detective Ferrera, but Audrey is tied up in this somehow.

I still have my swimsuit on under my tank top and shorts, so I tug them off, wrapping my phone up inside them. Then I set the wad on a boulder and hop in my inner tube.

I forgot my sunglasses, so out in the water, I shut my eyes against the harsh rays. I continue to drift, peeking only to steer every so often. For the most part, though, I let the water take me wherever it wills.

It isn't until my tube stops dead that I blink against the beating sun and sit up a little straighter. I'm in the shallows, just before the swimming hole.

I pick up my inner tube, tossing it onto the beach. Then I wade through to the boulders and start my ascent. Each touch of my hand against the rough stone causes a rush of guilt. I'm not supposed to be at Haver's Gorge alone. This rule has been repeated, recited, and etched on my mind since before I could swim. Any misstep over the slick, moss-laden rocks, any rock landing so much as an inch off target is a constant risk.

So when I hear splashes and laughter ring out through the gorge, I'm relieved—no need to worry about slipping all by my lonesome now.

When I reach the top of the rock, the wind carries a familiar deep voice across the gorge. "Paige?"

I shield my eyes and squint until Kurt Winfield's figure comes into focus on one of the lower rocks. In the center of the pool, two girls and a guy I don't recognize splash around and tread water. "Hey, Kurt!" I call out, wincing at the memory of our last couple of encounters.

"You're alone?" he asks. Even from a distance, I hear the shock and judgment in his voice. Kurt is a rafting guide, which makes him Clearwater Ridge's version of a Boy Scout troop leader.

"Yeah, came for a swim. Dylan is off at Berkeley's orientation."

"Well, come on in," he says, leaping off the rock and contorting his body into a dive position in midair. Nothing like Dylan's poised dives. But Kurt hasn't had years of training at posh schools and clubs. Like me, he goes to public school with mediocre athletic teams and education.

Once he surfaces, I wave a hand from side to side. "I changed my mind. I think I'll walk back."

Kurt swims a few strokes in my direction. "Hold on!" He keeps swimming, leaving me to hover on my boulder as the early evening wind grazes my drenched body, creating goose bumps all over my skin. Reaching the rocks, he climbs up to join me.

I can't help the prickle of fear as he nears me. The last time we spoke, Kurt wanted nothing to do with me. He can't actually push me off this rock, can he?

"Look, Paige," he says, taking one deliberate step forward as I take one precarious step backward. "I'm sorry I haven't been very helpful with the whole Audrey thing."

I stand in stunned silence. Before I can respond, he adds, "The truth is that I should've said something."

That prickly feeling moves up the back of my neck. I was right. Kurt *knows* something. He may have even lied. "Should've said what?"

"I should've told you to stop everything you and Dylan are doing. Because girls are going missing, and if you keep asking questions, you'll end up one of them."

23

Every centimeter of my body tenses. "Are you threatening me?"

"What?" Kurt flinches away from me, shaking his head. "No, of course not. The opposite."

"Well, it sounded like a threat." My voice is raised now.

"Hey, hey." Kurt lifts his hands. "I'm saying that this situation is more dangerous than you realize. Not that *I'm* dangerous."

"But you're keeping things from me. From the cops."

Kurt presses his lips flat and glances over his shoulder, though it's highly doubtful someone is hiding in the greenery of the ravine, listening to our conversation. Clearly, he's afraid though.

"Look, I know about Tripp," I whisper.

Kurt's eyes widen. "You do?"

"I know something happened the night of the party in the Pines. I know you and Audrey argued. And I know that she did something to exact revenge on Madison for the horse con."

"Oh my god," he says, staggering slightly. A jolt of panic bursts through me, and I reach out to grab his arm.

"Why don't we go sit down somewhere...safer?" Releasing his arm, I gesture toward the beach where I abandoned my inner tube.

"Yeah, okay," he says absently, still lost in his own head. My panic turns into pulse-pounding anticipation; I'm onto something.

Kurt clambers down, and I follow him to the beach. Rather than sitting, he paces, like he can't bear to keep still.

"You're covering for Audrey, aren't you?" I ask, plopping down into the gravel-strewn sand. I pat that space beside me, and to my relief, he sits. "At the party, you wanted to be the guy to help her, but she chose Tripp. After all, he'd been duped by Madison too. Or..." I think back to my brief memories of Kurt with Audrey at that party. The way he leaned close to her, almost stooping to meet her eyeline. I assumed they'd been having a romantic moment, but now I have a sinking suspicion he was begging. "Maybe you were trying to talk her out of her plan?"

Kurt lets out a frustrated sigh. "You've got it all wrong."

"Do I? What am I wrong about? The horse con? Madison and Tripp—only she was going by Rose Lambert? You arguing with Audrey at that party because she found out the girl who'd stolen all her money was right there, dancing in the next room? I saw Madison that night, you know. I remember now."

"You're wrong about Audrey!" Kurt spits. "She never wanted to hurt Madison. I mean, *shit*, Paige. Didn't you know Audrey at all?"

I blink, stunned by his words once again. Heat creeps into my cheeks. "But Madison is missing," I say, my voice sounding strangely robotic. "And Audrey had a motive to hurt her."

"Maybe she had a motive, but that's not Audrey. That night, she—" Kurt grasps at a chunk of brown hair as if to wrench it from his scalp. He turns to face me now, his tan skin leached of color. His eyes are unfocused, skittering from the swimming hole to the trees and finally landing on me as he says in a low voice, "She didn't hurt Madison Blake. But"—a quick glance at the trees—"she saw who did."

"What?" I barely hear my own voice. It's like the waterfall and the rush of the river—the entire world—has gone silent.

"Audrey saw something she shouldn't have. Wrong place at the wrong time."

"What did she see?"

Kurt starts to fidget, playing with a rock he found in the sand. "She saw someone attack Madison with a bottle and drag her outside. Audrey came to get me. She wanted me to follow them outside with her. But I couldn't. *That's* why we fought. I didn't want anything to do with it, so Audrey said she'd go to the cops."

"And why didn't she? Why didn't you help her?"

"You don't understand," he says, tossing the rock into the weeds. "It wasn't that simple. The person who hurt Madison is powerful, with a very powerful family. Reporting him would've put Audrey in danger. It would've put us both in danger."

"I think it's safe to say that whatever advice you gave Audrey didn't exactly *save* her from danger," I bite out.

"I know." Kurt wrings his head now, letting out a horrible

moan. "I thought I was protecting her. And maybe I could've, but Audrey being Audrey...she ignored my advice."

"What do you mean? She reported the incident?"

He shakes his head. "I don't think so. I'd convinced her that everything would be fine. This guy probably just wanted to scare Madison out of town after what she'd done. It wasn't until Madison's mother reported her missing that Audrey became...*obsessed* with the girl."

"Obsessed how? Like she wanted to tell someone?"

He nods. "To tell someone, to search for Madison. She was so overwhelmed with guilt from not doing anything that night, she spent the entire summer looking for her."

Overwhelmed with guilt. This is what caused Audrey's spiral. It's the reason she pushed me away, pushed Hannah and Dylan away. She couldn't risk my finding out what she was up to, so she moved me out of her room.

And now, the cycle continues. Is this why I'm spending my every waking minute searching for Audrey? Because last summer, I didn't help her?

"This guy," I say. But I don't need to finish the question. Because I already know the name that came up between Kurt and Audrey that night. Brent overheard it.

Tripp.

I think of the text on the burner phone. What are we going to do about Madison?

If Audrey was trying to find Madison, she wouldn't have texted this to the perpetrator two months later. That means 4477 could still be at large.

Like Solomon said, he could be someone Audrey contacted

to help her investigate Madison's disappearance. To help uncover the truth. Because Kurt refused, and Audrey either didn't trust me or wanted to keep me out of it.

"You were terrified of Tripp," I say. "But he's your friend. He's Audrey's friend."

"People will go to extreme lengths to protect themselves, Paige. I'm afraid that's what happened here, with Audrey."

Audrey's investigation got her in trouble. "You don't really believe—" But the thought slams into me so hard that I sway. I suck in air, my exhale an animallike, strangled cry.

This whole time, Dylan and I feared Audrey had done something terrible and was running from the law. We believed this, in part, because we couldn't wrap our minds around the Audrey of last summer. The girl who lied, ditched us, and stole money from her parents.

But there was another reason we told ourselves this tale about Audrey: deep down, we almost hoped it was the case. Because it meant that somewhere out there, at least she was still alive.

If Audrey never transformed into this horrible, villainous fugitive that Dylan and I invented—if she was still the same Audrey as always last summer, her intentions pure—then she might not be alive and well at all.

She may be dead, at Tripp Shaw's hand.

"Paige." Kurt gets up, the sand and leaves clinging to his damp board shorts. "Look, I was selfish. I loved Audrey once. At least, I thought I did, and I really was trying to protect her. But I was also looking out for myself. My life is here and I know what the Shaws could've done to run me out of town. Or worse. These guys—the *Tripps* of summer—they're my friends, but I'm not kidding myself. I'm never going to be one of them. I feel horrible for abandoning Audrey and for...Madison too." He leans in close enough that droplets from his still-damp hair whip into my face. "You have to be careful. These guys get away with this kind of stuff all the time. Not just with Madison and Audrey. They have the power to make people disappear." He takes a step back toward the rocks. "They're not like us."

Us.

He starts to climb, leaving that last word ringing through my ears, a reminder of how similar Kurt and I really are.

Of how little we belong in this world.

THE GIRL

It wasn't the words the boy said—those were perfect. "I want nothing more than to help you make this right."

It was his eyes. An almost lupine glint as he spoke that told the girl he was a liar. And she knew; she'd spent much time among liars.

She herself was a liar.

The girl got the distinct urge to look toward the door, just to make certain the path was clear.

Because something wasn't right with this boy. He'd offered her the guest bedroom, and she suspected he might wait until she fell asleep to double-cross her. She worried that despite her feelings for the boy—despite what she had believed he felt for her—he might betray her.

"I know someone who can help," the boy said. "I'll call in a favor."

The girl tried to nod, to say, "Thank you."

Only now something wasn't right with the girl either. Her

head felt funny, her mind foggy. Her face and limbs were going numb.

She glanced down at the red wine to find that it was blurring into a vision of glass and blood.

24
PAIGE

I make it to the house just as the sun dips behind the mountains and shut myself inside my room. Then I dial Dylan, who picks up before the second ring. "Hey, you," he says brightly.

"Hey." I try to match his tone, but it's useless. I take a seat on the bed and clear my throat. "How'd everything go?"

"Really well. I'm actually on my way to the hotel."

"Hotel? I thought you were flying home tonight."

"That was the plan, but my flight got canceled. Dad said he'd put me up downtown. I'm taking the first flight out tomorrow morning."

"Oh, that's too bad." My voice quivers. I'm already starting to fall apart. "I was hoping we could talk."

"We can talk now. Are you okay?"

"Not exactly. Remember how you said it might be fun to hang out with Brent today?"

"Yeah," he says, letting the word drag.

"Well, I did, and…" I've practiced telling him this. In a

way that's technically true but also makes it look like *his* fault that I stumbled upon all of this information. Only my mouth is refusing to cooperate now that it counts. "Some stuff came out, about Audrey."

"What kind of stuff?" The cheerful quality to his voice from a moment ago—all the starry-eyed hopefulness instilled in him from a day on his new campus—it's gone now.

I tell him everything. What Brent said about Audrey and Kurt arguing at the Summer Kickoff. That Tripp dated Madison Blake posing as Rose Lambert. That Audrey and Kurt argued about what she'd seen and how to handle it. How Audrey spent the entire summer attempting to track Madison down.

"So then, the burner phone…" Dylan says.

"I don't know. It could've been someone trying to help find Madison." A new thought skulks its way into my head. "Or it could've been Tripp himself. Maybe Audrey thought she could fool him into admitting guilt."

"By dating him?"

"Maybe. At this point, I don't think 4477's identity matters anymore. I think we have to tell the cops about Tripp and hope it leads to Audrey." I don't say the next part, that it seems like all we have left to hope for is a body. That Audrey and Madison are likely dead.

"Tell the cops *what*, though? What's your proof, other than hearsay?"

The way he says "*your* proof" stings. I thought we were in this together, but clearly, this new line of investigation is all mine. "The cops can find that. It's our duty to tell them about our lead."

"I don't believe any of it," he says. "Kurt lied to us before. Who's to say he isn't lying now?"

"I believed him, Dylan. He looked...scared."

"Well, I've known Tripp almost my entire life, and so has Audrey. He wouldn't hurt her."

"And Madison Blake? Would he have hurt her?"

"No," he snaps with enough force that I flinch.

"He got in my face today," I say, fingers clamping around the phone. "It was menacing."

"Wait—what? What did you say to him?"

"What did *I* say to him?" Indignation simmers in my throat. "Nothing! I mean—I may've asked this girl at his house about Madison, and he overheard."

"Paige," he groans.

"I would think you'd be more concerned about what I told you! We have to consider the possibility that he's capable of this. That he *did* this. He hurts girls and there's never been any consequences. His father is powerful enough to pay Madison's mother and Britta to say that she ran away in order to quash the investigation."

"That doesn't mean he did it! My family's got money, Paige. Does that make me a killer?"

My chest aches, and a swell of tears blurs my vision. I've never heard him so angry, especially not with me. "Of course not, Dylan. You know all I want is to find Audrey."

He lets out a sound somewhere between a sigh and a growl. "Okay, so let's say Tripp did this. That he's this big bad killer and that his daddy covers everything up. You're just going to ignore your *buddy* Kurt's advice? He told Audrey that if she didn't let it go, she'd get hurt. And now—" His voice breaks as realization sets in, and I desperately wish I was there to hold him. "Oh my god, Paige. What if she's really—"

"She's not," I say, despite my own lack of hope. "She could've found out Tripp was onto her, so she ran."

He's silent for a too-long moment. "Yeah," he finally says.

"That's why we need the cops on this. We've taken it as far as we can."

"Okay, but I want you to wait until I get home tomorrow."

"I don't think we should waste—"

"Paige, it isn't safe," he says firmly. "You can't waltz into the sheriff's station and accuse the son of the man who basically owns this town of murder. Tomorrow, my parents and I will come with you. Keep this to yourself for one night, and we'll all go to the cops tomorrow."

I consider this. It would be better to have Dylan's family vouch for my story. I've got no hard evidence. Kurt has made it clear that he's too chicken to make a statement.

And Tripp is already aware that I'm onto something. I should stay locked indoors this evening. "Fine. I'll keep it to myself, just for tonight."

"Look," Dylan says, his voice sinking. "I'm sorry I got upset. But this was exactly why I asked you not to dig into this without me."

"I know. I'm sorry too. I should've stayed home with Lucy and Nate and their bottle of rum."

"Rum?"

"You didn't hear that," I say. "Forget you heard that."

A long breath. "I'll see you in the morning, okay?"

"Yeah, okay." I hang up, thinking about my promise to Dylan. Is it the right decision? On the one hand, Audrey has been gone for ten months. Waiting one more night couldn't possibly make a difference.

On the other hand, Tripp suspected something today. He overheard too much.

If he and his father left even a tiny trace of evidence of their crimes behind, now's the time they'd get rid of it forever.

———

I hardly sleep the entire night. Instead, I lie in bed, brainstorming a concrete way to tie Tripp to Audrey's disappearance.

At 9 a.m. there's still no word from Dylan, even though he supposedly landed half an hour ago. I send off a quick text: Everything ok?

I shower and get ready for the day. When I check my phone, there's still no reply.

Downstairs, Mr. Covington is in the kitchen, scrambling eggs. "Morning," he says, waving at me with the spatula.

"Oh, hi." I find myself a coffee mug. "Did Dylan's flight get delayed?"

"Nope. He's taking a taxi back."

"Oh. So then, he landed?"

"Yep. Right on time." Mr. Covington scoops the eggs onto a plate. "He said he wanted to get in a workout at the club gym this morning, and then he'd be back."

I get a stab of disappointment. Dylan had time to tell his dad all of that, but he ignored *my* text? And then he went to the club to work out?

Footsteps sound on the stairs, which means the others are up. I don't feel like talking to anyone, so I take my coffee to the back porch. It's an uncharacteristically cloudy morning, lending a chill to the summer air.

Dylan knows that his sister's life is on the line. He knew how hard it was for me to wait even one night to go forward with what I'd learned about Tripp, and yet, he suddenly had this need to work out?

My hands start to shake around the mug. Either I'm antsy from the wait, or the caffeine is making me jittery. Dylan's obviously swept up in some spiral of denial. One of his best friends may have had something to do with his sister's disappearance. And instead of accompanying me to the sheriff's station, he blew me off.

I dial Dylan's number and listen as it rings and rings. There's no voicemail. I march through the house, grab my purse and Dylan's keys, and head for his truck. I have no clue how to get into the country club gym, but I'll find a way. Then I'm going to drag Dylan out of there and down to the station with me.

I've never actually been inside the club gym. On the way to the fitness rooms and the lockers, there's a small lobby with a desk where an attendant handles the sign-ins. This one is a muscular girl with a blond ponytail. "Good morning." She scrutinizes my unfamiliar face the way all the club staff does before breaking into a bright smile. "Need to sign in?"

"Yes, hi. This is my first time in here, so forgive me." There's a list of rules on the desk. I skim it quickly, my gaze settling on the line that reads, *Facility is available to all Clearwater*

Ridge Country Club full members, as well as seasonal and trial members.

"No problem." She looks at her computer screen. "What's your name?"

"Oh, no, I'm not a member...*yet*. I was thinking of doing the trial thing. I'd love to look at the facility before making my decision."

"Oh." The girl's smile falls. "See, your parents have to become trial members first. Then you have access to all the facilities."

I let out a sigh. "Well, my friends are members. Maybe they put me on the list? Paige Redmond?"

She starts typing, only to wince at me. "Sorry, I'm not finding you."

Frustration builds deep in my jaw. This is the second time this week I've been rejected by a club I never wanted to join. "Would you mind finding my friend, please? He can get me in."

She eyes me like I'm going to steal her precious list of rules and make off with it in her absence. Finally, she smiles. "Sure, what's the name?"

"Dylan Covington."

Frowning, she goes back to her computer as a girl around my age exits the main door to the fitness rooms. She's twisting her wet hair up into a bun, a gym bag hanging from one shoulder.

"I didn't sign Dylan in," the attendant continues. "But I'll just..." Her fingers clack over the keys some more, and she shakes her head. "He's not signed in. Are you sure he's inside?"

I nod. "He said he'd be here."

The attendant's lips twist. She must feel sorry for me, because she says, "Let me go check." She steps in the direction of the door when the girl with the wet hair stops in the lobby.

"You're looking for Dylan Covington?" She says it in a familiar way that sends my hackles on edge. She's pretty and fit, her clothes showing her every curve. A post-workout glow lights her cheery face.

"Yeah, did you see him back there?" I pitch a thumb toward the main door.

"No," the girl says, "but I saw him earlier when I parked. He was dressed for golf and walking with Tripp Shaw."

The shock rams into me so hard that I fail to respond as the girl hikes her bag higher on her shoulder and starts for the door again.

"Thank you!" I manage to choke out.

The girl turns to smile, and suddenly, I can't breathe in this perfectly air-conditioned room with these perfectly helpful people. I have to get out of here. I thank the attendant and step outside into the midmorning sunlight.

I stagger to what could either be a wall or a rock sculpture— but is definitely not meant to be a bench—and take a seat on it.

Dylan lied. He lied to his dad about being at the gym. And he lied to me.

Instead of heading straight home so we could go to the cops, he headed straight to Tripp. To warn him.

I'm so stupid. I thought that what Dylan and I had was real. I should've known that he's *one of them*. People like Tripp and Dylan will always choose each other. They'll always protect each other. I never should've confided my suspicions in him.

Then a truly terrifying thought bites into my brain. Dylan and I were together the night of the Summer Kickoff. Only he wasn't at my side the entire night. There was a good amount of time when Dylan left me shivering by the indoor pool to grab towels and a bottle of water. It had taken longer than it should've; that I remember. Long enough that I left the pool room to find my own towel. In the end, he came back with only the water. He said he'd gotten held up by someone at the party. But what if he lied?

Is it possible that the boy I've known my entire life—trusted my entire life—was complicit in what happened to Madison that night? Could he have gone to such lengths to help a friend?

Was golf today about Dylan and Tripp working out a way to cover their tracks so that neither one would go down for it?

I shake the thought away. Dylan would never choose Tripp over Audrey. He'd never betray his own sister like that.

But he betrayed me today. I feel the tears streaming down my face before I realize I'm crying. Then, because I can't simply allow myself to be sad and hurt—because I have to *do* something about it—I type out a text to him: I know where you are. I hope you realize what you've done

This time, I do get a response. I feel a slight zing of satisfaction that I've irked him. It's not what you think. Where are you?

At the sheriff's station I type out.

I send it, just to make him squirm. To show that if he can lie and double-cross me, I can do it right back. I really should go to the sheriff's station before Tripp finishes this clandestine meeting disguised as a round of golf and gets ahead of the whole thing.

That is, if he didn't already get ahead of it when I left his house last night.

On shaky legs, I force myself off my rock throne and into the parking lot. Dylan's keys are buried somewhere at the bottom of my purse. As I dig for them, my phone rings.

I should ignore it, but part of me wants him to hear from my own throat how done I am with his lies. I answer, not letting him get a word out. "Say hi to Tripp for me."

"You don't understand, Paige."

"Is he there?" I ask with a forced calm. "Right next to you on the seventh hole?"

"No," Dylan says in a low voice. "He's in the sauna. We finished our game a few minutes ago, but if you'd hear me out—"

"You went there to warn him."

"What? No. I came to talk to him because—where are you really, Paige?"

One-handed, I rifle through my purse again. Still no sign of the keys. "I've got to go, Dylan. I'm right outside the station." I hang up, stash the phone inside the purse, and continue my search.

Finally wrangling my keys free, Dylan's voice rises over my screaming thoughts. Only it isn't coming from my phone this time. I spin to see him outside the main building, hurrying toward me.

I unlock the truck with a trembling hand and jump inside. Once I've locked the door, I wait for Dylan to approach. On the outside, I'm gloating because he can't get to me; on the inside, I'm crushed that it's come to this.

That suddenly, I'm unable to trust the boy I love.

Dylan stands outside the passenger side door, eyes pleading with me through the window. "Paige," he finally says, voice sounding distant and tinny from the other side of the glass. "I'm sorry I didn't tell you about this. I knew you wouldn't understand."

"You had me make a promise—a promise I really didn't want to keep. But I did. And then, what did *you* do? You went running to the enemy."

Dylan glances over his shoulder. "Let me in, Paige. Let me explain."

I shouldn't. I don't trust him.

But the last thing I need is Tripp overhearing him shout about our plans through the tempered glass. I unlock the truck, remaining slouched and sulky in the driver's seat as he makes his way around to the passenger door.

Once inside, he keeps his distance. "Thank you for letting me in. I do know how bad this looks."

"Do you?"

"I was hoping to get some answers and ask for forgiveness later." He adds in a wry tone, "I'm sure you have no idea what that's like."

"I did what I did for Audrey," I spit. "You did this for your *friend*, Tripp, who may have killed her."

"No, I didn't. I came here because we flat-out didn't have enough proof to go to the cops. Not against Tripp Shaw. I know Tripp golfs here three mornings a week. I thought maybe, if I brought some Irish coffee onto the course to get his lips a little looser, he might spill. I asked him about Rose while my phone was recording."

I cross my arm, surprised by this revelation but also a little skeptical. "You did?"

He flashes a mini bottle of Jack Daniel's from the pocket of his golf jacket. "Courtesy of my seatmate on the plane."

"And did you get anything out of Tripp?" I sit up a bit straighter.

He sighs. "He claims he broke up with Rose right *before* the Summer Kickoff."

I shake my head. "That's a lie. She never would've come to the party if he'd just broken up with her. How is it possible that only I, and maybe Audrey, saw Madison that night?"

"I don't know," Dylan says. "According to Tripp, when Rose got all shy about coming to the party, he realized they weren't compatible. He claimed that the girl didn't know how to have a good time because she's this *uppity bitch*—his words—that didn't want anything to do with a kids' party."

I scoff. "Right, so Madison's the snob. He's making it sound like teenage drama when he beat that girl, or worse."

"But we can't prove it."

He's right. For all of our efforts, we lack even a single piece of hard evidence of Tripp's involvement. "Last night, you said your parents could help us. That with them backing our story, the cops would have to take us seriously."

"I'm not so sure anymore, Paige. Even with my parents, we can't walk into the station with nothing but hearsay on our side. You're forgetting that if we can tie Tripp to this—and it's a big *if*—it's only to Madison Blake's murder. It's a whole different thing to tie him to Audrey's disappearance."

I tip my head back against the headrest. "But we have the

burner phone and Kurt's account, if he'll talk. We know Audrey was digging into Madison's disappearance."

"It's not enough," Dylan says. "The Shaws run Clearwater Ridge. They're its biggest donors—Mrs. Shaw runs the annual charity event. If the sheriff's department shut down Madison's investigation without just cause, there's a good chance it's because the Shaws paid them off."

"So then, what are we supposed to do?" I hate this feeling of helplessness. Of being so close to the truth and not being able to see my way around this massive Shaw-shaped roadblock.

Dylan dares to lean ever-so-slightly closer, trying to meet my eyes as he offers his upturned hand.

I don't put mine in it. Maybe he was trying to help, but I still feel betrayed. "What made you change your mind? About Tripp?"

He takes a deep breath, lets it out. "Time, I guess. A night of tossing and turning, regretting what I said to you last night. When I came here this morning, part of me still hoped you were wrong about him. But I owed it to you and to Audrey to make sure. And then…" He clears his throat, like the words need help getting free. "I forced myself to remember some things, some not-too-pretty moments with Tripp that I've ignored over the years."

"Like what?"

"Just—" He lowers his head. "Today, for example. When he asked the caddy to choose his club for hole three and then the shot didn't go so well. Tripp lost it, threw the club, called the kid names, then told him he'd lost his tip. That's Tripp." I think back to the game in the pool yesterday. The way Tripp implied he would get the lifeguard fired just for doing his job.

"He's a poor loser on the football field," Dylan continues, "but he plays so damned well everyone puts up with it. I've always stood by, tolerated that behavior from him. And I'm not saying it makes him a killer, but…I guess it makes me think something as big as losing money to a fake girlfriend might be enough to make him snap. I had to come here, to try to get the truth. But I'm really sorry I did it in secret. If you really want to go to the station, I'll go with you. I'll back up your story."

Finally, I look into his blue eyes, my resolve crumpling. He does have a point. Right now, it's our word against Tripp's. What we really need is Tripp's admission that Rose scammed him. A motive, coming from his own mouth.

"No," I say, "you weren't right to keep me in the dark. You're right about needing more proof though. We'll go back in there and talk to Tripp again. But we need a new angle."

25

Dylan texts Tripp to meet us in the club restaurant. Once he finishes up his lengthy, postgolf ritual, Tripp joins us, hair wet and cheeks pink from the shower.

"Paige." Grinning, he takes the seat across from Dylan. "How lovely to see you again so soon."

My muscles tense. "How was the game?" I ask sweetly, loathing the fact that I have to make small talk with the guy who may've hurt my best friend.

"He crushed me," Dylan says with a laugh. "Five over par compared to my failure to even break a hundred."

"You'll get him next time," I say, patting Dylan's arm, even though I have no idea what those scores mean.

The waitress attends our table now. The boys order coffee and full breakfast plates. My stomach is too knotted to eat, but I order some pancakes just to blend in.

"Sounds like you two worked up an appetite driving those

little cars around," I say playfully. "Or was it from standing around, waving that golf stick?"

"It was getting up at five a.m. to swim laps." Tripp gives me a smug half smile.

I press my palms flat onto the table. "Five a.m.? It's summer!"

He shrugs as the waitress appears with the carafe, sliding his mug over the tabletop like the helpful boy that he is. "Growing up, my dad never really let me sleep in. Said he had to instill a strong work ethic in me. Now, I wake up early even when he's not there to drag me out of bed."

"That's admirable," I say. "I think I had a dream about waking up early to swim once."

Tripp rolls his eyes and sips from his steaming mug. "What are you guys up to the rest of the day?"

"We'll probably get started on Paige's podcast," Dylan says, reaching for the cream.

"You're going through with that?" Tripp asks, his tone mocking. "I thought you said it was just *a stupid idea*."

"I told her it was a good one." Dylan stirs the cream around. "Don't you think?"

"It's a bit reaching," Tripp says. "Just because a few bored old people are spouting off conspiracy theories doesn't make it a mystery. Who would you even interview?"

With a mischievous smile, I flick my eyes in Dylan's direction.

Tripp squints at me before glancing off to my right. "Is there someone else in—I don't understand."

Laughing, I grab Dylan by the bicep, making his coffee cup

wobble precariously over the stark white table linens. "Him! Dylan is going to be my first witness."

"Dylan? He didn't even know Madison."

"Nope." I lean in and lower my voice. "But he met *Carolyn Davis*."

"Who the hell is Carolyn Davis?"

"Madison Blake, of course," I say, taking up my coffee. "Carolyn Davis is like...an alias or whatever."

"Seriously?" Tripp opens his mouth to say more, but the waitress arrives with our plates, forcing him to fiddle with the silverware instead.

"Is there anything else I can get for you?" she asks.

"No," Tripp practically growls before collecting himself. He smiles politely, pushing his spine back into the seat. "We're perfectly fine, thank you." When she wanders away, he tips forward again. "When did you meet Carolyn?"

Dylan cocks his head to the side, brows furrowed. "Right after we arrived, I guess."

"This summer?" Tripp's voice climbs, both in volume and urgency. His right eye twitches slightly.

"Uh huh," Dylan says. "She's basically Satan incarnate. The girl tried to offer me information about Audrey for a fee. Said I couldn't tell anyone she was helping me. I had to leave the money in a shoebox behind the Clearwater Ridge border sign. And I almost did it too. Luckily, I didn't stick to the secrecy rule and told Paige about it. We planted an empty box behind the sign at the allocated time and waited." Dylan smacks a fist into a palm. "And guess who shows up to collect the box."

"Madison Blake," Tripp breathes.

"Yep."

"Did you film her? For your…show thing?"

"It's a podcast, so no, we didn't film her." I say. "And I mean, I didn't come up with the podcast idea until after we witnessed Madison in the act. Can you believe she would try to take advantage of a grieving brother like that?"

"I don't understand how you can be sure it was Madison," Tripp says, staring intently at the tablecloth now.

"Oh, I saw her photo when she was allegedly missing," I say, furling a hand. "You know, on the corkboard in Carlson's."

"But I don't think—what did Carolyn look like?"

I bite my lower lip and pretend to think back. "I mean, she didn't look *exactly* like the photo. Her hair was different, longer maybe."

"Did she have anything on her face?"

I frown. "What do you mean? Like makeup?"

"Could you see a scar?" He points to his own cheek, dragging an index finger down it at an angle.

My head wrenches back in genuine shock. "Madison Blake didn't have a scar in the photo."

"N-no," Tripp stammers. His face reddens, a sheen of sweat glistening over his forehead. "No, you're right. Madison Blake didn't have a scar. But apparently, there's this new con artist in town who's taken her place. This one has a scar—that's what Sheriff Bolton told my father—so I thought the person you saw could've been her."

"No scar," Dylan says.

Tripp eases back into his seat, picking up his fork again.

"Pretty sure it was Madison," Dylan continues. "She

wasn't too happy to open that box and find it empty." His voice is easy and assured. But I glance down to find his free hand gripping the hem of the tablecloth as if for dear life.

I understand how he feels. My own hands are clammy. My coffee is burning an acidic hole in my gut.

Tripp gave up a very important detail, only it wasn't about some new con artist in town. He gave up a detail about Madison Blake.

As of last summer, she was sporting a new scar down one side of her face.

Just like someone else we know.

26

After breakfast, Dylan and I hop in the truck and book it out to Devil's Den.

"This entire time," I say, still trying to wrap my head around it, "Madison has actually been alive?"

"Posing as her best friend, Britta," Dylan says. "Madison must've hidden up in the Den, knowing Tripp would never show up there."

"He seemed petrified by the idea that Madison Blake might still be around."

"Because of what he did to her," Dylan grits out, pounding a fist over the steering wheel. "That scar? Madison didn't have it before she went missing. It wasn't in any of her photos."

I nod. "Because Tripp did it to her with that bottle. Audrey witnessed it. She must've tried to go forward with what she saw that night, and Tripp caught her." *Just like Kurt warned her*, I think with a shiver. "If we can get Madison to tell Detective Ferrera what really happened, they'll have to look into the

Tripp lead. Clearwater Ridge royalty or not, that bastard had a motive to hurt Audrey."

We reach the familiar rugged path that winds up the mountain. Before leaving the club, we debated calling the Al's Mart number. But we couldn't risk spooking Madison. Plus, part of me needs to look her in the eye again. To see whatever I missed the last time we were in the Den. If that girl was really Madison Blake, she did quite a job making herself look like someone else.

After parking in the tiny lot in front of Al's Mart, we race inside. To my dismay, the blond clerk with the scar—Britta, Madison, whoever the hell she is—isn't behind the desk. Instead, there's another girl, this one's hair dyed black with red streaks. Like the first clerk, her name tag says *Britta*, and she's wearing a full face of makeup.

For a moment, I wonder if it could be the same girl. If she somehow managed to cover the scar and change her hair.

But we get closer, and I note that unlike the first clerk with the thin ovular face, this one's cheeks are full and round.

I had my whole shakedown ready in the truck. Now, I'm at a loss for words. I look to Dylan and back to the girl, who's now on her phone, typing out a text.

She glances up, meeting my eye, and an uneasy sensation squirms through me.

Something's wrong.

A faint *ding*, a phone alert, sounds from behind a closed door off to my right, and I move toward it. "Dylan, stay here with her." My ears hum and my skin buzzes as a sense of hyper-alertness takes over. I open the door, heading through it as the desk clerk begins to shout after me.

"Hey! You can't go back there!"

But I'm already inside. It's dark, but I catch a wink of sunlight before everything returns to pitch black.

I rush toward that vanishing flash of light, feeling my way along the wall until I find a doorknob. Giving it a twist, I wrench open the hidden door and burst into the blinding sunlight.

I squint, making out the figure of a girl in the tall grass behind the mart. She sprints toward the tree line, blond hair whipping in her wake.

I pick up my speed. "Madison, wait!"

She's about to slip into the thick woods, and my heartbeat falters.

But the moment before I lose her for good, the girl stops. Her back is to me, wisps of hair settling and fists curled at both sides. Stomping her boot, she curses under her breath.

Then she spins around, that scar I saw the other day—the one Tripp drew down his own face with an index finger—on full display now. "Why the hell couldn't you let this go?"

"Because my best friend is missing." I gesture back to the mart. "I know your friend Britta can relate." I move toward the girl with the cautious gait of a hunter stalking prey. "Look, I'm only trying to understand what's going on. Please, talk to me."

Shoulders hunched, Madison takes a step in my direction and slumps down in the grass. I inch closer, making out the dark roots at her scalp that I must've missed the first time we spoke.

But the girl in front of me exudes none of the carefree grace I witnessed when she danced at the Summer Kickoff, nor the radiant glow from that photo in her mother's living room. Even up close, it's hard to believe that *this* is Madison Blake. The sharp planes of her face don't match the soft curves from that photo. "Guessing I don't have a choice in the matter."

"I know you want to help me." I venture closer yet, kicking a rock aside to create a bare patch of land before sitting down in front of her.

"Yeah? How do you figure?"

"You warned me about Tripp. You could've blown me off yesterday, but you told me to stay away from him."

"And I hope to god you listened."

"He seemed pretty convinced you weren't around," I say, feeling like my every word could detonate. "Madison, what did he do to you?"

At this, her eyes widen. "Oh my god, you—you didn't tell him I'm alive." Her breath comes in shallow, labored rasps. "Please, please, say you didn't tell him."

"We didn't tell him," I assure her, reaching out like I'm trying to console a friend before remembering that she's a stranger. Shame sweeps through me; we might not have blown her secret, but in trying to poke Tripp for answers, we came dangerously close. Our invented grifter, Carloyn, didn't have a scar, so she couldn't have been Madison. This detail seemed to put Tripp's mind at ease. "He thinks you're dead?"

The grass rustles behind me. "Everything okay, Maddie?" Britta asks, approaching us slowly. Dylan is a few feet behind her, equally cautious as he treads closer.

Madison's fingers move to her temples, pressing until the pink skin blanches white. "I have no idea. Depends on what these two idiots did."

They join us in the grass, Dylan at my side and Britta across from him. It's like a campfire circle in the weeds.

"We know you dated him as Rose Lambert," I say. "We know he cut you with a bottle and dragged you outside his house the night of the party. I'm guessing he figured out your game and wasn't too pleased."

She lets out a sharp laugh. "That's an understatement. How do you know he cut me?"

"Audrey saw," Dylan says. "Her ex-boyfriend Kurt said she witnessed the attack and wanted to help, but he convinced her not to. Audrey didn't give up though. She spent all last summer trying to track you down, and we're pretty sure that's what got her…"

"Killed," Madison finishes, sending a chill up my spine. "I swear, I had no idea. I never even met Audrey face-to-face. She wired me the money for the horse, but to an anonymous account. I figured we were done. If I knew she was putting herself in danger because of me, I would've…"

She trails off, and beside her, Britta makes a face. "Like you told me, a whole year after you disappeared."

"I *apologized* to you," Madison says, eyes gleaming in the sunlight. "Look"—she turns to us now—"I had to make it believable. I had to make sure *no one* was in the loop. Not Britta, not even my own mother. Because if Tripp and his father came knocking, everyone involved had to sell it. Everyone had to believe that he'd succeeded in getting rid of me."

"What happened, Madison?" I ask. "Tripp really liked you, didn't he?"

Taking a long breath, she yanks a blade of grass up by the

roots. "I don't know how he figured it out. But at that party, he lured me into the laundry room, saying it was the best make-out room in the house and that I looked so hot in my dress."

I picture it, the short white dress that twirled as she danced.

"But I never even got inside the room. He was behind me when I heard the sound of the glass shattering. When I turned to look, he sliced my face open with the broken bottle." Her hand darts to the scar, fingers following the jagged, puckered path it takes from her temple down to the corner of her mouth.

"Kurt said he forced you outside," I say softly.

She nods. "He was trying to throw me out. Out of the party, out of his life. He dragged me to the woods behind his house and told me to get lost. But I was so"—she grits her teeth—"*angry* that he cut me. That he'd ruined my face. So I fought back, and not with my fists." She lets out a soft, bitter noise. "I aimed for that massive ego. I laughed at him, made fun of how gullible he'd been. Told him I'd never had as much success with any guy as I'd had with him."

Her eyes lower. "And it worked. Too well. His entire face turned all red and...twisted, and he punched me in the stomach. Knocked the wind out of me. I remember him raising the bottle again, over my head. Then everything went black."

I shiver at the image. "You can't remember anything else?"

She stares down at the grass. "I think I woke up in the car, but I couldn't see. It was too dark, like I was in his trunk or blindfolded. But my face and head hurt so much, I couldn't tell. When I tried to breathe, the scent of my own blood hit me hard. And there was something else—a sweaty, grassy scent that mixed with the blood."

Tripp's golf stuff. Dylan says he plays three times a week. Even if he didn't leave the equipment in the trunk, that smell would linger.

"I woke up the next day on the shore of the river. I had no idea what time it was or where I'd ended up. There were bruises everywhere—not just on my head. My ankle was sprained, my arms and legs were sliced up. For months, there was an imprint of his football ring on my stomach." She lifts her shirt, showing a faint blossom that could be anything at this point. "I think he tossed me into the river, assuming I was either dead or would be soon. My arms were bound in that trunk, you know? I mean, I was unconscious. I should've drowned." She clears her throat. "But somehow, I ended up on land."

"He tried to murder you," I breathe, struggling to understand how any human—much less someone I know—could do this to another human. "But he failed. You fought."

"He succeeded at one thing," she spits, pointing at her scar. "He left me completely disfigured."

"You never went to the police?"

"And say what? I'd stolen thousands of dollars in fake tuition, and surprisingly, my mark was unhappy about it?"

"You might've done time," I say, "but at least Tripp would be in prison for what he did. Now Audrey is missing, maybe even dead."

"Are you delusional?" She lets out a harsh laugh. "Tripp Shaw wouldn't be in prison! Why do you think they pulled the plug on my investigation?"

"Your mother said you called her," Dylan says hesitantly, "and told her you were fine."

Madison nods maniacally. "Oh, yeah, I called her. By then, *somebody* had already offered her a hundred grand to tell Sheriff Bolton she'd made a mistake. To say that I'd run away."

"And she took it?" I ask in horror. "Your mother just... took the bribe?"

"Not at first." Madison glares at me. "But once I called and she told me everything, I convinced her to take it. Why not get something out of the Shaws, after everything *golden child* Tripp had done to me? If anyone asked, she was supposed to say that I'd gone somewhere far off and secret. She'd heard from me on unfamiliar, untraceable numbers."

"So then," Dylan says, frowning, "why are you here? If you were scared for your life, why didn't you stay hidden?"

"The same reason I run cons in the first place," she says, the fire in her voice suddenly dwindling. "My mom." Her lips tremble, and for a moment, I'm afraid she's shutting down.

But she clears her throat, channeling her sadness into something else. Something that causes a tightening of her jaw and a fierce spark in her eyes. "She's all I have, and two years ago, she was diagnosed with lung cancer. The second my dad found out, he split. Just left us both. Mom can't work full-time anymore. The treatments leave her too weak. So, she lost her medical insurance, and now her bills are completely out of control. I had to help her."

I picture Delilah Blake in her living room, thinning hair tucked beneath a long scarf. The dull skin that had been covered by makeup in the hotel lobby. The scent of cigarette smoke, the sooty remains in the ashtray. Her frailness as she walked us to the door. The rattling cough she couldn't control.

Audrey may have been one of Madison's first—if not *the*

first—targets. All because a woman got sick, her husband bailed, and a young girl was left on her own to deal with the fallout.

"What about the hundred grand?" Dylan asks. "Couldn't your mother have paid someone to take care of her?"

Madison offers him a patronizing grin. "One hundred grand sounds like a lot until you get cancer—especially if you've been battling for two years, like my mom. Without me, she'll stop seeking treatment, quit the meds. She'll let herself die alone."

I think back on everything Madison's mother said about her daughter. *I hate to think this about my own child, but it seemed like she was either in trouble or about to be. I hear the whispers in town, and sadly, I think those people are right. Madison went somewhere else, to try her old tricks on new people.* Woven in were some morsels of truth, no doubt. She must wish her daughter had an honest, respectable career, rather than the one she's chosen.

But most of what Delilah Blake said was a lie. She said all of it to protect a daughter who's sacrificing everything to save her.

Sadness creeps in, suffocatingly thick. They've both gone to such lengths to save each other, and yet, Delilah hasn't tried to save herself. She hasn't managed to quit the thing that could kill her.

"And you thought no one would recognize you in the Den?" Dylan asks. "Where have you been staying?"

"She's staying at my place for now," Britta says.

"So yesterday," I say, thinking back to when I sat in the truck, desperate for answers, "when I called the mart, it was *you* who answered?"

Britta nods. "Gave you my number too. I had to track Maddie down and show her the photo. You should've seen her face." Britta wraps her arms around herself, though it's a scorching ninety degrees here in the sun. "I never should've let her work some of my shifts. It's just...no one who knows me ever stops here. There's a bigger mart up the road, closer to the housing tract. This place only ever draws the kind of people who aren't in any position to talk to the cops. Sometimes the occasional lost traveler or, well, *you*. When Madison's cons failed, she needed money to pay for her mom's next treatment. Ever since my grandpa left me this place, I've had errands to run, shelves to stock, and no money to hire another employee. So I figured we could hide Maddie here for a bit, she could work, and it would be a win-win."

My arm tickles, and I brush something I hope isn't a tick off into the grass. "Everyone we've spoken to says you were adamant that Madison was missing."

"That's why she came to me in the first place," Britta says. "A couple weeks ago. I nearly had a heart attack, mostly because she didn't look like my friend anymore. But she had Maddie's voice, and"—a dry laugh escapes—"Maddie's attitude. She said if I didn't shut my mouth, I was going to get us both killed."

"So you really thought she was dead," Dylan says.

"I mourned her," she says, voice breaking. "Everyone else kept saying she was fine, but I was crying myself to sleep. Now, I understand why she had to do it."

"Britta, did the Shaws ever offer you any money to keep quiet?" I ask her. "Because that would be huge, if we could—"

"No." She shakes her head. "I don't think they were ever very worried about me. When you come from the Den, your voice doesn't hold much weight. Not against the likes of the Shaws."

"Well, do you think your mom would come with us to the cops?" I ask, turning to Madison.

"Cops?" Her mouth drops open. "Are you—no way!"

"Please." I don't want to beg, but what choice do I have? Getting the Blakes on our side is our last hope. "We have to make a strong case against Tripp."

"He thinks I'm dead," Madison snaps. "Why would I do a single thing to change that?"

"Because he did something to Audrey. She tried to help you. She knew you were in trouble, and she did everything she could to find you. And then, when she went to the wrong person with the truth…I don't know. I'm hoping she fled. But what if he hurt her? What if she's still out there, and Tripp has answers? You'd really let him get away with whatever he did to her? With what he did to *you*?"

"It's too risky. His dad has the whole sheriff's department in his pocket. You think my mom was the only person that man paid off?"

"No," Dylan says. "That's why we need your help. You can tell your story. Get them to question Tripp about my sister."

Madison yanks out another blade of grass and shreds it, string by string. I understand her hesitation, and yet, part of me wants to reach over and slap that blade out of her hand. Audrey's life is on the line here.

Finally, she sighs, letting the decimated grass blow with her breath. "I may have taken photos of my injuries."

"You what?" My heart leaps in my chest.

"I don't know why. Thought I might need them." She licks her chapped lips and navigates through her phone. "Maybe I hoped that one day, there'd be a way to get this son of a bitch." Wincing, she hands it over.

I flip through the photos, my insides turning at what I'm seeing. The slash on Madison's face, oozing with infection after she was left to die in the river overnight. I pause on an image that's zoomed in on two parallel red lines on her wrist. "Is this from where he bound your hands?"

She nods gravely. "One of the marks is. The other is from my bracelet. It must've snagged on a branch or something in the river and gotten yanked off."

I continue flipping through, resisting the urge to look away. Madison's body took a severe beating—both from Tripp and the rocks. There are cuts, scrapes, and bruises covering nearly every inch of her.

When I get to the photo of Madison's stomach, I stop. "This is what we need," I say, my heartbeat kicking up.

Blooming vibrant purple and blue, Madison's bruise matches a very particular shape.

It's a football. Exactly like the one on Tripp's championship football ring.

THE GIRL

The girl awakened in a sea of white.

For the splinter of a moment, as streams of bright light punctured her vision, she wondered if this was heaven.

But she rubbed her eyes and forced herself upright, discovering it was merely a bedroom with crisp white walls and bed linens. Sunlight played through the slits in the window blinds. A dull ache started up behind her eyes, and when she touched a decorative pillow, her finger sank into it. The girl was very much alive.

As she yawned and stretched, the memory of the previous night began to stitch itself together. The boy had given her wine, but it was laced with something. Dread spiked in her chest. She pulled back the sheets to reveal a nightgown, silky and pure as a lily petal—one she couldn't remember putting on. Frantically, her gaze combed the room in search of her belongings.

She had to get out of this house.

Before the girl could climb down from the bed, there was

a knock at the door. Panic tore through her. The knob turned slowly, the boy's clean-shaven face appearing in the sliver. "You awake?"

The girl attempted to smile. "Just woke up."

"You must be feeling pretty lousy." He pushed the door open and stepped into the room. "Was that your first time drinking so much red wine?"

The girl only remembered drinking half a glass. "Did I drink a lot?"

He chuckled. "Here." As he stepped closer, it took every ounce of the girl's willpower not to flinch. But he merely set two painkillers and a glass of water on the bedside table—the white bedside table. It was then that the girl realized how very strange the room was. Almost like a child's room, though the boy was nearly grown.

The girl eyed the glass of water. She was starting to doubt her own memories. But if they were real, she couldn't trust a drop of anything he gave her.

"I want you to know," the boy said, "I called in that favor to my friend in the sheriff's department. He's going to handle everything." He smiled, and it was the same smile that had won her over weeks earlier. It was the smile that had drawn her to him, that made her heart hurt with longing.

But here in this stark white room, the smile made the girl's skin crawl. She knew the boy had never called anyone to help her. It was a lie. "Thank you. I really appreciate it." She got down from the bed, locating her clothes, which were slung over the armrest of a creamy wingback chair. "You'll let me know what he says, right? I should be going."

"Oh?" The boy pressed deeper into the room, his figure casting a large shadow over the bright wall.

The girl glanced down at her nightgown, snowy white like lamb's fleece.

On the wall, the shadow shifted. It stalked forward, long arms stretching as it overtook the girl, swallowing her whole.

A beast, devouring the lamb.

27

PAIGE

Dylan and I are in the kitchen making popcorn when we get the news.

"Tripp Shaw has been arrested on charges of attempted homicide." Mr. Covington's expression is a tangle of relief, shock, and fear.

"And they can tie him to Audrey?" Dylan asks.

"Tripp is a person of interest in her disappearance," Mr. Covington confirms.

We're hearing this before everyone else—before the news crews and the town of Clearwater Ridge. Detective Ferrera wants the Covington family to be the first to know that our account has been taken seriously.

And it was all thanks to Madison Blake and her mother coming forward.

Madison is nervous. Not just about her own crimes against the Clearwater Ridge folk, but that her mother will be charged for accepting the bribe and hiding Tripp's crime. But the detective assured her that none of that is on their radar at the moment. Right now, they're attempting to trace Audrey's burner phone—to see if 4477 is someone else who may have answers.

Most important of all, they're attempting to find out what Tripp knows about Audrey.

Dylan and I had some explaining to do about the burner phone and how we'd figured out Madison's part in all of this. We told the truth, mostly: we were worried about Audrey. We were sorry we didn't go forward earlier, but we feared the authorities couldn't be trusted.

And they couldn't be. At least, not the Crown County Sheriff's Department. We can only hope that the detective isn't involved in the Shaws' cover-up. That part of her work here is to dig up the bad seeds and toss them out.

"Kurt spoke to Ferrera as well," Mr. Covington says. "He admitted to being your informant regarding that party in the Pines."

I share a look of relief with Dylan. We kept Kurt's name out of our account, which made our story rather flimsy. But Dylan texted Kurt, letting him know we were going to talk and giving him one last chance to do the right thing. It looks like he finally took it.

"Will they offer Tripp a deal?" I ask.

Mr. Covington nods. "If it comes to that. The detective spoke of lowering the charge to attempted manslaughter *if* he pleads guilty and tells us where to find Audrey."

"Why manslaughter?" I ask. "That hardly seems fair."

"If everything happened the way you two pieced it together,

Tripp attacked Madison in a fit of rage. He'd just learned that he'd been duped by someone he had strong feelings for."

Still, it isn't justice. We don't know what that maniac did to Audrey.

"So now, we wait," Dylan says. He pushes the bowl of popcorn toward his dad, who declines, reaching instead for the whiskey bottle in the cabinet. He pulls down a glass, filling it halfway.

The poor man's face is pale and vacant as he stares out the window, then tips back the caramel-colored liquid. "Yeah, we wait." Finished, he sets the glass on the counter and wanders out of the room.

Dylan takes a seat on one of the barstools, the popcorn bowl before him untouched. "Wow."

"We've got him." I move behind him, resting my hands on his shoulders.

"Maybe. Just remember that we're dealing with the Shaws."

I know what he means. Kurt made it sound like the Shaws had done worse in the past. Tripp's dad isn't likely to let him throw in the towel and take the deal. His every instinct will be to save his son and attempt to restore the family's good name.

He'll put up a fight.

———

It's dark when the doorbell rings.

The house has been quiet since we got word of Tripp's arrest. Everyone's been on edge, waiting on news. I don't think anyone expected Detective Ferrera to show up on the Covingtons' doorstep in person at this time of night.

From the look on her face, I can tell it's bad news.

Mrs. Covington must see it too because she lets out a sob and buries her head in her husband's chest.

My heart stops. But before I can figure out how to process anything, Detective Ferrera shakes her head. "It's not Audrey," she says from the porch.

Dylan finally pushes past everyone congregated in the foyer to motion her inside.

"It's—we didn't get the answers we'd hoped for out of Tripp Shaw."

"He didn't tell you what happened to Audrey?" Dylan leads her to the living room, offering her the couch. Everyone else trickles in, the Covingtons taking the far end of the couch, my parents the formal chairs near the doorway. Lucy and Nate join us last, lowering onto the rug. I stay standing, feeling Dylan's warm fingers thread through mine. Lightly, I squeeze back, a silent assurance that this time, we face it all together.

Detective Ferrera looks tired. The makeup beneath her eyes is smudged, and her always-slick bun is loose and disheveled. More than that, though, she looks defeated. I always got the sense that easing up on this case wasn't her choice. Today, she wanted to believe we had answers about Audrey almost as much as we did. "No," she says finally.

"That son of a—" Mr. Covington snarls, but the detective cuts him off.

"I don't think Tripp knows where Audrey is," she says. "He claims he had nothing to do with her disappearance. He's willing to take a polygraph."

"So his father can pay the examiner to fake the results," Mr. Covington spits.

"I assure you, this investigation as well as Madison Blake's are now in my hands."

Mrs. Covington sniffles beside her husband. "Why do you believe him?"

"Because I've been doing this for twenty years," the detective says. "Tripp may not be a good kid. He had a very violent response to finding out about Madison. But I don't think he's lying about this."

"What did he say about Madison?" I ask timidly, knowing it isn't my place to ask questions here. "Will he at least go down for attempted murder?"

"Well, that's the other thing." The detective stares at her lap, pressing the pleats of the navy blue fabric with her palm, like she's trying to iron them out. "He claims he never moved Madison from the woods behind his house."

"What?" It's Dylan who shouts now, dropping my hand to take two large strides into the room.

The detective lifts a hand. "His story matches Kurt Winfield's to the letter. Tripp claims he cut Madison's face with the broken bottle and then pulled her outside to the woods. But that's where the story differs from what we all assumed went down. Tripp says he only intended to hurt her a little, just enough to run her out of town. But he never meant to knock her unconscious with that bottle."

She takes a deep breath, letting it out slowly, as if that will defuse the tension in the room. "When Madison didn't wake up, Tripp panicked. He left her there in the woods and went back inside to the party. He swears he never returned to the woods until he woke up the next morning. And that's when he discovered she was gone. Since she failed to turn up again and was reported missing, he assumed his plan had worked—that she'd been scared enough to disappear."

"Let me get this straight," Dylan says animatedly. "Tripp admits to beating her to a pulp, so badly that she's disfigured—unrecognizable even." Dylan's face is red, and he's inching so close to the detective that I move to tug him back toward me. "Sorry, sorry," he says, pressing his index fingers to his temples. "He admits to doing all of that, but *not* to trying to drown her in the river."

"Not to driving her to the river nor to dumping her in the river," Ferrera says. "Tripp claims Madison was unconscious but very much alive and breathing when he abandoned her."

"How is that any different?" I ask. "Those blows could've easily killed her. He just went to sleep? Knowing a girl was unconscious in the woods?"

"We still may have a case," the detective says in a dubious tone. "It would've been easier, obviously, if he'd copped to dumping her body in the river."

"So, you think he's telling the truth about Audrey, but not about Madison?" Mr. Covington asks, throwing a hand up. "I'm sorry, but I'm lost."

"No, no." The detective runs a hand through the wisps of hairs that hang loose around her face. "I don't know how to explain it, but he sounded truthful regarding both accounts."

"But he's not being truthful," Dylan snaps. "He's lying. He wanted Madison dead because she made a fool out of him.

Shaws don't lose. No one steals from *them*, uses *them*. Tripp couldn't let her get away with it, so he tried to kill her. This whole time, he thought she was dead! He had his father do everything in his power to make sure nobody tried to find the body."

"If Tripp's lying," the detective says, "the truth will out. We have investigators checking his trunk for Madison's DNA."

A wave of nausea runs through me. I picture Tripp stuffing Madison's body—unconscious yet clinging to life—in his trunk. Her waking up in excruciating pain to inhale the scent of Tripp's golf gear mixed with her own blood.

"He'll have wiped it by now," Mr. Covington says. "It's been a year."

The detective gives a vague head tilt. "In the morning, we'll start by checking out Tripp's alibi."

"Alibi?" Dylan asks.

"I can't elaborate yet. Let me check it out, and then we'll see if he was only bluffing about the polygraph."

"But what about Audrey?" Mrs. Covington asks. "What about *my* daughter? You've mentioned this Madison girl over and over again—trying to prove what Tripp did to this"—her mouth contorts into a grimace—"*lowlife.*" A prickling heat rushes over the back of my neck. "I want to know how you're going to find my daughter. Is it possible that this is all just another dead end?"

"I don't see how it could be," Detective Ferrera says, a twitch in her right eye the only crack in her composure. "Tripp denies having communicated with Audrey through a burner phone. As of now, we know where both phones were purchased. The next step is attempting to learn *who* purchased them. We will, of course, check for evidence of Audrey's DNA in the car." The detective picks herself up from the couch. "At this time, however, we simply don't know how all of this relates to your daughter."

28

Deep down, we all knew Tripp's car would be clean. It still feels like a blow to the gut.

Mrs. Covington breaks down and has to be carried upstairs by her husband for a "lie-down."

When Mr. Covington returns looking haggard and weary, he asks Dylan and me to have a seat in the dining room. He checks that the coast is clear and shuts the door. "I trust everyone to keep these things quiet, but the detective worries that some detail could leak to the media and interfere with the case. She mentioned something else on the phone—I haven't told Eleanor yet. But this bullshit alibi Tripp fed the cops has apparently checked out."

It's like having a brick dropped onto my chest.

"What was the alibi?" Dylan asks, clutching the edge of the table.

"He claimed that, in addition to a party full of people who can account for his whereabouts, three kids stayed over until late the next morning. He never left their sight long enough to load a body into the car and drive her to the river."

I arch a brow because this all sounds bogus. These kids would've fallen asleep at some point. "What if Tripp drove Madison out in the morning?"

"I asked about that. Investigators got a rough timeline from Madison. She limped a mile into town and saw that it was nine forty-five a.m. on the town square clock." He picks at his graying hair in exasperation. "There's just no way to swing it. Madison would've already been awake at the river by the time these kids left Tripp's house.

"Anyway," Mr. Covington continues, "all three kids corroborated the account, and one kid confirmed actually having eyes on Tripp the entire night. He said he was on something that kept him up all night, and Tripp never left the house."

"That kid lied," Dylan says, pounding a fist against the table. "Tripp did what he's done all along—paid someone else to parrot his story."

"Who are the kids?" I ask.

Mr. Covington shakes his head. "Ferrera couldn't give me any names."

"This is unbelievable," Dylan spits. "We *had* him."

"It'll go to court," Mr. Covington says. "But if Tripp's not even willing to budge on this for a lighter sentence, he's never going to tell us what he did to Audrey." He wipes an eye and stands, shoulders slumped in defeat. "I'd better go check on Eleanor."

"Is there anything she needs?" I ask, wanting to be useful. "Some tea, maybe?" This whole situation has me feeling helpless.

"That'd be nice. Thanks, Paige."

Dylan and I move to the kitchen. While I start the kettle, he pulls a bottle of rum from the liquor cabinet.

"What are you doing?" I ask, searching for the tea bags.

"We both know she doesn't want tea," he answers, grabbing a lime from the fruit bowl. "Unless it's Long Island."

Great. So I'm useless, even at this. "Maybe we can find out who these three kids are," I suggest. "We know Madison had more marks in town. Maybe Tripp chose other guys who wanted to punish her."

"Maybe," Dylan says. "I think I just…need to clear my head of all of this for today. It's too much."

"I get it," I say. We both need a break. Our heads are anything but clear at this point. Detective Ferrera is doing the best she can. If she tracks down whoever purchased those burner phones, we'll have a sparkly new lead.

He runs the knife steadily along the lime. "I'd like five minutes alone with Tripp," he grumbles, pouring the rum next. Finished, he slams the bottle onto the granite so hard that I flinch. "Just five. I'm sure I'd be able to make him talk."

"Hey, hey." I move behind him, wrapping my arms around his waist. "This isn't you. How about you take that up to your mom and then we'll go for a drive?"

"I don't know, Paige," he says, continuing to mix the drink. "I'm not sure anything's going to help." He takes the glass and, shrugging off my arm, skulks across the kitchen.

"Don't do this again, Dylan," I say, still facing the window where he left me. "Don't push me away."

There's no response. Only the sound of his footsteps trailing off down the hall.

I start to clean up the mess he left on the counter, returning the rum to the cabinet. As I'm wiping the granite clean, I hear his voice behind me. "I'm sorry."

I turn to face him, wet sponge still in hand. "I know. But I'm not letting you do this again."

Dylan shuts his eyes. "I can't believe he actually wrangled his way out of this. I was so sure we had him."

The defeat in his voice, the slump of his shoulders—it presses on my chest. "And we still might." I toss the dripping sponge back onto the counter and walk into his arms.

"Even if we don't," he says, chin dusting my head, "I won't shut down. We're a team."

I look up at him, meeting his eyes. "Dylan, talk to me. You know I understand." For the first time this year, I start to say the thing I've kept buttoned up inside. "Last summer..." I start to backtrack, fear creeping back in and clogging my throat.

I force the fear out, along with the words. "Last summer you pulled away. You said it had nothing to do with Hannah. So what was it?"

Dylan looks shocked and then slightly annoyed. "Nothing, Paige. There was nothing."

"Then why? I needed you, and you needed me. So why did you shut me out? Why does it feel like you're doing it again?"

Dylan pulls back, his face darkening. "Paige, I don't want to—"

"I need to know, Dylan. You're upset about Audrey. I get that. But why do you always choose to go through it alone? No one deserves that. No one—"

"*I* deserve it!" he snaps, spinning away and grabbing his head. "I deserve to go through it alone because it was my fault! Okay? Is that the answer you were searching for?"

"What? No, Dylan. Audrey's disappearance wasn't your fault." I reach out to touch him, but he jerks free.

"She tried to talk to me," he says, voice raw. "Audrey. That conversation I got caught up in when I left the pool room? That was her. She came and asked me to help her with something the night of the party, and I refused."

"What?" My voice barely rises over the sound of the ice maker. "Why?"

"I wanted to be with you." He turns enough for me to see his face, twisted with grief.

I try to make sense of his words. But it's like they're shifting and floating around, rearranging themselves.

"Audrey was always against us," he says. "I know you saw it too. I figured it was some ploy to get me away from you the second she spotted us happy together. So I basically shook her off me and told her to get lost."

My breath hitches. How could he have been so coldhearted?

Then I remember my own skepticism toward Audrey during the party. In fact, I'd been so worried that she would pull something to ruin that night, if she'd asked me for help, I may not have bought it either.

Dylan leans an elbow on the bar top, fingers threaded through his hair. "My little sister counted on me to help her, and I didn't. I blew her off to be with you."

I think back to our phone call with Hannah, to the horror on Dylan's face when she told us everything had started the night of the party. Was that the moment he realized the true consequence of his decision?

"If I hadn't been so selfish, this would've all gone differently. I'd have known exactly what Audrey was doing last summer. But the truth is, I didn't care. Not even after the party. She wasn't talking to you, which meant I got you all to myself. I think I *liked* that she wasn't around all summer."

My legs start to go numb, and I reach for the barstool to steady myself.

"When Audrey went missing…it didn't seem right being with you. I didn't deserve to be happy. Not when I could've stopped everything."

"You made a mistake," I say quietly. But on the inside, I'm raging. The only thing I wanted all summer was for Audrey to confide in me. Instead, she chose to confide in her brother, who turned her away.

No wonder Audrey tried to handle it all on her own. I want to get off this stool and march out of here. To abandon him, the way he abandoned Audrey.

But what would that make me? Here he is, trusting me with this horrible secret that he's kept to himself all this time. If I reject him for it, I'm no better. "You made a mistake," I repeat, reaching for his hand now. "I forgive you. But I think what you really need is to forgive yourself."

He squeezes back, shaking his head. His eyes flood with tears that make my chest sore and tight. "No," he says. "That's not what I need." He inhales, a horrible sound that's both a breath and a cry. "I need *Audrey's* forgiveness. I need my sister to come back, so she can give it to me herself."

All I can do is hold him. All I can do is wipe his tears with my fingers, run my hand over his back, kiss his cheek. Allow my touch to remind him that he is loved.

Because the thing he needs—I don't believe it can ever happen.

Audrey isn't coming home.

29

In the evening, Dylan and I watch the stars on the back deck. We listen to the distant hum of the river and owl's call, high overhead. I try to get him talking about orientation, to get his mind off of everything. It works a little. Despite everything he's gone through the past two weeks—the past year—deep down, he should still be excited to head off to college.

I don't tell him what I overheard my dad whisper to my mother earlier today: "I think it's time to go back home and give them some space."

I can't blame my dad. The air inside the Covingtons' house feels so taut and brittle. It's almost worse than last year. At least then, we all believed Audrey might return. We were on edge, but hoping that the stillness would be broken by the sound of her footsteps in the doorway. Her voice in the foyer. A phone call with good news.

Now we're waiting on a different type of call. The one that says all hope is lost forever.

Mom thinks we should be here, helping the Covingtons through everything. But I'm not so sure anymore. As much as I hate to leave Dylan, it feels like we're in the way. And the guilt weighs heavy; I presented Tripp Shaw like some neatly wrapped gift, the answer to all of their questions about Audrey. I gave the Covingtons hope, only for it to be snatched away.

Dylan finishes off his beer, and I hand over the one I've merely been peeling the label from. When his phone buzzes, he reads the message with a sigh, then passes it over to me. "Guess the cat's out of the bag."

I take it and read.

> **Brent Haywood:** you hear about Tripp? He tried to murder Madison Blake?

Dylan takes the phone back, typing out a message as I lean over to watch. Yeah, I heard

> **BH:** Did they ask to interview you too?
> **Dylan Covington:** Yep, everyone who was at last year's Kickoff
> **BH:** Mine's tomorrow. I'm going to vouch for my boy. There's no way T did this

Dylan lets out a low growl. "Not helping our case, buddy." But before he can text a response, there's another buzz.

> **BH:** Soccer Saturday?

"That guy's relentless," I say. "He just wants to show you up at something, since you always lap him in the pool."

Dylan runs a hand over the back of his neck. "Maybe it would be good for us. We could run off some of our frustrations."

"And I hear it's a contact sport." I grin. "So we can kick out a few frustrations on people's shins, instead of smacking rum bottles against expensive countertops."

He side-eyes me. "I'm in if you're in."

———

The weekly pickup game is located at a lovely park with bright green grass that looks like it gets watered three times a week, even in a drought.

I'm wearing running shorts, a tank top, and long socks like the players do on TV. Except my socks are really just knee-highs with little birds on them that I borrowed from Lucy.

Brent is lending us a couple pairs of cleats. He drops them on the grass in front of us. "I'm making sure we're on the same team, Paige," he says. "Gotta keep the two MVPs from the winning tennis volleyball water polo team together."

"That we do," I say, taking the smaller pair of cleats, which is still a size too big.

"Traitor," Dylan says, play hitting my arm. "You would turn against me, just like that?"

"He's a real soccer player, so yes. In a heartbeat."

Brent laughs. "We'll pick teams in a few."

He heads over to practice shooting on the goalkeeper, and I whisper to Dylan, "Aren't we supposed to get little shields for our shins?"

He gestures to a girl who's warming up with bare legs. "It's a pickup game, not the World Cup. I think we're fine."

"So I'll politely ask the other team not to kick me in the shins."

"Exactly." He stands and starts to run in place. "Want to pass the ball around? Get a little practice in?"

"I mean, how hard can it be? It's like water polo, only with your feet. And, like, without the water."

Dylan goes off to borrow a ball and then returns, dribbling toward me. I start to jog backward into the open space. "Pass it," I say, waving my arms.

He does, harder than I was expecting. I sprint to where it's headed, leaping with my foot extended to block it.

But my foot wobbles in the too-big cleat. A burst of pain shoots from my ankle up the side of my leg. I cry out, and before I know it, my entire body crashes into the grass.

"Paige!" Dylan rushes over, crouching beside me.

"Ouch," I say, rolling over to grab my ankle.

"You twisted it. It just—" He makes a diving motion with a hand. "This is not good."

Brent hustles toward us now, stopping to bend over and inspect my ankle. "What the hell, Paige? The game hasn't even started yet."

"These limbs aren't what they were in my youth," I groan.

"Let's get her to my place," Brent says. "I'll pull the car closer." He hurries to the parking lot while Dylan takes a look at my ankle.

Gently, he unlaces the cleat, loosening it enough to wiggle it off. The second he touches my sock, I slap his hand. "The sock stays. I think it's keeping all the inside stuff…inside."

"That doesn't sound good. And it's not the only place you're banged up." He points to my elbow.

Sure enough, my elbow and the side of my leg are skinned and bleeding from the fall. "Soccer is a *brutal* sport."

"I don't think what you did actually counts as soccer. Can you walk?"

"Maybe?"

He helps me up. When I put the slightest pressure on my foot, pain rockets through me again. "On second thought, no. Cannot walk."

"Don't step down on it," he says, looping my arm around the back of his neck. I use him as a human crutch, hopping on my one remaining cleat through the grass until a sparkling black Tesla pulls up.

Brent gets out, quickly jogging over to shout goodbye at the rest of the group. Dylan helps me inside, propping my foot up on the back seat. "Sure you don't want to stay?" I ask when Brent dives back into the driver's seat. "Dylan can take me back to his house."

"Or to a hospital," Dylan says, still holding the open door. "Looks pretty swollen."

Brent shuts his own door and turns on the ignition. "We might be able to avoid the hospital if we get some ice on it, ASAP."

"Fine, but you're not touching the bird sock. It's part of me now."

"What if it's broken?" Dylan asks.

Brent shrugs. "Sprains can swell up pretty bad. Let's see how it goes. Grab your truck and meet us at the house. Oh, but pick up some ibuprofen first. I used up the last of ours this morning." He leans back, with his elbow on the armrest. "Went a little too hard with the old man's bourbon."

Dylan nods, his concerned eyes on me for another beat before he shuts the door.

Brent shifts the car into drive, and we take off through the parking lot and onto the road, each little bump sending a new wave of pain through my ankle. I shut my eyes and focus on breathing. Despite the air-conditioning, I'm sweating from the pain. It feels stuffy—so much so that I'm gagging on the scent of my own bloody extremities.

And another scent mingles with the sweat and the coppery tinge to the air—one that curls my insides. *Grass*.

My brain starts to scream. *Soccer Saturday*. Brent's words when he ran into us downtown. *A bunch of us are there every week, rain or shine*.

The Summer Kickoff was on a Saturday. What if that scent Madison caught while she was trapped in the trunk wasn't Tripp's golf stuff? What if it was Brent's soccer gear?

The grass from his cleats and the sweat from his shin guards, mixed with her blood.

I think of Audrey in her riding gear. Solomon swore she stopped riding his horse months before she went missing. But she kept wearing her riding gear.

That paralyzing sensation coils around me now. It's been years since I've been to Brent's house. *House* is the wrong word for it; it's a ranch, spread over an enormous plot of land, practically its own freaking kingdom. As a kid it felt like we drove up a winding road for an eternity to get there. Then we'd spend hours in the trees, playing games. The woods sprawl for days back there.

And the ranch has its own private stables.

I try to find my phone to send off a text to Dylan. But my heart plummets.

Amid all the chaos and anguish, I left my bag on the field.

30

"I forgot my stuff," I say. "We should go back."

"I'm sure Dylan grabbed it," Brent says, sounding unbothered.

"But what if he didn't?" I'm struggling to talk through the pain and the panic.

"I'll text him to make sure." Before I can argue further, he says, "Siri, text Dylan Covington."

Siri asks what he'd like to text and Brent says, "Paige forgot her bag. Can you grab it? Send." He glances back at me. "There. He'll bring it to my place. We're almost there."

"We are? I thought your place was way out in the middle of nowhere."

He laughs. "We moved a couple years back."

"Oh." That tightly wrapped feeling eases. "So it's not the amazing mansion with the horses?"

"Nope. Just a regular old mansion."

I let out a breath. I'm being paranoid. Having a delusional

fit because I hurt myself. Brent had nothing to do with Madison or Audrey. Why would he? Brent and Tripp are friends, but this is attempted murder we're talking about. And I know Brent; other than the Covingtons, he's the only person in Clearwater Ridge I actually like.

He navigates the car up a long winding driveway. It's paved as smooth as silk, and my ankle is grateful, up until he hits the brakes. I let out a moan.

"Sorry," he says before exiting the car. He comes around to the back and helps me out.

"You lied. This place *is* amazing," I say, hobbling at his side up the porch steps. Truth be told, the pain is causing the stone facade with timber columns and gables to blur. But I'm sure it's amazing.

"Thanks." He unlocks the door and leads me through a massive foyer with marble floors. "I'd show you the tennis courts, but I think maybe you should stick to water sports after all."

"But no horse stables?" I say, double-checking.

"What's with you and the horses, Paige?" He helps me down a long corridor and into a wood-paneled elevator. "I didn't even know you rode."

"No, I don't. It's just—where are we going?" The door shuts, and my heart rate speeds up.

Brent presses the button to the second floor. "My bathroom. It's practically a physical therapy office. We'll do an ice soak and get you patched up."

The elevator stops, and he hefts me down the hall to a blindingly white bathroom.

I glance down at the blood pooling along my elbow and the side of my leg. "I don't suppose you have something a little less...white."

"Don't worry. Helena will take care of the mess." He sits me down on the edge of the porcelain claw-foot tub and turns on the water. "Rest a minute. I'll get something to help with the pain."

"I thought you said you were out of—" But his footsteps are already clomping down the hall.

He returns a moment later, raising a bottle of whiskey high. "This will help with the pain."

"I didn't realize you were a Civil War doctor. Will you have to take the entire leg or only the ankle bit?"

"It's just until Dylan gets here." He pours me a shot in a diamond-patterned glass and hands it over.

"Thanks." I hold it without taking a sip. "That was really fast. You keep a bottle of whiskey in the hallway?"

He flicks his head toward the door before scrounging around in the cabinet. "The game room is next to mine. There's a bar."

"Ah."

"And an ice machine, which is what we'll need next." He turns off the cold water and heads back out the door. I hear the rumble of the ice machine down the hall.

He returns a moment later with one of those silver buckets they have in hotels. "Okay," he says, dumping the ice into the tub. "Let's get this sorted." He helps me turn and place my foot into the tub.

"I don't wanna—"

"Do it," he says sternly. "Ten minutes in."

I obey, silently vowing never to touch a soccer ball or step onto a soccer field again. That's when I take a sip of the whiskey.

Once my entire foot has gone through the gamut of intense pain to numbness and back to pain again, Brent guides me to his room to perform Operation Sock Removal. He has me sit on his chaise lounge with my foot outstretched. "If I don't make it, take my bundle of letters to my family and tell them I fought hard."

He rolls his eyes and starts in with the scissors.

Once the sock is off, Brent gingerly wraps the ankle with a bandage from his sports kit. "That feel okay?"

I nod. "Thank you, Doctor."

"Wonder where the hell Dylan is."

"Do you think maybe he went to your old place?" I ask. "Actually, that would be kind of funny. Him showing up there and the new owners just staring at him."

"Oh, we still own the ranch," Brent says, standing. "Dad didn't want to get rid of the horses or the land. He wanted us to be closer to town while we're here. You're welcome to ride the horses, since you keep asking about them."

"Who runs the ranch if you and your dad are here?"

"We've got a hired hand who keeps it up, and sometimes I help out. Oh, and Dylan wouldn't have gone out to the ranch. He came over here last summer for a poker night." He's looking down at his phone. "Speaking of Dylan." He shows me Dylan's truck parking on his fancy camera app. "I'll bring him up."

"Okay." I smile, stuck in this chair while my brain races at one hundred miles per second. Brent still has access to the house with the stables. To the massive expanse of woods that the police likely never checked after Audrey went missing.

I think back to that ride in the car, the scent of blood mixed with grass.

What if Tripp is telling the truth about leaving Madison in the woods? Could Brent somehow be the one behind everything? If he'd been the one to help Audrey—if he was planning to end her investigation for good—the utter secrecy would've necessitated the burner phones.

But what motive did Brent have for hurting Madison Blake in the first place? Was it simply to help his friend Tripp cover up his crime?

Something about it doesn't quite stack up. Brent was the one who threw out Tripp's name in the first place. At the club, he mentioned overhearing an argument between Audrey and Kurt. An argument about Tripp. Brent wouldn't have pointed me in a direction that would only lead back to himself.

Unless Brent actually overheard more than he let on.

The door opens, and I flinch. But it's only Dylan, with a bottle of ibuprofen.

"Are you okay?" he asks, nearing me. He drops a couple of the painkillers into my palm. I force them down, even though I hate swallowing pills without water.

"Ankle's patched up like new," I say. "Though I can't say the same for Lucy's sock, may it rest in peace. Where's Brent?"

"He's going to whip up some snacks or something. He sent me up in the elevator. Why?"

I take a deep breath. "This is going to sound crazy, but when I was in Brent's car, I had what's either an epiphany or a near-death delusion."

"Well, you weren't anywhere near death, so…"

"It must've been an epiphany," I say, nodding. "What if Tripp isn't lying about having left Madison in the woods behind his house? What if he really doesn't know what happened to Audrey?"

"No, Paige, don't let him get to you too."

"Look, Brent's family still owns the ranch. What if *that* was where Audrey was riding all summer? It would explain why Lenny, the stable manager, and Solomon hadn't seen her most of the summer. And what if Brent was the one supposedly helping her search for Madison?"

Dylan frowns. "Just because his property has stables?"

"No." I cringe; I have no desire to see his reaction to this. "Because of the way the car smelled. The grass and the sweat and the blood. It was exactly the way Madison described it."

He lifts a hand. "So?"

"So Brent plays soccer every Saturday. The Kickoff party last summer was on a Saturday. Brent's soccer gear was most likely in his trunk—or had been—earlier that day."

"The trunk where Madison was stuffed on the way to the river," Dylan muses, gaze drifting over to the shelf beside the chaise. It holds Brent's collection of books, trophies, and knick-knacks, including a framed photo of him and his ex, Larissa. "I don't think a scent is enough, Paige. I know Brent. He's the definition of calm and collected."

"You thought you knew Tripp."

He sighs. "We're supposed to be taking a rest from investigation mode. And you need to take a rest in general. You're in terrible shape."

"Thanks." I punch him softly in the arm. "But I really think we need to take this seriously."

"It's Brent," he says dismissively. "My mom has a million photos of all of us kids, covered in dirt, running around the ranch. How can he—" Dylan cuts off abruptly, his face paling.

"What is it?"

He doesn't say anything for a minute, only glances back at the bedroom door.

"The ranch," he says, lowering his voice. "Remember when we were younger and we used to play in the woods behind the house?" I nod. "One time I wandered off alone, a little too deep into the trees, and there was this…trapdoor. I finally made my way back and asked about it, and Brent said it was off-limits."

"Okay," I say, trying to swallow and wishing for a glass of water.

"Well, one day, I guess Brent's dad forgot to lock the trapdoor. Nate and I found it again during a game of hide-and-seek and couldn't resist opening it." He checks the bedroom door again, then lowers his voice. "It was like…a bunker. You know, concrete walls. There was a ladder, and we took it down."

"What was in it?"

"Just boxes, storage. Nothing important, which is why I forgot all about it. But it was big, Paige. Big enough to hide a person."

"Oh my god." A light-headed feeling settles over me. "What if he—do you think Audrey could still be alive?"

"Maybe. We have to find the key. If Brent's using that bunker, he'll have it."

My gaze drifts over to the door. "But he could be keeping it anywhere. At the other house, even."

Dylan's face sets in determination, all angles and hard planes. "Then we'll check the other house."

I don't feel good about this, and it isn't just because I'm dizzy and in pain. "Why don't we tell Detective Ferrera to check the bunker?"

"Because all we have is a hunch. She'd need a warrant and she wouldn't get one. But if we go check the bunker in the middle of the night, while Brent is *here*, no one will ever have to know. That way, if we're wrong..."

"No harm done," I say, turning over the idea in my muddled head. "We should start looking for the key." I point to the antique desk across the room.

"What if he comes back?" Dylan hisses.

"Help me to the door. I'll play lookout."

He gapes at me like I've lost my mind. "No way. He could come back any second."

"Just—help me, Dylan." I start to scoot down the chaise, careful not to bump my wrapped ankle as I swing my legs over the side. Dylan ducks so I can loop my arms around his neck. He walks me over to the cracked open door, and I stand on my one good foot, leaning against the frame for support. "Go to the desk," I whisper.

Dylan starts rifling around. "I don't know about this," he huffs under his breath. He checks all the drawers and the little caddy holding pens and pencils.

"The bookcase," I say.

He obeys, crossing the room to search the shelves. My eyes are on the hallway as Brent's belongings clack around behind me.

When I glance back, he's staring down the contents of a wooden box beside the photo of Larissa. "He really isn't over her, is he? He has a box of like…mementos. There's a dried flower, a bracelet, a lipstick, and a little folded love note."

"He made a shrine to his ex. Cute. But is the key in there?"

"I don't think so." Dylan continues to comb through the box. "Just a bunch of junk. There's a Crown County Fair game ticket, a ring, and a"—he wrenches his hand back—"is that a lock of *hair?*" Cringing, he removes a photo album from the bookcase and opens it. "I think the flower could be the one she's holding in this photo of them at the Hilltop," he says after a moment. I turn my attention to the hallway again, hearing the riffling of the pages as Dylan browses the album. "But it's weird."

"Weirder than a lock of hair in a box?" I whisper.

"Maybe. The album is full, but all the photos look like they're from the same two dates. It's like Brent only went out with Larissa a couple of times."

That can't be right. Brent made it sound like the breakup had been really hard on him. If he'd only gone out with Larissa twice, why would he keep all this stuff? I turn to find Dylan inspecting the silver bracelet, and my heart skids to a halt. "Let me see the album," I say, motioning him over.

He passes it off, and hurriedly, I flip through the photos.

Dylan is right. Brent and Larissa are on a date at the Hilltop, Larissa wearing the same elegant black dress and delicate gold chain necklace for half the photos in here. In the second half, she's dressed in shorts and a crop top at the fair. The gold chain dangles from her neck, and on the hand used to show off a large ice cream cone to the camera, I notice several stacks of gold rings like the one in the box. No bracelet, nor even a piece of silver jewelry to speak of.

Madison had a bracelet though. One she claimed was torn from her wrist the night she was left for dead.

"Dylan," I say, my pulse starting up again just as the elevator creaks at the end of the hall. The door rolls open, and footsteps sound in the hallway. "Put the bracelet in your sock," I mouth.

"What?" he asks, confusion etched on his forehead as he glances toward the door.

I point to my wrist, then to my lone sock. "Hide it," I mouth.

His eyes widen, and he bends, stuffing the chain away just as I swing my body into the doorframe. "There you are," I say to Brent, smiling.

"Paige." He frowns. "What are you doing up?" He slips past me, carrying a tray with one of those silver lids like an old butler.

"Ibuprofen makes me jittery," I say, demonstrating by attempting to do a one-footed dance.

Brent hoists a brow and looks to Dylan.

"Hey, man," Dylan says, holding up both hands, "you're the one who said she didn't need a hospital."

"Well, sit down, Paige. Helena made us some brunch."

Dylan guides me back to the chaise as Brent delivers

a heaping plate of waffles and bacon, setting it on my lap. "Syrup?" He holds a glass dispenser by its shiny silver handle.

The nice-guy routine. He plays it so well.

I fell for it on the pool steps two summers ago, when Brent told me about how Larissa dumped him, and we laughed and talked until I started to shiver. I fell for it again a few days ago at the club.

What if Audrey fell for it too? What if Brent offered to help her dig into Madison Blake's disappearance, but he lied? He couldn't help, because all along, the person who tried to murder Madison and cover it up...was him.

And now, Audrey's body could be hidden somewhere in all those acres of woods.

31

The second Dylan gets me settled in his truck, I send Madison a photo of the bracelet and call her.

"Paige?" she answers, and I put the call on speakerphone.

"Look at the photo I sent you," I say as Dylan starts the truck, backing it down the long driveway. "Is that your bracelet?"

"Oh my god," she rasps.

An anxious whir starts up in my chest. "It was in Brent Haywood's bedroom. Madison, this is really important. Do you know Brent? Did you do something to piss him off?"

"No," she says quickly. "I mean, he was a mark a couple years back. His family is the richest in town every summer, so I had to try. I flirted with him at the Hilltop. He seemed down about some ex-girlfriend."

"Larissa," I say.

"Right. Well, at first he was pouty and didn't seem into me, but then he seemed...a little *too* into me. He wanted me to leave with him in his car. I got a bad feeling. Like whatever

I tried to pull on him, he'd be one step ahead. Anyway, I told him I needed to go to the bathroom, and I slipped out the back door. Took an Uber home."

The thought sends a queasy sensation through me. Madison was the only one of us to catch on to Brent's act. And yet, even with her smarts, she wasn't able to outrun him in the end. "So you tried to con him, then gave him the slip."

"Look, I swear, I only let him pay for one drink, then I never saw him again. How the hell did he get my bracelet?"

"I don't know," I say. "You were unconscious after Tripp hit you, right? What if Brent overheard Audrey and Kurt talking about you? About what you did to Tripp and what he did to you. Brent could've gone outside to see for himself."

"But why would he try to drown me in the river?"

I look to Dylan, whose expression is grave as he focuses on the road. "I don't know," I say. "It doesn't seem like Brent. But if he saw you at the party and recognized you from the Hilltop—if he knew you'd tried to scam him. Or if he was upset that you refused his advances that night..."

"Oh my god," Madison breathes. "My *name*."

"Your name?"

"Rose Lambert," she says. "I used the alias Rose Lambert that night with Brent." She lets out a frustrated huff. "When things didn't go anywhere with him, I figured I could use the name again. That was when I met Tripp."

"So then," Dylan says, "if Brent overheard Audrey and Tripp talking about Rose, he would've recognized the name of the girl who ditched him that night at the Hilltop. He could've gone outside and found you passed out in the woods."

"That sick freak," she bites out. "And you think Audrey figured out it was Brent?"

I let out a long sigh. "Maybe. Brent could be the guy from the burner phone. Let's say he was helping with her investigation, but she somehow figured out Brent's role in everything. He might've tried to cover up his crime."

"So," Madison says, her voice quavering, "what are you going to do?"

"The Haywoods own two properties," I say. "One here in the Pines, and then a ranch out in Saddlewood. I think we should head to the ranch while we know Brent is here. But..." I hesitate, because all I really know about Madison Blake is that she's a liar and a con artist. Can I trust her to carry out my plan?

Then I remember what she did for Audrey's investigation. Despite her fears, Madison went to the cops and told her story. She did it partly for herself, but also for Audrey, the girl who was lost trying to help her. In the end, she's earned a scrap of trust. "The plan would obviously work better if we could keep eyes on him," I finally say.

"You want *me* to do it," she huffs as though she's already decided against it. "You want me to spy on the guy who may've tried to murder me."

"Look, Dylan and I have to be the ones to search for Audrey."

"And why can't we give both of these jobs to Detective Ferrera?" she asks. "You found the damned bracelet in Brent's room!"

"It's *your* bracelet, not Audrey's. And we can't prove we

found it there. We just want to go to the property and look around a bit. If we find any evidence that Audrey was ever there, we'll drop the bracelet off on Ferrera's desk and tell her to start looking."

Madison groans. "Fine. I'll borrow Britta's car."

"Thank you, Madison," I say. "I'll text you Brent's address. How fast can you get there?"

———

After swinging by the Covingtons' place for Dylan's shoes and a toolbox, he parks half a mile down the road from the Haywoods' ranch property. Then we wait for Madison's text.

When my phone finally dings, nervous excitement buzzes beneath my skin. "She's there. Let's go."

The truck bumps along the dirt road that runs through Saddlewood. It winds for several minutes, though not nearly as many as my child brain had spun up, before we reach the paved turnoff to the Haywood property. "There," I say, pointing to a large oak tree off the path.

Dylan parks beneath it. After helping me down, he digs a crowbar from the toolbox in the back of his truck. He strides around to the front, stopping to frown at the scene.

I see what he means. The blue hood peeks from under the leaves, easy for the ranch hand to spot if he comes in or out. Dylan looks down at my foot next, his expression growing even more dismal. "You're going to have to wait here."

"What? No way. I can walk with a little help."

"And if this ranch hand spots us? What then? You can't run."

"We'll tell him we're Brent's friends and we came to look at the horses."

Dylan's footsteps clomp along the road. "And I suppose he simply lets us proceed instead of having us arrested for breaking and entering."

I scoff. "At the most, we're trespassing. That's got to be—what? A slap on the wrist?"

"That doesn't sound accurate."

"We just have to find that bunker," I say. "Then we'll break in with your fancy tools."

"These are very basic, regular tools." He slaps the crowbar against his palm. "I wish we had that key."

"It's probably in the house. Maybe we should split up. I can search the house for the key—"

"No way." He slips out from beneath my arm and spins to face me. Both of his hands are on my shoulders, his face wild with fear. "Paige, no. If we're right about all of this, Brent tried to *kill* two girls. You don't think he'd kill you too if he knew what you were up to?"

"Madison's got eyes on him," I say, my ankle throbbing anew.

His lips purse so hard they turn white.

"Fine, I won't break into the house."

We reach a fork in the path, and Dylan tugs me along to the left. "The other one leads to the stables."

The lay of the land is coming back to me now, though I was on the property years ago. Sure enough, after clearing a copse of trees, the sprawling house with a stone facade and four chimneys comes into view. A second story towers toward the back. Lush vegetation surrounds the place—green shrubs, spruce trees, and flower beds. It seems like more than the ranch hand is maintaining the place in the Haywoods' absence.

I scan the area again. "I think we're good," I whisper. "But Dylan. You'll have to leave me here."

"What?" He stops again.

"I was wrong about my ankle," I admit. "I'm not going to make it to the bunker. You go find it. I'll wait here."

Dylan remains where he is, eyes brimming with concern. "You'll stay out of sight?" He glances to the pines off to the left.

"Of course. I've got my phone." I pat my back pocket. "If Brent so much as walks to the mailbox, Madison will text."

He wraps his arms around me, kissing my hair. "You'd better be careful," he says, voice worn. "I can't lose you."

"You won't," I say. "Promise."

With a final, wary look, he turns and walks off in the direction of the trees.

I wander over to a rock nestled among the pines and finagle my ankle onto it. Rest and elevation—that's what I should be doing.

I hear a babbling, lapping sound and remember the man-made pond around the back of the house, with its trickling waterfalls and colorful fish. When we used to come here years ago, this place had seemed like an amusement park.

I wait on the rock long enough that the shade shifts away, leaving me exposed to the sunlight. At this late hour in the day, it should feel nice, but my nerves are on edge.

When my phone dings in my back pocket, I reach for it so frantically that I fumble it. Recovering it, I read the message, heart thumping.

It isn't a text from Madison though. It's from Dylan.

Found the bunker but I can't get it open.

My body slumps, disappointment weighing on my bones. The helpless feeling is back. The only way we're going to get into the bunker without a warrant is to find that key. I promised Dylan I would stay put, but this is Audrey. We might finally learn the truth about what happened to her.

This is just one more promise to Dylan that I'll have to break.

I ease my foot down from the rock and, wincing, stand. A few yards away lies a long, fallen branch, and I hop over to it. Stooping as best as I can, I grab it from the forest floor and prop it under my arm. With the branch as a makeshift crutch, I hobble along, leaving the cover of the trees and finding the pathway to the house.

I reach the manicured lawn, making my way around the side of the house. Spotting a breach in the hedge, I duck through, moving along the wall. I reach a window, my best chance at sneaking inside, and drop the crutch to the ground. Then, using my good foot, I perch my fingers on the sill and push up onto my toes.

But a noise startles me. I drop down, nearly losing my balance. I think it's coming from inside the house. Someone's in there.

Gritting through the pain in my ankle, I use both feet to get a look this time. I can't see anyone. Just a shockingly white bedroom.

There's something strange about the room, apart from its starkness. The blankets on the bed—they're folded with one end tucked into the other. Like pillows. My mind starts to race, hope and terror clashing on the way to the finish line.

Audrey was here.

She may still be here. I wedge my fingers into the nook between the bottom rail of the window and the sill. Then, throwing all my strength into it, I try to pry it open.

"Can I help you?"

The deep voice hits me so hard I lose my grip on the window and crash down onto both feet. Pain shoots through my ankle, and I scream. I roll back into the wood chips covering the soil, clutching my ankle.

"Are you okay?" the man asks, pushing through the shrubs to kneel beside me.

I nod, though my eyes are flooded with tears and my nose is running.

Through bleary eyes, I look up, finally taking in the face of the man hovering over me.

It isn't some ranch hand, some stranger.

This man, with his dark hair and sage-green eyes is Oliver Haywood. Brent's brother, who was supposed to be off in Morocco, playing cards.

THE GIRL

When the girl woke again, she was no longer in the white room. Instead, she lay in the dark. She scrambled to find a source of light, but her hand scraped against a cold rough surface.

Wrenching away from the wall, the girl stood, backing blindly into the void. Something rattled below her. A prickle of fear crawled up her spine as she bent down and felt about her ankle, discovering that it was chained to the metal bed frame.

The prickle turned to sheer horror. Behind her, a noise sliced through the silent cell, and the girl swirled around. Only the darkness loomed before her.

There it was again. A sound like a footstep over the concrete floor. "Hello?" the girl called out. "Please, help me."

A bright light shone in her eyes, fluorescent and biting. Covering her face, the girl took a step back. Her chains rattled.

She lowered her hand and squinted into the light, her eyes adjusting.

A few yards away stood a figure. Despite the frenzied

rhythm of her heartbeat, the figure remained perfectly still. It made the hairs on the back of the girl's neck stand up.

The boy.

"I'm very sorry about this," the boy said, and he did sound sorry. She thought she might persuade him to let her go.

"I don't understand," the girl said. "What did I do wrong?"

"Nothing." The boy frowned. "You didn't do anything wrong. I wish things didn't have to be this way."

Behind the boy, something stirred.

Another figure lurked in the shadows. Like a specter, he stepped forth, draped in a cloak of darkness. When the light touched his features, the girl gasped aloud. She backed straight into the bed frame, the sharp edges of boxy metal digging into her bare calf. "Nice to see you again, Larissa."

This boy's voice sent the girl's mind reeling backward in time. It took her to the night of the Bad Stuff. Back to the pain in her body. Back to the pain in her heart.

Back to all that blood.

And now that she saw both boys standing side by side beneath the crackling light, an earth-shattering sense of dread overcame the girl. It knocked her off her feet, forcing her to sink down onto the bed.

She wondered how she could've missed it before. Sure, at first glance the boys looked almost nothing alike. Their hair color was different: one's nearly black, the other's a dusty brown that turned honey-blond in the summer. Only one wore glasses. One was slim, while the other had the muscular physique of an athlete. With a shiver, she remembered the feel of those strong athletic hands wrapped around her neck.

But they shared a square jaw. And though the shade of green was different—one boy had the gray-green of a calm lake, while the other possessed the brilliant emeralds that haunted her nightmares—the almond shape and the hooded lids were the same.

Brothers.

The Haywood brothers. The girl had known of a brother. Brent had spoken about his well-traveled enigma of a sibling. Yet the older brother traveled a lot, and the couple had only dated a short time. The girl hadn't exactly met the family.

Brent had been charming once, just like the boy. The girl had drifted into town without a cent to her name. She'd never known money or a life where dreams were part of the picture. She was to live in the same box-shaped house with rotted beams and faded paint until the day she died. Or at least, in a similar box. When she'd asked about college, the girl's mother had laughed. "Don't think a girl like you will be needing a fancy education."

When she applied anyway, somewhere far away from the box and her parents, her father had slapped her.

Still, the girl had looked out the window every night. There, she saw the glimmer of a dream on the horizon. She hoped and prayed that if she could escape those two horrible people and their box-shaped house, she'd find the life she dreamt of. She'd find a voice of her own.

So the girl left the parents who had never cared for her while she was around and would never look for her now that she was gone. She set off in search of something bright and new.

Brent had been everything the girl's parents weren't. He

was playful and present where they'd been absent and neglectful. Generous where they'd been stingy. Doting where they'd been lazy and detached. And he was the most handsome boy who'd ever paid her attention.

Brent had even introduced her to all of his friends. He was perfect—as long as she let him lead. As long as she fell in line.

Then came the night of the Bad Stuff. The moment the girl rejected Brent's advances after a night out at an expensive restaurant, he changed. Like a mythological beast, he grew teeth and claws before her eyes. And he used them on her. He used them until there had been so much blood, the girl couldn't see out of one eye and her arm was broken.

Brent had told the girl to leave Clearwater Ridge for good. He said if she didn't, he'd finish the job he'd started.

The girl didn't want to fall in line. She didn't want to get out of town.

She wanted justice. For what the boy had done.

What a fool the girl had been to believe she could ever win. What a fool to fall for both of these boys. To believe not once—but twice—that a blackened heart had softened to hers. To escape from one wolf, only long enough to clean up the blood and allow the wounds to heal.

To believe that finally, she'd found a savior. Someone who had promised to love her and help her find a voice in a town where girls like her were voiceless.

She'd failed to realize a truth as old and deep as the dense woods overhead.

Wolves travel in packs. They're as fiercely protective of their family unit as they are wild and predatory.

All the girl had managed to do was run from one ravenous wolf, straight into the jaws of another.

Together, they descend upon her now. Not with gnashing teeth and claws, but with a silver blade that glints beneath the fluorescent light.

The girl's screams are buried far below the earth.

32

PAIGE

"You're hurt," Oliver says, helping me to my feet.

"I'm okay, just a—I was playing soccer with Brent this morning."

"Oh?"

"Yeah," I grit out through the shooting pains. "It was a disaster." Finally remembering the excuse I'd pocketed in case I came across the ranch hand, I add, "Brent said it would be cool if I ever wanted to see the horses, only I wasn't sure exactly how to get to the stables."

"He told you to come now?" Oliver squints up at the near-setting sun. "It's a bit late. And you're in no condition to walk out there." He leads me around the house to the front door. "Let's get you inside, and I'll take a look at that foot."

"Ankle," I say. "Brent thinks it's just a bad sprain."

"Even so, you should stay off it. I'm surprised Brent didn't tell you that."

"Oh, he tried. I'm stubborn. And I could've sworn he said

he'd be here tonight. But"—I tap myself on the forehead—"it's been quite a day. Guess I misheard. I'll get back to my truck."

"Where did you park?" Oliver asks, glancing at the circular driveway.

"Down the road a ways. I promise, I can walk. I just got a bit...frightened. I couldn't find Brent, so I started looking for him."

"I'll drive you home," Oliver says, taking my arm to lead me up the stairs. "But first, let's sit you down and get you a drink. You're looking pale."

Anyone would look pale if they'd just seen the ghost of their missing friend. Did Audrey fold that blanket? The feel of Oliver's sturdy hand on my arm sends a shiver through me.

Why did Brent say his brother was out of the country? Could Oliver be 4477?

And where is my friend now?

Oliver opens the front door, and we enter a large, brightly lit foyer with wooden beams and a winding staircase. When we reach the living room, he helps me onto a comfy chair. "Stay put. I'll be right back."

"Actually, would it be okay to use your bathroom?"

He smiles and stoops to help me up again. When we reach the first door on the right, he says, "Here we are. I might even have a pair of crutches somewhere. I'll go check."

"Thanks." I watch long enough to determine he's headed for the stairs before shutting the door behind me. Then, pressing my ear against it, I listen.

The sound of his steps fade away, and I ease the door open. I tiptoe down the hall in the opposite direction he went. The white room was on this side of the house, but I'm not sure how many windows I passed before reaching that gap in the bushes.

I try the first door, peeking inside to find an office. I shut it and limp along, using the wall for support. At the next door, I try the knob, finding it locked.

"Audrey," I whisper through the wood. "Audrey, are you there?"

My heart thumps so loudly in my chest, I'm worried I won't hear her answer. It's an answer I'm desperate to hear as I push my cheek against the door. I inspect the lock, but it's nothing I could pick, especially not before Oliver returns.

I need backup. I pull my phone from my pocket and type out a text to Dylan and Madison: Oliver is here and he has–

I hear the creak of wood just before the phone is knocked from my hand. It lands with a crack, skittering off down the hall. By the time I throw my hands up to ward my attacker off, it's too late.

The rag is shoved hard against my lips, crushing my teeth against the soft inner flesh of my mouth.

Blood touches my tongue. Fumes burn my lungs and my nostrils as I fight to inhale.

I begin to fall.

AUDREY

LAST SUMMER

My head is splitting in half. It's like the worst hangover I've ever had combined with getting a brick dropped onto my skull.

When I pry my eyelids open and attempt to sit up in bed, the pain is quickly overshadowed by the chilling realization that I don't know where I am.

And it's pitch dark.

I grab at my dress, at the bed linens. Everything feels familiar, as if my body and the bedding from Oliver's place were somehow transported to this dark and dingy location while I slept.

But I hear the clank, along with a sharp digging sensation at my ankle, and an entirely new sense of horror sweeps through me.

I'm chained to this bed.

A light flicks on from several yards away. I squint to find a single buzzing overhead light strung from what looks to be a corridor beyond this room, casting its yellow light over the concrete walls and silhouetting the figure in the doorway.

I jerk back, causing the cuff to dig deeper into my ankle.

The man steps forward, entering the room and flicking on another fluorescent light. When I see his face, relief floods my chest. "Oliver," I breathe. "You've got to get me out of here. I think my—"

But Oliver doesn't rush forward to free me. His expression remains as calm as a windless sea.

The terror slithers back, coiling around my lungs until I think I may pass out. "Where am I?" I look past him, through the doorway to the long corridor leading to darkness. "How did I get here?"

Then I remember the aching pain in my head.

"You drugged me," I say, bits and pieces of the previous night coming back to form a mottled, impressionistic version of events. We were having dinner. There was wine.

But Brent interrupted our meal, asking to speak to Oliver.

They went outside for privacy, only I snuck to the balcony and listened at the sliding door. It was open a crack. "What the hell are you doing here?" Oliver spat.

"This is what you get for not answering my calls," Brent said. "If you don't pay that lady, the cops are going to find the body."

I shivered at the words: *the body*.

"Pay her?" Oliver said. "You really think Madison's mother will stop looking for her daughter if we throw money at her?"

"If she doesn't, we'll have to take care of her another way," Brent had hissed.

"I'm sick of cleaning up your messes," Oliver said. "First Larissa, and now—"

"Don't bring Larissa into this. She was *my* girlfriend. You never really cared about her."

"No, but I do care about Audrey. So you can't screw it up. Knowing you, you'll leave a money trail that'll lead right back to us."

"I'll send the note and the money anonymously," Brent said. "She'll never know it was us."

"And Madison's mouthy friend? Britta? What about her?"

"She's not a problem. She's townie scum. The cops don't care what she has to say."

"This better be the last time your temper gets out of control," Oliver said.

"It will be," Brent said. "I just—you heard what that bitch did to me at the Hilltop. She thought she could dance her trashy ass over to our side of town, drain us dry, and give up nothing in return." He let out a cold laugh. "Little tease. I had to put her in her place."

"Which was the ground, apparently," Oliver said dryly. "Next time, you're on your own. You deal with Madison's mother and let me deal with Audrey. I've got a handle on things with her."

"Well, good," Brent said. "Because I have half a mind to—"

"If you so much as *breathe* on Audrey," Oliver cut in in a low voice, "you'll be in the ground with Madison."

"Whatever, dude."

I could tell the argument was winding down, and I'd heard enough. Queasy, I eased the sliding door shut.

But it *clicked*. A deafening sound that resounded through the night. Wincing, I tiptoed away from the door and toward the stairs, praying they hadn't heard.

Once I reached the main floor, I considered sprinting out the door and into the night. But before I could make a decision, Oliver's footsteps thudded on the stairs. When he reached the dining room, a sadness touched his eyes. "I'll get you a new glass of wine," he said, removing mine from the table.

"I haven't finished that one." My heart thumped so fast I could barely string a sentence together.

"This wine is terrible," he said without looking at me. "I'll open a new bottle."

He returned a moment later, setting a full glass of red wine before me and the new bottle on the table. Then he poured himself a glass.

I didn't drink mine. I knew better. Oliver was helping his brother cover up a terrible crime, and now I knew about it.

We continued to eat, Oliver's eyes lingering on my full glass. "Sure you don't want to try the wine? It's an excellent vintage. My father actually knows the winemaker."

"Thanks, but I'm already a little dizzy. Actually, I think I'll head home before I get too tired to make the drive." I stood up, wiping my sweaty palms on the sides of the dress in case he tried to hold my hand for a good-night kiss. Because somewhere in my panic-stricken, muddled brain, I still believed a good-night kiss was in the realm of possibilities.

"Then I should give you a ride. I can't let you drive if you're not feeling up to it." He smiled at me, and it seemed so genuine.

Now, my stomach turns at the memory.

"No, I'm okay. Thanks though. I only had that half glass. Probably just tired. Thank you so much for everything." I picked up my steps, hearing his own trailing close behind. "I'll text you in the morning." I made it as far as the front door before he caught up with me, his hand shooting past me to land on the door.

I fought with the knob, letting out a whimper as his hand held it shut.

"I'm so sorry, Audrey," he said, breath riffling my hair.

I struggled further, but his arms wrapped around me, dragging me back toward the table. With one strong arm, he held me to his body, unfazed by my attempts to kick and squirm free of his grasp. With his free hand, he grabbed the wine bottle. "Please, don't make me do this," he said, arm tightening around me, fist tightening around the bottle. "Just drink the wine, baby."

"No!" I screamed, knowing there wasn't a soul around for miles. No one but Brent, who had just stormed into the room to help contain me.

The last thing I remember is Oliver putting the glass to my lips.

Now, I rub at my head, about to ask for water when my gaze skims the floor. A plastic water bottle and two painkillers already lie there.

I glance down at my dress. It's the same one I wore at dinner. Oliver had surprised me with it, and I changed from my riding clothes into its gorgeous white silk-chiffon fabric.

I survey where the light spills over the clean bed linens next. Their silky feel is familiar, as is the white fluffy pillow. It's the one I used in Oliver's guest room all the times it became late and he thought it best for me to stay the night. He'd been so gracious—nothing but respectful—and I put my trust in him.

Somehow, though, the same care he'd taken with the guest room and all the candlelit dinners shows here and now in this frigid, dimly lit space.

Only it isn't care at all. I don't know what it is—what *he* is. But I know I was wrong about him all along. I scramble back on the bed until my spine hits the hard wall.

Suddenly, I know exactly where I am. Beneath the ground. In the bunker Oliver said was simply his father's storage space.

But the room is empty, apart from the bed. The only thing being stored here is me.

Cautiously, I scoot forward and lean down to grab the water and the pills. But as my hand lights on the neck of the bottle, I see the dark splatter marks covering the floor. Brownish-red in color, the splotches are faded yet stamped in the concrete, as if someone attempted to scrub them clean before abandoning the job.

Panic clogs my throat, but I force my eyes to meet his. "Madison. You—" I start to hyperventilate, incapable of doing anything but point at the stains.

"No, Audrey," Oliver says at last. "No."

I can't wrap my mind around any of it. It's the same deep, soothing voice that drew me in weeks ago. The same concerned look that softened my heart. The same handsome face I fell for.

And yet—I don't know this voice, this expression, this face at all.

"I didn't kill Madison," he says. "I didn't even have her down here."

"I don't understand. Is this—" I check my head for a wound. Did he strike me with the wineglass after all?

My head is fine. I check my arms and legs, but the blood on the ground is dried and old. It can't be mine.

"What happened to Madison?" I croak out.

"Not really sure, to be honest. She'd taken a beating from Tripp after you outed her."

Guilt writhes in my chest. It was my fault. That was the reason I couldn't let it go, not when Kurt warned me not to get involved. Not even when all hope of finding Madison seemed lost.

I'd recognized her the night of the Summer Kickoff in the Pines. I'd found Tripp and told him that a thief had infiltrated his party and he should kick her out. That was when he informed me that said thief was his girlfriend, *Rose Lambert*. The girl he'd been wanting to introduce me to. I had to break the news to him that *Rose* was none other than Madison Blake. She was a con artist from Shadow's Pass, and she'd taken my money. I suspected she'd taken his too.

All I'd wanted to do was help a friend. I had no intention of hurting Madison. Sure, I was devastated in the beginning. I'd gone so far as to track her down. But when I saw where she came from, the way she helped her mother from the hospital exit to the car, I let it go. The way I saw it, she took the money that I'd stolen from my parents in the first place. It was everything I deserved.

But I wasn't simply going to stand by and let her play with Tripp's emotions like that. So I told him who Rose really was, and he thanked me. He said he was going to break up with her.

I went to track Tripp down later in the night—to be a good friend and offer a listening ear if he needed one—and that was when I witnessed him cut open Madison's face with the beer bottle.

I watched him yank her outside.

Then I stood, half-concealed behind a door, unsure what to do. When I finally gathered up the courage to tell Dylan, he blew me off. He'd been upset with me since learning that I'd stolen from our parents. Though I never really saw it as stealing, more like borrowing. I convinced myself that Mom and Dad were so well off, they'd never notice the money was missing. The following summer, I'd find a better job—maybe something at the club—and pay it back. No harm done.

Only that's not how things went down, and my brother's perception of me became irrevocably altered. When he blew me off at the party, I went to Kurt. We weren't together anymore, but I believed he'd help me do the right thing.

Instead, Kurt instilled a sense of helplessness in me. A sense of fear. He told me that when it came to boys like Tripp Shaw, there was *nothing* I could do. I had no voice. And if I refused to accept this, I and everyone around me would lose everything.

That was why I couldn't tell Paige. It was why, halfway through my attempt to tell Hannah, I chickened out. My brother was a boy like Tripp Shaw, a boy who should've been able to help. And yet, I'd failed to get through to him too. So I allowed Kurt's words to echo in my mind. Already, they were proving true. I was helpless, voiceless.

I did try talking to Kurt again, the day after the party. I'd never had any intention of getting my job at the rafting company back. I thought maybe, in broad daylight, he'd at least help me look for Madison. Just to make sure she was okay. But he refused, and I left to track her down on my own. I hoped that Tripp had merely scared Madison out of town. I knew that if I was going to help her, I'd have to do it under the radar. I couldn't tell anyone, especially not Paige. She's always been the do-gooder. She would've gotten us both killed.

Then I ran into Oliver. Not for the first time; we'd known each other from a distance, having both spent summers in Clearwater Ridge. But he'd been much older, so we'd never really spoken before. I'd gone back to Shadow's Pass, to the place I'd tracked down Madison last summer after she took my money. I only wanted to speak with her mother, but the woman wasn't home. A man approached me on the street then. Tall and lean like a shadow. He came closer, asking what a pretty little thing like me was doing there.

That was when Oliver pulled up beside us. He pretended to be my friend, acted like I was with him. He asked me to get in the car. It had been a couple of years since I'd seen Oliver, but I recognized him. And given the alternative, I jumped at the offer.

After I thanked him, Oliver explained that he was on his way to the feed and supply store in Shadow's Pass. We fell into easy conversation on the ride back into town. He dropped me off at the river, like I'd asked. When he asked me to meet him in the woods beyond the town strip the following day, I felt a swell of warmth and excitement. He was a gorgeous older boy, and he wanted to spend more time with me.

I never planned on telling Oliver about Madison, but the more I got to know him, the more I opened up.

He had means, the Haywoods being one of the wealthiest summer families in Clearwater Ridge. He had connections in the county sheriff's department even. And unlike Kurt, he wasn't scared off by the thought of Tripp. "The Shaws can't touch me," he'd assured me.

So I trusted him, even when he suggested we communicate through prepaid phones. "It will be better if no one finds out you're looking into Madison's disappearance," Oliver said. "You've been obstructing justice. You could get time."

Then there was the age gap: my sixteen years to his twenty. The harder I fell for Oliver, the better it made me feel knowing that my parents would never pick up my phone and see his text messages.

Eventually, I knew that our time together had become less about Madison and more about *us*. I wasn't willing to let her go, but I was okay with allowing her investigation to consume less and less of my life. Oliver had made an unbearable situation—and all of the guilt associated with it—slightly more bearable. I loved him, and I believed with everything in me that he loved me too. I believed he would do anything, including face and expose Tripp Shaw, for me.

Until I overheard that conversation on the back deck.

"I know it didn't end with Tripp," I say now. "I know Brent killed Madison."

"Yes." Oliver stepped closer yet. Every muscle in my body tensed. "But not down here. And honestly, I'm not even sure she's dead. Someone would've found the body by now. My brother said he left her to drown in the river." He rolls his eyes. "As if her body's simply going to sink to the bottom and disappear. So you see, I really did want to locate Madison as much as you did. I was tasked to *take care* of her." He sighs, fingers jangling the set of keys at his belt loop. "But then, another task came my way. Once you started digging around. Once you couldn't let her go."

"So it was all a lie. There was no *us*." My vision swerves, Oliver careening over and bobbing back up again like an inflatable tube man. Or maybe it's my entire still-dehydrated body that swerves, because my head scrapes the wall.

Oliver rushes at me, stooping to grab the water. "Audrey, no. It wasn't a lie. I did find you that day in Shadow's Pass because Brent asked me to keep an eye on you. He was worried you'd start mouthing off about Madison having been at that party. When he saw you staring at the missing poster in Carlson's a little too long, he asked me to step in. So yes, I followed you that day, when that"—he grits his teeth—"piece of scum came at you on the street." He reaches up, calloused hand grazing my cheek. My entire body clenches until he lowers it. "But I really did fall for you. I've loved every minute we've had together."

"Whose blood is it?" I take the bottle from him, my thirst screaming out. The seal breaks in my fingers with a satisfying click; it's safe to drink. I point to the large brown stain on the concrete floor. "If it isn't Madison's blood, whose is it?"

His forehead furrows as he considers his answer. He could easily make something up in an attempt to appease me, but it would fail. He wants to win my trust back, as if that's a possibility. "Another of my brother's fatal mistakes, I'm afraid."

I think back to the heated conversation between the brothers on the deck. "Larissa Swanson."

Oliver nods, his expression somber. "I had to do some

cleanup there. My brother's anger got out of hand again. He can become somewhat of a self-righteous asshole when provoked. And violent," he adds quietly. "A mean streak against women that he inherited from our father."

Oliver's gaze goes distant, his mind clearly stuck on the past. I remember the white room in his house, the one I fell asleep in before waking up here. How Oliver's mother liked to keep everything crisp and bright, and though she passed away, her sons couldn't quite bear to touch it. I think of the pain in his eyes whenever he spoke of his mother. Of what might've happened to that poor woman in those stark white rooms.

But Oliver runs his fingers through his dark hair, those gray-green eyes zipping back to mine. "Brent thought they were at the point in their relationship where things should"—he pauses, carefully choosing his words with a tact that seems utterly at odds with his behavior down in this bunker—"move to the next level physically. When Larissa disagreed, Brent's violent side took over." Oliver shrugs, as though his brother's actions were inevitable. "I found her much the same way I found you. I never planned to hurt her, only to get inside her head. I had to see what she was planning to do about Brent. And in the end, she forced my hand."

I can't look away from the bloodstain that spreads wide as a lake. It would've been so much blood. "You killed her."

"Yes, but I never loved her," he says, as if this should be reassuring. "She was merely a project—something I had to fix to save my brother. I didn't struggle with it the way I'm struggling now."

Struggling. About the fact that he has to kill me.

"That's all I am to you? Your next cleanup project? Just more collateral damage in the wake of your brother's crimes?"

Oliver's head wrenches back, like he's truly gutted. "No, of course not." Like he could actually have a soul to crush after everything he's done.

And everything he's about to do.

"How come no one's come looking for Larissa?" I ask.

"She was a drifter, a nobody. She tried to leech off Brent, the same way Madison tried to leech off him. She wasn't like *you*, Audrey. You'll have the entire country searching for you. That's why I'm glad we decided to stick with the burner phones. But Larissa? We buried her body in the woods nearby. For a while, I stayed on alert, thinking I'd catch a news article here or an evening news report there. Thinking someone would miss her enough to follow her to this town." He lets out a long breath. "No one ever did."

They made her disappear. *Worse*. They made it seem like she'd never existed.

I have to get out of here. I know he doesn't have a soul. Still, I do the only thing I can in my powerless state; I beg. "Please let me go, Oliver. Please, please let me go. I promise to keep Brent's secrets. We can still be together."

He frowns at me. "Baby, I wish I could. Believe me, that's all I want. If you hadn't eavesdropped last night, you'd still be up in the main house with me. But I have to watch out for my little brother. He needs me."

An ice-cold terror streaks through me. "You're not going to leave me down here."

"I'll be back tomorrow," he says, leaning toward me like he

might reach out. "Oh, I almost forgot." He straightens, moving back into the corridor and disappearing into the darkness.

When he returns a moment later, he's carrying a bag. "I got that cheeseburger you like from the diner."

"No, no, no, Oliver. I don't want a cheeseburger. I want the hell out of here! Please! I swear I won't tell anyone!"

He ignores me, grabbing a bucket from the corner and dragging it closer to the bed. "I'll get you your own light tomorrow," he says apologetically before flicking off the overhead light.

"Oliver!" I call out, tears streaming down my face. I can't see him walk off down the hall, but his footsteps plunk on the ladder rungs. I stand, yanking against the chain with my foot until the cuff carves a mark and my ankle screams out.

For a second, light spills into the void as the lid is lifted.

Then it clanks back down, shutting me in with the darkness.

33
PAIGE

The first thing I see when I wake up is blood. An entire pool of fresh sticky red blood a few yards away. I take my first full breath, and its metallic scent, combined with the reek of urine, overtakes me.

I check myself for injuries. Apart from the ankle, though, I'm clean. My right wrist has been chained to a corroded pipe that runs along the wall from one end of the concrete cell to the other.

I scan my surroundings, from the empty bed across the cell to its cracked concrete walls splotched with mold, before my gaze darts back to the blood. Realization tumbles down on me like an avalanche, crushing that last glimmer of hope I'd held on to all this time. Burying me beneath a thick layer of sorrow.

"Audrey," I croak out. This must be where she died. Where the man who chloroformed me must have killed her. "Oh, Audrey, no." The grief mounting in my chest, the sobs filling my throat—they spill free now, along with my tears.

Footsteps thud over the floor, and I stiffen. It's him.

But I turn to the doorway to find the man holding a girl.

Clothed in a filthy dress, the girl's long hair is matted with grease. When the man nudges her forward, the short dress ripples, a swirl of brown and crimson stains shivering in the light's glow. For a second, I think the girl is a ghost.

Then she meets my eyes with hers—the same sky blue as her brother's, though the spark has drained after so much time in this dim, drab cell.

Audrey.

A torrent of emotions hits me at once. *She's alive.*

But the hope and relief are quickly tempered by that familiar feeling of dread as I watch Audrey, helpless in this man's grip.

My tears still flow, though not for the same reason. This girl, my best friend who was once vibrant and lovely, is nothing but a shadow of her former self. Her normally sun-kissed skin is ashy, hair thinning and scraggly. Her bones look frail enough to crumble at the slightest touch.

Oliver helps her gently along, and I can see that her wrist has been bandaged. With newfound horror, I gape at the pool of blood.

"You're awake," Oliver says gruffly to me while easing Audrey onto the empty bed across the room. He takes her ankle, and to my shock, she doesn't fight as he secures it with the chain that dangles from the bed. "Audrey had a bit of an episode when you arrived. But she's better now."

"What did you do to her?" I growl, getting up onto my knees despite the pain in my ankle.

"*I* didn't do anything," he says, standing. "I would never hurt Audrey." His gaze skims over me slowly. "You, on the other hand…" The callousness to his voice sends a chill through me.

"Well," he says, taking a step backward, "I'd imagine you two have some catching up to do." With a disgusted glance at me, he turns and skulks off down the corridor.

A minute later, the bunker lid clanks into place.

"What happened to your wrist?" I ask, scrambling toward Audrey over the rough concrete until the chain yanks me back.

"He was going to kill you," she says, her voice as thin and feeble as her body. "He had a knife. I couldn't think of any other way to stop him, so I sliced my wrist on the bedpost." I look to where the exposed metal peeks through the acrylic veneer.

Nausea swells in my stomach. "I don't understand. How did that make him stop?"

She licks her dehydrated, scabbed-over lips. "He thinks he loves me. He doesn't trust me with his and Brent's secrets, but he can't let me go. That's why he hasn't killed me yet."

"You could've killed *yourself* on that bedpost, Audrey," I scold.

She stares at the blood-coated floor. "It's all I've wanted since I got here."

I try to reach for her with my free hand, my fingertips falling short as the chain digs deeper into my other wrist. "No, Audrey. Everyone's been looking for you. We miss you. We…" I sniffle. "We *need* you."

Her gaunt face contorts into a pitiful expression. "I'm

sorry. I'm so, so sorry. I never meant to put everyone through this. I was just...trying to right a wrong."

"It's okay, Audrey. You wanted to help Madison, even after what she did to you."

She blinks. "How do you know about that?"

"We've been searching for you, Audrey. Dylan and me. We found that burner phone, and everything led us here."

"You never should've come," she says, cradling her wrist. "I've already made enough of a mess. I don't deserve your help."

"How can you say that?"

"Because I was a coward!" she cries. "If I'd done something to help Madison the night of the party, none of this would've happened. I could've saved her. Now, Madison's dead, and you and I are both going to die here."

I open my mouth to tell her about Madison, but then it dawns on me. "Audrey, are we being watched? Are there cameras?"

"I haven't seen any."

Even so, I check all four corners and the ceiling, then mouth the words. *"Madison isn't dead."*

"What?" Audrey's eyes, darkly rimmed and sunken into her skull, widen.

I can't say any more. It would be putting Madison at risk. "Maybe Oliver's not a killer," I say instead with hopeful naivete. "You're still alive. Maybe there's a way we can—"

"He murdered Larissa Swanson," Audrey interrupts softly.

"What?"

She points to a dark brown stain only a foot from the fresh red pool. "Oliver and Brent."

The nausea rises, pushing into my throat. I'm going to be sick. All those mementos, those sentimental items in Brent's room, were they just...*tokens*? Things a killer takes from a victim?

I remember Dylan suddenly. He was up there, trying to break in. How did Oliver miss him when he brought me here? He could still be hiding somewhere in the woods, capable of breaking us out of here.

Unless something happened to him.

I think of my phone, of that half message I typed out. The one that was never sent. Oliver must've taken my phone, which means he probably knows what we're up to.

The nausea reaches its peak. I hunch over, hands on my thighs as I gag. I continue to dry heave, but nothing comes out.

Gathering my bearings again, I look at Audrey. "Did Oliver say anything about—" Remembering that there could be surveillance, I mouth the name: "*Dylan?*"

Her eyes widen, and she shakes her head. "Is he—"

I flick my eyes upward, then whisper, "He knows about the bunker. He was trying to get in."

She nods. "I heard something earlier." But her lips twist into a frown, and I know what she's thinking.

Where the hell is he?

I have so many questions. So many details I need Audrey to share so I can formulate a plan to get us out of here. "How often does he come down here?"

"Once a day usually. He brings food and..." Her shoulders hunch and her eyes avert to the corner. "Empties the bucket."

"So he might not come back today." That's good. It gives us time.

Though Audrey's had nothing but time, and she's still stuck down here. And Oliver seems to give her a lot more freedom than he'd ever allow me. "So he takes off the chain when he comes down?" Her brow furrows, and I add, "When I woke up, you weren't chained. He had you back there, somewhere." I point to the dark corridor that leads to the exit.

"Oh, no. He only moved me away from the bed so he could sand the post smooth. That way, I couldn't try *this* again." She lifts her bandaged wrist. "Actually, it was the farthest I've traveled since he brought me down here."

At this thought, a paralyzing fear wracks my body. These past ten months, Audrey has never even seen the sun. No wonder she's so pale and decrepit. I want to break down, to throw my body onto the cold concrete and sob.

But I have to pull it together for Audrey. She's endured a day like this—a fear this sharp and a reality this bleak—three hundred times over. I can do it once. My mind is fresh, my body strong, apart from this damned ankle.

And Dylan is out there somewhere. Though if he were okay...

The nausea surges again. Dylan must've been pounding away on this bunker when Oliver dragged me here. If he were truly okay, he'd have come for us.

In the meantime, I have to try to get us free. I glance over to Audrey, who's white and leaning an elbow on to the bed, too weak to hold herself upright. "Just lie down, Audrey. I'll figure something out."

I examine her setup from across the room, only the light beside her bed to illuminate things. If there were a way to break her free, she would've found it by now.

I, on the other hand, showed up here unexpectedly. Oliver had intended to kill me, until Audrey put a kink in that plan. Between having to tend to her wounds, her bed, and securing me, he must've been flustered. If there's a weakness, it will be on this side of the cell.

I check my chain, tugging on it and inspecting the links.

Moving on to the keyhole in the cuff next, I debate what might fit inside. But my pockets are empty, my hair held back by a simple elastic. I get low to the ground, but the floor seems to be swept clean.

What I need is a small piece of metal. "Audrey," I ask. "Does Oliver ever bring you anything besides food? Like pens for drawing or journaling?" If I could break off the metal clip of a pen, I might be able to reconfigure it into a tool to pick the lock.

"Just books." Cheek still flat against the pillow, she points to a stack on the floor beside her bed.

"We need something hard and malleable enough to pick our locks."

"There's nothing like that down here," Audrey says, almost like she's checked out completely on Operation Get Free. "Once he left the toothpick in my burger from the diner. But I broke it in half trying to pick my lock."

I picture the wood splintering, all of Audrey's hopes breaking apart along with it. Before I can dwell too long on that devastation, I crawl down the length of the ancient pipe that I'm cuffed to. I lean my ear against the rough, corroded metal to determine what's flowing through it. "Are these water pipes?" I ask Audrey.

"Yeah," she says, sitting up ever so slightly. "But they don't work anymore."

I tug on the pipe. It makes a clanking sound but doesn't budge. Standing, I hop along the wall, looping my cuff until it hits the seam where two pipes have been welded together. This time, when I yank on the chain as hard as I can, the pipe groans. And it shifts.

It lets out a hiss as liquid spurts from the crack into my face. I shut my eyes against whatever bacteria-laden sludge is still left in the pipe. Then I yank again, harder this time, screaming out against the pain in my wrist.

The seam cracks apart. Not clean through, but enough that my cuff slides into the breach and hope flutters in my chest.

There's a problem however; one more tug will snap my wrist in half. "Audrey," I say, craning my neck to find that she's completely upright, watching me with a transfixed sort of awe. "Throw me your sheet."

She gets to work tugging the linens free. Balling up the top sheet, she tosses it over to me. I reach for it with my feet, ignoring the burst of pain in my injured ankle, the one I'm putting all of my weight on now.

I tuck as much of the fabric inside the space between my wrist and the cuff as possible, creating a cushion. Then, shutting my eyes and gritting my teeth, I give the chain one last tug with all my might.

The pipe breaks in half, letting out a crack like a gunshot in the small cell. More green liquid drips down onto the concrete.

Heart pounding, I slide the cuff down the remainder of the pipe to freedom. All I can do now is pray that Oliver doesn't

have cameras. If he does, I'll never have time to get Audrey out
of here.

I wrap the excess chain around my arm and limp over to
Audrey. "I'm going to find the key to your cuff," I assure her,
pulling her into a quick embrace. "I'm not leaving."

"It isn't down here," she says, her voice shrill with panic.
"Oliver has all the keys with him."

"Well, then, I'm going to find something to pick the lock."
I turn, dragging my injured foot toward the doorway.

"Paige, you can't worry about my lock. You have to get
out of here."

"Stop it, Audrey. I'm not leaving you."

"You don't understand," she says, words coming in a rush.
"He won't kill me. He can't. But before you woke up, he told
me—" Her voice catches, and a large tear rolls down her cheek.
"He said my little stint had only bought you some time. But
that when he returned, he was going to…*kill* you."

The room goes silent, the only sound Audrey's words echo-
ing in my head.

I'm a dead girl.

"You have to get out of here," she pleads. "Maybe you
can find help for me once you're safe, but you can't risk staying here another second. Paige, do you understand what I'm
saying?"

Ignoring her, I reach up to flick on the overhead light. I
enter the dimly lit corridor, passing the ladder and glimpsing a
smaller cell opposite this one.

I enter it, finding the storage room that Dylan described
sneaking into years ago. Other than the sink, which must've

been what the pipes were for at some point, it's filled with boxes. I rummage through them, looking for something to pick Audrey's cuff lock. But it's only old riding gear, file folders, and junk. I start to move to the other side of the room when I spot something out of place among the boxes.

A black and red toolbox. Either it's always here, or Oliver left it behind after fixing Audrey's bed.

I hurry to it. There has to be something in here I can use to pick the lock. I pry the lid open and rifle around, searching for something small and narrow. But a grating noise catches me in the gut.

The bunker lid.

Heart pounding, I grab the heavy metal wrench and hobble through the corridor as fast as my pulsing ankle will allow me. My teeth are clamped down hard onto my lower lip, holding back my scream. The taste of blood seeps onto my tongue.

I look at Audrey, putting an index finger to my lips. Then I slip behind the wall, metal wrench poised high, grip tight around the handle. *This is it.*

Oliver has come back to kill me.

There's a thud against the concrete floor, followed by footfalls in the corridor. They echo the pounding of my heart as I quiet my breathing and wait.

He steps into the cell, and I aim for his skull.

34

"Wait!" Audrey screams as the wrench slices through the air.

I pull back just before hitting the man in the head. The man whose wide blue eyes fasten on mine now.

"Dylan?" I drop the wrench to the ground and rush toward him. "What the hell? I thought you were Oliver!"

"Not Oliver," he says, throwing his arms around me, kissing my hair, and squeezing so tightly my vision blackens. He loosens his grip to look me over before tugging a set of keys from his pocket.

A gust of excitement and terror rushes through me. "How did you get those?"

"I snuck into the house and stole them off the key hook." He turns to Audrey, pausing only for a second to take in this new version of her, to let his gaze linger on her bandages before kneeling to work on the lock.

"So, then, where's Oliver now?" I ask.

"Hopefully, still in the house." The cuff clicks open, and

Dylan pries it from Audrey's ankle. She gapes at the naked space and the raw red mark the cuff left behind. Dylan tugs her to her bare feet and delicately enfolds her into an embrace. At the sight of them, tears prick at my eyes.

But the moment ends as Dylan draws back to take her hand. "Come on," he says. "Madison texted that Brent is on his way."

Bile rises in my throat. I dart a glance toward the corridor, black beyond our fluorescent light.

"Then let's go," I say, motioning them onward.

"Your chain," Dylan says, making to toss me the keys.

I shake my head. "There's no time. Let's just get the hell out of here." I tighten the chain looped around my arm, knowing we can't afford to have it clanking around in the woods. Then I stoop to grab the wrench and hobble onward.

Dylan pockets the keys and aids Audrey along behind me. I glance back to see her struggling on withered legs like she's never taken a step in her life. "It isn't much farther," Dylan assures her. "When we make it to the woods, I'll carry you."

We clear the corridor, reaching the alcove below the lid. Dylan props Audrey up against the wall and tugs on the hem of my shirt. "Let me go first. I'll check that the coast is clear."

I nod, handing him the wrench as he brushes past me in the narrow space. He left the lid open, but it's dark outside. Only the faint glow of the moon spills onto the concrete.

Dylan clambers up the ladder, poking his head through the opening. "I think it's clear," he whispers down to us. "Can she make it up?"

"Yeah," I say, despite my doubts. I tug Audrey along toward the ladder as Dylan crawls out onto the forest floor above.

"Help her to me and I'll pull her through," he says.

I do, placing one hand on each side of her frail, trembling body as she eases a foot onto the rung. "You've got it," I tell her.

Audrey grunts, hefting herself up until she has both feet on the ladder.

Overhead, I hear Dylan's voice again, so distant and muted I can't make out the words.

"Dylan?" I call out.

A grunt sounds above, followed by a low voice. Then a thud.

My heart slams into my rib cage. "Audrey, wait," I hiss, tugging her down toward me and staggering back as I catch her. She turns in my grasp, her eyes wide with terror.

"I'm going up there," I whisper, steadying her against the wall.

She clamps onto my wrist, but her grip is weak. I shrug it off easily before hurrying into the storage space, where I scrounge up a hammer and another wrench. I don't even feel my ankle anymore, only the pounding of my heart. I pause before Audrey again, forcing her to take the wrench as I mouth, "*It will be okay.*"

Then, sucking in one last, deep breath, I tuck the hammer beneath my arm and pray that wasn't the last promise I ever make.

My feet are rubber over the rungs, my palms sweaty. When I reach the surface, I squint into the silvery wash of moonlight, steeling myself for whatever's to come.

Then I see him. *Dylan*. Sprawled out over the forest floor.

I choke on a scream and heft myself out of the bunker. Never stopping to catch my breath, I get to my feet and swing the hammer like a madwoman. Someone is out here in the dark. But I have to help Dylan.

"Dylan," I say, sliding down to the earth beside him.

He lets out a groan as I turn him over. "What happened?" I glance back toward the bunker's opening. I can't let Oliver slip inside. Audrey's alone down there, practically defenseless.

"Brent," Dylan mumbles, trying to sit up.

I help him, my fingers touching something wet and sticky that runs down his back. Panic churns inside me, but I ignore it. I scan the woods again, every tree a potential person in the darkness. Every sound makes my heart leap. He could be behind any one of these trunks.

When I start to pull Dylan to his feet, his eyes widen.

I don't think. I simply let go of Dylan, spin, and swing the hammer.

It lands with a sickening crunch. My target lets out a grunt. In my gut, I know that sound was a skull.

But he's still on his feet, swaying and staggering. I can't wait for him to recover. I strike again, right over the hand he's raising to defend himself.

He goes down this time. Night-blackened blood streams down his face so thick I can barely tell that it's Oliver.

"Are you okay to hold him?" I ask Dylan, who's standing now.

"Yeah, go get Audrey."

I nod and make a mad dash to the bunker. "Let's go!" I call, clambering down the ladder.

Audrey's wrench clangs to the ground as she lunges forward. I resist the urge to leap the remaining distance, not wanting to render my ankle completely useless. When I hit the ground, I help Audrey up the rungs, following close behind. At the top, I give her a strong push toward the earth.

She's still picking herself up when I make it to the surface. "Dylan!" she screams, wobbling forward.

I sprint past her to where Dylan has Oliver's arms secured behind his back. "He's alive?" I ask. Guilt over hitting him is already crushing my airways.

"Yeah," Dylan says. In the moonlight streaming through the treetops, I see that there's something wrong with his eyes. The blue is nearly eclipsed by the fast-growing black of his pupils.

"Oh my god, Dylan," I breathe. "You need a hospital."

"I'm okay," he says as Audrey's labored footfalls and strident breaths draw near. "Just get her to the truck."

"Okay, but what about—"

A *click* pierces the forest, turning my blood to ice. I've only ever heard this click in the movies, the sound of a trigger cocking back.

When I turn, Brent is standing a few yards away. The barrel of his rifle is pointed straight at my head.

I step back, knowing the effort is futile. Maybe it's dark enough that he'll miss me, but he'd easily hit Audrey. She can't run.

"Wait a minute," Dylan calls out to Brent. "We're friends. You don't have to do this!"

I glance at Audrey, standing with her shoulders drawn in close. If I can lead Brent away, maybe she and Dylan can get to freedom.

There isn't time to debate. I pivot on my good ankle, taking one large stride away from Audrey. Before I land another step, the blast tears through the night.

Everything darkens. Sound dies.

I drop to the ground.

35

The rough twigs on the forest floor bite into the soft flesh of my palms. I hear breathing from somewhere in the forest. Then, as the leaves near my lips rustle, I get a rush of relief; the sound is coming from my own mouth.

"Paige." Dylan's voice, followed by the crunch of branches as he nears me.

I look up, past his concerned expression hovering over me. Past a seemingly unconscious Oliver to where Madison Blake is standing, her pistol still poised.

Before her on the ground, Brent Haywood's body lies unmoving as the blood pools around his head.

Sirens sound in the distance.

In the hazy moonlight, Madison's gaze skips about the bloody scene. It finds and latches on to mine.

I'm too stunned and broken to mouth the words *thank you*, much less produce them over the siren's wail.

From the look in her eyes, though, I know she hears me.

THE FOLLOWING SUMMER

There's a party the evening we arrive in Clearwater Ridge, only it isn't at Tripp Shaw's house.

I doubt the Shaws will ever throw another party in this town.

Though Tripp didn't go down for attempted murder in the end, he's doing time for assault. Not even Mr. Shaw will be able to clean the stains off the family name.

Tonight, ours is a party of five. Just Lucy, me, and the Covington siblings. And while there is beer, there's no music, no dancing; only the whooshing of the river, the chirping crickets in the undergrowth, and the call of the owl high overhead.

"Who's swimming?" Audrey tiptoes into the river, letting out a squeal. The full moon shines overhead, casting an ethereal glow over the rippling water. "Come on! We have to at least stick our heads under. If I do it, you all have to do it."

It's nice to see her back to her old bossy self.

The night wind rustles the bearded wheatgrass and spruce

needles. Lucy and Dylan follow Audrey through the rocks like puppies, but I hide behind Dylan. "Don't tell her where I am," I whisper as the cold nips at my arms.

He merely reaches back to grab my hand and lift it in the air. "Paige is in."

"I did not agree to this," I whine, attempting to wiggle from his grasp.

"We'll do it together, Paige!" Audrey yells. "Ooh! Dylan can take our pic!"

"No, see, Dylan wants to go in." Finally, I slip my fingers free and shove him toward the water.

Audrey makes a pouty face but pulls her brother by the hand.

I grab my phone and switch on the flash, snapping a photo as the two of them shut their eyes and lower beneath the frigid water.

Audrey comes up shrieking, only to snap back into perfect composure a second later. "Did you get it?"

"Yeah," I say. "You look like you're crying. I'm posting it."

"You are not!" she shouts, lunging toward the riverbank.

I laugh, grateful to be back in this place once again—not just in Clearwater Ridge, but as friends who can feel at ease around one another.

Audrey's been putting in the work, going to counseling, focusing on nutrition and exercise. She's back to smiling, to eating more than one meal a day, to sipping her parents' beer on the riverbank. The hollows in her cheeks have filled in, the color long since returned to her skin.

Those are the parts of her that are on display for all. But

I know there are other parts buried beneath the surface. Parts that remain raw, like weeping wounds. I know that Audrey will never truly be her old self again. It's impossible to reverse the changes that were carved into her being as she lived ten months beneath the ground, under her abductor's control.

I'm learning to love both parts, the old and the new. I'm grateful to have her back—back to speaking to me, back to laughing with me. We're sharing bunk beds again this summer. In fact, this past year, we've been closer than ever. Facing down death together in a concrete cell bonded us in a way most people will never understand. There isn't a day that's gone by that we haven't video chatted or at the very least texted.

"Your turn, Paige!" Audrey calls, motioning me toward the water. "Or I'll tell Dylan about that guy in your chemistry class."

My mouth drops open.

"Guy in chemistry class?" Dylan asks, tone bordering on amused and concerned.

"Just this guy," I say, nudging a rock with my toe.

"*Lab partner*," Audrey says in a singsong voice.

"Just this *lab partner* who asked for my number last semester." I glare at Audrey. "It's not like I gave it to him."

Dylan's brows arch in mock judgment.

"What? You're telling me you never turned down a college girl all year?"

"Never needed to," Dylan says, prompting me to put a skeptical hand on my hip. "I hung a sign with your photo and the word *taken* from my neck every day."

"Good," I say, trying not to giggle and failing miserably.

He wades through the rocks, water rolling off his skin as he makes his way over the sandy bank toward me.

There's a devious smile on his lips, and I start to back up. "You're going to throw me in now, aren't you?"

"Maybe." He steps closer. "You'd deserve it. You're not nearly as committed to this relationship as I am."

"Show me photographic evidence of this alleged sign, and I'll throw myself in."

He pulls me toward him by the waist, dripping water all over me. "How about I just throw you in?"

"I'd like to see you try." I loop my arms around his neck, and he leans in, pressing his lips to mine.

When we part, he blinks as though dazed. "What were we talking about?"

"You were going to get me a beer."

"Oh, right." He smiles, and his lips dust my hair again before he makes for the cooler.

I've missed him. He visits me whenever he has a break or a long weekend, but it's been hard with him in college and me still finishing up high school. I applied to Berkeley, in hopes that we could finally end the long-distance thing. To my astonishment, though, I got accepted into my top choice: the premed program at Stanford. I accepted. It's only an hour's drive to Berkeley. We'll see if he and I can continue to make things work.

Audrey exits the water now, shivering as she wraps a towel around herself.

Dylan cracks open the beer I'll never drink and passes it to me. "You coming?" he asks, moving toward the water's edge to join the others. "You can't avoid the night swim forever, Paige."

I glance at Audrey, who hops onto a boulder, moonlight painting silvery highlights in her blond hair. "In a minute."

I wander over to take a seat beside her. "I thought you were done trying to sabotage my relationship."

"Oh, Paige." She pats my wrist gently, then steals my beer. "Don't you see that there's nothing I could do to screw up your relationship with Dylan?"

I think she's being sweet until she adds, "I mean, if he can see past the way you dress and the fact that you talk like you lived through the prewar era, there's absolutely nothing more *I* can do."

I glare at her. "You know, a lot of people like the way I talk."

"You mean the ones in the nursing home."

"Yes."

Grinning, she tips the can to her lips and takes a long slug. Then, lowering from the rock, she sticks the can in the grass. She wanders away, her form lithe and shadowlike in the twilight as she stoops to pick the violet wildflowers that grow there. "I told you it would happen though, didn't I? You and Dylan."

"No thanks to you."

She returns unsmiling as she piles the flowers in her lap and begins weaving them together by their long stems. "That night at the party two summers back. Before all the...bad stuff."

I nod for her to go on, wrapping my arms around myself to ward off the chill in the air.

"Dylan asked me if there was a chance you liked him, and I laughed." She rolls her shoulders around like there's a soreness deep down, one she can't quite reach. "I laughed because it was so obvious. You'd been in love with him since you were, like, eight!" She continues to twist the vines together. "That was what I tried to tell you in the kitchen, before Kurt walked in and everything sort of…you know. I always supported you. You two are perfect together."

"I kind of figured out how he felt," I say, drawing squiggles in the condensation around my bottle, "when he kissed me in the pool."

Audrey shakes her head. "I truly underestimated you." She turns to place the finished crown of wildflowers on my head. "Now you're queen of the river."

I hop down from the rock to curtsy, and she applauds.

We haven't had a moment like this, just the two of us in person, in ages. Fortunately, there will be plenty of moments in our future.

Audrey is joining me at Stanford in the fall. Horrified at the thought of getting held back for missing her junior year of high school, Audrey worked double time getting caught up. Then, applications were a breeze. Every university wanted the girl who survived a kidnapping ordeal.

We're going to be roommates, which means she's already going wild with all of her visions for decorating our dorm room.

Her plan is to major in political science. Ever since her rescue, Audrey has become interested in the justice system. She's been a huge advocate for Madison Blake, who's also serving time for numerous accounts of fraud. Thanks in part to Audrey's testimony concerning that night in the woods, Madison got a lighter sentence; she'll be out on probation in a few months.

I can never condone Madison's crimes; she stole and lied and manipulated people. It doesn't change the fact that I also see her as a hero. When push came to shove, she risked her freedom and her very life to step out of the shadows and face down the man who tried to kill her.

She did that to save us.

I've written to her at the prison a couple of times. Each word scrawled on paper felt awkward and forced, but I want her to be okay. I'd like to think that after she serves her time, there's hope for her future.

A few months back, her mother passed away. Madison was devastated. After all, she'd sacrificed everything to help the woman. To persuade her to keep up her treatments. In the end, Madison blamed herself for her mother's death. She believed that if she hadn't been imprisoned, she could've somehow altered the course of events.

The three of us plan to visit Madison while we're in Clearwater Ridge. The county prison is only a short drive. We want her to know that her bravery that night in the woods hasn't been forgotten. We remember. Every single day we're grateful for what she did. If she hadn't gotten in Britta's car and followed Brent out to the ranch, I'm not sure any of us would be alive to tell the story.

When the sheriff's deputies found us outside the bunker that night, Oliver was badly beaten but alive.

Brent wasn't quite so lucky. Apparently, swindling wasn't the only skill Madison's father imparted on her before he skipped town; the girl knows how to handle a gun. The bullet she fired struck Brent's brain, killing him instantly.

Next month, Oliver will stand trial for his many crimes, including kidnapping, unlawful imprisonment, and the murder of Larissa Swanson.

Not long after Audrey told the cops about Larissa, they uncovered her body buried in the woods. The Covingtons held a small ceremony in town last summer. We said goodbye to the girl whose life was cut short, whose family hadn't cared enough to report her missing four years ago. We laid flowers on her grave. The entire time, I held Audrey's hand, trying not to think about how easily the girl now buried in Clearwater Ridge Cemetery could've been my best friend.

It's taken a while to get to this place. To be able to look Audrey in the eyes without falling apart. Dylan and I had created a horrible story about Audrey—a story that kept us from doing the right thing last summer. We believed that Audrey had changed the summer she went missing. That she disappeared due to this new darkness, these new faults.

The truth is that Audrey disappeared because she's the same girl she's always been. Her only downfall was the big heart that made me friends with her years ago.

"Let's just stay here tonight," Audrey says, her head flopping back. "Sleep under the stars."

"That could trigger my lumbar spinal stenosis," I say, parroting a condition I learned from Betty Watkins at the nursing home.

I understand how she feels though. This is our last summer before college, and we have to somehow make up for all the time we missed out on last year. To hold on to every single drop of sunshine, coconut suntan lotion, and river spray. Every spoonful of chocolate ice cream at Carlson's and every petal of the wildflowers that grow along the bank.

Audrey turns to roll her eyes at me.

I'll never know how a force of nature as bold as Audrey could've lost her voice the way she did last summer. How she could've let her fears consume her so completely that she chose to hide, to stick to the shadows and work apart from the people who love her most.

But I guess we all lose our voice sometimes. We all let the lie get to us—the one that says we never had a voice in the first place. That we'll never be heard above the voices that run our towns, our world: the loud, the powerful, the just plain evil.

I know that they're out there. The wolves. They howl and circle, haunches raised and fangs bared as they prey upon the weak.

But I know that together, even the frail and meek can fight back. The softest voices will join, creating a sound to rise above the howls.

Creating a chorus loud enough to crush the wolf.

Read on for a sneak peek at

THEY'RE WATCHING YOU,

another page-turning thriller

from Chelsea Ichaso!

EVERY SECRET SOCIETY HAS ITS PRIVILEGES...
AND ITS SACRIFICES

THEY'RE WATCHING YOU

CHELSEA ICHASO

AVAILABLE NOW

When a secret society has you in their sights,
it can lead to power, privilege... or death.

ONE

"You do realize you're going straight to detention," I say to my lab partner Gavin Holt. He's wearing a white button-down shirt adorned with his signature bow tie—all the boys wear ties. It's a requirement, though Gavin is the only guy on campus who insists on the bow variety.

But this time he's gone off the rails and paired it with plaid pajama pants. Strictly against dress code. Torrey-Wells Academy, named after its two founders, has a bit of a double standard when it comes to attire. Guys have to wear slacks and a tie to classes, chapel, and to the dining hall; girls can wear pretty much whatever they want as long as it covers the necessary parts. For example, I'm wearing sweatpants and a ratty TWA sweatshirt—my daily uniform—and am in no danger of violating the code. Apparently, when the school opened up to girls back in the seventies, the board found altering the academy handbook too much of a bother.

Which is fine with me.

Gavin shrugs but scoots his stool closer to the lab table to hide his lower half. "I woke up late."

I roll my eyes.

"And then I had a small Pop-Tart smoke alarm emergency."

"Well, you look like you're ready to crouch by the Christmas tree and unwrap a package of Hot Wheels."

"You're one to talk, Sweatpants Girl."

Fair enough. I scan the list of ingredients again. "I guess this means I'm getting the water. Try not to blow anything up while I'm gone." I grab the beaker and head over to the sink. There's a sixty-six-point-six percent chance that Gavin will ignore my warning and blow something up while I'm gone, if we're basing this on stats from our last three assignments.

With a wave of my hand, the fancy steel faucet turns on. The Lowell Math and Science Building, constructed four years ago thanks to a rich donor named Lowell who made his money genetically modifying crops, is a state-of-the-art facility. No penny was spared, from the touch screens the teachers use in place of whiteboards to the observatory fit with a massive telescope. Handle-less water faucets were important too, I suppose. Water starts spewing out the sides of the beaker before I realize I've been gazing off into space. I shut it off with another wave and dump some of it, glancing over my shoulder at Gavin.

His lips are quirked, eyes squinting at the tray full of materials. He's definitely contemplating lighting something on fire. I watch as he adjusts his glasses, picks up the spatula, and begins prodding at the sodium metal without his gloves on. A sudden wave of frustration rolls through me. My best friend, Polly St. James, should be sitting here next to me, not Gavin.

If she hadn't left, I wouldn't be so stressed about my grade in this class. Whereas some teachers tend to show leniency toward the athletes, Dr. Yamashiro is extra strict. To keep the GPA required for my financial aid, I can't get anything less than an *A* on this experiment. Or on any assignment, for that matter. But with Gavin for a partner, I might have to settle for getting out of the building alive.

I return, setting the beaker onto the glass tabletop with a clank. Water droplets splatter the ingredients list as well as our findings sheet.

"You okay?" Gavin asks, leaning closer, his jade eyes narrowed behind his lenses. His scent is sweet with a hint of smoke, like he downed an energy drink on the way here or tried to ignite a Jolly Rancher.

"Fine. Put your safety goggles on."

He obeys, placing the goggles over his glasses, and I add a few drops of phenolphthalein indicator to the beaker. But he nudges me with an elbow, and I almost fumble the dropper. "Well, you don't look fine."

I take a deep breath and steady my hand. I'm not about to tell Gavin that life pretty much sucks now that my only friend has abandoned me. I'm not about to tell Gavin that I suspect something bad might've happened to Polly—that she didn't just up and run away like her parents and the police say.

I would never tell Gavin Holt that my eyes are stinging with tears because even the best-case scenario means my closest friend chose to leave me and never return my calls or texts again.

"I'm just tired and sore. Still recovering from hell week." Every year, at the start of lacrosse preseason, Coach makes us attend 5 a.m. practices before classes, and again at 5 p.m. after classes. It helps to get us in shape. It also makes every inch of my body feel like it's melting off.

"And maybe a little upset that Polly is…" Gavin pushes a strand of dust-brown hair off his forehead. "You know, gone."

"Maybe." But the truth is I started losing Polly months ago.

A few weeks into our Form III school year (Torrey-Wells Academy can't very well call us juniors and seniors like every other school in the United States), Polly was suddenly too busy for me. Even though we're roommates—we've been room-mates since Form I—I didn't see her as much. Polly's straight As always came with a healthy dose of cramming; this year, she never felt like studying. Then there was the staying out and sneaking back into the room after curfew, reeking of booze. It wasn't like her.

At least, it wasn't like the Polly who was friends with me. She'd vaguely mentioned her wild-child days, but people change. We were content to drink soda from the vending machines and spend Saturday nights in our pajamas.

Until she started getting buddy-buddy with Annabelle Westerly and joined chess club. This has to be the only school in the country where chess club is cool, and it's all thanks to Annabelle. Polly and I used to joke about how Annabelle Westerly's endorsement could probably make pin the tail on the donkey the next school fad. But suddenly, Polly wasn't laughing much with me anymore.

She was laughing with Annabelle, who's trouble veiled in designer labels and a posher-than-thou lexicon.

Then two weeks ago, Polly wasn't laughing with anyone. She was gone.

ACKNOWLEDGMENTS

To my brilliant editor, Wendy McClure—thank you for your wise input as we took this story from a pitch to the book readers can hold in their hands. Thank you for your enthusiasm, encouragement, and for being such a delight to work with all the time.

To my fabulous agent, Uwe Stender—for your belief in my writing and unwavering support along the way.

A huge thanks to the team at Sourcebooks: Erin Fitzsimmons, Thea Voutiritsas, Jessica Thelander, Aimee Alker, Theodore Turner, Karen Masnica, Rebecca Atkinson, Michelle Lecumberry, and Jenny Lopez. Casey Moses, thank you so much for the fantastic cover!

I am forever grateful to my dear friends and critique partners, Julie Abe and Laura Kadner. You two have earned a lifetime supply of cupcakes.

To my early readers, Laura Kadner, Heidi Christopher, and MK Pagano—thank you for your honest feedback and encouragement.

To my parents, George and Rebecca Kienzle—for listening and cheerleading through all of the publishing highs and lows. Alec, thank you for helping out with edits on the last book! To my Ichaso and Lewis families, your support means the world. And a special thanks to Andres for answering my golf questions.

To my husband, Matias—for always being my first reader and the person who talks me through every single new idea or plot struggle. I couldn't do this without you.

Kaylie, Jude, and Camryn—keep writing your stories. You have far more imagination than I ever did at your age. Thank you for thinking that my job is cool and for being the best people ever.

To the book bloggers and influencers—thank you for supporting my books. Every post and photo means so much to me.

And of course, thank you, dear reader! You're the reason I get to keep writing, and I'm endlessly grateful that you picked up this book.

Finally, all gratitude and praise to my Lord and Savior.

ABOUT THE AUTHOR

Chelsea Ichaso writes twisty thrillers for young adults, including *Little Creeping Things*, *Dead Girls Can't Tell Secrets*, and *They're Watching You*. A former high school English teacher, she currently resides in Southern California with her husband and children. You can visit her online at chelseaichaso.com or on Instagram @chelseaichaso.

sourcebooks
fire

Home of the hottest trends in YA!

Visit us online and
sign up for our newsletter at
FIREreads.com

· ·

Follow
@sourcebooksfire
online